Tiopa Ki Lakota

Tiopa Ki Lakota

D. Jordan Redhawk

P.D. Publishing, Inc.
Clayton, North Carolina

ISBN-13: 978-0-9754366-6-0
ISBN-10: 0-9754366-6-X

First Printing 2000 (ISBN: 1-930928-03-3)
Second Printing 2004 (ISBN: 0374137855)

9 8 7 6 5 4 3

Cover art and design by Stephanie Solomon-Lopez
Edited by Barb Coles/Linda Daniel

Published by:

P.D. Publishing, Inc.
P.O. Box 70
Clayton, NC 27528

http://www.pdpublishing.com

Acknowledgements:

Many thanks to the Bardbrains – you know who you are, Albert White Hat Sr. – who gave me much food for thought, and Charlotte – for starting the ball rolling so many years ago.

Special thanks to Steph Solomon-Lopez for a beautiful cover!

My editors have done a wonderful job over the various editions and deserve special thanks – Day Petersen for the first edition, Nancy Ashmore and K Simpson for the second edition, and Barb Coles and Linda Daniel for this latest edition.

First and foremost, however, was the extensive editing and rewriting under the direction of Cindy Cresap for the second edition. With her expertise, the story of Anpo and Kathleen became so much more than the original tale ever was. The book is one of my favorites now and I owe it all to her. Thanks, Cindy!

Naturally, this book is dedicated to my wife, Anna Trinity Redhawk. All that I do, I give to you.

PUBLISHER'S NOTE:

A glossary with pronunciation for Lakota names and words is located at the back of this book beginning on page 260.

Part 1: Wi Ile Anpo
Sun is Burning at Dawn

Chapter One

1761

The warrior, Wanbli Zi, quietly smoked a pipe at the fire. Before him the fire crackled and popped, warming the lodge. He was not alone.

Three women worked there as well as his uncle who sat nearby. The first woman – his wife's mother – sat near the fire, her aged hands carefully sewing a pair of moccasins. She had come to visit through winter, and would return to her family's band when the snows melted. The next – his first wife – finished preparing the evening meal, dividing her attention between two small girls and a baby in her arms. The third and youngest – his second wife – assisted with shy docility. She had only come to his family after the summer gathering, and remained uncertain of her new status.

Of the children, the younger was four winters, playing with a toy person among the sleeping furs. The oldest was nine winters, on the verge of learning her place in society.

His first wife handed the eldest girl a clay bowl of stew. "Here. Give this to your father."

With an eager smile and nod, she carefully took the steaming bowl, and approached the warrior. "*Ate?*"

Wanbli looked up from the fire. "Yes, *cunksi.*" He took the food from her with a smile. "Thank you, little one. Now go help with your sister."

Stopping only long enough to give her father a hug, the girl returned to the duties of keeping her little sister occupied.

He set the bowl near the fire to keep it warm, and finished smoking in contemplative silence. His uncle, one of the finest arrow makers in the band, set aside the thin strips of feathers he used for fletching to eat.

Beyond the buffalo robes of his wife's lodge, a late winter snow drifted to the ground. Around this lodge huddled the winter camp of the Maka band of the Oglala Lakota. Thirty *ti ikceyas* lay around a large cleared area in a near circle. The only open space in the hoop stood at the eastern side where the entrance faced the rising sun. At the exact opposite of the entry stood a larger lodge, used as a meeting place for the elders.

Finishing his tobacco, Wanbli emptied the ashes into the fire, so the spirits could share the sacred smoke, and set the pipe into a rack. His second wife now fed the younger child and his older daughter sat nearby, watching everything with large brown eyes as she ate her meal.

His first wife, the mother of his children, postponed eating as she bared her breast to feed the baby. He watched, remembering his pleasure when Gi presented this newest person to him a few short days ago. Three daughters, all beautiful like their mother. Not many men were blessed with such. Perhaps some day he would also have a son to teach hunting and tracking. He eyed his second wife in speculation. Even if he had no son of his seed, he vowed to consider adopting or capturing one. Surely someone had an over abundance of children, and would be willing to allow Wanbli to adopt one. Or perhaps he would find a child during a raid on an enemy encampment, one he could raise as his own.

He heard a knocking of wood on wood outside, someone tapping the stick put there for this purpose. Calling a welcome, he was surprised to see the shaman push aside the leather covering and step inside. Hiding his puzzlement, he invited the visitor to sit in the honored place beside him.

The shaman, Inyan, declined an offer of food and drink. Instead, he opened a pouch, producing a pipe and tobacco as flakes of snow melted across his shoulders and hair.

Wanbli refrained from raising his eyebrows at the pipe. The bowl was of polished stone, white and gleaming, while the stem was dark wood, carved with a likeness of a mountain lion. This pipe was very old and important, used only in rituals, and Wanbli wondered why the shaman brought it to Gi's lodge. What could be so vital as to bring about its use?

He and his uncle sat in silence, watching as Inyan carefully loaded the bowl with tobacco.

The shaman crouched forward and, with nimble fingers, used two twigs to lift a burning ember, lighting the pipe. The glow from the fire lit his fairly unlined face. He was young to be a shaman; only thirty-four winters. His father had taught him since he was a boy and, with the elder's death this past winter from the coughing sickness, the younger had taken over his father's duties in the camp.

He sang a song of joy as he offered the smoke to the four directions, his voice soft. Then he touched his lips to the stem, using his free hand to guide the smoke towards his head and behind. Smoke was sacred and of the spirit. It imparted wisdom, and those who smoked could see their words, only able to speak truth under its influence.

The shaman handed the pipe, stem first, to the warrior who

repeated the process of smoking and guiding the cloud closer. It then passed to Wanbli's uncle who did the same. The men sat in silence, finishing this ritual. When the bowl held nothing but ashes, Inyan tapped it into the fire, releasing the last of it for the spirits that lived in their world.

Wanbli waited patiently, knowing that soon Inyan would make his words known. Still, curiosity beat strong in his heart, and it thumped with relief when the shaman began to speak.

"I sat in meditation for four days," Inyan said. "I wished to ask the spirits of winter questions about the coming seasons, hoping to understand what our future holds. Instead I received a vision of a newborn child." He leaned forward and peering intently at Wanbli. "Your woman's child."

Inyan's eyes snared Wanbli's. A sense of waiting filled him, certain something of great import directed the shaman's vision.

"I saw a female *igmu*, giving birth to a human. When the baby cried out, I could hear the scream of the mountain lion in the voice, and knew it to be a girl child. I stepped closer, the mother lion ignoring me as she licked the afterbirth from the baby's frail body. In the baby's heart burned the fire of a warrior. I could hear it in her voice, see it in her eyes."

Wanbli frowned. "What does that have to do with my wife's child?"

"The baby born of the lion is your wife's daughter."

He leaned onto his backrest, trading a glance with his uncle. "The lion is a strong spirit for a girl child," he said. "Do you foresee what will happen to her as she grows? Will she find a man strong enough?"

The shaman carefully rewrapped the pipe in his hands. "Her destiny does not lie in women's work," he said softly. "She is *wicakte*, a two-souled person."

The warrior looked at his uncle in puzzlement.

The older man shrugged. "It has been so before, though not for many, many winters – a woman raised as warrior and hunter for her family. She could be this thing."

"Yes," Inyan agreed, putting the now bundled pipe back into its leather pouch. "And you will have a son, to care for you – to hunt when you can no longer, to protect you from war, to support you in your elder seasons."

Wanbli sat in silence, contemplating this odd turn of events. The two other men remained quiet, giving him space to think. If what Inyan saw was a true vision. No man would be able to tame his daughter. No man would want her.

After a time, Wanbli waved his first wife close, reaching for the newest member of her lodge. The lively bundle squawked once at the interruption to her feeding. He instantly covered the baby's mouth with his, counseling silence which she obeyed.

With surprising gentleness, Wanbli further unwrapped the bundle, revealing his daughter. Her tiny hands balled into fists, she flailed them around, shivering in the cooler air. He held a finger out and one fist swatted it before grasping with a strong grip. She brought the digit promptly to her mouth and he could feel tiny gums against the finger pad.

Dark eyes stared back at him.

Inyan was young to be shaman. The possibility remained that he misinterpreted his vision, though Wanbli could not see how any other conclusion could be made. His wife's was the only child born in the last two moons, and no other woman in their village carried one. The shaman seemed certain of his understanding; why else would he come bearing the sacred pipe? Perhaps he did so to indicate the importance of his words.

Wanbli studied his offspring. She still held his finger and suckled, though hunger would not be abated in such a manner. Despite this, she remained silent, watching him as he watched her. He smiled.

He looked to the two men at his fire. "This is Cinksi, my son of the heart. She will grow strong. She will learn the arts of war and how to speak with the spirits. She will become a fierce hunter and provide for her family."

1767

Cinksi fought her natural instincts to fidget. Her father's activities were quite interesting. The pack of boys rampaging past distracted her with their whooping as they brandished small weapons at one another.

"Watch closely," Wanbli said, drawing his daughter's eyes back to the task at hand. "This is the knot we use." He slowly demonstrated as he tied the wet rawhide strip on the spear haft. Once complete, he turned it to study the handiwork. "When the rawhide dries, it will tighten and the spearhead will not fall out." He used his other hand to gesture the girl closer.

She scooted forward on the buffalo robe and peered at the spear. With careful hands, she tried to wiggle the head but it held fast. She looked at her father, impressed. "It is already so strong, Wanbli! Even *wakan tanka* could not move it when the rawhide dries."

The warrior chuckled. "If the great powers were to want this spear in pieces, it would be so, child," he said.

The boys trotted past, intent on some game, and Cinksi's attention again wandered from the spear. She watched as they disappeared behind the lodge of her father's second wife. Craning her neck, she tried to see past the structure, but they remained out of sight.

"Cinksi."

She turned back to her father. He held a second, smaller spear in his hand, one that was not there when she first looked away. A miniature version of his own, the antler tip was blunted. Cinksi's joy spread across her face as he handed the small weapon to her.

"For you, Cinksi. Now, go. Show the *hoksila* that you are stronger and wiser than any of them."

Cinksi needed no further prodding. She took the spear and raced away to catch up with the boys.

They huddled behind the furthest tent on the north side of camp. There were seven of them, ranging in age from six to nine winters, dressed in breechclouts and moccasins. They heatedly debated something among themselves, their voices trailing off as the newcomer's presence was noticed.

Cinksi slowed to a walk when she got close to them. Her heart beat loudly in her chest as seven pairs of eyes stared at her. She could hear her father's voice in her ear. "*A true warrior feels fear yet moves through it, becoming brave.*"

"Become brave," she murmured to herself. The girl threw her shoulders back, and raised her chin to stare haughtily back as she marched forward. She wore only breechclouts and moccasins, as well, looking every inch like another boy. Stopping before the biggest of them, she glared up at him and set the butt of her new spear on the ground by her foot. A small puff of dust arose from it and settled back down.

The taller boy examined her much like she was a particularly fat bug underneath a rock. "Who are you?" he demanded, knowing the answer. No one was a stranger in the camp.

"I am Cinksi. My father is Wanbli," she said, her tone regal.

He looked her up and down. With a playful tug at her breechclout, he snickered, "I heard you were a *wicincala*."

The others chuckled as well, but the girl in their midst refused to be daunted. She did not flinch away from the tugging on her clothing. "I am not a girl. I am *wicakte*."

Immediately losing interest in her, the boy said, "Go home, little *wicincala*. We do not play with toy persons here." His dark eyes fell on the spear she held. "And you do not play with weapons." He plucked it from her hands.

Cinksi stared at him, stunned. She watched the boy heft the spear her father had given her, checking its weight and balance as he turned away. The other boys in the group were laughing, preparing to follow. It was utterly inconceivable that the boy would do such a thing, let alone think he could get away with it. The world seemed to slow down as the adrenaline of anger sparked the fire the shaman had seen so many winters ago.

No thought crossed her mind. At first frozen in place, her next awareness was of dust, a startled grunt, and aggressive movement. Teeth gritted, Cinksi fought for a good grip on the boy, attempting to wrest her spear back from him. Before she could do so, however, arms grabbed hers and pulled her off. She struggled against her captors with a growl.

The boy did not appear angry. He rose to his feet and dusted himself off. His friends held Cinksi tight, though she did not fight as hard for release. Still, she made anger noises in her throat, and they seemed loath to release her. The others stood back in awe as they watched the altercation.

The spear thief crouched down in front of her, studying her curiously. "You are crazy, *wicincala*," he said. "You should not fight me. I am older and stronger and bigger."

She lessened her scuffle a bit and glared back at him. "I am not *wicincala*!" she insisted. "I am *wicakte*, and I will still fight you! Until the day I die!"

"But, you will lose, Cinksi."

"I do not care! Someday I will be bigger and stronger and then I will win."

He picked up the spear that had fallen to the ground at her attack. He looked it over carefully, brushing it off a bit and adjusting a feather adorning it. "All this for a spear?"

The girl's nostrils flared, her lips twisted into a scornful expression. "My father gave me the spear as a gift. It would dishonor him and myself to let it be stolen from me." She left unspoken the thought of who else would be dishonored.

Looking to the boys holding her arms, the boy said, "Let her go."

Cinksi nearly stumbled at her sudden release. She caught herself and pulled her small frame upright in a proud stance. "I will fight you now."

The boy silently handed her the spear instead.

Frowning, the girl took the spear back into her possession. Her dark eyes narrowed as she studied her tormentor.

"My name is Nupa. My father is Wi Sape. I return this spear to you."

The rest of the boys stared at him as if he had grown two heads.

Cinksi thought about it for a few seconds before taking the child's weapon from him. "I will still fight you," she offered in a calmer voice.

Nupa smiled at her. "If you wish. Can you and I have a peace? Until you get older and stronger?"

She considered his request with utter seriousness. "Yes. You and I can have a peace until then."

"Good!" He straightened and looked at the other boys. "Cinksi stays with us." He inhaled deeply of the summer air. "I go hunting!" he yelled before turning and running off.

The boys hared off after him, accepting his leadership. Cinksi hesitated. *That was much easier than I thought it would be.* Then she raced after them, adding her own voice to their whooping and calling.

Chapter Two

After two moons running with the boys, Cinksi became an accepted and well-respected member of their pack. She and the oldest boy, Nupa, developed a fast friendship. If one did not think of some sort of mischief to get into, the other did. And, despite her age and size, Cinksi became very adept at beating the boys on all levels of physical prowess.

Currently, the eight of them played near the camp in the tall grass. Despite the appearance of being alone, those warriors assigned to keep the peace during a hunt, the *akicita*, kept close eye on their antics. Less than a mile away a herd of buffalo grazed, coloring the hills black with their number. The herd had been sighted three days ago, and the entire camp had traveled to this spot. Now the village awaited the decision of the men who would lead the hunt. Until that decision was made, no one was allowed away from the village for fear of spooking the animals; those who might be foolish enough to try would face the wrath of the *akicita* and clubmen.

In response to the excitement, the pack of children had begun their own hunting party, preparing to swoop down on the buffalo – a mangy bitch and her three puppies. They had split into two groups to outflank their quarry, Nupa leading one and Cinksi the other.

A drop of sweat trickled down the girl's intense face, but she did not wipe it away. Her party had closed in on the left flank and she did not want to move and give her position away to the dogs. It had taken the better part of the morning to gain this spot, a small hillock with a dip in the center that hid the small family beneath her from general view. The inexperienced hunters had flushed the mother and her pups twice already. One more time and Cinksi planned to forget the elusive bitch and return to her mother's *ti ikceya* for something to eat.

On the other side of the dip, she saw a spear head slowly raise. It waved gently side to side, two times. In response, she used hand signals to her party, preparing them for the attack. Then she heard Nupa's whoop and the eight of them surged forward, hollering at the top of their lungs as they "hunted" the dogs.

The puppies scattered in clumsy surprise, yelping in fright at the sudden cacophony about them. The boys and Cinksi pretended to thrust spears into them as the trio scampered away. Their mother, a mean spirited animal, got hold of one boy's spear and a tug of war ensued. Eventually, the remainder of the hunting party ignored the pups, laughing at the antics of the boy with the spear as the dog growled and gnawed her way on the haft.

Nupa aimed a kick at her, to distract her from her chewing, and she pulled away to snap at his moccasin before trotting back towards her offspring. Once she was sure all her pups were present and unharmed, she urged them away from the gaggle of attackers, keeping a watchful eye.

Cinksi threw herself down onto the grass, peering up at the deep blue sky. Most of the others followed suit. The only boy to remain on his feet studied the damage to his weapon.

One pulled a water skin from his shoulder and took a long drink before passing it along. "I wonder how many buffalo my father will kill?" he asked.

"Your father is a good hunter," another said. "But my father and brother will kill more than him."

Nupa had his turn at the water skin before handing it to Cinksi. "I had a dream last night. A vision."

This information garnered the attention of the group, several sitting up to peer at the oldest boy closely.

"What did you see in your vision?" Cinksi asked, intrigued.

"My father, Sape, killed two bulls. Your father," and he nodded at the girl beside him, "killed a bull and a cow." He went around the circle and pointed to each of the boys, informing them how many kills their fathers and brothers had made.

One boy looked suspicious. "Are you certain it was a vision, Nupa?"

Indignant, the older boy puffed his chest out. "Want to bet on the outcome of the hunt?" There were no immediate takers.

"I bet my spear that you are wrong," the smallest boy finally said with a stern expression.

This became the catalyst and each child made bets of their personal items and toys. Those who thought Nupa's vision true put up their items to back his. Cinksi's wagered the spear her father had made in support.

They heard the village crier, and Nupa rose to his feet, he being the tallest, to see over the small hollow of grass they lay in. "There's a decision! A decision has been made." He looked down to the pack, anticipation in his dark eyes.

The eight of them stood and trotted toward a camp now humming with industriousness.

All those who would hunt leapt onto their best horses, milling about as the rest of the people gathered their belongings in preparation for travel. The crier's voice rose above the noise, counseling haste and quiet.

As the children neared the activity, the crier saw them. Knowing the type of antics young boys urged themselves to do, he sang aloud a caution to them as he passed, warning them to not defy the *akicita* by attempting to follow the hunters, to remain with the village as it moved nearer the hunting ground.

Cinksi paused in surprise, the thought having not occurred to her before. She glanced at Nupa to see his skin redden. Watching in curiosity, she considered the prospect, but she and her friends were not the only ones to hear the crier's voice. A pair of clubmen glared at them, and an *akicita* ordered them to attend to their families. No one would disrupt *this* hunt. Rather than invite disaster, Cinksi obeyed, leaving her friends as she rushed to her father's fire.

Wanbli was not there; he already gathered with the hunters who started away from camp. Instead, Cinksi found her mother, Waniyetu Gi, supervising the packing of her lodge. As was proper for a child of her age, Cinksi helped her mother and sisters with the last of it before they all assisted Hwa, Wanbli's second wife. Soon, their belongings tied down to horses and dogs, they followed the trail others began, on the way to a hill where the people would oversee the hunt.

While it was a short trip – the sun had hardly moved when they arrived – the hunt was mostly over. Cinksi helped unpack, casting longing looks at the valley before her. Clouds of dust arose from the stampeding herd and hunters. Away in the distance, more rose to the sky as final kills were made. Dark forms littered the ground, too many for the child to count as she worked. She clambered up the poles of her mother's lodge to tie the skins in place, and paused to stare until Hwa called her down.

A scout returned from the hunt, news of its completion on his lips. The crier took up his call, urging everyone to gather tools, and begin the task of making meat. All members of the village proceeded to the killing fields with an excited buzz. They picked over the carcasses of the animals slain by their hunter husbands and sons and brothers, identifying each by markings on the arrows and spears used.

No one was exempt from work. Once a family butchered the kills of their family, they assisted those who had fewer hands. Even the children were involved, skinning, cutting, or loading meat onto carriers to return to camp.

Soon, the task was done, and everyone returned to the village. The boys gathered with their older male family members as the excited tales of the hunt were discussed. The smell of roasting meat filled the camp, promising a wonderful feast. Several men sat at the council fire, smoking pipes and filling the boys' ears with stories.

Cinksi hung on her father's every word as he described waiting on the ridge above the valley. She could almost feel the dry wind as her father received the signal to attack and swooped down on his best hunting pony to harry the herd.

The buffalo had startled, initially milling around in surprise at the sudden danger before settling on a course. They had stampeded and the sounds of their hooves on the hard packed earth were like the thunder in a clouded sky. Her father had pulled his horse near a well-grown bull and had let his arrow fly. The buffalo had stumbled and fell to its death as he continued on to his next likely target. The second was a pregnant cow that had not died immediately. Her father had stopped his chase and put the cow out of her misery, a dangerous task as the wounded animal thrashed in terror and pain. By the time he finished, the hunt had completed, the remainder of the herd stampeding off.

As the stories trickled through, some of the older girls arrived with the raw livers of the kills. Cinksi's eldest sister trotted up with a breathless smile and handed three of the livers wrapped in a skin to her father, her head lowered with proper decorum.

Wanbli took the delicacy, thanking his daughter. He settled the bundle on the robe he sat upon, and pulled a knife of obsidian from the sheath around his neck. With great care, he sliced the two larger livers into chunks and passed them to others around the fire even as they did the same with their prizes. Strong in spirit, the liver of the animals endowed the Lakota hunters with strength and courage. In this way, all the men of the camp could partake of the spirit, even the elder big bellies who did not participate in the hunt.

The smallest liver, which came from the fetus within the cow Wanbli had slain, was held up in front of Cinksi. The warrior looked down upon his youngest daughter with grave intent. "This is the liver of the unborn *tatanka*, whose mother was killed by my hand. Tonight, we will all feast on it after it has been boiled."

Cinksi's heart was full of love and adoration as she listened.

"Today, however, I give this liver to you, my *cinksi* of the heart, so that you may grow strong and brave." The warrior handed the small organ to his daughter.

Her eyes widened in surprise. "Thank you, Wanbli," she said, delight in her voice. Turning to look at her friends, Cinksi saw their envy of her father's gift. None of the boys had been given pieces of liver, only her. Deciding to show her gratitude, she pulled a miniature replica of Wanbli's stone knife from her pouch. With great care, she cut the unborn buffalo's liver into eight pieces, sharing it with her friends.

Once the boys had their pieces, she bit into the meat left in her hand, savoring the saltiness of the fresh blood, the tenderness of the organ's texture. Cinksi could almost feel the surge of energy from the unborn buffalo's spirit fill her as she finished her treat.

She heard the men's murmur of approval, a slight flush coloring her skin at their regard. A quick glance at her father showed his pride at her actions, and she sat a little taller. Then another warrior spoke, telling his tale of the hunt, and all eyes were upon him.

By early afternoon, the hides were staked out and meat cut into strips to dry in the sun. A happy and excited atmosphere filled the air as the camp prepared to feast. The women cooked, and the men went about the business of warriors and hunters – caring for their weapons and horses. The shaman left in search of solitude for a vision quest.

Cinksi ran after the pack of boys as they scampered off to reenact the hunt as they had heard it.

"Nupa!" the girl called. "You were right! My father *did* kill a bull and a cow!"

They all considered what their fathers and brothers had told them of the hunt, comparing it to what Nupa had seen in his vision the night before. Eerily, the eldest boy was correct in all of his accounts.

"You are a shaman," a boy said, his dark eyes wide. The others agreed with him.

Nupa shook his head in scorn. "No. I do not wish to be a shaman. I had one dream. Nothing more."

"Maybe your vision means you should start a society," Cinksi said.

Around her, the boys gave their heartfelt approval to the idea.

"A ritual and a song must be made," one added.

Another boy spoke up, fingering the feathers on his spear, "And a special dance."

"You need to ask Inyan for a song," Nupa said. "Songs are sacred, as are rituals and dances. If this is done, the spirits must support the society."

The pack bowed their heads together, ideas filling the air around them.

Chapter Three

1773

Hooves approached, and Cinksi looked up from her task of braiding a hairpiece from leather, horsehair, and three small feathers. Nupa rode toward her. Considered a warrior now at fifteen winters, he carried himself tall and proud on his pony.

It was common speculation among the old women of the village that Cinksi and Nupa would marry when they became old enough. The pair had been constant companions from the first, stirring up trouble wherever they set their minds and leading the pack of boys to all sorts of altercations. However, both of them had already decided that this would not happen. He had no interest in marriage and knew that she would turn him down if he asked. Nupa wanted a woman like his mother, not to live with another warrior. Cinksi could not conceive of doing women's work, not even for her best friend.

The pair found this amusing, however, and played it up upon occasion – becoming doe-eyed towards one another before suddenly bursting into an argument that caused the both of them to tumble to the ground, wrestling. As time went on, Nupa won far less frequently and Cinksi grew stronger. The elders simply shook their heads and smoked their pipes while the younger members of the camp bet on their favorites.

"*Hau*, Cinksi!" he called as he neared.

The girl grinned and waved at him, tucking her project back into a pouch, and jumping from a rock to her old pony. She noticed several other young men riding closer, relieving the older children of their duty to guard the herd as night grew closer.

They pulled up next to each other.

"How was the day?" he asked with a smile.

"Bad. Nothing happened."

Nupa laughed, his voice still sounding strange to her ears now that it had deepened. "Nothing happening is a good thing, Cinksi!" he insisted.

"Not if you were out here," she grumbled good-naturedly. Glancing at the other riders who were out of hearing range, she asked in a low voice, "Do you know when we are to reach summer camp?"

"The big bellies say sometime in the next two days." Nupa looked around at the change of guard. "Go home, Cinksi. Your mother is making stew. I almost stopped at her lodge to eat before coming here."

Cinksi chuckled. "I am surprised you still live with your mother. You spend much more time with mine." She dodged under his expected swing and brought her arm around to touch him on the back as she kicked her pony forward. "You are slain!" Then she rode away. Fast.

Soon she arrived at her mother's *ti ikceya* and jumped off her pony. She stopped to scratch the reddish brown horse on the forehead before turning him back towards the herd. With a gentle slap on his withers, the pony trotted back the way he came, heading for the remainder of the herd and good grazing. The girl watched him go with great fondness.

He is getting older. *Not as young and spry*, she mused as she turned towards the lodge. *I will need another soon.* She remembered the day her father had presented the horse to her. He gifted it to her for saving her sister when another band attacked theirs. It still saddened Cinksi that she had not been able to save her eldest sibling, clubbed to death by the falling logs of the lodge. *At least my oldest sister's spirit is free now.*

Cinksi moved to the fire pit in front of the lodge and sat down beside her father.

Wanbli was seated to her left, the *tiopa*, the opening of the lodge, to her right. He glanced at her, flashing her a quick smile before returning to fletching an arrow.

Three women sat across the flames from her. The youngest appeared to be no older than Nupa, a beautiful girl nearing full maturity, and sharing many characteristics with Cinksi. The next was much older and resembled them both, with hair turning gray like her husband's. A third, of an age midway between them, quilled a pair of moccasins as the others bustled over the fire and the evening meal; her belly swelled gently with new life.

Cinksi's mother filled a wooden bowl with stew and handed it to Wanbli who made appropriate noises of gratification as he set his arrow aside. She gave a second bowl to Cinksi.

"Wanbli, tell my *ina*, that I thank her," she said, accepting it. "It smells very good." Cinksi immediately dug into the repast with a great show of enjoyment as her father did as she requested.

According to Lakota custom, an older boy of her age could not speak to or look directly upon the women of his family. To do so would show dishonor, not only of the women but to the man they looked to for support. Because of Cinksi's altered status as *wicakte*, she had recently begun to adopt the traditional male role, though it still felt odd to avoid her father's second wife and her own mother in day-to-day conversation. Fortunately, the taboo did not extend to her sister, as siblings were encouraged to be close and support one another through life.

"What did you do with your day?" Wanbli asked as he ate.

The girl shrugged. "I stayed with the horses; they are fine. The travel has done them good. That fat pony of Hwa's has even lost some weight." Looking up from her bowl, Cinksi cast a quick eye at her father's second wife, grinning.

As was proper, Hwa did not address the young *wicakte* directly. Hwa said to Gi, "I have heard my pony is fat, but he is not old and staggering upon ancient hooves."

Cinksi frowned at the comment, but what her second mother said was true. "My pony is getting old. I will have to find another."

Wanbli nodded solemnly. "Perhaps at summer camp. You will have to train your own this time."

"Do you think I could trade?" she asked, finishing her stew.

"Possibly. You might want to wager instead. Or race or wrestle. You do all these things well." His gaze held a fondness for her.

"I will do that, then," Cinksi decided, holding her bowl out to Gi for more. "Nupa says we may be at summer camp within two days." She saw her sister blush at her friend's name and smiled. *Perhaps Nupa will be my brother-in-law!*

"It will be good to have a rest from our travels, good to see friends and family once more." Wanbli finished his meal and, in an exact echo of his daughter's gesture, he held the bowl out to his women for more.

Before the meal concluded, a young girl of seven winters dashed up to the fire. She carried a toy person clutched in one arm, and red stains covered her mouth. "*Ina*! I found berries!" The child produced a small pouch of the fruit, and gave it to Hwa.

"It appears more berries found their way to your stomach, Hinhan," Cinksi said to the girl, finishing her stew.

Blushing, the newest arrival bowed her head as she was given a bowl of food. The women counteracted Cinksi's words with gentle noises of approval. Hinhan, bolstered by their voices, glanced at her older half sister, a shy grin echoing the one on Cinksi's face.

"Where is Wakinyan?"

Wanbli picked up his pipe from its stand and filled the bowl with tobacco. "I do not know," he said of his uncle, the old man living with them since the death of his wife many winters ago. "He may have gone hunting or visiting. He did not say."

After the meal, the women cleaned up and proceeded to work on their projects. Gi sewed a shirt for her husband. Her daughter, Hca Wanahca, ground a bone needle to a point on a well-worn rock. Hwa continued quilling the moccasins, occasionally pausing to rub her belly.

Wanbli, finished with the fletching of his arrow, rose to his feet. He nodded at Cinksi, who stood as well, and the pair of them drifted over to the main fire where the men of the camp gathered. There, the men smoked and talked, telling stories, gambling, and singing songs. Many of the older boys sat among them, listening, learning. When the hour grew late and the fire burned down, the men drifted off to their women's lodges for the night. Tomorrow they planned to be up early and on their way, one day closer to summer camp.

Cinksi ducked into the lodge and glanced about. The fire pit was in the center, her father's robes across, and opposite the door from it in the respected place. Her mother was already rolled up in her robes to the right. Further past her, Hca pulled a wooden comb through her long hair.

The younger girl averted her gaze, visually avoiding her sister as she went to her sleeping robes near her father. Living in a *ti ikceya* with a number of people, avoidance was a common practice within. It was the only way to guarantee privacy. Respectfully, the younger girl's family returned the favor and did not look towards her as she pulled off her shirt and prepared for sleep.

For a long time, Cinksi lay in her robes, her hands behind her head as she gazed up to the juncture of the logs at the top of the lodge. Soon they would arrive at summer camp and the Sun Dance.

Only those who felt they needed to prove themselves to the spirits or show their appreciation for help would dance. Cinksi knew of three in her camp who planned to participate. The ritual of the Sun Dance was of a fluid nature, changing and evolving over the seasons as the people changed and evolved. Sometimes, even *wicincala* were allowed to dance though she had never seen it happen in her lifetime. Cinksi wondered exactly what she could do if she called upon *wakan tanka* for assistance and received it. Maybe she would ask the shaman to teach her the secret rites of the Sun Dance.

Cinksi drifted off to sleep, hearing the drums and songs of the Sun Dance, feeling the sun on her face as she danced, feeling the tug of the ropes where they were attached to her shoulders and back.

~ * ~ * ~ * ~ * ~

Cinksi awoke in the pre-dawn hours of morning. All was silent and peaceful, the sun not yet beginning to grey the sky. She rolled over onto her side and brought her arms around her middle. Her belly ached considerably; it felt as if someone had put a rope around her and pulled it tight. The pain came and went, cramping.

Unsure of what was happening, she worriedly considered calling to her mother, asking for the medicine man. Then a fresh cramp hit unexpectedly, and she moaned a little. She rocked in agony until the pain let up.

There was moisture between her legs. *Did I wet my robes?* she wondered, her fears gaining ground. *I have not done that since I was a baby!* Cinksi's hand delved beneath her breechclout, feeling a heavy slickness. Pulling her hand out, the embers from the fire pit showed only a dark stain on her fingers. The girl squinted in the dim light, trying to understand just what the substance was. They widened as she understood.

I am bleeding! she thought. Another cramp hit her and she moaned again, her heart pounding in fear. *I am going to die!* Once the pain subsided again, she struggled out of her robes, crawling towards her older sister, to wake her, to get help. *I do not want to die!*

Cinksi frantically rousted her sister from sleep. She whispered her fears, explaining that she was bleeding to death.

When the older girl comprehended the reality of the situation, she urged the younger to wait in her robes. "I will take care of you, *mitankala*," she whispered.

Cinksi did as she was told, wondering why her sister did not wake their parents, did not call the medicine man and the shaman. She watched in pain as Hca slipped a dress over her head and moved away from her bedding to rummage around in the herbal stores their mother kept.

"Here," Hca murmured as she returned. She handed her a root. "Chew on this while I make a tea for you. It will help with the pain." The older girl kindly caressed Cinksi's head and smiled. "It will be fine. Trust me. You are becoming a woman now." She then moved to the remains of the fire and stirred up flames to heat some water.

Chewing on the root, Cinksi watched, frowning. *I am becoming a woman? This is the bleeding time?* Many questions filled her mind regarding this new insight and she resolved to ask her sister and mother about them as soon as possible. Another wave of pain hit her and she gasped and rocked.

Hca returned a few minutes later with an herbal tea to help with the pain. She insisted that Cinksi drink it all before it cooled to get the healing benefits from the herbs.

The pain backed away and the younger girl relaxed, a weariness stealing over her. Before she could rest, however, Hca urged her up, telling her to get dressed. The two left Gi's lodge as the eastern horizon grayed with coming dawn.

Hca led her sister to the *isnatipi*, the place of solitude for bleeding women. She entered, tugging Cinksi's reluctant hand. Once they were inside, she taught Cinksi the proper way to position herself, taught her to use the absorbent materials provided to catch the menstrual blood.

Soon Cinksi laid alone, her older sister returning to Gi's *ti ikceya* without her.

There was only vague discomfort now, and she felt the fluid seeping from within her. She would remain here for as many days as it took for the bleeding to end. While the village traveled, she would remain with the *isnatipi*, away from the men. Here was her power, a power that no man held, the power of giving life.

She had been raised as a *hoksila*, a boy. How would things differ when this was over? Would her father decide she could no longer be a warrior? Would he shun her, and tell her to learn how to sew moccasins for he and Wakinyan as befitted a proper maiden?

Worrying this new state of affairs, Cinksi drifted asleep.

Chapter Four

"*Wicahca?*" Cinksi asked, using the formal term of respect. She stood near the fire of Inyan Ceye, waiting for his acknowledgement.

The shaman looked up from sewing a small pouch of fox fur. "*Hau,* Cinksi. Sit with me." He set aside his task and smiled warmly at the girl.

Gingerly, Cinksi sat to the left of the shaman in the honored place. She frowned to herself as she considered what to say. Once her bleeding had ended, she had attempted a vision in the manner of all women — taking the bundle of material with her blood on it, wrapping it carefully in a soft skin, and placing it in the limbs of a tree overlooking summer camp. Cinksi had sat from the dawning of that day until the moon had set that night. No spirits had spoken to her.

Inyan kept his counsel, waiting for her to speak.

The silence continued for some time. It grew more comfortable as the sun moved across the sky rather than distressful. Cinksi mulled over her reasons for approaching the shaman, finally speaking up. "*Wicahca,* I would seek a vision."

The shaman nodded solemnly. "You did not receive one on the hill?" he asked.

Cinksi blushed and ducked her head, unaware he had seen her. "*Hiya.* I did not." She held back from speaking further, uncertainty trapping her tongue.

"Tell me your thoughts, Cinksi," Inyan said. "I cannot help you if you do not."

Her face flushing further, she said, "I do not see why the spirits would give me a vision that way, *wicahca.* I did not seek a vision as my father did or his father before him." She stared at the fire pit before them. "I know that I am not *hoksila,* but I feel the spirits would want me to seek a vision as the other *hoksila* have. If I am to be a warrior, that would be the only way the spirits will speak to me."

The shaman nodded with the same serious intensity. Again silence filled the space as they both contemplated this turn of events. After some time, Inyan said, "Then I must instruct you on seeking a vision, Cinksi, so that you might hear what the spirits have to say to you."

She looked up in surprise, a glow in her dark eyes. "You will help me, Inyan?" she asked, her voice almost a whisper.

"*Hau*, Cinksi. Now, go. I must prepare to teach you the way."

"*Ohan, wicahca*!" She jumped up, barely tempering her excitement. "Thank you!"

"Do not thank me, young warrior," Inyan intoned, though his dark eyes sparkled with humor. "It is you that must be clear and centered and able to receive a vision from *wakan tanka*."

Her heart flew with the eagles as she left the shaman's fire. Since her bleeding clouds filled her heart and mind. Was she a warrior? Or was she a woman? Her father treated her as always when it was over, not once indicating she should move her sleeping furs to the women's side of the lodge, though he had avoided her while she bled, even when the village traveled to another camp. During her stay in the *isnatipi*, her mother and sister had stayed near, treating her as one of them. Yet, once it was done, they returned to their normal behavior, not speaking to or looking at her directly.

Cinksi thought of the *winkte*, the two-souled people. Neither man nor woman, they embodied both. Born male, they nevertheless took on feminine aspects. She knew of only three among her people, residing in other camps.

She knew of no one like her, none who were *wicakte*, born female and embodying masculine aspects. It seemed when the bleeding time was upon her, she would be a woman, but in all else a man.

Perhaps the spirits will honor me with a vision and show me the way of things.

~ * ~ * ~ * ~ * ~

Cinksi left the *oinikaga* tipi, her body slick from the steam inside. She wore only a breechclout and moccasins, as was prescribed by Inyan, shivering as early morning air caressed her heated skin. It felt odd to not wear a shirt; since her breasts began to develop a few moons ago, she had begun to wear one all the time.

Outside the rounded lodge, she picked up a leather bag, that she slung across her shoulders, and a buffalo robe she covered herself with. These were the only things she would take on her quest.

It was still dark, the coolness in the air despite the season causing her to tremble again. Cinksi pulled the robe tighter around her shoulders and moved into the darkness. Inyan had told her to walk toward the rising sun until she found a high place for her final preparations. When she asked how she would know it was the right place, he had answered, "You will know."

"I will know," she repeated to herself.

Time passed and soon the sun was high. She removed the robe, not expecting to meet anyone out in the wilderness of the northern plains. Rolling hills rose around her and she considered which would be the proper place to make a stand. She stood at the base of a hill and saw a boulder thrusting from the earth. The shadows from the sun overhead gave it a dangerous appearance. As she stared at it, she realized it resembled a cougar.

Inyan had seen the *igmu* in a vision before she was born. This must be the place the spirits wanted her to use.

Cinksi climbed the hill. Her stomach indicated that it was now nearing the evening meal as she reached its summit and looked around. The boulder stuck out of the hillside perpendicular with the ground, leaving a slight hollow in the prairie grass at its base. *This will do well,* she thought.

She removed the pouch and set it aside with the robe. As the shaman had instructed, she cleared a patch of ground of all life. The area was longer than she was tall and as wide as her reach. Her chore complete, she gathered the robe and pouch and stepped within.

She could not leave until the spirits blessed her with a vision, or until she gave up.

Cinksi spoke the ritual words she had been taught by Inyan as she opened the pouch. Carefully, she drew out four tiny bundles about the size of her thumb. Each was attached to the twig of the plum tree and had been made by the shaman for her quest. With further chants, she stood the twig in the ground on the western side of the cleared area, then the southern side, followed by the eastern and northern edges. These were the spirit banners and would protect her from harm.

Next out of the pouch came a fur-wrapped pipe, a quantity of tobacco and a few other herbs. She gathered the herbs together into a small pile, and also loaded the bowl of the pipe. The final item from her pouch was a smoldering ember kept safe in the hollow of an antler. Cinksi lit the herbs, the sweet smell of sage and rosemary filling the air around her.

Using the ember to light the tobacco, she offered the pipe to the western sky. "Spirit of the West," she called, "I am Cinksi and I seek a vision." She took a puff of the smoke, directing the excess cloud over her head, and waited.

Nothing happened.

Cinksi was uncertain how long to wait. Inyan had told her that she was to allow some time in between requests to give the spirits time to contact her. *I cannot wait too long. My ember will burn out and I will not be able to complete the ritual.* She debated this for some time.

Coming to a decision, she turned to the east and followed the same procedure, offering the pipe, calling out a request, smoking, and waiting. This was followed by supplications to the Spirits of the North and South with the same results.

The girl sighed. The spirits desired to see her resolve in this matter. She decided to take the next course of action.

"Spirit of the Sky, I am Cinksi and I seek a vision."

Nothing.

Frowning, Cinksi finished the ritual. She asked the Sun for a vision, its flaming visage beginning to dip behind the hills as the evening drew to a close. Then she asked the Earth itself for a vision, the final and most significant request. The girl finished just in time as the coal she used finally burned out.

She crouched down in the clearing, her face against the ground. Cinksi wrapped her robe around her and concentrated on receiving a vision from the spirits.

~ * ~ * ~ * ~ * ~

It happened the second night, moving into the third morning. The only truly frightening time had been wolves howling nearby, but none had approached Cinksi. The spirit of the *igmu* residing in the boulder kept her from harm.

She found it hard to focus on her desire for a vision. Especially at first, when her every thought was on food and warmth. When she was not asleep, she concentrated on a vision, searching the area around her for a sign from the spirits. None was forthcoming.

The girl felt dizzy from lack of food and water. If she did not receive a vision soon, she would have to make the choice of dying here or giving up. It wasn't unusual for someone to return to camp after a vision quest without finding what he or she sought. Cinksi could not believe that *wakan tanka* would set her on the path of a *wicakte*, yet not speak to her.

Cinksi faced the east. As the sun rose before her, it occurred.

The Sun flared into a brilliant white light. She had to squint to peer at it, one hand raised to shade her eyes. As the light faded, she saw a cloud of dust rising and felt the ground beneath her shake as a thousand buffalo stampeded. They ran towards her position, led by the most sacred animal of all, the white buffalo.

Watching in dazed awe, Cinksi saw a warrior woman swoop in from the south, screaming her cry as she attacked the white buffalo with a spear. The warrior's hit was solid, and the white buffalo stumbled, mortally wounded.

The remainder of the herd simply disappeared, as did the warrior woman. The white buffalo staggered closer to Cinksi, blood pouring from its side, its nostrils flaring wide as it panted for breath. It fell just outside the cleared area, looking so real she could almost touch it. Even the hair about her shoulders lifted from the wind of its fall, dust sour upon her tongue. The Sun flared again, and she lost the image, covering her eyes with her arm. When the light faded, she looked again to find the white buffalo gone.

In its place knelt a strange woman with pale skin. Her hair was long, longer than Cinksi's, and a yellow the color of the Sun itself. Her eyes were the blue of a deep lake, still and clear. She wore the buckskin dress all of Cinksi's women wore and moccasins, her hair flowing freely in the breeze.

This strange apparition rose from where the white buffalo had fallen, blood pouring from her side where the buffalo had been wounded. She walked gently closer to the girl staring at her in wonder, her movement making no sound. Then she put a hand to her wound, bloodying her fingers. Reaching forward, she brushed the blood onto Cinksi's face, two thunderbolts beneath the dark eyes. As the Sun flared again, the girl saw brilliant blue staring at her intently, and heard the word whispered into her ear.

"*Mahasanni.*"

The light returned to normal. Cinksi looked frantically around for the woman or the white buffalo and found nothing. With shaky fingers, she touched her face. Again there was nothing.

Trembling, the girl gathered her pouch and robe. She must return to camp to ask the shaman to help her interpret her vision.

Chapter Five

Cinksi sat anxiously as she awaited the verdict of someone wiser than herself. Inyan had heard her tale and now smoked in reflection. He passed the pipe to her, stem first, and her heart thrilled. With her vision, she had finally become an adult member of her people. It warmed her as she took the sacred smoke into her lungs and returned the pipe to the shaman.

"It is a complicated vision, Cinksi," Inyan commented once the smoking was done and the ashes given to the fire. "I do not presume to understand what the spirits wanted someone to know."

"I understand, *wicahca*."

The shaman nodded. "To see the white *tatanka*, to see yourself slay him...I think this is a vision of your future. And so the rest of your vision must be your future, as well."

She frowned, her dark brows furrowed. "But, the yellow woman? Is she my future? Why did she call me *mahasanni*? Only the closest of couples call one another such."

"I do not know. She is a stranger to us. She may be a stranger to our ways. But she is involved with the *tatanka*." Inyan stared into the flames of the fire. "Perhaps on your path as *wicakte*, you will acquire both wives and husbands; perhaps she is one."

Cinksi carefully thought this over. The idea of joining with another – be it man or woman – seemed odd to her. She had only just become an adult; marriage was too far in her future to contemplate.

"You will hurt this yellow woman as you did the white buffalo."

For some inexplicable reason, Cinksi's heart twisted in sadness to hear these words, driving away her puzzlement. "Will I kill her, too?" she asked, not wanting to hear the answer.

"I do not know. She speaks to you with love even after wounding. Maybe she sacrifices herself for you in some manner. The details are unclear."

Her soul felt weighted with unhappiness. The yellow woman had been so intriguing, so wondrous, more so even than seeing her adult self kill the sacred white buffalo. Cinksi wondered if it was possible to change the future.

"You have had a very powerful vision, *wicakte*," the shaman said. "Not many receive such strength. Use the power well."

"I will, Inyan." Roused from her melancholy, she said, "My father plans a celebration feast tomorrow."

"I look forward to celebrating with you."

~ * ~ * ~ * ~ * ~

The following day when Cinksi awoke, she discovered gifts from her family displayed at her place by the fire. A fine yellow shirt, painted and quilled with designs from her mother; two pairs of moccasins with red suns upon a white background from Hca; a third pair painted blue and green from her half sister, Hinhan; and a set of breechclouts and leggings from Hwa, her second mother.

Pleased with the items, she made sure to praise the women of her family to her father and his uncle within their hearing. The women responded in kind, chattering among themselves over the young warrior's attractiveness.

The crier wandered the village, announcing a grand feast held by Wanbli; that all were welcome. Soon, the news was picked up by heralds from other villages in the great hoop of summer camp, and it promised to be quite an event. Cinksi flushed upon hearing her name spoken among the people, the cause of the celebration known among the thousands of Lakota camped there.

Her village worked industriously, the women assisting Gi and Hwa with cooking and preparing for the celebration. While Wanbli had announced the feast for his family, the Maka band showed their appreciation of the *wicakte* in their midst by helping. Those born with two souls illustrated the balance of nature with their existence, and were most sacred. That this one had visions of *tatanka ska*, the white buffalo, boded well for the future of the village.

Rather than hold the feast at Wanbli's fire, people migrated to the central fire of the Maka in order to accommodate the larger number of expected guests. As afternoon wore into evening, food flowed freely and many joined the celebration. The fire burned high as drummers and singers entertained the people. Men danced the songs as women trilled their joy. Someone began a woman's tune, and the dance shifted to females.

At a break in the festivities, Inyan stepped into the firelight. He wore a buffalo helmet and a cougar mantle, his face painted into a fierce visage of white and black. Red lightning bolts slashed across his cheeks. The music stopped as he walked once, twice, a total of four times around the fire, arms wide and head thrown back.

"Today is a very good day," he said, his usually gentle tones rough as he projected to the large crowd. "Today a young *wicakte* met with the spirits, and returned with a powerful vision of the future. Of her future."

Cinksi's skin darkened as her family and strangers murmured in appreciation of her vision. The attention, while pleasing, came near to overwhelming her. Inyan continued speaking, fortunately, and drew the people's ears.

"Now is the time this young person, this *wicakte*, be given a name to show her appreciation of the spirits and their message."

Her mouth almost dropped open as she stared at the shaman. *A new name? Not even Nupa has received a new name, and he is older.*

"I have spoken with the spirits of my ancestors, the buffalo, and the spirit of the *igmu* that sits within this young heart. They have told me that Cinksi is no more. She will be known as Wi Ile Anpo."

Women trilled their happiness and men whooped in support of this new name. Anpo, who used to be Cinksi, could not help but flush further. Her village's crier took up her new name and sang it aloud, his words caught by other heralds until all in summer camp would know.

Wanbli entered the circle of firelight with the shaman, a handful of carved sticks in his hand. "I give away five of my best horses to whoever presents one of these to me," he said, his voice rich with pride. "I give these in the name of my *cinksi* of the heart, Anpo." He threw the sticks into the crowd.

Anpo remained still, pleased at her father's generosity as well as her new name. Perhaps the vision did not bode as ill as she first perceived.

Part 2: Winyan Ki
The Woman

Chapter Six

1773

"Kathleen, where's your brother?"

The girl sighed deeply and rolled her eyes in adolescent exasperation. "I don't know, Mum." She glanced over her shoulder at the cabin window. "'Twas supposed to be cutting wood for Da!" Returning her attention to the peas she snapped into a bowl for the evening meal, she mumbled under her breath, "I don't understand why I'm to know what he does every waking moment."

"Because you're the eldest and the one with the responsibility," her mother reminded her, a faint smile on her face as she stepped onto the porch. She ignored her daughter's blush and patted her gently on the back. "I'll finish these," she said, taking the bowl of vegetables. "You go find Stewart and tell him his da could use help with the tilling."

"Aye, Mum," Kathleen muttered. She stomped off to locate her errant sibling.

There were not many places he could have got off to on the frontier. The prior year the McGlashans finally paid off their indentured owings after seven years of servitude in Boston. They had joined a group of like-minded individuals heading west in search of freedom and land to call their own. Their new home, a two story cabin with two rooms and a loft, had only recently been completed, and work had begun on the land in earnest. Things had been hard last winter, but it had looked up through summer – the soil was fertile, the land green and growing, and a natural spring ran near enough that a well wasn't necessary. Their nearest neighbor was the widower Adam Stevens three miles to the north. A bit further away were four or five other homesteads and the closest sign of civilization over six days travel to the east.

Kathleen could not help but recall her father expounding on the wonders of the New Country back in Ireland. She had been so disappointed when the milk and honey he promised did not flow from the rivers and trees. She remembered she was supposed to be searching for her bratty brother, and pressed her lips and brows together in a scowl.

She circled the cabin to find her brother nowhere near the wood-pile as expected, the ax imbedded in an old stump. "That brat!" She stood with her hands on her hips, surveying the area around their home.

A large stand of maple shadowed the northeastern side of the cabin. Kathleen saw her father in the field to the west of the homestead, urging their cantankerous mule to pull the plowshare.

"Stewart!" she called.

From a distance, she heard his voice. "What?"

Turning towards the small barn, she marched toward it. The door stood wide and she stepped in, stopping to allow her eyes to adjust to the dimmer lighting. "Stewart?"

"Aye, Kath, I'm right here."

Kathleen could make out a smaller form over by a stall. "Da's looking for you, Stewart. He wants you to help with the plowing." She moved closer to her little brother. "What're you doing in here, anyway?"

The eleven-year-old boy, three years her junior, hung on the partition between the stalls and grinned over his shoulder. "Watching Caleb." He waved a hand at the animal in the stall.

Kathleen leaned against the railing, peering in at the new addition to their farm. Their milk cow had given birth that spring to a calf. It had immediately captured the younger McGlashan's fancy, and he spent near as much time with the animal as he did with his family.

"He's growing like a weed," Kathleen said.

Stewart's grin widened. "Aye, he is," he said proudly, as if he had something to do with the natural growth spurt of a young bull.

Kathleen cocked her head in exasperation. "You better get out to the field. Da's looking for you."

The boy sighed and brushed unruly blond hair from his eyes. "Guess you're right, sis." He waved at the calf. "See you tonight, Caleb," he said before pushing away from the partition and heading for the door.

From outside, their mother's voice could be heard. "Kathleen!"

"Ah, I'm in trouble again." Her eyes flashed angrily at her brother's laugh.

Stewart patted her gently on the arm. "When aren't you in trouble, lass?" he asked. "You've been on the wrong side of Mum's temper so long, I don't think you'd know what 'twas like to not be." He scampered off before she could smack him.

Growling, Kathleen watched him go and wondered why what he said was so true.

"Kathleen Sarah McGlashan!"

"Aye, Mum! I'm coming!" She lifted the hem of her dress and jogged back around the house.

~ * ~ * ~ * ~ * ~

"I don't understand why I have to get all cleaned up, Mum!" Kathleen complained. Promptly upon her return, she had been put to work heating water for a bath. She now soaked in a medium sized barrel the family used for a tub, lavender scented steam rising about her as she made a half-hearted attempt at washing. "It's not even Saturday."

Rachel McGlashan bustled about the main room of their home, putting the final touches on some cookies before sliding the tray of them into a small Dutch oven in the fireplace. "I've told you, lass. We're having company for supper."

Kathleen frowned, brushing at a strand of yellow hair that had evaded tying atop her head. "Does Stewart have to clean up, too?"

"Aye. He'll have to clean up some as well," her mother replied, an odd tone in her voice.

Something did not seem right. *Who could be coming? The only neighbor near is the widower Stevens.* Kathleen had never had to do this the last time he came for dinner. The teenager worried the problem as she finished her bath.

"Here, love, let me help you wash your hair," Rachel interrupted her daughter's thoughts.

Now I know something's fishy! Mum hasn't helped with my hair in...well, in forever!

"I've always loved your hair, lass," Rachel murmured, once she'd begun lathering the blonde tresses with soap. "It's so much thicker than my own."

Uncertain, Kathleen murmured, "Thank you, Mum."

"You've grown into such a beautiful young woman, too. Every day you look more and more like my mum." There was a comfortable silence. "Do you remember your Gram?"

"Aye, Mum. She had white hair and taught me to play the tin whistle."

Rachel smiled at the memory. "Good. I'm glad you do. She was a wonderful lady. When she was much younger, her hair was as bright as yours is now."

Despite herself, Kathleen closed her eyes and exhaled slowly, the strong fingers massaging her scalp relaxing her. "What's really going on, Mum?"

The older woman remained silent for a moment. "Widower Stevens is coming to dinner."

"But why am I getting all cleaned up then?"

"Kathleen," her mother started, "he's a lonely man. His wife passed away two years ago, and he's out there on that farm by himself with no sons to help out."

The teenager's brow furrowed as she considered this statement.

For some reason, she did not understand what her mother was attempting to say.

The older woman continued when her daughter had no response. "And you're not going to find many other choices out here in the wilderness for a husband, Kathleen."

Blue eyes flew open as the full weight of her mother's comment hit her. *Marry him! She wants me to marry him!* "But...but, Mum," she sputtered, pulling away and turning to peer in horror over her shoulder. "He's an old man!"

Rachel's mouth pinched together in irritation. "He's not that old, lass. He's only twenty-eight." To forestall further comment from her eldest child, she held up her soapy hands in warning. "And a good provider. Why, he's got a good ten acres of land in seed now, and it's growing every year!"

"I don't care *how* much land he has!" the teenager yelled. "I'll not marry him!"

The older woman sighed explosively and rose to her feet. She picked up a nearby towel and wiped off her hands, speaking all the while. "It's not like we're trying to marry you off today, Kathleen! We're only inviting him to break bread with us, give the two of you a chance to get to know one another. You're too young to be married yet."

Kathleen brushed soapy bangs from her eyes. "I am?"

"Aye, lass. Do you think we're that barbaric? To wed our oldest child to a stranger at fourteen?" Rachel sighed again. "It's just that there's not many options for a pretty young lass out here. We can only do the best we can."

"Aye, Mum." Kathleen ducked her head in shame.

"Promise me you'll give him a chance, Kathleen." When her daughter stared back, Rachel returned to kneel by the tub. "Promise me. It's not Widower Stevens' fault, either. Don't be taking things out on him."

The slumped shoulders were far more eloquent than the words murmured from Kathleen's mouth. "Aye, Mum. I promise."

"Good!" Rachel rose to her feet, a smile on her face. "Now, rinse your hair, love, and I'll help you dry off and get dressed." She moved away to check on the cookies, humming under her breath.

Kathleen heaved a heavy sigh and did as she was told.

~ * ~ * ~ * ~ * ~

Her mother had dressed her in her Sunday best and helped put her hair up. All the while, Kathleen was regaled with hints of how to carry herself in the presence of their dinner guest. When the rest of her family came back from the field, the responses were mixed. McGlashan was properly awed at the beautiful young woman blushing by the fireplace. Stewart giggled at her, however, and Kathleen lost her decorum to chase after him as he bolted out the door. Despite the stern commands from their father to return, she caught the little monster and knuckled his head for his disrespect.

Widower Stevens, a tall, thin man dressed in dark clothing, arrived on a horse at the required time. The men immediately gathered together and began discussing the weather, the crops, and the animals. Stewart kept himself underfoot, trying to entice the visitor to the barn to see Caleb.

Kathleen watched surreptitiously from a window. *He's not a bad looking man,* she finally allowed. *If we were to be married, our children would be blond. And he appears to be gentle and kind.* The teenager turned away, catching her mother watching her, a smile on her face. With a grimace, she returned to stirring the pot of stew.

Everyone sat at the table for the evening meal, though the women stayed on their feet while they served the men and boy. Conversation ranged through various topics from the standard day-to-day existence to the rumblings from the colonies to the east.

"You know, there's talk of revolution in the colonies," Stevens commented. He smiled up at Kathleen who refilled his mug of ale. "We get news so late here, though, I doubt we'd hear of anything 'til years after the fact."

"Aye," McGlashan nodded. He pushed back from the table. "Stewart, get my pipe. There's a good lad." As the man opened the tobacco pouch and began packing the bowl, he continued. "I'd heard that a British ship ran aground last year at Rhode Island. 'Tweren't long before the colonists themselves burnt it out."

"Things are getting volatile, and that's for certain," Stevens said. "Out here, though... Not much call to get involved. Don't reckon that the British will get this far into the wilds."

"Probably not," McGlashan agreed.

"But, Da," the boy piped up. "Didn't the British get this far up north? They were fighting with the French up by the lakes."

Their guest nodded. "True, lad. But, now they've got all the land between here and there full of colonists who aren't happy with the way things are going. At least up north they had the support of the colonies."

The talk continued on as the women gathered up the remains of the meal. The men eventually wandered outside into the night to smoke and chat some more of politics and the like. Rachel used the time wisely to speak with her daughter.

"See, Kathleen? That wasn't so bad now, was it?" She scraped the remains of the meal onto a single plate.

Reluctantly, the teenager nodded. "Aye. 'Twas all right."

"And you see what I meant? You could do worse out here for a future husband, you know."

"I know, Mum. I know."

Chapter Seven

1775

"Dinner was wonderful this evening, Kathleen."

"Thank you, Mr. Stevens. I'm glad you liked it. I recall you mentioning a fondness for cabbage at your last visit."

The couple sat on the front porch of the McGlashan homestead, enjoying a rare warm autumn evening. Inside, Kathleen's family cleaned up from the meal and settled in for an evening before the fire. Tonight, Rachel had made certain their visitor was aware of her daughter's contribution to supper. She seemed to enjoy Kathleen's embarrassment, gently chiding her for not being proud of the dish served.

Stevens' weekly visits had become a regular occurrence, as were the after dinner discussions between the couple. As time progressed, they were gently pushed together by Kathleen's parents, neither of them ignorant of the reasons. Everyone within a thirty mile radius of the McGlashans knew they paraded their daughter before Stevens in an attempt to make a good match for her.

Having grown comfortable with the weekly arrangement, Kathleen blinked when Stevens leaned forward to take her hand. For two years he had refrained from physical contact, as was proper for their relationship. Startled into a closer inspection, she noted his blue eyes seemed more intense than usual, and she felt her heart tremble with dread.

"Kathleen," he said, "I would like to ask your father for your hand in marriage." When she did not respond, Stevens continued. "It seems the right thing to do. Neither of us have many other options out here. And I'm not getting any younger. I can't promise you that it'll be an easy life, but it can be a rewarding one."

She swallowed, her heartbeat fluttering in her throat. *Well, it's finally come.* Kathleen's brow furrowed as she attempted to consider his request. All she noted, however, was that his touch felt sweaty and a bit oily.

Stevens squeezed her hand with tender affection. "I'll not expect an answer this trip, Kathleen. I know it's an important decision for you. I don't want you to feel pressured into something you don't want."

"Thank you, Mr. Stevens," she murmured in a low voice.

Releasing her hand, he brought his fingers up to her chin and raised her head to look at him. "Please, Kathleen. My given name is Adam. I'd much rather hear such from your beautiful lips."

The intimate touch felt sinful and improper. Kathleen was not sure whether to be offended or not. After a long pause, she slowly nodded. "Aye, then. Adam."

Stevens' smile widened, and he rose to his feet. "'Tis time for me to be heading home. You'll confer my thanks to your family?" He settled his wide brimmed hat on his head.

"Certainly...Adam," Kathleen responded, blushing at the use of his first name. She stepped off the porch with him towards his horse. Once there, she watched in astonishment as he kissed the back of her knuckles.

"'Til next week then, my Kathleen." He mounted his horse and, with a tip of his hat and a grin, he wheeled about and trotted away.

Kathleen crossed her arms in front of her and watched him until he left her sight. Alone except for the call of an owl nearby and stars sparkling above, she drifted back toward the cabin. At the door, she heard her father reading the Bible aloud to her family.

She had to tell them about Stevens' question, and to do so would change everything. Already, she imagined her mother's face lighting with the news. Her father would be gruff, putting on an air of paternal protectiveness to hide his pleasure. Loath to speak to them just yet, she retreated to the chair she had vacated moments earlier.

The proposal had finally come. Kathleen knew her mother had expected it for a few months. Stevens, a well to do bachelor, had stopped visiting the two other homesteads housing eligible women the previous year. It seemed no secret to the farmers in the area that his hat was set for the pretty McGlashan girl. Kathleen scowled to herself as she recalled the embarrassing speculation at a barn raising this past summer. The women and girls could speak of nothing else, teasing her outright or whispering with delicious joy over the rumors.

Kathleen sighed. She knew she was supposed to be happy. Potential husbands were few and far between out here on the frontier. In fact, she knew of no others within twenty miles. One lived on the other side of the Ohio, further into the frontier than most had gone, his homestead taking tenacious hold in a dangerous valley. If Kathleen ever wished to realize her dream of a dozen babies, she could do no worse – Stevens seemed a kind and even tempered man, not prone to fits of temper. Intelligent and well read, he could debate politics with the best of them. She knew little of his previous wife; he seemed reluctant to discuss the topic in mixed company. Kathleen only knew he had had one, lost to fever long ago.

But her dreams...her dreams said Stevens was the wrong choice.

Kathleen knew what her future held. The man who haunted her had dark eyes and hair, unlike Stevens. Where the widower kept his sandy blond hair cropped close, the man in Kathleen's visions had long hair, tied back at the nape of his neck. If she closed her eyes, she could almost see him standing before her in a fine suit, a smile on his handsome face, looking every inch the proper gentleman out for a stroll on the streets of Boston.

If only the dream was reality. Instead, she remembered her mother's words, expounding on Stevens' ability as a provider. Her father marveled at the man's intelligence and canny wisdom. Even bratty Stewart seemed enamored of Stevens.

"I wish you'd all just shut up!" she mumbled.

"I've not said anything."

Kathleen turned to see her little brother standing at the door. She sighed and rolled her eyes. "I was talking to myself, Stew." She stared out into the dooryard, hoping her sibling would take the hint and go back inside.

Such was not the case. The youth approached and sat in the chair beside her. "Da sent me out to see if you're well. Is Mr. Stevens gone then?"

"Aye, he is."

He cocked his head, a lock of yellow blond hair dropping into his eyes. "Did he hurt you somehow? Take advantage?"

Kathleen heard the muted warning in Stewart's voice and stared at him. "No," she said. "No, he didn't." The expression of concern on his face was so unfamiliar, she wondered if he was a changeling. Curious, she asked, "And what if he did, Stew?"

Eyebrows so like hers knitted together. "Then I'd have to get Da's musket and set Mr. Stevens straight." He sat a little taller and puffed out his chest in manly resolve.

Kathleen studied him. "Why?" she whispered, trying to comprehend.

"Why?" Stewart asked, confused. "Because you're my sis, that's why! He might be the only man out here for miles, but that doesn't mean he can have sport with you." He shrugged. "I mean, I like him and all, but I'd still defend your honor."

A small smile crossed Kathleen's face. "Even if he'd make me a good husband? A wonderful provider and father?"

"Aye. Even then. If you'd none of him, then none of him you'll have, if I have any say over it."

"But, he's smart and friendly and kind and generous," Kathleen added, bringing up all the things she'd been told by their parents.

"And so is my bull, Caleb," the youth said sarcastically. "But that's neither here nor there." He placed a hand on her knee. "What's wrong, Kath?"

"Mr. Stevens...Adam has asked me to marry him."

Stewart blinked at her. "Have you made a decision?"

"No. I haven't. But he'll be expecting an answer next week after dinner."

"Well, Da always says two heads are better than one. Maybe I can help you?"

Kathleen snorted. "I don't think so, Stew. 'Tis not like I'm trying to find different solutions to a problem. A simple yes or no will do him fine."

"Aye, Kath, but you're obviously unsure. Maybe talking it over with me will help set things straight in your mind." He looked at her with an open face, nodding gently.

Perhaps he's right. What can it hurt? You need to give Mr. Ste–Adam an answer. She nodded, and Stewart sat back with an air of expectation. "All right then. What do you want to know?"

He pursed his lips and scratched idly at his neck. "Do you love him?"

Another snort. "I don't know, Stew. I don't think so. I like him well enough and all, but I don't think I love him."

"Well, then. Does he love you?"

A wry grin quirked her lips. "I'm sure enough of that to say no. Adam feels the same way I do, I believe."

Stewart frowned. "Maybe we're going about this the wrong way." He picked up a twig and began peeling the bark from it. "Kath, what do you want to do with your life?"

"I've never given it much thought," she said with a shrug. "I've always known I'd find a man, get married, have babies. I've always wanted to have lots of babies." Her eyes grew distant, searching her memories and dreams. "'Tis funny, you know? I can remember dreaming of having lots of children and raising them up in my own home. But, for the life of me, I can't remember of ever thinking of a husband to share my life with." She wondered if she should tell him of the man in her dreams, but decided against doing so. It was only a wisp of fancy, not real life.

"Well, you can't have one without the other," Stewart smirked.

"Hush!" Kathleen said with a smile, bumping her shoulder against his.

"So, you like him. And he likes you. But having a husband isn't all that important to you," he summed up.

"Aye, that about covers it."

"Then I'd say your best option would be to marry him. At least there's a basis for friendship – 'tisn't like you hate each other. And then you can have all those babies you've wanted."

"True," Kathleen agreed, though deep in her heart she felt the wrongness. *But, logically speaking 'tis the truth all around.* Still, somehow she knew this was not the path her life would take. She could feel it to her bones. *And until my life goes another way? Sit here at my parents' home? Become an old maid?* Kathleen turned to look at her little brother. She smiled reassurance and patted his hand. "Thank you, Stewart. You've been a big help this evening."

"You can always talk to me, Kath," he promised. "We've had our differences in the past, but I've grown up some. Things are different from when we were children."

The fact that he was still a child in her opinion caused a glimmer of laughter, and Kathleen stifled it. "Aye, Stew. You're right. Things are different." She rose to her feet. "We'd best be for getting inside before it chills."

Seeing that the conversation was over, the boy stood. "That's the fair truth of it," he said, walking to the door.

Kathleen felt a wave of love for her brother, enhanced by the golden light from inside when he opened the door. *Maybe things would work out just fine after all.*

Chapter Eight

The perfect excuse for a party, plans began in earnest almost before Stevens left the following week. While McGlashan continued working the crops, Stewart took their mule around the outlying area and issued invites to other families. He was on the road for three nights and returned with several happy responses to attend. After Stewart's return, Stevens left for the nearest township to make arrangements with a magistrate to officiate over the nuptials. The journey was six days in either direction, so the McGlashan clan juggled the work of both farms.

In Kathleen's home, preparations became fevered.

"Oh, Mum!" The teenager sighed in exasperation. "I've tried this dress on a hundred times!" She stood on a stool near the fireplace as her mother fussed around the hem of a green gingham outfit.

Rachel tugged on the hem to readjust the waistline, studying her daughter's clothing with a practiced eye. "Aye, and you'll be trying it on a hundred more 'til we get it right," she insisted, mumbling through the pins in her mouth. "Now, stand still, lass! Or you'll be lopsided at your wedding!"

Glowering at the ceiling, Kathleen mumbled, "Aye, Mum."

The older woman continued to pin up the hem of the dress, humming away. When finished, she stepped back to observe her handiwork before finally giving the girl permission to step down. "I've heard the Heinrich's will be here with bells on the day before," she said, gathering the gingham in hand and rustling over to her chair by the fireplace.

Kathleen pulled another dress over her shift. "Why the day before?"

"To help with the cleaning and fixing. Mrs. Heinrich makes a fine potato cake, if you recall." Rachel sat down, the dress in her lap, and strung a needle with thread. "She and her children will come and Mr. Heinrich will stay behind until the following day." Adjusting the cloth, she stopped to wipe a strand of graying blonde hair from her eyes. "I think we'll set them up in the barn. I'll have Stewart muck it out the day before."

Kathleen finished dressing and moved to the table where the fixings for an apple pie were set out. As she began paring the apples, she asked, "How many will be attending?"

Rachel rocked gently in her chair. "Oh, looks to be about a dozen, no more. The Heinrichs, that new couple down south of here, said they'll come, and the Anders clan. 'Twill be an exciting day for you, Kathleen! You'll look so pretty in your wedding dress." She beamed at her daughter.

"Aye," she responded dutifully, not feeling all that excited at the prospect of becoming Mrs. Adam Stevens. More like...dread.

The days passed too quickly for Kathleen. Her wedding day dawned bright and promising. The barn held most of the Heinrich family, soon to be joined by their father and eldest brother later in the afternoon. A wagon had pulled up the previous night, the young Cooper couple from down south bedding inside. Kathleen's nearest neighbors, the Anders, were due at any time.

The homestead was packed to the rafters; women and girls clustered around inside the cabin fixing their best dishes for the festivities. The men and boys milled about outside, smoking pipes, looking over McGlashan's farmstead, and listening to Stewart constantly pressure people to look at Caleb the bull in the north field.

At a little past midday, Stevens arrived with the magistrate in tow. The pompous little official puffed about the small clearing designated as the wedding site and praised the makeshift tables laden with food. Meanwhile, the men dragged the groom to the barn. Once there, he was given a shot of homemade liquor that made his pale eyes water, and gussied up for the ceremony. The women fawned over the bride, pinching her cheeks, helping her into her dress, discussing the attributes of the new husband-to-be, and generally making Kathleen all the more nervous for their efforts.

Stewart, dressed in his finest, burst into the cabin. "Are you ready then?" he asked, raising his voice to be heard over the clamor of the women.

"Yes!" Rachel called from behind the crowd.

The women parted, revealing Kathleen. The green gingham dress was long and full, a high waist accentuating the bosom. Long sleeves puffed out on the upper arms, closing in to fit tightly around the forearms and wrists. Handmade lace had been attached to the cuffs and low collar, and additional material had been used as a belt, a bow tied in the back. Her blonde hair was piled high on her head, with ringlets and spit curls spilling down here and there.

"Kath! You look..." Stewart blinked. "You look incredible, lass."

Kathleen blushed a little, not used to compliments from her bratty sibling. "Aye. Thank you, Stew."

He stepped forward, his eyes shining with some unknown emotion. "If you weren't my sis, I'd marry you myself."

She drew herself up at the giggles from the women around her and glared down at her brother in sisterly exasperation. "Like I'd have you, you brat."

"Kathleen Sarah McGlashan!" her mother said into the shocked room.

Stewart blinked again, coming to his senses. A grin split his face, and he punched Kathleen on the upper arm. "Aye. I'm a brat. But it beats being a lily livered canary whistling on the pipes all day."

Rachel sounded even more distressed as she gasped, "Stewart Franklin!"

The siblings ignored her and swept each other up into an embrace.

"You look fantastic, Kath," he whispered.

"Thank you, Stew," she whispered back.

Outside, the sounds of Mr. Heinrich's accordion filtered through the still open door.

"There 'tis then," a woman nearby piped up. "Time to get a move on, younglings."

Kathleen released her brother and gulped down the sudden overwhelming fear that threatened to crowd out all thought. Stewart pecked her once on the cheek and ran back out the door, preparing to take his place as Stevens' best man. The women around her filtered out to take their places with their husbands and parents with the exception of Mrs. Anders and her young daughter. These were to be Kathleen's matron of honor and flower girl.

Rachel gave her daughter a quick, reassuring hug and a kiss. "You'll do fine, lass," she whispered. "You look so beautiful!" Blue eyes already glistening with unshed tears, she hugged Kathleen fiercely to herself once more. Then she bustled out the door to take her place with the rest of the wedding party.

Mrs. Anders looked to the young bride. "Kathleen?"

She fought down her rising bile and forced a smile to her face. "Time to get married."

~ * ~ * ~ * ~ * ~

The ceremony went off without a hitch, her mother and half the other women crying in response. The groom looked resplendent in his best suit, the buckles on his Sunday shoes shining brilliantly. When he had seen his bride for the first time in all her splendor, his eyes glinted with unshed tears of happiness.

After the wedding, everyone gathered for a feast and fest. The clearing in front of the cabin was utilized as a dance floor as McGlashan and the Heinrich's boy pulled out fiddles and joined Mr. Heinrich's accordion. While there were more women than men at the function, that did not stop anyone from merrily dancing away. Having little experience with it, Kathleen felt a bit odd. Whenever she and her brother danced, she usually led. It was difficult to give way to her new husband.

As the afternoon got on, gifts were unwrapped – a quilt from her mother, a matching set of braided leather bracelets from her brother, an ivory pipe that had belonged to her grandfather and was given to Stevens. The guests had also brought various and sundry gifts to help the new couple start their home, despite the fact Stevens' home was already well stocked after years of use.

Afterwards, the newlyweds said their farewells. The guests loaded their gifts and Kathleen's personal belongings onto a cart and Stevens helped his young wife into the box seat. As they drove away, the sounds of the merriment continuing behind them, Kathleen realized she had never even seen her husband's home before.

Three miles passed, and the sky was beginning to darken. They arrived at a tidy little homestead. Stevens spoke of where the well was located, where the fields were, what he hoped to plant next spring. Kathleen listened with half an ear, peering at the small cabin as he pulled up in front.

"Here, Kathleen," Stevens said, wrapping the reins around the brake and hopping down. "Let me help you into the house. I'll unload the goods onto the porch and put up the cart after." He came around and reached up to her.

Swallowing, flutters of nerves whirling through her stomach, she rose and let her husband sweep her down to the ground. He placed her arm through his crooked elbow and guided her up the steps.

"'Tis just a small home, sweetling. But, 'twill easily be added on when the babes come." Stevens pushed the door open and paused, peering down at her with a soft smile. For the second time, the first being the wedding ceremony, he kissed his bride gently. "Welcome home, Kathleen."

"Thank you, Adam," she said, casting her eyes down and blushing. She clutched at him and let out a tiny shriek as he scooped her up into strong arms.

"I've got to carry you over the threshold, sweetling," he laughed, doing just that. Once inside, he set her down, supporting her as she regained her balance. "Here. Let me light a lantern for you."

The dark interior brightened as the lamp was lit. Stevens settled the glass over the flame and stepped back, surveying his home. With a rueful grin, he glanced at her. "'Tisn't much at the moment, sweetling. This old place hasn't seen a woman's touch in far too long."

Despite her nerves, Kathleen curiously glanced around the single room. A fireplace was on the opposite wall, cold and dark. To her left was a row of cupboards from wall to wall standing waist high. The resulting counter space was covered with a fine layer of dust, a small collection of books, and the usual clutter of a home. In the far right corner stood a large wooden framed bed, neatly made up. She swallowed anxiously and avoided looking at it.

Stevens stepped forward and gave his wife a quick peck on the forehead. "I'll be back soon, sweetling."

The sounds of items being set onto the wooden porch filtered through, and Kathleen continued her perusal. She removed her shawl and noticed pegs hanging from the wall beside the door. Hanging it there, she settled her hands on her hips.

The table wasn't filthy, exactly. She considered the state of her brother's belongings and snorted. *Aye, Adam's a bit neater and that's a fact.* There were two benches on either side of the table and a chair at one end. The lantern glowed from the center, illuminating the small cabin.

Kathleen moved around the room, clucking at the film of grime that seemed to invade every nook and cranny. The mantel above the fireplace held a small silver frame. It was the only thing that was not layered with dust. She picked it up and peered at it closely. The picture inside was a tiny painting of a woman with dark hair and somber grey eyes.

"My first wife, Amanda," Stevens said softly.

Startled, Kathleen jumped, nearly dropping the artwork. Her husband reached around her and smoothly caught it before it could fall to the floor. With a blush, she turned and began apologizing. "I'm sorry, Adam."

"Don't be, love," the man said. His blue eyes held a measure of tender sadness. He settled the frame back on the mantel. Almost absently, his other arm wrapped around her and he held her close. "What's past is past and I'll not discuss it this night." Stevens grinned down at her. "'Tis our wedding night." He ducked down for a kiss.

The butterflies in her stomach raged as they fluttered about.

~ * ~ * ~ * ~ * ~

When all was said and done, it was not near as bad as she had made it out to be. As Kathleen lay on her side, staring at the wall of the tiny cabin, she still cried in silence. She missed her mum and da and even bratty Stewart. She missed her home.

Behind her, sprawled on his back, Stevens slept. Blissfully ignorant of his new young wife's distress, he snored gently.

It had hurt, at first. Her mother had told her it would. Kathleen knew she would be sore for the next day. Despite that, it had become an interesting sensation. *But, did it have to take so long?* she asked herself, wiping tears away. She wondered how often she would have to submit to her husband, how often he would want her in that way. *'Twill be worth it in time. We'll have lots of wee babes roaming 'round.*

Kathleen thought of her bed in her parents' cabin, thought of hearing her brother as he talked in his sleep, thought of waking up to hear her mother preparing breakfast, and her da groaning about getting old before his time. Another spate of tears flowed across her cheeks, and she clutched the quilt her mum had made to her chest.

1777

Kathleen tightly twisted the cloth in her hands, holding it over the tub of water. When she had satisfactorily removed most of the excess moisture, she tossed the damp item into a nearby basket. She dipped back into the tub and retrieved more clothing.

It was a beautiful spring afternoon. The air still held a hint of winter crispness, but all signs pointed to the last frost being behind them. Blue jays chattered to each other in a nearby stand of pine trees. If she concentrated, she could hear her husband in the fields behind the cabin, cussing at the horse he worked.

Today was laundry day, an all day affair. Before her were two large wooden tubs, one of them set on a table, holding the soapy water she had used to clean their clothes. The two buckets she had used to transfer water from the well lay nearby. She rinsed the final load in the second tub on the ground, stirring the clothes with a large stick before pulling each piece out to wring dry.

And that's the last of it, she thought with a happy sigh. Using her apron, she dried off her hands and used a corner of it to wipe the sweat from her forehead. *At this rate, I might be able to take a bath before dinner.* Kathleen picked up the heavy basket of wet clothing and brought it to the ropes she had had her husband string up between the cabin and the trees not long after their marriage. Most of their clothes already hung there, flapping in the light breeze as she prepared to add more to their company.

It had been a good marriage to date. While she did not exactly love Stevens, she had grown rather fond of him. He was always so gentle and kind, trying his best to not show his disappointment as yet another month went by and still no children. Kathleen could not understand what the problem was. Their intimacy was a regular thing – twice a week, except during her monthlies. As time went on, their lack of off-spring had begun worrying them both.

"If God deems it, Kath, you'll be blessed," her mother's voice whispered in her head. Though, having children denied her because God deemed it so was not a comforting thought.

Kathleen shook off her somber thoughts. *Adam doesn't want you sad, lass. Finish the chore, take a bath, and get his dinner to the table.* Instead, she focused on happy times.

The previous Sabbath had been spent at her parents' home. Stewart had not been there, having gone down the way a piece to have dinner with the Anders and the eldest daughter he was sweet on. So, the two couples enjoyed a quiet evening of conversation and food. The only fly in the ointment had been the talk of the local natives in an uproar.

"Apparently, a fellah down south of here cheated one of them when he traded," McGlashan said, puffing on his pipe on the front porch.

Stevens nodded sagely. "Anyone we know?"

"No. Unless you know a man named Silas?" At his son-in-law's negative response, McGlashan shrugged. "Well, anyways, to make a long story short, the Indian weren't happy with the situation and killed him."

"That's murder!" Kathleen said, shocked.

"Aye, 'tis, lass. As his brothers thought, as well. So, they went out a'hunting and caught a few of this Indian's friends. From there things just escalated."

Frowning, Stevens finished sipping his coffee. "Do you think we'll have any trouble up here?" he asked.

"No, I doubt it. Seems the savages are sticking to their neck o' the woods. Haven't heard of them coming any further north."

Kathleen scowled at herself as she hung one of her husband's shirts. "Nothing like cheery thoughts, lass," she said aloud. Pushing the conversation from her mind, she hummed to herself as she hung the laundry to dry.

Once finished, she looked up at the sun, wiping her hands on her apron. *Adam will be in for a break soon. He's nothing if not methodical.* With a grunt, she tipped over first one and then the second tub of water. When they drained, she leaned them up against the table to dry and retrieved more water from the well. After transferring two buckets to the cabin, Kathleen scooped up the basket and went inside.

The basket was returned to the foot of the bed, ready to catch their dirty clothing for the next laundry day. Deciding she had no time for a bath after all, Kathleen opted to have a quick washing. She partially poured one of the water buckets into the kettle over the fire and stirred it into the mixture of stew that had been simmering all day. Placing the second bucket on the table, she pulled a coveted bar of lavender soap from the cupboard along with a rag and a piece of linen.

Kathleen hung the apron up on the hook by the door and returned to the table. Undoing the buttons on the front of her dress, she bared herself to the waist and dipped the rag into the water. She rubbed the bar of soap onto the wet cloth and proceeded to scrub her body, gasping at the initial coolness against her overheated skin. Once a fine lather had been achieved, she submerged the rag back into the bucket, swirling it around to rinse it out. Again, she scrubbed, wiping the soap from her skin. The piece of linen was used to dry off.

As she shrugged back into the arms of her dress, she heard the door behind her open. "Adam! I didn't hear you on the porch, love," she said, reaching for the buttons at her waist. "Sit down and I'll get you something to drink."

Two things happened simultaneously. The sound of her husband's musket reached her ears from out in the fields, and a rough hand grabbed her by the shoulder and spun her around.

Kathleen looked up into the dark and dangerous gaze of a native warrior. Eyes wide, she clutched her dress to her chest, covering herself, and stepped back. "Get away from me!" she whispered urgently, unable to make her voice work any louder.

The warrior looked at her partial state of undress and a wicked grin crossed his face as he stepped forward.

Part 3: Kawita
Coming Together

Chapter Nine

1777

"*Hau, tanksi.*"

Anpo opened her eyes, and peered up at her friend. "*Han, tiblo.*" She sat up, the buffalo robe falling away as she stretched in the dawn light.

Nupa grinned as he handed her a piece of dried meat. "The *hoksila*, have come to watch the herd. You and I will return to camp." He turned away to roll up his sleeping robes and tie them with a thong.

Rubbing sleep from her eyes, Anpo inhaled deeply. She bit off a chunk of the meat before rising to follow her friend's lead. "Do you think they have decided on the hunt?" she asked, by way of conversation.

"I do not know. It has been three days, and Inyan returned yesterday with a vision." Nupa adjusted the thong on his robes. "It must have been favorable. Else they would not still be talking."

Anpo nodded in agreement. Finished with her bedding, she glanced about. The ponies quietly grazed about the clearing. Here and there, boys took up positions to guard the herd until such time as the camp decided to move or until she and the *koskalaka*, returned for another all night vigil.

Nupa clapped her on the arm. "You and I will go to your mother's *ti ikceya.*" He shouldered his buffalo robes.

"Are you interested in the food or my sister?" Anpo asked, leading the way.

Nupa followed along, his smile rueful. "The food is good, but Hca Wanahca is very easy on the eyes."

They laughed in the early morning sunlight.

Breakfast consisted of boiled grains and dried meat. The two sat at the fire of Wanbli Zi as his women and daughters served them. Gi made certain her daughter, Hca, provided food for the fine young warrior eating with them. Wanbli studiously ignored the fawning his eldest engaged in. Hinhan, Anpo's half sister by Hwa, kept Anpo's bowl full. She was now twelve winters, flowering into a beautiful young woman. Soon she would turn many heads, and Anpo felt a sense of pride for her. She watched Nupa become stoic and strong under Hca's gaze, his chest puffed out as he tried to impress the woman with talk of great deeds.

"Did the night go well?" Wanbli asked.

"*Hiya*. Nothing happened," Anpo said. She ignored Nupa's expression. They had had this discussion before.

Wanbli looked upon Anpo with fondness. "Nothing *can* be a good thing, daughter."

She lifted her shoulders in a shrug, humor on her face. "So I have been told."

Nupa shook his head in feigned disgust.

"A rider came during the night. One of the scouts," the older man commented, changing the subject.

The two young warriors' ears perked up in interest. "Did they find *tatanka*?" Anpo asked. Her friend leaned forward, all thoughts of the beautiful Hca gone as they waited for an answer.

Wanbli made an agreeable noise in his throat. "It has been said that they saw not only buffalo, but also the camp of Wicasa Waziya Mani. The council is preparing to issue an invitation for a mutual hunt." His eyes pinned his youngest daughter. "It has also been said that the *tatanka ska* is with the herd."

Anpo leaned back, a breathless sensation washing over her. She heard her friend gasp at the pronouncement. *It is the time of my vision!* Thoughts and questions whirled around in her mind.

"You will kill the sacred white buffalo, *tanksi*," Nupa said.

"You have seen this?" Wanbli asked, aware of the young man's occasional visions.

Nupa nodded again. "I have." Turning to his friend, he draped an arm around her shoulder and quickly hugged her. "I am proud for you, Anpo! You will bring the camp much honor with *wakan tanka*!"

Anpo accepted the embrace, thoughts racing through her head. *And what of the woman with hair like the sun? Will she bring honor? Or pain? Is she real or spirit?*

~ * ~ * ~ * ~ * ~

As the day wore on, it became more and more difficult for Anpo to concentrate on her task. At other points in the camp, young warriors loitered about, appearing nonchalant as they awaited word from the elders. Those officials, who kept peace during the village moves, kept close eye on the hot bloods. Tension filled the air.

Anpo kept an eye on the council lodge as she knapped a flint arrowhead in front of her mother's *ti ikceya*. Her father counseled with

the other big bellies, his first year as one of the elders who led their
people. From somewhere nearby, she heard young women giggling as
they went about their tasks. Despite the potential excitement in the air,
her thoughts remained focused on the *winyan*, the woman from her
vision of four winters ago.

*The white buffalo disappeared. In its place knelt a strange woman with pale
skin. Her hair was long, longer than Anpo's, and a yellow the color of the Sun
itself. Her eyes were the blue of a deep lake, still and clear. She wore the standard
dress that all of Anpo's women wore, buckskin and moccasins, her hair flowing
freely in the breeze.*

*This strange apparition rose from where the white buffalo had laid, blood
pouring from her side where he had been wounded. She walked gently closer to
Anpo who, stared at her in wonder. Then the woman put a hand to her wound,
bloodying her fingers. She reached forward and brushed the blood onto Anpo's face,
two thunderbolts stabbing down her cheeks. As the Sun flared again, Anpo could
see those brilliant blue eyes staring at her intently and hear the words whispered
into her ear.*

"Mahasanni."

Anpo shook the vision off. It had been like this since she had originally had it – the sudden sensation of falling back in time, of being on
the hillside again, seeing the woman with yellow hair and hearing her
voice. The shaman had told her that it was uncommon for a vision to
have so much power, but that this stranger must be *wakan* for all of
that.

At midday, Gi fed Anpo a bowl of the stew that simmered over the
fire. Anpo's sisters arrived, baskets of berries on their hips, and they ate
lunch. The camp sat quiet and still in anticipation.

Much later, the covering of the council *ti ikceya* was thrown aside as
several men exited. In response, the young warriors of the village
drifted toward them, eager to hear their words. The crier, Petala, immediately began to sing.

"Two are called to invite Mani's village to hunt, two young warriors
who represent our people, two will ride south and west."

Wanbli stepped into the sunlight and looked to his woman's lodge.
Spotting his daughter watching, he waved her to him.

Anpo blew out a suspenseful breath and rose, brushing the remain-
ders of her meal from her breechclout, and covering the flint work with
a piece of leather. She trotted to her father. "*Ohan*, Wanbli?"

"The elders ask you to go to Mani's camp with the invitation," the
older man said. He turned toward the sound of someone approaching.
"And you, Nupa."

The crier's words rang across the gathered village. "Anpo and Nupa go to Mani with the invitation. Anpo and Nupa ask Mani to join with our people to hunt *tatanka ska*."

"I am honored to go." Despite pride at being asked and joy that her friend would accompany her, a silvery-cold trickle of fear lodged in Anpo's heart. *I will see my future.*

"As am I," Nupa said.

Wanbli, pleased with his daughter's standing, ushered the two warriors into the council lodge to speak with the elders.

~ * ~ * ~ * ~ * ~

When Anpo woke the following morning, she discovered new clothing at her place by the fire. Of the four pairs of moccasins, the finest were white, the tops painted with red sun symbols. There were buckskin leggings of a natural tan color, the fringe painted white with designs in red and yellow – the lightning, the sun, and the buffalo alternated down each side. A yellow leather shirt held the same white strip of designs down the front from each shoulder to the hem.

In the early morning darkness, Anpo clothed herself. It was said that how a warrior looked was an indication of how much he was loved. And, despite the one obvious difference between herself and the other warriors in camp, the women in her family outfitted her well. She bundled the remaining moccasins together to take along.

All the occupants of her mother's lodge were awake. Gi prepared breakfast while Hca wrapped food for her younger sister to take on her trip. Wanbli sat at his fire, leaning against his backrest as he smoked. Anpo combed her hair until it glowed in the amber light and tied it back, high on her head. She affixed two feathers to her scalp lock; the first a yellow tail feather of the eagle, standing upright; the second a feather painted green, dangling down.

Gi clucked disapprovingly when Anpo presented herself for breakfast. She spoke to her daughter, Hca, loud enough for Anpo to overhear. "My man's *cinksi* of the heart wears an old breechclout. I have a far more fitting one for her."

Anpo watched Gi from the corner of her eye as the woman rummaged through furs. She returned with an expanse of white leather.

"This was to be hers after she killed the *tatanka ska*, but I give it to her now," Gi said with a smile. She gently laid the skin beside her youngest daughter.

"Anpo will look very handsome," Hca said.

Amazed at how much faith her mother had in her, Anpo picked up the soft skin with awe. It blazed white against her dark skin. Her family

looked prudently away as she removed and replaced her old breechclout.

"My *ina* and *cuwekala* take very good care of me, Wanbli," Anpo
said to her father.

"As is their way," Wanbli said.

"They must know how much I appreciate their hard work."

The women hummed in acceptance of Anpo's thanks.

"It is time," Wanbli said, putting his pipe in its holder.

Anpo scooped up her spare moccasins and weapons. She stepped
out into the cool morning air, her father close behind.

Three men stood nearby with the ponies – Nupa and his father, Wi
Sape, and the shaman. Anpo approached, adjusting her pouch and
knife.

Inyan stepped forward with a bundle of fur. "Here is the invitation
for the leader of their camp. You will enter and speak to no one until
you are spoken to at their council fire. Go right to their council and
nowhere else. Give Mani our invitation and wait there until tomorrow.
He will give you his answer for you to return here in the morning." He
handed the bundle to Nupa who obediently tied it to his saddle.

"Ready?" Nupa asked with a grin, handing her pony's reins to
Anpo.

"*Ohan!*"

Wanbli smiled at his daughter's enthusiasm. "Remember. Leave
camp and go south for a time. You will come across a large pine tree,
split in two. From there, go west. The camp's cook fires will guide you
the rest of the way. You should be there when the sun is high."

The warriors nodded in understanding and hopped onto their
steeds. They heeled their ponies and fairly flew out the eastern
entrance. The big bellies watched them go before quietly returning to
their lodges.

~ * ~ * ~ * ~ * ~

Once out of sight of camp, the two slowed to a trot, pacing themselves. Anpo handed her friend a piece of dried meat that her sister had
packed.

"You look nice," Nupa commented. "Is that breechclout new?"

Anpo nodded. "*Ina* gifted me. She was going to wait until I killed
the white buffalo, but chose to not wait."

He nodded. "The color is unusual and looks good."

"Hca called me 'handsome'," Anpo said with a wry snort.

Not seeing the humor, her friend studied her. With a slow, grudging respect, he nodded. "You are handsome, *tanksi.*"

They cantered along a few feet before his silence bothered Anpo. She asked, "What?"

Nupa shrugged. "My next words would have been 'You will make some woman a fine man'." He shook his head. "But, you are not a man. You are a *wikoskalaka.*"

Frowning, Anpo asked, "I am *wicakte.*" She readjusted herself in her saddle. "I have been this way all my life."

"But do you not want...?"

"What? To join with a man?" She snorted at his nod. "Whatever for? I can hunt better than most men. I have learned how to scout and fight better than most men. Besides, I do not think a man would have me."

"*Tanksi...*"

"*Hiya, tiblo!* You know I speak true." They traveled a few more minutes, both deep in thought. "Would you have me?" Anpo finally asked.

Her friend sat straighter in his saddle. "I would."

She burst into laughter at the stoic, tragic face he held. "But, I would not have *you, tiblo!*" She dug her heels into her pony's withers, causing it to rear up and shoot away.

Nupa was only a second behind her, putting away his feelings of relief and dismay to race after his best friend.

Chapter Ten

"But, what will you do, *tanksi*? You will have no children to care for you when you are an elder."

Anpo sighed. Nupa would not stop worrying the matter. Every time she cajoled, teased, and changed the subject, he always brought the conversation back to this.

They had made it to the split pine and worked their way west through rolling plains. There were no stops for meals; instead they ate on the backs of their ponies. They had only stopped once at a creek to allow their steeds to drink. The sun neared its zenith, an indication they had not much farther to go.

"You know as well as I, *tiblo*. I will adopt. Then I will have a son to teach." Seeing her friend's glower, it occurred to her what his concern was. "You are worried that I will have no man? No one to sleep with?"

"I am worried that you will have no *woman*," he conceded. At her guffaw, he bristled. "Do you know how to cook for yourself? Tan hides? Sew? Do all the things your mother and sister do for you?"

"So, you suggest I find a woman who will share my robes?" Anpo couldn't help herself. She chuckled joyously at the thought.

Nupa scowled at his friend before the humor finally invaded his good senses. Soon, he laughed as she.

"*Tiblo!*" she said when she had controlled her laughter. "I will wait for you to marry Hca and live with you!"

Snorting at the absurdity, he said, "*Hau!* *You* will be my second woman then!"

Soon, smoke from many campfires could be seen in the distance. They stopped long enough to go over themselves and their ponies, straightening clothing and dusting off leathers. Nupa pulled out the bundle that Inyan had given them.

"Are you ready?" he asked.

Anpo nodded. "*Ohan, tiblo.* You and I will be welcomed."

They rode for the camp of Wicasa Waziya Mani, circling round until they reached the eastern entrance. Several warriors around the camp heard their approach and stood ready with weapons at hand.

Women and children hovered nearby, the young ones excitedly moving around to get a better view of the newcomers.

As they entered the main clearing, Anpo saw a flash of yellow at one lodge. A vague familiarity tickled her mind, tugging her away from her course. She pulled her pony up short and spun around, searching for the color. Anpo saw nothing but warriors beginning to take umbrage at this break from custom.

Nupa stopped as well, alert to whatever caused his best friend consternation. Unable to see anything, he edged his steed closer and caught her eye.

The intense look of warning from him brought Anpo back to her senses. They were unable to speak until the headman of this camp had received them. She gave a curt nod and proceeded to the largest lodge with Nupa.

Upon their arrival, they jumped off their ponies. Nupa opened the fur given him by their shaman. Three items nestled inside – a medicine bundle created for this meeting, a small pouch of willow bark, and an invitation wand with intricate designs stained on its wood. Anpo's status as *wicakte*, a two-souled person, conferred the leadership and honor upon her. Therefore, despite his greater age and experience, Nupa handed her the wand, holding the other things still cradled in the fur.

Several big bellies arrived from various points around the village. One by one, they stepped into the oversized *ti ikceya*. A boy stepped forward and took their horses, while a young warrior, younger than Anpo, held the *tiopa* covering aside for the visitors to enter. It took a few moments for their eyes to adjust to the darker interior. The honored place to the left of the leader was left open for them. Anpo sat down, her friend beside her.

She looked about the fire, noting many familiar faces. She had seen most of these men at the summer and winter camps, when all the Lakota gathered together. While she was probably just one of the many, many young warriors in the world, these were the leaders of the people. Anpo nodded respectively towards the chief and held out the invitation wand.

Mani, the head of this camp, was a young man. His hair was still dark and his body hale. With powerful grace he accepted the wand, nodding in return to the pair of young warriors. This was followed by the medicine bundle and willow bark.

He smiled as he showed all the elders present the invitation. No one spoke. An older man unwrapped a pipe and prepared it for those gathered. He wore the regalia of a shaman, and the elders showed him deference. With the bowl loaded with tobacco, he handed it stem first to Mani.

All in the tent partook of the smoke. The ceremony calmed Anpo's natural excitement at being part of this important meeting. She knew this was a test for her; to see if she had the ability to carry herself with proper decorum as befitted a *wicakte*. In the silence she reflected on the pipe, the representation of both male and female such as herself. The bowl was woman, its womb filled with the spirit. The stem was man. Only the two together created smoke, causing a man's words to be seen by all.

When the tobacco was spent, Mani thanked the young warriors, and introductions were made all around. "So, you have found the buffalo?" he asked in a deep voice. "Is he near?"

"*Ohan, wicahca,*" Anpo answered with the proper feminine response. A rustle flowed through the lodge as all became aware of exactly who they had before them. The elders knew of the *wikoskalaka* who acted as *koskalaka*, though they had not recognized her on sight. Anpo ignored the disturbance, having dealt with the surprise many times. She had learned long ago to not give credence to the immediate discomfort her presence caused. It faded with familiarity. "Our scouts have seen *tatanka* a day's ride away from here, half a day from our village. Our leader, Wagmiza Wagna, asks that your people join with ours in a hunt four days from now."

Mani nodded, his dark eyes intent on the young warrior. "Be welcome in our village. You will be guests at a feast, and the elders will council on your invitation."

Anpo and Nupa thanked him for his generosity before leaving the lodge. Once outside, they saw their ponies had already been led away to this camp's herd. Their belongings had been placed in front of a *ti ikceya* nearby, the lodge they would be sleeping in that night.

"Why did you stop when you and I arrived?" Nupa asked as they sauntered to the lodge, all eyes of the camp upon them.

Anpo shrugged. "I do not know. I thought I saw something. I was trying to find something again."

They arrived at the *ti ikceya*, a small and nondescript dwelling for visitors such as themselves, and pulled their sleeping robes out. In a matter of moments they reclined in front of the fire pit, watching the remainder of the camp as they went about their business.

Nupa pulled a water bag from his things and took a long draw. Handing it to his friend, he continued his questioning. "What did you see?"

"I cannot explain, *tiblo.*" Anpo sighed, taking the bag and drinking deeply. She wiped her mouth and sealed it, leaving the bag between them. "I am not sure if I saw something or felt something."

The young man nodded solemnly. "I understand. The same happens with my visions – I see, but I do not. They cloud my mind."

"*Ohan!*" Anpo exclaimed, sitting forward. "That was my feeling. Like my vision."

Their discussion was interrupted as other young men drifted closer. Soon several sat about the fire, smoking and exchanging stories and news.

~ * ~ * ~ * ~ * ~

That evening, there was much rejoicing at the visitors' arrival and news. The women of the camp attempted to outdo one other with the food they cooked, the *hoksila* jostled for position nearest the strangers, and the warriors entertained themselves and their guests with gambling and games of skill.

As darkness grew, and food disappeared, Mani stood and held his arms high overhead. "Hear me!" he called to his people until they quieted. Anpo and Nupa listened just as attentively. "This village has been invited to join with Anpo's and Nupa's to hunt *tatanka*. The elders have decided." With true showmanship, he paused, his dark eyes glittering in the firelight.

The camp collectively leaned forward, holding its breath.

"We will join you," he smiled, looking down at the seated guests. "Tomorrow morning you will return to your camp and tell Wagna that we will soon arrive." Mani turned to the shaman and received a medicine bundle and small pouch of willow bark.

At the leader's nod, Anpo quickly rose, her friend a heartbeat behind her. The items were handed reverently over to her.

"This is our answer," Mani said.

With extreme care, Anpo wrapped the pouches in a fur and tied them with a thong.

The camp erupted in whoops and cries. More wood was laid onto the flames, and drums were brought out. Hunters began dancing, enacting how they would hunt the buffalo in the days to come. Rattles and pipe also joined the din, making for an exciting stir of sound.

Nupa looked longingly at the young men, and then back at his friend who had returned to her robe.

"Go, *tiblo*," Anpo said. "I have the bundle. I will dance at our camp before the hunt." Seeing the war of wanting to enjoy himself fighting his desire to keep her company, she scowled at him. "I said go. Do you think you will be allowed to impress all the *wikoskalaka* when my sister is nearby?"

He blinked at her before a slow grin crossed his face. With a whoop he leaped into the fray and began dancing.

Anpo watched him with a fond smile. But her eyes kept being drawn to the darkness surrounding the fire, looking for something that was not there. *If this is the time of my vision...where is she? Will she be a powerful spirit? Or real?*

~ * ~ * ~ * ~ * ~

Kathleen slumped on her sleeping robes in the *ti ikceya*. The day had been a busy one, and she was very tired. *Aye, you should be, lass. You helped put up enough food to feed Boston proper.* Outside the lodge, she heard wild drums and the people singing as they danced. She thought she heard pipes, as well, but could not be certain. Nearby, an old toothless woman sewed two pieces of leather together and sang softly in a whispery voice. She was the only other person in the tent, an aging guard to keep the new young slave trapped.

'Tisn't like there's anyplace to go, Kath, she thought to herself with an ironic twist to her mouth. She stretched out and covered herself with her robes, trying to get comfortable on the hard ground.

As far as Kathleen could tell, it had been well over a month, nearing two, since she'd been kidnapped from her homestead in the east. The man who had brutally raped her in her cabin had taken a liking to her fair skin and kept her. There had been many nights over the course of several weeks in which Kathleen had been sexually assaulted. The two women who had lived with that man beat her regularly for the slightest infraction of their unspoken and vague rules.

All Kathleen wanted was to curl up and die by that point. She had tried to get a knife from one of the women, smuggling it into her dress while helping prepare the meal and intent on using it to join her husband. One of the woman had seen it and beat her senseless. Then her man had done the same.

Things had changed dramatically about two weeks ago. In the early morning hours, a monstrous uproar had been heard in the camp. There was screaming and yelling. The tent Kathleen had been in had caught fire. The man had already gone outside to fight the attackers, and the women soon followed to escape the flames, leaving her inside to roast.

Kathleen still did not remember how she had gotten out of the inferno. Outside had been a mass of confusion, and it was all she could do to stay out of the way of stampeding horses and wild-eyed natives. Through the din of smoke and noise, she had heard hooves beating hard on the ground and suddenly she had been swept up and across a wooden saddle.

She had been with her new captor and his family ever since, moving steadily west.

Kathleen rolled onto her side, facing the fire and watching the old woman at her task. *Could be worse, lass.*

Her treatment had gotten infinitely better. There were no beatings, though the man had slapped her once when she had gotten hysterical. The women were rather kind. The grandmother across the fire occasionally swore at her or some such when she had done something wrong. Kathleen could not tell what was said, and it was probably just as well. There were also two children in this tent and, for one who knew she was barren, living with them had been a joy.

However the brutality of Kathleen's kidnapper had left its mark. The man – *my new husband?* – had tried to bed her four times, and four times he'd gone away in disgust. The first time, she had gotten hysterical, and he had slapped her. Afterwards, when he climbed into her robes, his naked body against hers, she froze. She could not move, could not breathe, nothing but a ceramic doll to be posed, to be used. This was obviously not something he wanted. He would leave her robes, going to his wife's bed.

You've got to get over this, lass. If you don't have any worth, then you're a dead woman. Unbidden, tears welled up in her eyes. With the lack of abuse came time to reflect and feel. Kathleen knew her husband was dead. She had seen his body when her attackers had dragged her from the cabin. It was only recently she had the opportunity to mourn. *Adam needed to have someone to love. Needed to have children. And I wasn't able to give him either.*

Another concern was her family. There was no indication that there had been an attack on the McGlashan homestead, yet it still worried her mind. *Aside from you, lass, there's no sign of an attack on your homestead either.* Every night, as these strange people prepared for sleep, she prayed to God that her mum and da were all right, that they and Stewart had survived the horrid attacks up and down the frontier.

So the last two weeks had gone. Sleeping, eating, packing, moving. Followed by unpacking, preparing food, eating, and worrying. All with the occasional odd anxiety attack thrown in for good measure. Kathleen did not know where the camp was heading, just that they continued to travel west and west and west.

Today had been different. The arrival of two young warriors had been interesting. Kathleen wished she spoke the language better so she could hear what was going on. Her skill was rudimentary; on a comparable level with the toddler she lived with. It was not all that dissimilar from her previous captor's tongue. Still, Kathleen did not let on exactly how much she understood, not yet. Who knew what good would come of her subterfuge? Perhaps an opportunity to escape would arise.

There were preparations for a feast, and there was music and dancing outside now. Quite a bit of excitement. *I wonder who they are? Someone important from the looks of things.* But she had been hustled into the tent as soon as the strangers entered the camp, and been out of sight ever since. *Maybe they're worried you'll get stolen again. Seems to be the way of it here.*

Unable to fathom the whys and wherefores, her deep blue eyes slowly closed, tears drying on her cheeks. The old woman's voice weaved through her mind as she drifted off to sleep, singing a counterpoint to the sound of her gram's tin whistle.

Chapter Eleven

"*I am near, mahasanni.*"

Anpo's eyes flew open, and she surged up from sleep, looking wildly around for the pale woman.

Nearby, Nupa stirred in his robes but did not wake.

It was a dream, nothing more. Anpo's heartbeat slowed, and she scrubbed sleep from her face as she sat forward. The whispered words had seemed so close. Was the woman of her vision truly close? Close enough to breathe words in Anpo's ear? Her gaze darted about the murky lodge, half afraid of seeing the bearer of that voice, those words. A wave of disappointment followed, at odds with the dread.

Outside the *ti ikceya* she heard movement as others awoke. Reaching over, she nudged her friend, rousting him. "*Han, tiblo.* It is time to go."

"*Hau, tanksi.*" Nupa grinned before stretching and yawning. As he stood and dressed, he said, "I cannot wait to arrive home! A great hunt awaits!"

Anpo said nothing as she collected her belongings and packed them up. The sacred bundle given them by the chief was still in her possession and would remain so until she arrived at their own camp to give it to Wagna.

Sensing his friend's somberness, Nupa peered at her. "Are you all right, *tanksi*?"

She regarded him with a troubled expression. "I cannot drive the pale woman from my mind, *tiblo.* She haunts me waking or sleeping. If this is the time of the vision, I wish she would show herself! The waiting is hard!"

Nupa reached out to take her upper arm and squeeze it gently. "Visions are never easy, especially those of such power. Be patient, *tanksi.* All will come to pass as the spirits intend."

Anpo gave a half-hearted snort. "I hear your words with my ears, but if I close my eyes, I see Inyan."

"I am not a shaman!" Nupa insisted as he pulled away from her. "I would not make a good one." Hearing another snort, he rolled his eyes.

"Being shaman is more than visions, *tanksi*. Do you think I have the patience to sit for hours on end, awaiting the spirits? To work so diligently on harvesting leaves and grass?"

The sudden sight of the great warrior, Nupa of Wagna's camp, picking flowers in a field filled Anpo's mind.

He frowned at her as she rolled on the floor, howling. "I do not understand why you are laughing."

~ * ~ * ~ * ~ * ~

The people of Mani's village packed their belongings in preparation for the journey when Anpo and Nupa left. The ride home was uneventful, if quiet. Anpo's mind constantly mulled over her dream and vision. The longer the day, the more the feeling of anticipation grew within her heart. It was as if she knew the vision was coming to fruition in the very near future. Nupa tried to ply her with jokes and conversation, but failed miserably. He finally left her to her thoughts and followed along quietly.

By midday, they returned to their camp. *It is good to see home,* Anpo thought as they rode into the eastern entrance. Familiar faces surrounded them, eager to hear of their visit. They stopped at the council lodge, and the leather covering pushed aside as they dismounted. A big belly stepped out and gestured for them to enter.

Shuffling around the fire pit, the elders opened up the honored place beside Wagna. This was the first time Anpo had ever been inside this lodge. She and Nupa sat to their leader's right, two dark heads in a field of gray. A pipe was lit and, after several minutes of smoking, the chief spoke.

"You have an answer, Anpo?"

"*Ohan, wicahca.*" She held out the bundle she carried.

Wagna took the fur and carefully opened it. His creased face remained stern though his eyes held a smile. He held up the fur to show the medicine bundle and willow bark pouch. "Our invitation is accepted," he said to the gathered men.

"The camp of Mani will arrive before the sun goes down this night," Anpo said, her lips holding a humorous twist that Nupa's echoed.

"I will have a feast in their honor to welcome them to our camp," Wagna said. He turned to the young warriors beside him. "You have done well, this day. I offer you to sit with me at the feast."

Anpo kept a neutral expression on her face, though she could feel the desire to drop her jaw. Beside her, she almost felt Nupa thrumming with excitement. "I would be...very honored, *wicahca*," she said.

"And I!" Nupa said. He nudged her with his shoulder.

~ * ~ * ~ * ~ * ~

Anpo and Nupa were minor heroes for the day, constantly pestered by the *hoksila* with questions, given extra little treats from the women's cook fires, quizzed by the other *koskalaka* and *wicasa* as they lounged around and smoked.

In preparation for the new arrivals, several of the women moved their lodges to accommodate the extra people, expanding the camp outward. Women and girls prepared a variety of foods for the feast. The men spent their time dressing in their finery, carrying on discussions of past hunts and speculating on the rumored *tatanka ska*.

As the sun lowered in the western sky, anticipation swelled in the village. Boys, already excited at the day's promised events, got into mischief as they dared each other to go in search of Mani's people. A few of them met the sharp tongues and heavy clubs of the *akicita* who patrolled the village to keep the peace before a hunt.

Three riders, Mani and two of his advisors, came from the north, circled around to the eastern side, and slowly made their entrance into the village. They wore their finest clothing, carrying feathered regalia that told everyone who saw them of their daring and exploits. At the council lodge, they hopped off their ponies.

"*Hau*, Mani," Wagna said grandly, his arms wide.

The younger leader held out the invitation wand delivered to him the day before. "*Hau*, Wagna. I am honored that you have asked us to hunt with you."

As the three visitors were urged into the council lodge, several young men and women ran to the herd and hopped onto ponies, thundering away to the north to assist the oncoming village. It was not long before the new arrivals were present and setting up their lodges in spaces so recently vacated. While the women and children put up *ti ikceyas*, the men and boys gathered at various fires to greet old friends and exchange news.

Anpo sat at her father's fire, sharpening an antler spearhead by grinding it against a rock. Wanbli was in the council lodge with the rest of the big bellies, and her mother was speaking to her *maske*, her best friend, who resided in Mani's camp. Anpo was unsure where her sisters and second mother were. *Probably helping someone set up a* ti ikceya, she thought. *Or fawning over the young warriors. I wonder if Nupa feels anxious?* A grin crossed her face.

As if the thought called him, Nupa ran up to her, excitement in his bearing. "*Hau, tanksi*! You must come with me!"

She rolled her eyes. *"Hiya.* I am busy now." She did not relish the idea of playing games of chance; her mind worried the vision of her future and took most of her attention.

"Hoh, tanksi! You must. There is something I must show you."

"Can you not wait until later, *tiblo?"*

Nupa shook his head no. Though his face was solemn, his eyes sparkled brilliantly.

Anpo set her spear to one side. She knew from experience that to deny Nupa in this mood would only strengthen his resolve. He was nothing if not stubborn when he set his mind. Acting disgruntled for his benefit, she rose from her seat and mock-glared at him. "Lead on."

His smile was radiant against his dark face, and he turned away with a gesture for her to follow.

In moments they arrived at a visiting family's *ti ikceya.* The setup of the lodge was complete, and an older and younger woman prepared the cook fire, setting out the various accouterments needed for day-to-day life. Several young men and women from Anpo's village loitered about, casting surreptitious glances at the tent.

Intrigued at the interest shown this one lodge, Anpo looked to her friend. "What do you wish to show me?"

"You will see. Be patient." His face was aglow.

Anpo returned her gaze to the *ti ikceya.* She noticed that the other members of her camp began watching her, more so than usual. *I do not understand. I am no different than yesterday.* Her brow furrowed.

The old woman of the lodge glanced around at the collected people who failed to appear nonchalant in their rude stares. Muttering curses under her breath at their impudence, she marched over to the *tiopa,* and pushed aside the covering. Calling inside, she bid the occupants to come out into the daylight.

Despite herself, Anpo picked up the anticipation of the others. Their eyes intensified as they watched, their glances more and more centering on her. Just as she was about to speak of this strangeness to Nupa, something moved at the lodge and she found her gaze drawn there.

A small child of about four winters climbed out. Behind him was an older *wicincala.*

"They are only children, *tiblo,"* she murmured to her friend.

"Hiya, tanksi," Nupa responded. There was more movement at the *tiopa,* and he grasped his friend's arm. "Look!"

Hesitantly, a pale woman stepped out into the waning sunlight. Her hair was long, longer than Anpo's, and was the color of the Sun itself. It was tied back at the neck, but flowed freely below that, hanging to her waist. Her skin was so light as to be almost white in color with a slight golden tint to it. She wore the standard dress of the women of Anpo's people, buckskin and long, with moccasins on her feet.

She is here! Anpo could not begin to describe what she felt. All time stopped, no breath came to her, her mouth open in shock, and her heart beat hard in her chest. She watched the stranger be guided to the fire where the old woman set her to work cutting roots.

"Is she the one?" Nupa asked.

Rousing from her stupor, Anpo inhaled deeply to fill her aching lungs with air. Her mouth snapped shut, and it was all she could do to simply nod in response. Even though the woman had yet to look up at the surrounding camp, Anpo knew. *She will have eyes the color of a deep lake.*

Nupa grinned widely and squeezed her arm again. "The time of your vision is near," he said. "The sacred *tatanka ska* will be yours before the hunt is finished!"

The old woman, tired of being stared at, harangued the young men and women of the camp, picking up a piece of firewood to threaten them. They scattered and moved off, abuzz at this new topic of conversation.

Nupa dragged Anpo away. She put up no fight, her mind in an uproar.

~ * ~ * ~ * ~ * ~

Kathleen peered at the people moving away from the old grandmother who yelled at them. *You're lucky you've not made her angry, lass,* she thought, watching the ferocious old woman threaten to beat people with her stick. When finished, the elder turned to glare at her household, and Kathleen dropped her eyes. She diligently cut the vegetables she had been given, hoping to not get hit. *She hasn't hit me in all the time I've been here,* Kathleen reasoned, attempting to allay her fears.

Once the danger had passed, she relaxed into her task. She could almost pretend she was still in the cabin, preparing a nice supper for her husband. The women and children speaking to one another brought back reality, their language a foreign noise impinging on her daydream, though she prided herself on comprehending it more and more.

Kathleen did not know where her captor had gone. He had disappeared once they reached this camp. She continued her chore, wondering why they had joined with this other band of natives and what would happen now.

Unbeknownst to her, a pair of dark eyes watched her every move.

Chapter Twelve

Anpo felt like a child as she spied on the pale woman from behind someone's *ti ikceya*. She remembered sneaking through camp with the other children as they stalked people and dogs among the lodges. *You feel like a child because you act like one.*

Once Nupa returned her to her mother's lodge, Anpo scooped up a robe and covered her face. The gesture was a universal one among their people, and he accepted her desire to be alone. Her youngest sister, Hinhan, and mother witnessed Nupa's shunning, and both found other things to do away from the lodge. Anpo could not remain at her father's fire, however, her emotions swirling about in her heart with the ferocity of a summer cloudburst. She returned to stare at the physical manifestation of her vision, crouching behind the *ti ikceya* to peek at the visitors' hearth.

She is a dream come to life! she thought. *She is real! Not a spirit!* Anpo chewed her upper lip in uncertainty. *What does this mean?*

"What do you see?"

Anpo shot to her feet so fast, she nearly toppled over. A warm hand grasped her upper arm to steady her, and Anpo turned to gape at the interruption. She swallowed. "Inyan!"

The shaman wore a crooked smile. "*Hau*, Anpo," he said. "I ask you again. What do you see?"

Her attention darted back toward the fire pit. The sun was on the verge of setting, and the flames of it sparked the color of the strange woman's hair. A yellow glow erupted about her head, illuminating the fair skin.

"I see my future, Inyan," she whispered, her lack of the honorific *wicahca* a measure of her unsettled state.

"Come with me, Anpo." When she did not move, he tugged her upper arm, pulling her away. "We must talk."

Anpo tore her gaze from the vision and flushed at her strange behavior. *What is wrong with me?* Still, she did not want to speak with Inyan; did not want to leave this spot. It was as if she had spent so many years seeing the vision, the reality of it seemed impossible. She needed to drink from the woman's essence, to touch her, to verify she was real and not a fevered dream.

Anpo wondered if she would die from this wanting.

The shaman led her to his woman's *ti ikceya*. Rather than sit outside in the public eye, he drew Anpo through the opening and sat her on his left.

Anpo remained in a daze, unaware of her surroundings. She did not notice the unspoken communication between Inyan and his wife, the old woman leaving them in privacy within her lodge. Not until she heard her name, did she realize the shaman had lit a pipe, and now held it toward her, stem first. She received the pipe, and they smoked in silence. The ritual served to ground her anguished emotions.

"She is the one," Inyan stated.

Swallowing hard, Anpo nodded. "*Ohan, wicahca.* She looks just as I saw her four winters ago." Her eyes narrowed in confusion. "Can that be? She is not much older than I."

"This confirms that you did, indeed, see the future in your vision, Anpo. Tell me, do you now look as the warrior woman who slew the *tatanka ska?*"

She contemplated his question, remembering the vision with acute clarity. "I do!" she said, her voice a strangled whisper. Before Inyan could respond, she focused on him intently. "If I can see my future, why can I not see why the woman calls me *mahasanni?*"

He tilted his head. "What *wakan tanka* wishes you to know will be told you. That is the nature of visions."

She bowed her head in thought.

"You have questions, Anpo. They rise off of you like smoke from a fire. I will give you what wisdom I have."

Anpo tried to focus her thoughts in some constructive manner. "I do not know what to ask, *wicahca.*"

"Look into the flames, Anpo. Use the fire to burn away the confusion and clear your mind."

She did as he suggested, staring into the fire pit, meditating on her emotions and thoughts and soul. A long time passed and Anpo could feel herself calming, her breath deepening as she relaxed.

The tatanka ska had disappeared. In its place knelt a strange woman with pale skin. Her hair was long, longer than Anpo's, and a yellow the color of the Sun itself. Her eyes were the blue of a deep lake, still and clear. She wore the standard dress all of Anpo's women wore, buckskin and moccasins, her hair flowing freely in the breeze.

This strange apparition rose from where the white buffalo had laid, blood pouring from her side where the white buffalo had been wounded. She walked closer to the girl staring at her in wonder. Then the woman put a hand to her wound, bloodying her fingers. She reached forward and brushed the blood onto Anpo's face, two thunderbolts across her cheeks. As the Sun flared again, Anpo could see those brilliant blue eyes staring at her intently and hear the words whispered into her ear.

"Mahasanni."

"When we hunt, will my killing the sacred *tatanka ska* hurt the white woman?" Anpo asked, her voice distant.

"I do not believe so. When she spoke to you in your vision, she used the phrase, '*mahasanni*'. She will know you well before she is wounded."

She turned to look at Inyan. "She belongs to another, *wicahca*. Why would she call me this? I cannot be a man to her. I may be *wicakte*, but I am also *wikoskalaka*, as is she." Her brow furrowed as she tried to comprehend the meaning of the vision.

"You are *wikoskalaka*, Anpo. As is she," he agreed, nodding. "Perhaps because of the sacred *tatanka* that she will come to you. And perhaps you are destined to be close...closer than even *maske*."

"Is that possible?" Anpo asked, her voice low.

"I believe so." Inyan filled the bowl of his pipe with crushed, dried leaves.

I do not want to hurt her. I will not hurt her! "I will not go on the hunt."

The shaman paused in his task for a split second before continuing on. "Wi Ile Anpo, are you a warrior and hunter for the Lakota?"

Dark eyes blinked at the man. "What? *Ohan, wicahca!* Of course!"

"But you will not hunt for your people because *tatanka ska* is waiting for you?" She shied away from his question, and he continued. "You will deprive your *ina*, your *ate*, your *tiospaye*, of much needed food for the coming winter?"

"*Hiya, wicahca*," Anpo muttered, dropping her head in shame. "I will not deprive my family."

"To know the future is not easy. To know the future is harsh for one so young. But you cannot do anything to stop the future from coming." He lit his pipe and puffed on it in contemplation. "Did the white woman die in your vision, Anpo?"

"*Hiya*, Inyan. She was wounded by my hand and bleeding."

"I know that you do not have experience in the way of *wicasa* and *winyan*, Anpo," the shaman said, treading carefully. "You do not know that couples hurt each other very deeply."

"My parents have not hurt each other, *wicahca*," she said.

"Not with weapons, *hiya*; but with words, with actions. Their feelings have been hurt and, though they might not bleed from a wound, they bleed inside." Inyan shrugged. "That is the natural way of things for people to grow."

Anpo digested this bit of information. "You believe that I will hurt this woman, and not be by my weapons?"

Leaning forward, he stared at her intently. "Do you believe that you are able to hurt her with a weapon?"

Anpo sat back in shock. "*Hiya*! I cannot!"

"And you do not even know her yet," Inyan said sagely. He offered the pipe to her, and they smoked in silence.

"With *tatanka ska* she will come to me. We will come to know each other well. Then I will hurt her somehow, enough to make her bleed within," Anpo said. "But she still cares for me, still calls me *mahasanni*...." Her face took on an expression of wonder. *I do not know if I am worthy of this gift.*

Inyan nodded in agreement. "That would seem to be the way of your vision, Anpo."

They finished the pipe, no more words between them. When it was complete, he asked, "Do you understand your vision more fully, Anpo?"

"*Ohan, wicahca*, I do." She rose to her feet and smiled at the elder. "Ask anything of me in return for your aid in this matter."

The shaman stood as well, albeit with less ease, a grin on his face. "I ask that you be happy, Anpo."

Her smile softened at unseen emotions and images. "I will, *wicahca*."

~ * ~ * ~ * ~ * ~

Her talk with Inyan had given her much to think about. Regardless of the situation she found herself in, Anpo's natural good spirits returned by the time she arrived at her mother's *ti ikceya*. She found the women of her family putting the final touches on their preparations for the evening feast.

When Anpo did not give any signal to be left alone, her older sister, Hca, smiled at their mother. "My *mitankala* returns to the fire. Perhaps she is hungry."

Anpo squatted down and collected the spearhead and stone she had been working with earlier in the day. To avoid speaking directly with the women, she kept her attention on the weapons of war, telling them, "My belly rumbles with emptiness."

Gi used a carved wooden utensil and dipped out a bit of stew into a bowl. She set it beside her youngest daughter.

Anpo took the food and ate with an appreciative expression. "My *ina* always makes the best stew. At the feast, hers will be the most enjoyed."

Not to be outdone, Anpo's second mother, Hwa, sat fresh fry bread beside the warrior, and Hca placed a meat and berry mixture near.

Anpo dipped the bread in the pemmican, recognizing the taste of the berries they had eaten for lunch a few days earlier.

"They will make you fat and lazy, *tanksi*," Nupa said with a laugh.

Anpo waved her friend closer. "Come try my sister's *wansi, tiblo.* There is none better."

Nupa, not able to pass up an opportunity to flirt with his friend's sister, stepped forward with a grin. He received a piece of the meat and fruit mixture from the blushing *wikoskalaka*, rolling his eyes in gratitude.

Ignoring Hca's blush, Anpo glanced towards the center of the village. "The people are beginning to gather."

"*Hau*," he said. "You and I will join them."

They gathered robes to sit upon and wandered toward the group. Behind them, Anpo's family collected their offerings for the feast and followed. The men and elders from both camps already seated themselves. Soon, only those not guarding the herd of ponies sat at the council fire.

The leader of Anpo's village, Wagna, sat in front of the council lodge. To his left and in the honored space were Mani and his advisors. To Wagna's right were the two messengers, Anpo and Nupa. The older man stood and held his arms wide, garnering the attention of the people.

"Today is a very good day!" he exclaimed with a smile. "Our brave warriors, Anpo and Nupa," Wagna gesturing to the pair beside him, "have returned from their task, and brought Mani and his people to our fires." Here he turned to the younger leader who sat proud. "In two days we shall hunt the great *tatanka*. Perhaps our camp will be even more honored and one of our own will slay the sacred *tatanka ska*."

The gathered men yipped in excitement while the women trilled appreciation.

Anpo tried to control the blush she felt as most of the people from her village looked to her with knowing smiles and nods. *I may not kill the tatanka ska*, she thought. *The time may not be now.* But deep in her heart she knew that was a falsehood.

"Let the feast begin!" Wagna called.

The women of the joined camps began serving their men and brothers and sons. Among them, the white woman caused quite a stir. The warrior who owned her was the recipient of many a ribald joke as the evening wore on, all of which he accepted with good nature.

One warrior did not share the humor. Anpo ate her meal in silence, occasionally smiling and speaking with those who spoke with her. Rarely did her attention leave the blonde.

Part 4: Tatanka Ska Ki
The White Buffalo

Chapter Thirteen

1777

As the morning of the hunt dawned clear and cool, the warriors from the joined villages gathered together before the council *ti ikceya*. The two shamans worked together to call for the blessings of the Great Mystery upon the warriors surrounding them. Both leaders were anointed with a special mixture of sage smoke, to aid them in leading their hunters with certainty and swiftness. A final pipe was smoked among the elders and honored. Then came a loud outcry as the warriors leapt onto their hunting ponies and rode out of camp. *Hoksila* pelted after them, calling out good luck to their favorites.

"You will slay *tatanka ska*!" Nupa called to his friend as they rode side by side. Other warriors of their camp called out in agreement.

Anpo's face was grim. "Only if it is to be, *tiblo*."

He nodded. "It is to be, *tanksi*! You will be the honored one tonight!"

The party halted on a hilltop. Below them, a herd of buffalo grazed, easily four hundred head. The sacred white animal was invisible among such a number. Anpo looked back and saw the lodges being taken down as the village prepared to follow their hunters to the killing fields.

Her hands wept and she dried them on her pony's mane. She had only been on one previous hunt, her experience a poor one. Anpo's arrows had gone awry, merely wounding one young male. Would things be different this time? Would she achieve her vision of slaying the white buffalo? Or would she fail?

Mani called his hunters together. "My people will attack from the south! Wait until I signal!"

Time passed slowly for the hunters remaining. Anpo peered at the herd, trying to locate her destiny with little luck. She took a deep breath and closed her eyes. Collecting herself, she remembered the vision, remembered her talk with Inyan the day before. She had been surprised then to realize she looked as the warrior woman in her vision. Today there was one difference, however. Concerned, she looked at her weapons.

Anpo carried a bow and arrows. One shaft was already knocked, another held loosely in her hand until they prepared to attack. Yet in her vision, she hunted *tatanka ska* with a spear. Would her success rely on such a small thing? What would happen if she hunted with only her bow?

The thought of the white woman fading from her life, disappearing with Mani's village once the hunt was over, stabbed sharp in Anpo's chest. Inyan had said not to change her vision. Perhaps something horrible awaited her if she did not do everything as she originally saw it done.

"Nupa."

Her friend turned to her.

"Let me hunt with your spear."

Nupa cocked his head as he studied her. With no question, he handed the weapon to her, receiving her bow in trade.

Satisfied and relieved, Anpo swallowed against the flutter of her heart. Before she became too comfortable with her decision, a signal came from the opposing flank of the herd.

"*Hokahe wana!*" Wagna called, and the hunters of his camp swooped down the low embankment, screaming their cries. Simultaneously, Mani's warriors did the same, resulting in a cacophony of sound and motion that startled the closest buffalo.

There was an immediate if confused response from the herd. Those nearest the advancing warriors started and milled about anxiously, searching for the cause of their distress. The beasts further away began to gently drift in the opposite direction, instinct picking up on their danger.

The first warrior, Mani himself, reached the herd. He flew along on the back of his hunting pony, the reins in his teeth and a knocked bow in his hands. As he neared a large bull, he let fly his arrow, immediately reaching to his leather quiver for the next. The arrow hit its target, striking from above the flank and ranging forward and down. It was a clear and strong shot.

The buffalo's heart was pierced, and it shuddered before falling over. This signaled the herd. The smell of blood, the noise of their surroundings, the thunder of horses' hooves – all resulted in the sudden stampede as the animals tried desperately to get away.

Mani did not stop as his steed raced past the dead beast. He targeted another and shot again. Behind and on either side of the herd, the warriors did the same.

The first beast Nupa took with Anpo's bow was a yearling bull. His shot was clean and the animal died on its feet. As it tumbled over, disrupting the escape of its brethren behind, he whooped and urged his pony forward to his next target.

Anpo watched as her weapon worked well for her friend. Exhilarated despite the impending prophecy, she turned on her steed long enough to grin and whoop at her father's success as a bull fell to his arrow.

"*Hau*! Anpo!"

Her head whipped around, and she saw Nupa further ahead, yelling and gesturing wildly. Looking into the herd, the sacred white buffalo materialize in front of her.

Movement slowed to a crawl. While around them the herd stampeded, the white animal slowed to a walk. *He is waiting for me!*

Anpo looked about to see if any other warrior had noticed this strange behavior. Even as she pulled her horse in that direction, she saw three others veering towards the buffalo. One was a member of her own camp, an older man of an age with her father. The other two were from the joining village – Mani himself and Hehaka Yatke, the man who owned the white woman.

Their appearance became a catalyst, and time sped up. Anpo urged her pony until it flew toward the white buffalo that had eerily come to a halt. She took a deep breath to still her fluttering nerves, and threw Nupa's spear with all her might.

Time crawled again as she watched the spear spin towards her target. Over the sound of hooves she thought she could hear three bow strings loose their missiles. The buffalo turned its head, a dark, liquid eye regarding her. Then it started as the spear pierced its hide and drove deep – a true shot.

Anpo watched the animal shudder and topple over, her spearhead piercing its heart. Two arrows also stuck out of the hide.

Though the hunt continued around her, Anpo pulled her steed up and dismounted, moving to the sacred animal. "Thank you, *tatanka ska*, for this great honor. My family will use your bone and meat and hide to survive the coming winter. You will always be honored at my fire."

Around her was pandemonium. Warriors sped past, hot on the trail of the animals crazed with fear. Her pony pranced anxiously about at the ruckus. Despite the last of the herd stampeding past, none disturbed Anpo and her kill.

With a careful hand, she reached to the wound her spear sprouted from. Taking blood on her fingertips, she drew two lightning bolts across her cheeks. She remained in her place on her knees beside her kill, eyes closed as she continued to pay the sacred animal's spirit homage.

Eventually, the sound of approaching horses roused her. Anpo inhaled deeply, and stood. Several warriors from both camps arrived, whooping in excitement.

"*Tanksi*! I told you!" Nupa called, clearly elated at his friend's success. "You have brought this camp much honor with *wakan tanka*!" He hopped off his horse and ran forward.

Others from both camps clambered off their mounts to congratulate the young *wicakte*. Anpo flushed from their praise. There was a pause in the well wishing when the two leaders arrived. Both, elder and younger, approached the carcass and studied it, speaking softly to one another.

Mani bent, whispered something to the bull, and yanked the arrow that had been his from the flesh. His teeth were bright against his dark skin as he approached the waiting hunters. "You have done well, Anpo," he said.

Nodding, Anpo responded, "Thank you, *wicahca*."

More horses thundered up as the rest of the men arrived. One threw himself from his saddle and angrily marched towards the knot of warriors gathered at the beast.

"The *tatanka ska* is my kill!" Hehaka Yatke argued. "I am the honored one. Not some girl."

The men grew silent as Anpo was slurred. Even Yatke's chief turned to stare at his warrior, ashamed for his rudeness. "Yatke–" he growled, eyes flashing.

"*Hoh*, Mani!" the enraged warrior interrupted. "You might be willing to step aside for a *wicincala* pretending to be *wicasa*, but I will not! You saw the shot! You know I speak truly!"

"I know that you and I and two others all tried to slay the white buffalo at the same time. Two arrows and a spear pierced the animal's hide." Mani spread his hands wide, an apologetic expression sent Anpo's way. "I know that my arrow was not deep enough to kill. I do not think yours was either, Yatke."

The other man refused to back down. "I claim the *tatanka ska*," he insisted, arms crossed over his chest and chin jutting out in defiance.

"Then let the shamans ask the spirit of *tatanka ska*," a clear voice suggested.

Everyone turned to look at Anpo.

"The shamans will talk to his spirit and will know who slew him," she continued, her face relaxed though her gaze was hard.

The witnessing hunters murmured approval at the proposal. While the hunt was over, it was not official, and no wars or vendettas could be fought until it was. All seemed to find it a good idea except the disputer.

"*Hoh*! There is no need! A *wikoskalaka* could never throw a spear with enough strength to kill a buffalo!"

Anpo frowned. Around her, a good portion of the men from both camps growled, having seen her make this kill.

Yatke refused to back up when she stepped forward to glare into his face.

In a strong voice, Anpo asked, "Then you are afraid?"

His back stiffened more. Pushing his face until it was a mere breath away from hers, he said, "I am not afraid of you or old men."

Undaunted, Anpo asked, "Then you will abide by their decision?"

"If they decide against me, they will be wrong." He paused in thought. "But, I will abide by their words."

A flash of her vision crossed her mind – the woman with hair like the sun. "If the shamans decide in your favor, I will give you my best hunting pony. If they decide in my favor, you will give me the white woman."

A flash of confusion briefly crossed Yatke's eyes. As all awaited his decision, he weighed the options. Eventually, he smiled. "I agree. Let these *wicasa*," and he stressed the word, "be witness."

Wagna pointed to the nearest warrior still on his horse. "Go. Tell our shamans I have need of their counsel. And tell the rest of the camp this hunt is complete. *Wana*! Hurry."

The rider shot off at a full gallop, racing towards the approaching village.

Nupa remained at his friend's side as the men drifted away to look over their handiwork. He cast sidelong glares at Yatke, who stood alone. "His head is full of feathers," he growled. "Anyone could see that you have the honor here, *tanksi*."

Shrugging in feigned disinterest, Anpo looked over the field. "I told you, *tiblo*. I will have the honor only if the honor is to be." Her mind saw a head of golden hair, eyes of the deepest blue. *Is the honor to be?*

Her friend refused to respond to her skepticism.

Soon, the rider returned, two other ponies following him with the wise men of the villages. Behind the three, the camp approached, ready to make meat and prepare the evening's feast.

Inyan climbed from his steed. "There is a dispute?" he asked, looking at Anpo.

Before she could respond, Yatke spoke up. "*Hau*! There is." He waved vaguely in Anpo's direction. "This...this...*wikoskalaka*," he sneered, "thinks the white buffalo is hers. But she is not strong enough to slay him."

The shaman raised an eyebrow at Anpo who nodded. Turning to his comrade, a man about a dozen years senior, Inyan smiled. "You and I will speak with *tatanka ska* so that we might ease these warriors' hearts and minds." The two strode over and bent to their task.

As the women and girls picked over the carcasses, identifying their men's kills by identifying marks on the weapons, the two older men pored over the white buffalo. Each took out a rattle and other tools of their trade. They began to chant with much rattling and fanfare as they joined forces to speak with the dead animal's spirit. Nearby stood a gaggle of boys watching the proceedings with avid interest.

Anpo stood tall and proud, keeping her anxiety and anger under control. *You are better than most men,* she thought. Catching movement from the corner of her eye, she watched her opponent pace. *Definitely better than this man.* She could feel the flow of strength from Nupa and her father who stood behind her.

No one stood behind Yatke.

When most of the slaughtering was finished, the two men completed their spiritual quest. Both dusted off their robes and put away their shamanic instruments. Their voices were low as they conferred. Apparently coming to an agreement, the pair approached the disagreeing parties.

The elder shaman of Yatke's camp spoke up. "We have come to a decision. Will you abide by our words?"

Anpo bowed her head in agreement. "I will abide by your decision, *wicahca.* And I will keep my part of the wager."

"And I," the other warrior spouted, stepping forward with irritation that she had spoken first.

Nodding, the older of the shamans stepped back, gesturing towards Inyan.

"We have walked the land of the spirits and spoken to many who witnessed this hunt," the younger shaman intoned. "We have found the spirit of *tatanka ska* and asked him his opinion of this matter between two of our best hunters." Inyan eyed all who surrounded them. "*Tatanka ska* knows that the warrior in the yellow shirt slew him."

There was a moment of silence as his statement sunk in before Nupa whooped and pounded his friend on the back, nearly knocking her over in excitement. Anpo's knees felt watery, and it was all she could do to keep her feet as relief washed over her. Something else coursed through her blood – a trickle of fear.

Yatke stood frozen, a look of confusion on his face.

Mani approached and studied him. "I am witness," he said, bringing Yatke back to the present, and reminding him of his wager. "When you lose, do not lose the lesson."

Chapter Fourteen

The day began when Kathleen woke to voices outside the tent. Something exciting was occurring, and the men hollered fit to wake the dead. When she sat up, the old woman harangued at her from the fire, waving her out of the sleeping furs.

Herded outside, she discovered the people gathered around the central tent, as they had the night before. This time, however, most the men were mounted, brandishing weapons and yelling. Several stern looking ones with black stripes across their faces circled the mob. From previous experience, Kathleen knew these men were soldiers of some sort, assigned to keep the peace among their people. She figured they were failing miserably, considering the boisterous activity about her.

After some sort of ceremony, the mounted natives raced around in a circle before pelting out of the encampment. Before Kathleen could comprehend what everyone was going on about, the two women she lived with hustled her back to the tent. There she helped them break it down. Others did the same, women and children dismantling the tents and packing their belongings onto horses and dogs. Soon, the people were on the move once more.

Kathleen wondered if they were off to attack an enemy. *Perhaps soldiers have made it this far west!* She could not help but feel a thrill of anticipation at the thought. Maybe they would save her and return her to her home.

They halted before she could get too far in her musings. It seemed odd to travel such a short distance before setting up camp again; it could not have been more than two miles. A cloud of dust rose from beyond a hillock to the east, indicating the men had not gone far, either. Thoroughly confused, she wished she understood the language a little better. She concentrated on the discussions around her as she was instructed to pull out baskets, skins, and assorted cooking instruments. Her daydream of rescue faded away. *Something* was happening, but the atmosphere was too joyous for it to be a military skirmish, and she could hear no telltale musket fire from further away.

At mid morning, a lone rider returned. The clatter of hooves drew the people close, and Kathleen trailed behind, holding the boy child. She watched as the rider hurled himself from his saddle, and pelted towards the tent in the center of camp. Others seemed puzzled by his behavior, a low buzz of conversation rising about her. Within moments, however, the rider stepped back out of the tent. He spoke, loud and clear, and the crowd gave a weird ululating trill before becoming industrious.

Kathleen was divested of the child she carried and directed back towards the tent. From there, the two women managing her gathered the utensils and pushed some of them into her hands. She was surprised to find herself holding an obsidian knife. *Do they trust me with weapons now?* Further thought interrupted, she was pulled and prodded away from camp.

She noticed the other members of camp doing the same, a mass migration to the east. Within moments, the group crested the low rise. Scattered all across the shallow valley below were dead animals.

That's what was happening! Kathleen's final hope of being saved withered away as she made the connection. *They were hunting for game.* Kathleen was brought along until they came to an animal. The women with her began the slaughtering, urging her close and mimicking which way she should use her knife to cut the thick hide.

Nearby, a cluster of the men milled around, some with voices raised in anger. Kathleen looked up from her work and wiped her sweaty forehead on her shoulder. She was blood to the elbows and smears of the red liquid colored her dress and moccasins. *Butchering is hard work*, she thought. *I've always wondered why Adam was so exhausted when he finished with the venison.*

Of the voices that caught her attention, she was surprised to see that one belonged to the man with the yellow shirt. She had noticed him watching her since the two camps came together. Kathleen had thought him level headed and quiet, if a bit stern. The other belonged to the man she lived with, his face twisted in fury. *He must really be angry about something*, Kathleen thought fearfully. Memories of an abusive savage came to her, flashes of pain from her many violations, and she shuddered. She returned to her task, ducking her head in an attempt to avoid the memories, wondering what would become of her.

As if her thoughts called him, the man arrived and stood over her. The boy hugged his father's leg, and the girl chattered at him. He spoke to the women and reached down for Kathleen's arm.

Sudden terror filled her heart as he forced her to stand, removing the knife from her nerveless fingers. *Now, what? Is he still angry, then? Am I to be beaten for something? Does it start again?* She dared a glance at his face, swallowing relief at seeing none of the flashing anger she expected.

She flinched when he pulled her away from the others. Not wanting to upset him, she went dutifully along. Then she was placed in front of the man with the yellow shirt, her arm put in his hand.

It took a few moments for Kathleen to understand what exactly was happening. When she did, an icy hand gripped her heart, and her blood pounded in her ears. *He gave me away!* she thought with horror. *Oh, God! Now what will happen to me?* She heard a conversation between the two men, but she was frozen in fear. *What if this one's like the last? I don't think I can survive it again.* Visions of her previous rapist filled her mind, weakening her knees.

~ * ~ * ~ * ~ * ~

Yatke handed the strange woman to Anpo. "I do not give this woman to you to pay a wager. I freely give her to honor your skill as a hunter and warrior of our people." He released the woman's arm. "Ask me anything to pay the wager due you."

Surprised at his change of heart, Anpo stared at him. She said, "I will accept a pony so the woman can ride."

He nodded and stepped back. "A pony for the wager." He turned to walk away.

"Wait!" Anpo asked, "Does she have a name?"

Yatke shrugged. "I do not know. She is unable to tell us. We have used Jiji until she could speak our tongue." He continued away, leaving Anpo with her new property.

"Your vision has come true, *tanksi*," Nupa grinned at his friend. "You have the honor of *tatanka ska* and the pale woman with hair like the sun!" He peered over her shoulder to look at the stranger. "Does this mean you will not move in with your *cuwe's* family when she marries?"

The pale woman's arm trembled beneath her grip, and Anpo ignored her friend's teasing. *She is as scared as I! Why? Does she know of our destiny?* The stranger's fear bolstered her courage.

Hiding her face behind a golden veil, the woman stared at her filthy moccasins. Anpo put her fingers under the lowered chin, bringing the woman's face up until she could see familiar features. *Eyes the blue of a deep lake.* The world seemed to recede as their eyes locked. Anpo heard her friend speaking, but did not understand the words. She heard her father respond, and their presence dissipated as they left the two women alone. "What is your name?" she asked.

There was a flash of confusion, and the woman spoke.

The musical tone of the woman's voice and language set Anpo

back. A smile teased her lips. *Her voice sounds like the birds and the wind playing through the trees.*

She glanced quickly around, wanting to share this thought with someone, but no one was there. All of her people now helped to butcher and gather the carcasses for the trip back to camp. Her mothers and sisters worked on the white buffalo now that it had been decided the honor was Anpo's.

She returned her attention to the white woman. "What is your name?" she asked again. This time, she patted her chest and stated, "Anpo." Then she placed her palm onto the woman's chest.

The woman seemed to understand her intent. A demure smile crossed her lips, pleasure at being asked. "Kathleen," she said, patting her chest as she said the unfamiliar word.

Anpo nodded. "Ketlin," she repeated.

"Yes!"

Anpo sucked in a breath at the brilliant smile she received and could not help but return it. She brought the woman to her family. "Wanbli," she said, interrupting the family's labors. While her words were to her father, they were for her mothers and sisters. "This is Ketlin. She is my woman now and will help your women. They will need to teach her what she must know."

Hca rose to her feet. "I will teach her." She held out her hand to Kathleen "When we are finished with *tatanka ska* I will have Ketlin bring the liver to my *wicakte* sister."

Kathleen was soon involved in slaughtering the white buffalo, her gaze taking in the new people surrounding her.

Anpo did not help, stepping back to observe her woman. Her mind and heart were numb, yet joyous at the same time.

Nupa approached his friend with a wry smile on his face. "You look like *hehaka* just when he realizes he is being hunted, eyes wide and frozen in stillness."

Shaking herself from her reverie, Anpo said, "I look no different from you when you eat at my father's fire." She gestured toward her older sister with her thumb.

His eyes narrowed and the smile faded. "Is that the way things are between you and the white woman?" he asked. "Do you feel for her what I feel for Hca?"

Anpo grimaced, the good humor gone for the moment. "I do not know, *tiblo*. I only know that Ketlin and I have a destiny to share for good or ill."

Deciding to lighten the mood, Nupa laughed. "You have slain the *tatanka ska, tanksi*! Your destiny will be for good! I know it!!" He pulled her towards the remaining people gathered. "Come! They are nearly finished with their work. There will be a grand feast to celebrate!"

Letting the confusion and fears drift away, Anpo joined in his laughter. Her eyes continued to track the white woman's movements. *The vision lives, in reality as well as my heart. What will I do that will cause her to bleed?*

Nupa helped his family pack the meat and hide to the village, and Anpo did the same. In doing so, she barely noted her father had killed three of the animals. Her attention remained firm upon Kathleen.

The woman seemed no different from every other time Anpo watched her over the last two days. Her fear was evident in the tight shoulders, the furtive looks. She did whatever was asked of her when she understood the order; Hca had to pantomime an action only once for Kathleen to understand.

Anpo frowned at her mother's treatment of Kathleen. Gi, as first wife to Wanbli, held a higher place in Anpo's family. Her *ti ikceya* was the largest; she decided who would do what task to keep food in everyone's bellies and moccasins on their feet; hers was the final decision within the lodge. Kathleen's place was that of slave. She had no rights among the Maka village, not until she learned their language and knew her position.

Anpo wondered if her distaste for Kathleen's treatment came from knowing their future destiny. She had never considered different treatment for a slave. Yet the memory of those blue eyes staring through the brightness, the blood running freely from Kathleen's side haunted Anpo.

Once everyone returned to the village, the men left the process of making meat to their women. As a whole, they drifted toward the river, to clean themselves of dust and blood. The women would do the same downstream once they finished the immediate chores necessary to keep the meat safe from predators and spoilage.

Anpo went further upstream for her cleansing. Being neither male nor female, she did not bathe with either. As the water turned red with the blood of the white buffalo, she wondered about her feminine counterparts, the *winkte*. There were four of them now among her people, a sacred number, but none resided in Wagna's village. Were their lives as lonely, as different?

Did any of them marry men? The idea startled her, and she froze.

A warrior usually did not think of marriage until well past their twentieth winter. Anpo was sixteen, far too young for such seriousness. But the first of her vision had come to pass. The white buffalo had given himself to her, one already highly honored by her existence as *wicakte*. The yellow haired woman now belonged to her. Anpo did not think much time would come to pass before she and Kathleen joined.

How else could Ketlin call me mahasanni?

Mind full of questions and doubts, Anpo finished bathing. She climbed out of the river and used handfuls of grass to dry herself off before dressing. When she returned to the village, she noted many of the women had already left to wash. At her mother's lodge, the hides from her and Wanbli's kills were stretched and staked. Anpo went inside and changed into a fresh breechclout and pair of moccasins.

She saw the men beginning to gather at the main fire when she emerged and went to join them. Tales were already being told as the boys listened avidly to the descriptions of the hunt.

At Anpo's approach, Wagna made space for her. "Here, Anpo! Sit with me!"

Flushing, she looked at Mani who was being displaced from the honored position.

The younger leader smiled and gestured her closer. "*Hau*, Anpo. I would be honored for you to sit here between us."

A bit nervous, she sat between the two powerful men. Her initial uneasiness faded as the normal pattern of things asserted themselves. Pipes were pulled out, tales were spun, and around the camp women and girls prepared the feast.

Anpo's attention was drawn away from one of the speakers when she saw the yellow hair of her woman. *My woman.* She banished the thought, the complications of it too much to deal with for now. *Ketlin. I wonder what her name means.*

Chapter Fifteen

Once the majority of the work was completed, Hca gestured for Kathleen to follow the women to the river. Many *winyan* and children were already there, cleaning themselves and their clothing before the labor of preparing the night's feast. They chattered and laughed as they worked and played, enjoying a brief respite from their tasks.

Hca removed her dress, using her hands to indicate Kathleen was to do the same. Her mother, Gi, was already in the water, talking with her *maske* nearby. The other women of her *tiospaye*, Hwa and Hinhan, sat naked on the riverbank, scrubbing their leather garments with rocks to remove stains. Hwa's and Wanbli's son, Cetan, splashed in the shallows nearby.

Kathleen blushed as red as the blood splashed across her clothing. A hush grew over the women as she obeyed Hca's direction, all eyes studying her skin and hair and freckles with curious intensity. Noting the sudden quiet, Hca scanned the river. Seeing the stares, she planted her hands on her bare hips and glared back at them. "*Han*, you!" she called out. "Did your mothers raise you to be rude or is this something you learned as adults?" she demanded.

Several of them blinked at her before realizing they were being chastised. Most looked away; others appeared affronted by Hca's direct and challenging manner, though they turned their backs. Her mother made a disapproving noise, but Hca refused to be chided. This was her sister's woman, a powerful one if the vision was true. Despite Kathleen's status as slave, she had to be treated with more respect and deference.

Satisfied with being ignored by the others, Hca splashed into the water, waving the scared woman to follow. "Do you know how to swim?" she asked, mimicking the motion with her arms. "To swim?"

Kathleen swallowed and repeated the words. "To swim." She took a couple of strokes away and back.

Pleased with the response, Hca said, "Come, Ketlin!" She swam away toward the opposite shore, followed closely by Kathleen.

~ * ~ * ~ * ~ * ~

After bathing, Kathleen sat alongside her new friend and scraped the wet leather of her dress until most of the blood came away. The other women left her alone, and it gave her time to think of the day's occurrences.

It was not that these women were kinder to her. The eldest, while not as old as the grandmother who had been the bane of her existence the last few weeks, still appeared as stiff and stern with her, free with rude words should Kathleen not understand her orders. But the two women Kathleen had lived with before were too busy in their day-to-day existence, what with two small children in the tent to increase the workload. It followed that they were less inclined to be pleasant to someone like herself who had no idea what to do.

Her new living situation consisted of twice as many women, plenty of hands to cover the workload until she could learn. There was the older one and another maybe ten years younger. Hca seemed an older version of Anpo and was no doubt his sister. Finally, there was a beautiful young girl of perhaps ten or eleven, and a pudgy little boy barely out of the toddler stage.

Hca instructed her to put on the wet leather. Kathleen shivered in the breeze and wished she had different clothing to wear. She was led through the camp, back to the tent where they had brought the carcasses. As Hca held the leather flap aside at the opening, she thought, *My new home.*

The interior looked much the same as the last tent where she had lived. A fire pit stood in the center, robes and furs were strewn about for sleeping and sitting, various bundles here and there around the edges held a multitude of incomprehensible items. Kathleen remained standing just to one side of the doorway, and Hca climbed in and past her. The old woman also entered and closed the opening behind her. Kathleen wondered where the other woman and two children went. *Don't they live here, too?*

The old woman noticed her shiver. She spoke to Hca, gesturing at Kathleen with her thumb, something about her white skin being thin. Then she guided the newcomer further into the *ti ikceya* by an elbow.

"*Ohan, ina.*" Hca rummaged among some things, finding what she looked for. Obviously pleased, she turned to Kathleen and held up a dress. She spoke to the white woman and, when Kathleen stared with mild comprehension, she pushed the dress into her arms.

The dress was of buckskin and long. It was painted yellow, like Anpo's shirt. Running from shoulder to hem were two strips of white with red designs painted on them – a lightning bolt, the buffalo and the sun. Hesitantly, Kathleen took the offering. "Thank you, Hca," she said, though she knew the woman would not understand her. "It's beautiful." She looked down to her dress, formless and without adornment. Unbidden tears came to her eyes.

Hca's pleasure faded as she saw tears trailing from Kathleen's eyes. She frowned and stepped forward, speaking again.

The old woman looked Kathleen over with a critical eye and spoke. Her words were about Kathleen being hurt. She did not seem overly hostile toward the new arrival, though her tone was as gruff as the old woman in Yatke's tent.

Kathleen tried to hold back the tears as the women conversed over her. Obviously, they had a good idea of what happened to her before her arrival among them. She swiped one away with a vicious movement. *Now is not the time, Kath!* she thought, fighting her emotions. All was for naught, however, when an understanding expression crossed Hca's face. Kathleen was pulled into an embrace.

The kindness opened a floodgate, and all the pain and fear and worry of the past few weeks washed over her. Kathleen sobbed, her body shaking from the force of her cries. Slowly, she was lowered down until she and Hca were seated on some furs. The woman rocked her and sang softly as Kathleen cried.

The tears subsided. *Kath, you're an idiot.* She pulled away from Hca. As she hiccoughed like a small child, the old woman knelt beside them and wiped her face with a piece of soft leather, her manner somewhat brisk. Kathleen blushed at the treatment, feeling like a three-year-old. She had to admit to herself that she felt better for the emotional release, regardless of her embarrassment. *Not that these people can understand how silly I feel.*

Kathleen allowed herself to be undressed. The wet leather of the previous outfit no longer against her skin, she felt herself warm almost immediately. She gave a final shiver as she slipped the new dress over her head and smoothed it down. The other women were doing the same, each avoiding watching the other as they changed clothes. Kathleen averted her gaze, as well, giving them as much privacy as was available in a tent of this size.

When she finished, Hca tied a belt about her waist. She beckoned Kathleen toward her, producing a yellow belt to go with the dress. She tied it about Kathleen, drawing the formless clothing in at the waist. With a satisfied look, she stepped back to regard her handiwork. "*Ina?*"

The two women conversed, and Kathleen paid close attention to their words. *"Ina". That must mean "mother". That wasn't the word that the other woman used for the old grandma.* She worried the question, wanting answers but not able to get her inquiry across to the pair regarding her.

"Ketlin, *cunksi*," the old woman said, "Come." She waved them toward the covered opening, saying more before she stepped out of the tent.

Taking Kathleen by the hand, Hca led her outside.

Feeling a little more grounded from her bout of emotion, Kathleen followed, a sense of gentle wistfulness filling her. *Perhaps things will be better now.*

~ * ~ * ~ * ~ * ~

Anpo saw her sister and woman approach the gathering of men. No longer paying the least amount of attention to the current speaker, his voice droned into silence as she watched Hca speak to Kathleen. When the woman's gaze met hers, she felt her heart flutter. *Does her presence do this to me because of my vision? Or because of her power over me?*

She watched Kathleen approach with hesitant steps. The woman's eyes remained downcast until she knelt beside Anpo, a bundled skin in her hands. Kathleen risked a quick glance at Anpo when she was relieved of her burden, her skin reddening.

The delivery made, Kathleen prepared to rise. Anpo reached out and grabbed her wrist, forcing her to remain kneeling just behind and to one side. The pulse beneath her grip thumped with a rapid beat, and Anpo felt a slight flinch. *Do I have the same power over her?*

Opening the bundle, Anpo saw the liver of *tatanka ska*. She thought the irony of its delivery amusing. *Ketlin bringing this to me is truly fitting.* She pulled her knife from its sheath, ignoring Kathleen's startled gasp as she carefully sliced off a bit of the organ. Holding the small piece before her woman, she said, "Ketlin, you should share in the spirit of *tatanka ska*. Because of him you and I are together." Anpo watched the woman's skin go whiter with a vague sense of wonder. *Soon she will be the color of* tatanka ska *himself!*

Kathleen swallowed audibly before leaning forward to take the liver on her tongue. A surprised expression made Anpo grin. As Kathleen ate the morsel, Anpo turned back to the liver and sliced it up into small chunks. Taking one for herself, she handed the skin of meat to Wagna beside her. "Let all of us enjoy the strength and spirit of *tatanka ska*."

The men murmured acceptance of her generosity as the skin passed around until all had enjoyed a piece of liver from the sacred animal.

Hca stepped forward to touch Kathleen's shoulder, drawing her away. Anpo wanted to keep her there, but did not stop them from leaving. It would be unseemly for her to cling to Kathleen, much as she wanted to spend her every waking moment with her. There would be time for them to become acquainted later.

Reluctant, Anpo turned away from her woman, forcing herself to focus on one of the big bellies discussing past hunts and glories.

Chapter Sixteen

Kathleen's afternoon was quite educational. Hca made a fine instructor, not only about how to take care of the skins and meat, but the words involved. She took the time to point out each thing, touch it, and concentrate on Kathleen as she spoke the word. By the time the meal was ready, Kathleen was able to name everything properly. She received a laugh and a hug from Hca in reward, and could not help but grin foolishly for some time after.

When Kathleen prepared the first serving of food for Anpo, Hca helped by adding extra of the things she knew he enjoyed and frowning with a shake of her head for those that he did not. Kathleen understood what she was being said and refrained from giving Anpo anything not on the list of favorables.

The feast was a riotous affair, one Kathleen had never witnessed before. Even the previous night's festivities were not quite as active. She found the dancing and drums nerve wracking, reminiscent of many stories told among frontier families about Indians gone wild. There had been several such gatherings since her initial capture, but she had been kept in the tent each time. Seeing such ferocity served to quell her curiosity, and she wished she was safe inside a tent. Such was not an option for her. She remained meek, wanting to cower from prying eyes. However, it was her duty to serve Anpo, and places to hide were rare.

He must not have any other wives, Kathleen considered, attempting to keep her mind occupied with matters other than the obscene dancing about the bonfire. *Of course, he looks younger than Stewart, and he won't have a wife for another five or six years.* With the previous man, she was rarely called upon to serve him food. The mother of his children did that chore. *And since I was the second...wife? I wasn't needed to feed him.* Anpo did not seem to have any women about him other than his family. From what Kathleen could gather, Hca was Anpo's sister and Gi was his mother. The other woman with the children, Hwa, had to be a sister to Gi, or maybe another wife. Kathleen had heard on the edges of civilization that Indian men had more than one woman, the gossip properly scandalizing to ensure its continued circulation among white people.

As night drifted on, children and older folks left the fire and reveling to the younger crowd. Songs were sung, dances danced, and music played. Kathleen was glad to note these people did have a set of wooden pipes, and wondered if she would be allowed to play them herself some time. The food was eaten until there was nothing left. The food, the excitement of the day, all conspired to relax Kathleen. She knelt beside Anpo, her eyes drifting closed as exhaustion stole over her.

She roused to a touch on her shoulder, starting violently. Saying something, Anpo helped Kathleen to her feet, his face gentle. His expression eased the thumping of her heart.

She understood they were leaving as Anpo rose with her. He made some comment to the remaining people and walked towards the tent. As they drifted further into the darkness, Kathleen's fears grew again. *You know he'll want to bed you, Kath. You can't do to him what you did to the other. He'll give you away, sure as rain!* By the time they stepped into the tent, her heart pounded, and she had difficulty breathing, the panic attack building in intensity. *I don't know if I can do it!*

Anpo directed her to the sleeping robes Hca had indicated were hers. They were located between Hca and Gi to the right of the entrance. The coals in the fire pit were barely bright enough to light the way. Hca and her mother already slept nearby, two bundled lumps on either side of Kathleen and Anpo. Sitting Kathleen on her robes, Anpo stepped to the fire and stirred up a bit of flame. She wondered if perhaps her fears were misguided.

The glow backlit Anpo's muscular frame, and Kathleen swallowed anxiously. When he returned and sat facing her, she dropped her gaze, wanting more than anything to be anywhere else. Even back with the other man and his women was preferable to the here and now. *Oh, God! Here 'tis!* She felt hands on her shoulders as the man turned her in her place to face him. Now they were seated with the fire to her right. *He wants to see what he's got.*

Kathleen refused to look at him. She shivered uncontrollably, her muscles tight in response to expected pain. Several long moments passed with no movement from either of them. Obviously, he studied his new acquisition, though she wondered when he would touch her. Her trembling increased at the thought, and Kathleen bit back a sob.

The suddenness of Anpo's movement startled Kathleen, and she flinched back as he stood in a fluid movement. She held her stomach, rocking as his yellow shirt fell to one side, followed by the breechclout and belt and moccasins he wore. Terror filled her heart as dark skinned hands reached down and took hers. Her belly rolled with nausea, her skin beginning to sweat with the terror in her heart. After a reluctant struggle, Kathleen was brought to her feet.

She kept her eyes averted, her head turned towards the fire. Tears coursed down her cheeks, but she refused to sob aloud. Her new friend, Hca, slept nearby, and Kathleen did not want to wake her. Anpo still held her hands, warm and dry against her clammy flesh. *Why was he prolonging things? Couldn't he just rape me and be done with it?*

"Ketlin."

He said something else, but Kathleen did not understand the words. He reached out and guided her chin around. Again, she resisted before acquiescing. Rather than look at his nakedness, Kathleen stared over his head. He motioned in front of her face, two fingers pointing to her eyes that drew her attention despite her best efforts.

Anpo pointed into her eyes and then his own. Again he spoke.

Their eyes met and locked.

When this had happened on the killing field, Kathleen's fears had drained away. Looking into Anpo's steady gaze robbed her of her terror, replacing it with a vague sense of awe and wonder. As before, this same thing happened again. Kathleen's mind babbled she was going to be raped, but it was not sinking in. Then Anpo's hand gestured again, bringing her gaze down.

Kathleen spasmed in surprise and would have fallen had Anpo not kept her hand, lowering her gently to the robes.

He's a...a...woman! The vision of breasts and a light patch of dark curly hair played itself over and over in Kathleen's mind. *A woman?*

~ * ~ * ~ * ~ * ~

Anpo smiled at Kathleen's amazement. Again, she gestured down her body, drawing her gaze. "See, Ketlin? I am no different than you." She reached out and caressed her woman's cheek. "I will not hurt you."

Kathleen seemed to be at a loss. Tears dried on her face as she regarded Anpo. Finally, she bestowed her with a tentative smile.

Encouraged, Anpo let her attention roam from the deep blue eyes to the yellow hair. Leaning forward, moving slowly as to not frighten the woman, she reached behind Kathleen and unbound it. The color sparkled in the firelight, and her mouth opened a bit as she studied it with admiration, taking a few strands between her fingers and appreciating the contrast against her skin. *She is the same as my vision. The Sun has graced Ketlin.* This led her to follow the line of the woman's neck to where it disappeared into her dress.

The *cuwignaka* Kathleen wore was interesting. The designs painted on it were identical to the ones on Anpo's shirt. *The one my sister gave me.* Rather than have Kathleen remove the dress, Anpo moved on to the other exposed areas of her skin. She had heard from her mother that

Kathleen had been severely abused by the enemy before coming to Yatke. The women gossiped about her behavior in Mani's village, saying she had been hurt badly to react as she did. Anpo's vision flashed in her mind. She may be fated to hurt Kathleen, but she would do everything possible to thwart that destiny.

Despite the frustration of the clothing Kathleen wore, Anpo continued her inspection around it. She reached for the woman's hand and pulled until her arm was extended, revealing pale skin. Leaning close, Anpo peered at the fine almost white hairs that sparkled in the light. Her breath caused them to tremble and move. *Even her skin has yellow hair!*

When Kathleen pulled her arm away, it broke the spell. Anpo looked up blankly as the woman rose to stand in front of her. A puzzled expression crossed her face as Kathleen smiled at her. She watched as Kathleen removed her dress and sat back down.

She is...she is beautiful! Anpo watched the woman neatly fold her dress and set it to one side. She leaned forward and peered at the newly revealed flesh. Anpo reached out to touch the white skin, but stopped. By rights, she could do as she wanted with Kathleen. The woman was hers, her slave, someone to do the women's work to make things easier for her *tiospaye*. If Kathleen had been any other maiden, Anpo would not think twice about her treatment.

But this was the woman of her vision. Inyan had said many times over the years that she was a powerful force. Was Kathleen sacred? Would treating her ill exasperate their future? Having lived for years with the vision, Anpo was reluctant to cause Kathleen any more pain than was already ordained.

Kathleen noticed the hesitation. She took Anpo's hand and guided it to her heart. Now that permission was given, Anpo kept her touch soothing as she ran her hands along Kathleen's body. It was almost like gentling a wild pony. She felt the woman tremble beneath her palms, saw the pulse beating hard at her throat. The more contact she made, the less Kathleen jumped.

Anpo was impressed by the softness of Kathleen's skin, intrigued by the tiny hairs covering her body and the crinkly curls between Kathleen's legs that were slightly darker than the hair on her head. She enjoyed the contrast of her brown hand against Kathleen's flesh, more so on the woman's belly where it was whiter. By touching her, Kathleen became more real, more than the vision that had driven Anpo all these years.

Finally finished with her examination, Anpo sighed and straightened. *She is more relaxed now,* she thought as she studied the woman. *She knows I will not hurt her, as she has been hurt before.*

Anpo debated with herself. In the manner of her people, she slept as a man, a *wicasa*. Her robes were next to her father's on the other side of the fire. Kathleen's were located on the women's side of the *ti ikceya*, near Hca and her mother who would look out for her and teach her the Lakota way. When her father wished to share Gi's robes, he would do so, but return to his own to sleep.

Anpo did not want to leave Kathleen. The thought of taking her woman to the river, of bathing her pale skin in the moonlight, was an intriguing one, yet Kathleen still seemed skittish despite her new knowledge of Anpo's nature. Kathleen's fear from her mistreatment would interfere with what must be a joyous meeting of their bodies. Any intimacies between Anpo and her would have to wait.

The vision had been so vivid, had lived with her for so long....

She was *wicakte*, neither male nor female. Who was to say she did not belong here on this side of the fire and in her woman's robes?

With a smile, Anpo readjusted herself on Kathleen's robes. She gestured for her to lie down. "Ketlin. We must sleep."

Kathleen relaxed, a slight sigh escaping her lips. She climbed into the sleeping robes with Anpo. They settled comfortably together as the flames faded to embers. She spoke, her voice barely above a whisper.

The only thing Anpo understood was her name. The strange lilt of Kathleen's voice made her smile. She hugged Kathleen closer, enjoying for the first time the sensation of skin against skin. "Be safe, Ketlin. Know that I am here to protect you."

Part 5: Wounspe Ki
The Teaching

Chapter Seventeen

1777

Anpo slowly drifted to wakefulness, a peaceful dream tickling the edges of her mind. A strange and comfortable weight against her body wriggled in a pleasing manner when she inhaled and stretched. Her brow furrowed as she tried to remember what had happened. *Tatanka ska! Ketlin!* Her eyes popped open, and she peered down her body, heart fluttering.

Golden hair spilled out from and across the sleeping robes. Kathleen was draped across Anpo's torso, using her as a pillow. Her face peaceful in repose, one pale hand rested on Anpo's shoulder.

She is not a dream, Anpo thought. She studied Kathleen with a gentle expression. *She is real. And she is mine!* Anpo squeezed her close. Kathleen murmured something in her language and readjusted herself, draping a leg over Anpo's thigh.

Heart full, Anpo used her free hand to caress the yellow tresses, fingering their softness and enjoying the sensation of her skin against another's. *Is this what my* ina *and* ate *feel when they are together? This caring?* she wondered. Peering up to the logs at the center of the lodge, Anpo sent a thought to *wakan tanka. Please help me be worthy of this gift, this woman.*

Anpo heard movement outside, noises indicating others in the village were awake. Looking through the smoke hole above, she saw gray against the dark interior. Normally, this would be too early for her to be up. Most young warriors preferred to stay up late into the night and sleep through the morning. The unfamiliar sensations of sleeping with another, however, had roused her.

Kathleen murmured to herself, on the verge of waking. She inhaled and stretched, sinuously pressing against Anpo. The *wicakte* enjoyed the pleasurable feeling. *Why would any* wicasa *want to sleep separately from his woman...unless this is different because I am different?* Before she could pursue the possibility, Kathleen came fully awake with a gasp. She stiffened in Anpo's arms.

Not wishing to scare her, Anpo stopped caressing Kathleen's skin. The woman pulled back, arching away as she stared at her. They regarded one another for a still moment as the outside world diminished. Anpo saw the beginnings of a blush crawl across the fair skin, Kathleen's terrified demeanor returning as she shrank away.

"Ketlin," Anpo said, her voice soft and low. She brushed the back of her knuckles along Kathleen's cheek, ignoring the slight flinch. "I drown in your eyes, Ketlin. You are very beautiful. I am glad you have come into my life, and I will work hard to be worthy of you."

The gentle words washed over Kathleen and, though she probably understood not a one, Anpo must have expressed her gratitude and caring and happiness well. Kathleen reached out to her in a tentative mirrored action, lightly running her knuckles across the Anpo's skin. She spoke in her language, a slight crooked smile breaking through the trepidation.

Smile widening as she listened to the strange accent, Anpo sat up and gathered Kathleen into her arms. Kathleen accepted the contact, appearing to enjoy it as much as she. Nearby, Hca rose from her furs, reminding Anpo others would soon be awakening. She released Kathleen, who looked about their sleeping area, and located Anpo's clothing. They helped each other dress.

Anpo led Kathleen out of the *ti ikceya*. The fire was dark, having been allowed to die in the night. Sitting down in her customary place, Anpo gestured at the circle of stones and gathered wood. "Ketlin, prepare the fire."

Kathleen looked down at the cold fire pit. She spoke, her intonation going up at the end. If she asked a question, the tone would have gone down, and Anpo wondered what she said. Using sign language, she slowly repeated herself.

Puffing out a breath, Kathleen looked about them. Under her breath, she repeated Anpo's words, "Prepare the fire." Apparently coming to some understanding, she hiked up her dress and knelt beside the fire pit. Anpo watched as she scattered the last evening's ashes and stacked new wood. Proud of her, Anpo picked up a stick and went to the still smoldering council fire. With a bit of blowing on the coals, the stick caught flame, and she returned.

Kathleen dusted off her hands and sat back on her heels. She saw Anpo arriving with the burning stick. Again she spoke in her words as she watched Anpo bring the pile of kindling to life.

Once the fire crackled, Anpo looked about the hearth. She found their breakfast, some dried meat and leftover *wansi* from the previous day's feast. Anpo scooped up the food and a half empty water bladder. Sitting at her place, she waved Kathleen closer, patting the robe beside her. She doled out portions of the makeshift breakfast, and they ate in silence.

Watching Kathleen eat, Anpo mused about their future. *Things are destined to be difficult. But she will still care deeply for me.* Taking a draught from the water skin, she offered it to Kathleen who took it with a smile. *Maybe Inyan was true in his thought. I will only hurt her as one hurts another when joined. Like Wanbli and Gi.* Here, a certain wistfulness filled her heart. *I hope that is so.*

Around them, more and more people moved about. *Winyan* prepared breakfast for their families, younger children ate and planned their day, and older children got ready to relieve the *koskalaka* guarding the herd of ponies. People were sluggish, however, from their late night of celebrating the hunt. Inside her mother's lodge, Anpo heard movement, knowing the women of her family would soon join them.

Kathleen, finished with her meal, held up the water skin, hefting it gently. She rose and waved the container at Anpo, speaking her language. Anpo did not understand, tilting her head as she studied the woman. Again Kathleen spoke, this time pointing in the direction of the river. "You will go get water?"

Speaking once more, repeating Anpo's words, Kathleen seemed eager to please. Anpo considered Kathleen's demeanor and decided she was right. She did a quick mental scan of the area. The river was close to the village; Kathleen would be safe to go there without harm. *I do not know how much she knows, how well she can take care of herself.* With a murmur of approval, she waved Kathleen toward the river. She watched her leave, eyes focused on the lazy sway of Kathleen's hips until she was out of sight.

Anpo felt odd at the excessive interest she gave Kathleen, but could not control herself. She did not recall ever watching a woman in this manner before, and there were many beautiful maidens among her people. Certainly one of them would have caught her attention before now. Anpo compared Kathleen to other *winyan*, and the only difference between them was coloring. *Her color is not what I see when she walks away.*

Somewhat disgruntled at this, Anpo was glad when others of her *tiospaye* began to gather. Hinhan led her little brother to the fire, her mother, Hwa, close behind. While it was not the place of warriors to tend children, Anpo took Cetan from his sister. As she played with the boy, the women began the task of preparing a meal. Hca and Gi soon joined them.

They chattered amongst themselves, mother and daughter bringing Hwa up to date on the new addition. Hwa and her children lived in a nearby lodge, an extension of Wanbli's family, and she was eager to hear about Kathleen. It was Hca who teased Anpo by informing the others where her sister had slept the previous night. Anpo retaliated by explaining to young Cetan a warrior could sleep where he or she pleased, no matter *winyan's* gossip.

By the time Kathleen returned with a full water bladder, the women had taken Anpo's hint and moved on to other topics of discussion. Hca smiled welcome to the arrival, taking the water from Kathleen.

"Thank you, Ketlin," she said. She gestured her closer. "Come. You and I will help *ina* prepare the morning meal for Wanbli."

Soon, Kathleen was seated across the fire from Anpo, a bowl in her lap. She mixed together dried meat and berries with a measure of animal fat. Hca used her fingers to combine cornmeal and water, creating dough. Hwa then took flattened pieces and cooked it on a hot rock.

Wanbli came out of Gi's *ti ikceya*, adjusting his breechclout before sitting down in his customary position at the head of the fire. Cetan, ever happy to see his father, left Anpo to sit beside the man. The boy puffed his chest out, his expression stern as he emulated Wanbli's demeanor.

Other than a faint expression of approval at his young son's actions, Wanbli's words were aimed at Anpo. "You have done well for yourself, *cunksi*. When you were born, Inyan had a vision of you. You have gone farther than his vision. I am very proud."

Anpo's skin darkened, but she kept her father's gaze. "Thank you, *ate*. Your patience and teaching aided me."

He nodded, accepting her compliment. Gi handed him a piece of fry bread, still hot from the rock. With a practiced hand, he scooped leftover roasted meat into it and rolled it up. "Now that you have a woman, what will you do?"

"I do not know. I have no dowry of my own as I had not planned to join." Anpo accepted fry bread from her second mother, using some of the berries Kathleen stirred into the *wansi* mixture. "Ketlin will have to begin working on a lodge from the skins I bring her. She will be a buried woman until her lodge is complete."

Gi spoke up, directing her words to Hwa. "My youngest daughter has more than she knows." She shared a secretive smile with her Hca. "I have worked on her dowry from skins brought to me."

Anpo stared at her mother, food half chewed. Aware of the rudeness of her action, she looked away.

Her younger sister, Hinhan, spoke with a laugh. "She cannot live in her *ina's* lodge forever!"

Blushing, Anpo chewed and swallowed her mouthful. "I...I did not think to live in Gi's lodge forever, but..." She shrugged at Wanbli with a vague sense of confusion.

Gi continued on despite the interruption from the children. "I will give Anpo's dowry to Ketlin since she is her woman. She will have a *ti ikceya*." She took another piece of bread from Hwa's rock and handed it to her husband. "Ketlin will have her own lodge by the time we reach summer camp."

"Can a slave own a lodge?" Hinhan asked, her youthful voice puzzled at this change in custom.

"Ketlin is more than a slave," Gi said. "She is a powerful shamaness, a woman from the spirit world. She came to Anpo in a vision, and everything my *cunksi* saw has happened." She looked the white woman over. "Her existence has brought Anpo much honor, and we must honor Ketlin in gratitude."

Hwa, lips curled in amusement, said, "If Anpo opens her mouth wider, we can throw her food inside instead of waiting for her to chew."

Anpo's mouth snapped shut.

Wanbli, who had been silent through the conversation, spoke. "You will have to teach your woman manners, Anpo," he hinted, nodding in the white woman's general direction. "Before we reach summer camp."

Puzzled, Anpo turned to look at her woman.

Kathleen, finished with the mixing of the *wansi*, formed it into long rolls that she placed onto a nearby skin. Her shoulders did not hold their tightness as they had yesterday, and she sat taller than Anpo remembered seeing before. Apparently intent on the conversation around her, Kathleen stared rudely at Wanbli as he spoke.

With frightening suddenness, Anpo blocked Kathleen's view. She pointed two fingers closely towards the woman's eyes and cut them to the left in a sharp gesture. "*Hiya*! Do not look at *ate*, Ketlin."

Flinching away from the unexpected motion, Kathleen raised her arms in a defensive posture.

As Kathleen cowered, Anpo frowned. *Does she think I will hurt her? Hit her? Does Ketlin know that I am destined to hurt her?* Wordlessly, Anpo looked to her family, a myriad of emotions crossing her tanned face — puzzlement, fear, irritation, and the ever-present shame of her future actions.

"Anpo must go slowly with Ketlin," Hwa said softly. "She has been hurt so badly."

"She believes I will hurt her," Anpo stated, dropping her gaze. "And my vision says this is true."

Gi, in a rare moment, spoke directly to her daughter. "*Hiya*. I have seen this before in women who have been hurt by their men. Ketlin does not see you. She sees the man who hurt her. She is only afraid of his actions repeated."

Anpo knelt by Kathleen. The woman seemed to be trying to disappear into the ground, not looking at anyone. Reaching to touch Kathleen's temple, Anpo watched her shoulders tighten and she shrank further away. "How do I teach her? She cannot understand my words, and I cannot understand hers."

Hca took her mother's lead, addressing Anpo. "Use our sign language, *mitankala*. She does understand some of our words, but the signs make their meanings clearer. I used signs yesterday, and Ketlin was able to understand what she could see."

Studying the woman, Anpo wondered at the tears flowing from Kathleen's eyes. What kind of people cried so publicly? Was it a sign of strength or weakness? Among the Lakota, this type of behavior was limited to mourning the dead. Kathleen's power was foretold by Inyan winters ago, so Anpo decided it must be a sign of strength.

She leaned closer, hearing strange words muttered beneath Kathleen's breath. There was no doubt Kathleen was terrified. Anpo readjusted herself, sitting in front of Kathleen. "Ketlin. Look at me. You are safe here. I will not hurt you."

Hinhan eased over with slow movements and took the bowl of *wansi* and the skin Kathleen had been using. She gave Anpo a shy smile and moved away. The rest of Anpo's family quietly discussed their day, ignoring the proceedings so close by.

Anpo scooted closer and reached out a calming hand. She touched a trembling shoulder, caressing with a soothing motion. "Look at me, Ketlin," she said, using the same gesture and words she had the night before in the lodge.

Kathleen shivered at the touch, but she must have remembered. Neck stiff, her gaze flickered to Anpo and remained there.

Smiling at Kathleen, she tried to convey a sense of safety and ease. It seemed to work, as the woman relaxed, tears fading. Anpo kept one hand on Kathleen's shoulder, not wanting to lose contact. With her other, she used the two fingers pointing in Kathleen's eyes to accent her language. "Ketlin, look at me," and the fingers pointed at her own.

"Look at me," Kathleen repeated, her brow furrowing in concentration. Her shivering eased at Anpo's evident satisfaction.

"*Ohan*, Ketlin! Look at me. To look at me is good." Using the same motion, Anpo pointed at her sister. "Look at Hca. Good. She is a woman."

Again, Kathleen repeated the words, flinching a little as she did as requested. When nothing happened, she loosened up more, listened intently as Anpo continued the lesson. Anpo indicated everyone in her *tiospaye* that Kathleen was allowed to approach directly — all the women and young Cetan. Her expression became serious, and she lowered her voice. "Do not look at Wanbli, Ketlin. He is your *tunkasi*, my father. You must not speak to him or look at him."

Kathleen frowned at this information. It was obvious she did not understand why. Again Anpo wondered about Kathleen's people. Did they have no manners at all? Before she could follow the thought, Kathleen spoke. The only word she recognized was her father's name.

"I cannot think of a way to tell you, Ketlin," she said. "He is your *tunkasi,* and you are not to be close to him. I am dishonored if you are close to him. I cannot be close to your father for the same reason; he is my *tunkasi.*"

"She knows not to do so," Gi spoke up. "She will learn the why as she learns our words."

Reluctantly, Anpo agreed. "You speak truly, *ina.*" She caressed Kathleen's cheek. "I will not hurt you, Ketlin," she whispered.

"I will not look at Wanbli," Kathleen said, her words slow as she sounded them out. She cupped Anpo's cheek, her face earnest.

Joy filled Anpo's heart at the use of her language. "My woman is very intelligent," she bragged. "Hear her speak our words."

Hca handed a piece of fry bread to Kathleen. "Ketlin needs to keep her strength if Anpo is to stare at her from dawn to dusk," she said, teasing her sister.

Anpo pulled away, her pleasure not marred by jibe. "Gi should feed my sister more, as well, when Nupa is here for meals." Satisfied her mark had hit home, she returned to her place and scooped up her discarded meal. Soon Kathleen would understand their tongue, and they could truly speak to one another. What would they say?

Chapter Eighteen

The two villages remained together for many days as they waited for the meat to dry and the skins to cure. Soon the day came that Mani and his people collected their belongings. Several people gathered at the council lodge, wishing the leader and his elders well in their travels. Then they were on the move, slowly meandering towards the west and the future summer camp where they would meet again.

Kathleen watched them go with a mixture of sadness and joy. She saw the little girl she had lived with before Anpo on the back of a horse and waved, receiving one in return. *I'll miss the children*, she thought. *At least I don't have to worry about Anpo giving me back to him, though. It's not like I've done anything wrong really.* Kathleen turned to the tent where she lived. *The ti ikceya*, she reminded herself.

The past few days had been idyllic in comparison with the rest of her time with the native peoples. Aside from the occasional misunderstanding due to their differences, things had gone quite well. Her days were full of learning their language and ways, what a woman's duty was and how to go about it. It was pretty much no different than home. Her nights were quiet as she cuddled with Anpo and enjoyed peaceful sleep for the first time in months.

True, the work was just as hard, but the overwhelming fear of violence faded with the days. Gi frowned at her upon occasion, making that noise in her throat that signified disapproval. Kathleen struggled diligently to do everything she was asked, however, showing deference to the matriarch of Anpo's family. That seemed to be enough to appease Gi. Hca had become a good friend and teacher. She seemed very smart for a heathen, and Kathleen wondered what she would have been like if she had had regular schooling.

Kathleen still was not certain why she was forbidden to speak or look directly at Wanbli. The taboo seemed not to extend to other bucks, though she had observed Hca and the other women's marked reverence to most men in the area. It was a puzzlement. Being objective, she could honestly say the same happened in reverse; only children were allowed to approach either gender with little care, and those adults who were coupled spoke to one another. Kathleen could only think it had something to do with their living arrangements. With several generations dwelling in the same *ti ikceya*, it could get sticky mighty quick. *What would happen if a son brought a wife into the mix, and the father took her away for himself?*

She shivered at the thought, seeing the similarity between that vision and her current situation. At least this way Wanbli respected Anpo's...property. Kathleen had no illusions about her status.

And Anpo. She was a mystery. She seemed to waffle between acting gruff like the other native men and showing tenderness with just a touch or glance. Kathleen still could not understand why Anpo wore men's clothing. Hca had tried to explain her sister was *wicakte*, but the word meant nothing to her without knowing additional language.

"*Han*, Hca!" Kathleen called as she neared Gi's lodge. She smiled at her friend looking up from the task of sewing skins.

"*Han*, Ketlin! Come and help with your *ti ikceya*." Hca scooted to one side to allow room for Kathleen to sit, handing her the bone awl and sinew. "This is the final piece. I am almost finished."

"This will be as big as Gi's lodge?" Kathleen asked as she aligned two pieces of leather and bored a hole through them.

"*Ohan*, maybe bigger but not by much. Anpo's status among the people is an important one. Your lodge must show this." Hca watched Kathleen pull the sinew through the new opening. "Do not pull too tight or the hides will be uneven."

Kathleen nodded, smoothing the skins together. Hca began poking another hole, and they worked quietly as the camp returned to its natural rhythm. Kathleen saw Anpo and Wanbli at the council fire. Anpo's friend, Nupa, was with them.

Glancing sidelong at her companion, Kathleen spoke. "Is summer camp big?"

Hca made a positive sign, though she did not look up from her task. "*Ohan*. Our people have seven council fires, and we are but a small village of one of them." She looked at Kathleen. "There will be feasting and dancing and games! There will be a Sun Dance and ceremonies! There will be many things to do and people to see, Ketlin!"

She smiled at Hca's enthusiasm. "Many handsome young men?" she asked.

"Yes! Many of those." Hca laughed in delight and looked over at the council fire. "Many of those," she repeated.

"He likes you."

Hca's eyes widened. "I did not think you noticed." She shyly returned to her task.

Laughing, Kathleen stopped Hca's hands with her own. "Who

could not? He is always at Wanbli's fire, his eyes all big and round and..." She waved impatiently and spoke a few words in English.

"I do not understand, Ketlin," Hca said with vague sadness. "But you have learned our words well."

Only because you've been a wonderful and patient teacher, Kathleen thought. "Wait." She rose and pulled a stick from the fire. She drew a picture on the ground. "What is that?"

Hca frowned at the crude drawing. "An animal. But I do not know what kind."

"There is a white belly and a white tail." Kathleen tapped her foot in slight irritation. "I know! Our *cuwignaka* are made of this animal's skin!" She held up a fistful of the leather dress she wore.

"Oh! An antelope." Hca thought back over the conversation.

"Is that what this is called?" Kathleen asked. "*Nigesanla.*" As she committed the new word to memory, Hca's sudden laughter interrupted her.

"You are saying that Nupa looks like a deer when he looks at me?" she hid behind her hand, hooting, and Kathleen joined in her joy.

The two women received disapproving looks from others passing nearby as they giggled indecorously.

Nupa glanced over at the pair as they muffled their laughter, as befitted young women of their standing. Nudging his friend with a shoulder he pointed his chin at them and asked, "What do you think they are laughing about, *tanksi?*"

Anpo peered past him, her mouth curling at the joy she saw in Kathleen. *She is so beautiful.* "You, *tiblo.*"

"Me?" He stiffened, affronted, and looked back and forth between his friend and the women. "Why do you say me?"

Anpo scooped up a twig, its end glowing red, and lit her pipe. "Look at my *cuwe.* She turns red when she looks at you and laughs the harder." She puffed the tobacco, bringing the smoke up and over her head with her free hand.

Studying the women with pursed lips, Nupa saw Hca do what Anpo described. He stared for a moment before relaxing into confidence. He accepted the pipe offered him. "She likes me." He repeated Anpo's actions.

They sat with the elders and listened to them speak of things, of hunting, of wars past, of times when they were young *koskalaka.*

"What does having your own woman feel like?" Nupa asked.

Anpo's gaze flickered to Kathleen. "Different." She puffed on the pipe as she reflected. "I feel lighter and heavier now. I am happy yet I have more responsibility in my life. I have to look to the future and make decisions with someone else in my heart."

"I have missed your presence with the herd at night."

Anpo nodded. Having a woman had elevated her to a position of power that no one else her age had. She was no longer required to fulfill her duties as a youth, but now took her place as an adult in her society which meant guarding the horse herd at night was no longer a concern of hers. "And I have missed yours, *tiblo*."

The voices of the elders lulled the pair, their conversation ebbing. Eventually, Nupa spoke again. "Strange that you have a woman before me. I always thought I would be first to be joined." His expression was serious. "Strange that you would have a woman at all."

"I know. I find this strange, as well," Anpo agreed. "But you and I know that no man would have me." She tapped the ashes into the fire. "And I know that I would have no man." She bundled up her pipe to put away. "This way is best."

~ * ~ * ~ * ~ * ~

Kathleen woke first. She lay in the comforting warmth of her sleeping robes, the gentle thumping of Anpo's heart filling her ear. *Why did it never feel like this with Adam?* She splayed her hand against dark skin, seeing the contrast even in this murky interior.

Memories of her short marriage filled her mind – mornings of making breakfast for a husband who was kind, if not loving; days of doing chores and speaking out loud to herself because there was no one else; nights of intimacies that, while not forced, were not invited. Kathleen couldn't recall a single time she had awakened with Stevens as she did with this young woman. *Anpo's comfortable. Sweet. Safe, definitely safe.*

Beneath her, Anpo stretched and sighed, on the verge of wakefulness. Kathleen used the movement to snuggle closer without disturbing her rest. She inhaled deeply of Anpo's scent. *I just can't seem to get enough of her!*

Today was the big day. Today the *ti ikceya* would be finished. Today Kathleen would lead Anpo into her lodge and officially take residence. From what she gathered from Hca, Kathleen essentially offered marriage to Anpo, or something to that effect. *Married. To a woman.* Kathleen burrowed further into the warmth of Anpo's body. *Aye, lass, now there's a quandary for you. If you ever make it home, how're you going to explain a wife?*

One thing was certain – Kathleen was far happier with the prospect of being with Anpo than she had been while married to her husband. *Is this what I've been heading for all my life? Is this what I've been feeling was missing?* She remembered daydreams about the man in her future. He was tall and strong, long dark hair pulled back in a ponytail. Kathleen stifled a giggle. Anpo easily fit the description, missing only the fine suit and shoes.

The long arm wrapped around her shoulders tightened, and a voice spoke her name. With a smile, Kathleen peered up at her rousing warrior.

"Ketlin. Did you sleep well?"

"*Ohan*, Anpo. I did. And you?"

She grinned in return. "Very well." Anpo yawned and stretched before wrapping her arms around her woman and holding her close.

Kathleen squirmed a bit in discomfort. *My bosom is tender. Must be near my monthly time.* She resolved to quiz Hca on how native women took care of the problem as soon as possible.

~ * ~ * ~ * ~ * ~

Wanbli and Anpo wandered off after breakfast with the idea of bringing in some fish from the river. They took provisions for the day and their spears. As soon as they disappeared, the women began their preparations in earnest.

Kathleen found herself again in the shapeless dress she'd arrived in, her beautiful one taken by Hca and Hinhan to be cleaned. Hwa began a stew with Gi's assistance while Kathleen ground a bone awl against a rock. Gi occasionally stopped her work to inspect the awl until it was sharp enough to pierce a piece of hide.

"Very good, Ketlin," she said, setting the awl aside. "You work hard. You will take very good care of Anpo and honor her."

"Thank you." Kathleen colored a bit at the compliment.

"Now, you and I will prepare your lodge for tonight." Gathering together some things, she handed them to Kathleen saying, "These are yours now."

She blinked at the Gi. "Th–Thank you! You are so good to me!" Kathleen swallowed a lump developing in her throat.

A hand gently rested against a pale cheek. "You make my *cunksi* smile like the sun she is named after. You have learned our language and ways well. You will honor Anpo, your very existence giving her strength and power."

What did I ever do to deserve this? Then the tender moment was gone, and Gi was once again brisk.

"Come, Ketlin. You and I will prepare your lodge."

Kathleen was led off, her arms full of robes, heart happy.

~ * ~ * ~ * ~ * ~

Anpo hefted a leather satchel full of fish, pulling the strap over her head and across her broad shoulders. Her father carried another bag, this filled with the remainder of their leftover meal, and led the way back towards camp. The river had teemed with trout, and they speared many.

"Wanbli?"

"*Hau*, daughter."

"How long have you and Gi been joined?"

There was a pause as he considered the question. "We were joined a winter before our first child was born."

"I am sixteen winters. You have been joined..." and she trailed off, brow furrowed in consideration. "You were joined twenty-three winters ago!"

Wanbli's face remained calm, but a smile quirked his lips at the incredulous tone. "*Hau*, Anpo. That is right."

They walked in silence for a while.

"*Ate?*"

"*Hau, cunksi.*"

"Did you ever hurt *ina*? With your words or actions?"

"*Hau*, Anpo. That is the nature of living with another. To live with another and not hurt them is like trying to hold back the water in the river with only your hands." Wanbli looked at his child, seeing her serious profile. "All people get hurt in life, *cunksi*. We become strong as pain teaches us to overcome our weaknesses. Do not worry so."

Again there was silence.

"Did *ina* ever hurt you, Wanbli?"

"*Hau, cunksi*. As I said, that is the way of life."

Anpo regarded him with concern and curiosity. "Then why have you not given her away? Why have you kept her? Why has she stayed with you?"

"Because my *mahasanni* and I care for each other, Anpo. We are stronger together than we are apart."

Anpo sighed and nodded.

Wanbli settled a hand on Anpo's shoulder, walking closely beside her. "Be still in your heart, *cunksi*. Do not worry the vision so. The vision will not change and will only make you crazy with grief and fear." He nodded in front of them. "Look. We are almost to camp. You and I will bring our catch to our women, and we will eat well this night!"

She forced herself to smile, picking up her step to keep up with Wanbli's.

Chapter Nineteen

"Anpo will be surprised, Ketlin," Hca said as she braided long yellow hair.

"Why?" Kathleen turned to one side so the other half of her hair could be done.

Gi, who finished the last stitching on a pair of leggings, spoke up. "Because you are a slave and not a traditional maiden, Ketlin."

Kathleen was confused. "Someone like me cannot join with a warrior?"

"Slaves and *winyan* who are not of our people must learn our words, learn to please the man they belong to. And Anpo is *wicakte* and young to have a woman." As the braiding was finally twisted into place, Hca used a strand of sinew to tie it off.

"If a woman who is a slave pleases her man, learns our words, and gives him a child, she truly becomes Lakota and can join with him," Hwa said from her place near the fire.

"But, I cannot have children!"

Gi leaned close to peer at Kathleen, a small smile on her lips. "Whether you can have children does not matter, Ketlin. You make my *cunksi* happy and that is important. You have honored me and Wanbli by your attention to Anpo."

And what Mum says, goes, Kath! She fought back a nervous giggle.

"You have learned our words well," Hwa said. She used a callused hand to scoop cornmeal from the rock she used to grind it into a basket. Placing more kernels of corn on the rock, she continued her chore. "Anpo may be young, but she is *wicakte*, two-souled. No one remembers the last time one lived among us. Perhaps she is not young to have a woman."

"She is very powerful." Hca smoothed Kathleen's yellow dress, dry from its early morning cleaning. She handed it to the woman. "Not just as *wicakte*, but as a vision seeker and teller of the future. *Tatanka ska* has given my sister a great gift in you."

Kathleen accepted the dress and prepared to put it on. Before she could question Hca how an animal could be responsible for making her

Anpo's slave, the leather flap at the *ti ikceya* opening flew aside.

"They are here! They are here!" the young Hinhan exclaimed, ducking into the lodge.

"Be calm!" Hwa ordered her child, though there was a sparkle in her eye. She turned to Kathleen. "Are you ready, Ketlin?"

Swallowing on a suddenly dry mouth, Kathleen nodded. "I am ready."

"Good," she said, her reply crisp. Turning away, she shooed the other women back outside, following close behind.

Kathleen found herself alone in the *ti ikceya*. "Well, here goes nothing, Kath," she murmured. She twitched her belt to a better position and paced in front of the door.

~ * ~ * ~ * ~ * ~

As the two warriors approached Gi's lodge, Anpo noticed a flurry of activity as her family stepped outside. Suspicious at Hinhan's ill hidden excitement, she asked, "*Ate?*"

Her father gestured in resignation. "Do not try to understand them, Anpo. They are *winyan* and do not make sense."

Anpo considered this with growing concern. "I am *winyan*, Wanbli. Do I not make sense?"

Wanbli made an approving murmur in his throat and touched her shoulder. "You are *wicakte*, Anpo, born and bred. You make very good sense."

As they arrived at her mother's lodge, Anpo's mind worried his statement. *Is a* wicakte *so different from a woman?* Pulling the satchel from her shoulders, she held it out to her mother. "*Ina!* We have many fish for you."

Gi accepted the catch. Without a second glance at it, she set the leather bag on the ground near her normal work area. "Sit and rest," she said to her husband, knowing Anpo would also do so.

Wanbli smiled a greeting at his women and children, sitting in his place at the head of the fire. He pulled a pipe out as Anpo joined him.

Anpo asked, "Where is Ketlin?"

With an infectious grin, Hinhan leaped up from her seat tending the fire. "I will find Ketlin!" she exclaimed.

Anpo was puzzled. She looked to her father and remembered his statement regarding *winyan*. Her face cleared. *They make no sense.* Resolved to ignore the behavior, her attention was distracted when Kathleen followed Hinhan out of Gi's lodge.

Her yellow *cuwignaka* was clean with paint freshly applied to the designs. A dark brown leather pouch hung from Kathleen's waist, an antler knife handle protruding from it. Leggings wrapped her calves and new moccasins covered her feet, the tops of which were painted white with the sun design in red.

Just like mine, Anpo thought, her eyes drawn back upwards.

Long, blonde hair had been thoroughly combed and oiled with animal fat. Two long braids hung down her back. Around Kathleen's neck was a necklace of elk teeth and porcupine quills.

She is so beautiful.

Kathleen moved forward with startling grace and stood before Anpo. A flush blossomed across her skin, and the corners of her mouth curled up. She held out her hand. Anpo felt a tingle move up her arm at the contact of their palms. Then she was pulled to her feet and led away from Wanbli's fire.

Kathleen's *ti ikceya* was as yet unadorned. The fire in front burned merrily, a haunch of meat roasting over it. Kathleen led Anpo past it and inside. Here another fire burned, though it was low, enough to give light. Kathleen led Anpo to the head of the fire, seating her there. Anpo glanced around the lodge, finding her belongings already scattered among Kathleen's things – her sleeping robes to her right, Kathleen's to the left; Anpo's backrest tied in place where she sat; a pipe rack and her pipe easy at hand.

She watched as Kathleen removed the moccasins she wore. They were still damp from the river, and Kathleen set them near the fire to dry. Another pair of moccasins sat close by, and she pulled them nearer.

Putting the new footwear on Anpo's feet, Kathleen looked up and smiled.

Anpo's breath caught at the beauty. Despite the fact Kathleen was yet a slave in this society, she reached behind her and pulled the yellow braids to hang forward and down the woman's chest. This would tell everyone that they were joined, married. Anpo gathered Kathleen into her arms.

~ * ~ * ~ * ~ * ~

Anpo and Nupa stopped to water their ponies at a creek. Wagna's camp was on the move toward summer camp. Ahead and behind, a long line of their people traveled, following the signs left by advance scouts. Things had gone well, and there were no dangers to be had. Nightfall would be upon them, and both knew they would stop and make camp soon.

She pulled her pony away from the river and jumped upon him. "I wish to be at camp by dinner," she said as she settled into the saddle.

Grinning, Nupa looked up to her, making no moves towards his steed. "Such is the way of joining that you cannot be without Ketlin's company for more than a day?"

Instead of rankling at his teasing, Anpo laughed. "*Ohan, tiblo*! You will understand when you have a woman!" Whirling her pony around, she exclaimed, "I will race you to the leaders on the path! Whoever is first receives a gift from the other!"

Nupa blinked at Anpo for only a moment before vaulting onto his horse. The two sped away, whooping.

As all young warriors were prone to do, they used this race to show off. They flew toward the front of the line of people, sliding off their horses to touch the ground racing past and remount. Their people watched the spectacle, young men yipping with encouragement. Several young women giggled and whispered at their antics, which only drove the pair to further daring.

They reached their goal, swinging around the big bellies who led their people. To one side, they stopped and dismounted.

"I am first!" Nupa exclaimed. "You will give me a gift!"

Anpo nodded, her face a mirror of his own. "*Ohan, tiblo.*" She pulled a pouch from her horse and handed it to her friend. "Here is a pipe from the bone of *tatanka ska*. I finished carving the stem yesterday."

His smile faded to seriousness. "You honor me, *tanksi*," he murmured.

"I share my honor with my family, *tiblo*. You may not be blood, but you are family to me."

"Thank you, *tanksi*."

"Anpo!"

The two turned towards the voice, seeing Hca running towards them, her face serious.

Anpo stepped forward, all thoughts focusing on her sister. For Hca to approach her directly indicated something important occurred. "Are you well, *cuwekala*?"

"Ketlin, *mitan*, she is ill."

Her heart turned to ice. Anpo left her sister and friend to leap onto her pony, racing once more down the line. Behind her, Hca's voice followed. "The medicine man is with her, Anpo!"

A small knot of people gathered to one side of those who walked and rode. Anpo recognized Kathleen's horse with its load of poles and skins. Around this were her two mothers, her younger siblings, and the healer. Skidding to a halt, Anpo jumped from horseback, realizing the form on the skins was her woman. "Stand aside!" Anpo demanded, when her father appeared from nowhere to block her path.

"*Hoh*, Anpo!" he said, physically holding her back. "Let Osni finish."

Osni chanted a spell of protection over his patient. Anpo glared at Wanbli, but he would not back down. Hwa remained with Kathleen, her children watching the healer with fascination, while Gi approached Anpo.

"She will be fine, *cunksi*. Ketlin's stomach hurt her. I asked Osni to help ease her discomfort." Seeing Anpo less agitated, she said, "Do not interrupt the healer."

Wanbli nodded, not losing eye contact with Anpo. "Do not interrupt. Wait for Osni to finish. He will tell you what you need to know." When Anpo made no move, he stepped forward, forcing her with his presence to turn away.

Hca returned from the front, riding Nupa's pony. She dismounted, handing the reins to Anpo. "Nupa is coming soon, *mitankala*." She and her mother went back to Kathleen.

Anpo's mind swirled in turmoil, her heart pounding. Anger boiled beneath the surface. *I must see Ketlin! I must protect her!* She stared at her pony, trying to think of a way to help, not even sure what help was needed. Her father's voice filtered through, and Anpo focused her eyes on him.

"You can do nothing, Anpo. You can only wait. Being unable to help is hard, but you will not ease things with your presence."

"I must help Ketlin," Anpo said, voicing the thoughts racing through her head. "She needs me."

"She needs you to be calm. She needs you to be able to think." Wanbli sighed. "The mark of a man is that he may set aside his emotions in trying times, be calm and able to think, to reason. All that can be done is being done. Your presence will only complicate matters and show your dishonor of Osni."

Anpo blinked at him. "I do not know if I can, *ate*," she said in a low voice. "I do not wish to dishonor the healer...."

"Then do not. Be a true warrior, Anpo. Wait until he comes to speak to you. Do not speak before he does."

A strained look crossed her face, but she made an agreeable noise. Her back remained to Kathleen's pallet, yet all her attention was upon it.

Nupa arrived and took the reins of his pony. He said nothing, standing near his friend and her father, giving his support by his presence.

Osni continued his ministrations, chanting and rattling his instruments over Kathleen's prone form. Eventually, he finished the activity, speaking softly to the women gathered there.

He shuffled towards the men and *wicakte*, his many winters weighing heavily upon him. Osni was very old, having been old when Anpo was born. His skin was dry leather, his hair snow white and wispy.

Standing in silence, Anpo resisted the urge to grab the old man by the neck and wrestle information from him. She held back her desire to bolt to her woman. Behind her, she was comforted to hear her family speaking with Kathleen.

After long contemplation, the medicine man spoke, his voice as leathery as his skin. "Your *winyan* is ill, Anpo."

"Will she be alright, *wicahca*?" Anpo asked, trying to control her emotions.

"If she does as she is told, she will be fine." There was a long pause. "She is with child."

Stunned silence met his pronouncement as all three warriors stared at him.

"W–what?" Anpo asked in a whisper.

The craggy old face broke into a smile, his few teeth gleaming. "Your woman is with child, Anpo. She will give birth in a few moons."

Unable to remain away, Anpo spun on her heels and dashed for Kathleen. She heard Osni's raspy chuckle behind her.

Kathleen was wrapped in her sleeping robes, looking a bit worse for wear. Hwa and Hca had built a small fire to boil water, and Gi mixed herbs to alleviate her nausea. Kathleen looked up as Anpo neared, her heart jumping at the woman's expression.

Anpo knelt beside her woman, pulling a pale hand into hers. "Ketlin," she started, but couldn't think of anything else to say.

Kathleen chewed her lower lip and dropped her gaze. She tried to explain. "Anpo. I did not think I could have children...."

"Ketlin," Anpo repeated, and this time the voice was warm.

She peered at Anpo, amazed to see a wide smile.

"You are with child, *winuhca*," Anpo stated. "You will bear me a son or daughter!"

Kathleen blinked at her warrior. "You are happy?" she asked, apparently not expecting such a reaction.

"Happy? *Winuhca*! This is the best thing to happen to me in my life!" Anpo swept Kathleen into a hug, rocking her. "Thank you so much for this gift!" she whispered.

Unable to hold back the relief, tears spilled from Kathleen's eyes and she held Anpo tightly. "Thank you, Anpo," she whispered. "Thank you."

Part 6: Yuwipi Ki
The Sun Dance

Chapter Twenty

1777

The following morning Kathleen sat outside her *ti ikceya*, a mass of reeds in her lap. The base of a basket gave the vegetation some semblance of order, but the loose ends haphazardly filled the air above. Her tongue stuck out the corner of her mouth as she tried to remember which end went where from her lessons with Hwa, Wanbli's second wife.

A trio of women walked past, chatting amiably amongst each other and carrying water from the creek the village camped near the previous evening. Upon sighting Kathleen, they all called to her, bidding her a good day.

With a tentative smile, Kathleen returned the sentiment and watched as they went their way. *Well, lass. News certainly travels fast, eh?* Shaking her head with a small smile, she returned to her task of weaving reeds together. As Gi had said, all women were accepted as full members of the Lakota when they made their *wicasa* happy and bore them children. When Osni announced she was pregnant, every woman and *wikoskalaka* had shown up after camp was set with offers of assistance for the new young mother. It was a bit overwhelming. Yesterday, nobody would speak to her, and now everybody was a friend.

Despite Anpo's happiness at the news, Kathleen did not sleep well. Visions of the horrible abuse instigated upon her filled her sleep, making for a restless night. Anpo held her closely through the nightmares, soothing her fears and singing her to sleep.

There was little doubt in Kathleen's mind that the child she carried belonged to her rapist. The knowledge of it chilled her heart even as it soared to new heights of joy. *After two years, Adam and I couldn't have a child. I doubt it would have changed.* Plus her time with Yatke certainly would not have resulted in pregnancy. He never succeeded in bedding her while she lived in his woman's lodge, her hysterics far too aggravating for him to do so.

Kathleen sighed and tried to focus on the basket in her hands, but fears and uncertainty continued to plague her mind. Questions flickered through her thoughts, disappearing nearly as fast as they could form.

Just how accepting are these people? Will they accept this child as Anpo's? Will Anpo accept the child? The worst thought continued to upset her, the one Kathleen mentally cringed from each and every time it came up – *Can I accept the child of the man who raped me?*

"*Han, winuhca!*"

Looking up from her task, Kathleen smiled up at Anpo. She set aside the half completed basket, glad of the interruption to her morose wonderings.

Anpo, a wide smile on her face and two prairie dogs hanging from one hand, approached and sat down at her fire. Brandishing the carcasses, she said, "I have brought you *pispiza*. You can cook these this night."

"Thank you, Anpo. You are a very good hunter." Kathleen watched her flush from the compliment before bending to skin the animals. *Ah, she's a pretty one, she is,* came the fond thought.

Kathleen, with time to speculate on Anpo, had come to the conclusion that she was probably younger than her brother, Stewart, though not by much. Anpo did not react in the manner of the older men, seemingly still learning her way as a hunter. She still blushed when praised, smiled more often than others, and occasionally appeared uncertain of what to do.

Kathleen recalled Anpo's sister, Hca, telling her how unusual it was for one so young to have a woman. Of course, everything about Anpo was unusual from the men's clothing she wore to her use of weapons. Hca had tried to explain to her that Anpo was *wicakte* and sacred, but Kathleen's understanding of the language was not extensive enough for her to completely understand. All she could gather was that Anpo was unique among their people, and something about her having two souls. It was odd these people even knew of the existence of their souls; she had thought them heathens with no concept of God. From what Kathleen could gather, they did not know of God or the savior, Jesus. That would explain why they thought some people had two souls, which was outright ignorance. God only gave one soul to each of His children.

"Are you hungry now? I have grains boiling," she asked.

"I am hungry, Ketlin."

Kathleen used a wooden spoon to ladle some of the mixture into a clay bowl. She crumbled some dried herbs into it and stirred. Rising, she walked behind Anpo and knelt to set the bowl to one side, placing a hand on one sturdy shoulder to steady herself. Unable to resist, she stayed on her knees and leaned forward, using the strong back as support.

Feeling the pressure of Kathleen against her, Anpo stopped her butchering and turned her head to look over her shoulder at her. "How do you feel, *winuhca*? Are you still ill this morning?" she asked, referring to the morning sickness that plagued Kathleen.

She readjusted herself, becoming more comfortable as she leaned against Anpo. "No. I feel much better now." The morning sickness had been mild over the last few weeks. So much so that Kathleen had not realized what was happening, thinking it was the stress of her situation that upset her stomach. Once she received news from the healer about her delicate condition, everything fell into place – the nausea, the tender breasts, and the general sensation of bloating in her mid section.

"You must try to sleep this afternoon," Anpo said. She held her torso steady for Kathleen and returned to skinning the animals. "We will not be leaving for summer camp until tomorrow."

Loathe to attempt sleep without Anpo, Kathleen shrugged slightly and snuggled against the shoulder she rested on. "I do not know. Maybe." Her eyes closed.

Anpo finished butchering the carcasses with few movements of her upper body. Despite her desire to remain awake, Kathleen dozed in place, not rousing until she heard her name. She squeezed Anpo's shoulder gently. "I am still tired," she offered by way of apology. *These people did not have a word for "sorry". How did they ever apologize?*

As Kathleen pulled away, Anpo peered over her shoulder. "You did not sleep well. You must sleep this day. There will be no rest tomorrow until we reach summer camp."

Kathleen grimaced a little and gave a little shake of her head, looking away. "I cannot, Anpo." She moved back to the fire and stirred the sack of boiling grains.

"I must clean myself," Anpo said. "You fix the *pispiza*. You and I will both rest this day." Handing the meat to Kathleen, her face brooked no argument.

"*Ohan, winuhca*," Kathleen said. Her heart held a mixture of trepidation for the coming nightmares, and caring for this young woman who would insist on taking care of her. *Why do I feel so much more for Anpo than I did Adam?* she wondered as Anpo made her way to the creek. *And in far less time.*

After Anpo cleaned up and ate, and Kathleen had prepared the meat to be cooked for their evening meal, she took Kathleen's hand and led her into the lodge. The edges around the base had been rolled up a few inches to allow a summer breeze to cool the interior. Anpo removed her shirt and moccasins, leaving her breechclout. She settled down on Kathleen's sleeping furs, waving her close. "Come, Ketlin. You need rest."

Still shy even after two weeks of being in Anpo's custody, Kathleen tinted a little and glanced away as she removed her dress. She knew without looking that Anpo's gaze took in every inch of her fair skin as they always did. Kathleen still had not decided whether it was good or bad. *Certainly not like anything's going to happen, lass. At least you're safe in that respect!* A distant part of her heart mourned the thought. Finding the emotion odd, she pushed it away and lay down.

As Kathleen curled up with her, Anpo sighed. She turned on her side and cuddled closer, draping a long arm across Kathleen's waist. "Try to sleep, *winuhca.* I will be here when you wake."

Kathleen rolled over, facing Anpo and tucking her head beneath the dark chin. She felt an arm snake around her side and a hand rub her back in a gentle, soothing motion. As any tired child, reluctant to sleep, she forced her eyes to remain open. Noting the pulse jumping in Anpo's neck, her hands reached up to finger a necklace of quills and wooden beads hanging around it.

Anpo continued her caresses. Finally, she asked, "What is wrong, Ketlin? What worries cloud your mind?"

Kathleen sighed, the sound followed by a long silence.

"Ketlin?"

Frowning as she tried to formulate her thoughts into questions, Kathleen sighed again. She felt Anpo begin pulling away to peer down at her and hastily spoke to forego the movement. "What happens when the baby arrives?"

Anpo's body relaxed, and she returned to her position, blonde hair beneath her chin. "You want to know how our women have children?"

Kathleen said in a muffled voice, "*Ohan.*"

"When a woman is with child and ready to give birth, she calls her *ina*, to help her. The shaman or the healer helps with the birth if things are difficult. Some women have hard times, but most do not." Anpo paused. "Since your *ina* is not here, my *ina* will help in her place. If the healer, Osni, is called, he will chant spells and prepare you, giving you medicines if you need them. Inyan will seek a vision and protect the child from evil spirits that wish to invade once the new person is born."

"Then what?"

"Then the baby is born." Changing the topic slightly, Anpo said, "I was the first child of which Inyan had a vision."

"A vision? What did he see?" Kathleen asked, wanting to know more of Anpo. It also steered the conversation away from the terrifying prospect of bearing a child in the wilds, far from the assistance of a midwife or physician. She attempted to dismiss the trepidation, knowing if she had given birth in Adam's care there might not have been a midwife within a thirty-mile radius. Still, having some old man wave rattles and sing over her did not build confidence.

"He said that he heard the scream of the *igmu* when I first cried out. He told my father, Wanbli, that I would be a warrior and hunter."

Kathleen smiled and nuzzled closer, almost feeling the sense of pride drifting from Anpo. "Do you think he will have a vision with this child?"

"I do not know. Our child will be strong and may bring a vision to a shaman." She made a negative gesture. "But, the spirits do not make sense to me. What visions Inyan will see are a mystery and *wakan*."

Heart warming at the usage of the word "our", Kathleen asked, "Have you ever had a vision?" Her interest piqued when she felt Anpo freeze and watched the vein in her neck beat a double time as her heart rate increased.

"I have had a vision," she admitted.

"What was this vision?" Kathleen asked. "Unless you cannot tell me," she added hastily. "I do not want to...ah..." Her knowledge of the language failed her, and she floundered about for the word that would describe what she meant. In English, she said, "I don't want to insult you, Anpo."

"*Ah-ah*, shh, listen," Anpo said, squeezing her arms tightly around Kathleen. "You have learned our words so well. You will learn them all soon."

"Not bloody fast enough," Kathleen muttered, her Irish lilt again caressing Anpo's ears.

Chuckling at the tone, Anpo pulled her woman closer and rolled onto her back. "You must teach me your words, as well, Ketlin."

Kathleen found herself in her usual place, draped across Anpo. Still fighting the need to sleep, though unable to keep her eyes from drifting closed, she asked another question. "How did you see your vision, *winu-hca*? How did you seek one?"

Kathleen drifted asleep, hearing the low voice of Anpo telling her a tale of *koskalaka* and *wikoskalaka* and how each did vision quests. How a girl, upon becoming a woman, would make a sacred bundle of her first bleeding and place it in the highest limbs of a tree, waiting below for the spirits to speak. How a boy, guided by a shaman, would search for a high place, follow a certain ceremony, and wait for several days for a vision. How sometimes the spirits would not speak for a long time, or at all, yet other times seem to leap out at the seeker as if eager to finally be heard.

Kathleen did not know when she drifted to sleep. Her dreams were filled with quiet breezes across prairie grasses, a blue sky with a smattering of clouds, and the occasional call of an eagle far in the distance.

Chapter Twenty-One

Inyan put the final touches of paint on a hardened leather rattle. As he set the item aside, a shadow blocked the waning sunlight. He looked up at Anpo waiting a respectful distance from his fire.

"*Hau*, Anpo," he said, waving her forward. "Sit with me."

She nodded and approached, settling down to his left.

Inyan's woman, Maka, heard his voice and peered out of her lodge. She stepped out and offered Anpo a bladder of water. "Are you hungry, Anpo?"

Accepting the liquid, Anpo gestured no. "*Hiya*, Maka. I have already eaten. Thank you for the water."

Maka nodded and returned to her lodge, allowing her man and his guest privacy.

Inyan lit a pipe and waved a puff of smoke toward his head. He handed the pipe to Anpo so she could do the same. As they smoked in silence, he studied her, comparing her to the child she used to be.

Anpo sat strong yet relaxed, an inner peace seeming to fill her heart. Whereas once she was anxious and unsure when she visited him, today she seemed firm in her resolve. *The pale woman has centered this warrior,* he mused.

When the pipe was finished, he wrapped it. "What do you wish of me, Anpo?"

"*Wicahca*, I would tell you a story." At his signal to continue, Anpo inhaled deeply and began. "When I was a child, I thought as a child. I was foolish and did not know the way of adults. After I had my vision, I still was uncertain and unclear, still foolish." A smile curled the edges of her mouth. "As are all people who are that age."

Inyan nodded with an approving murmur, his eyes asking her to go on.

"Things have changed this season, *wicahca*. I am no longer a child. I have seen my vision come to life. I have slain *tatanka ska* and am joined with the yellow haired woman of my vision. I will become a parent, raising our child in the Lakota way." Anpo paused, her eyes searching the horizon as she tried to come up with the words. "I ask this once. I will not ask again." Anpo's face was solemn. "I will participate in the Sun Dance to thank the spirits for their attention, for filling my life with such joy. I ask you to instruct me in this ritual so that I might dance properly."

He examined the *wicakte* before him, again noting the differences in bearing and attitude that had developed in such a short time. "You have much to thank *wakan tanka* for, Anpo. Your fortune has been good." He contemplated her request.

The Sun Dance was the most sacred ceremony of all. Its purpose was for a dancer to give the ultimate sacrifice in thanks for extreme danger narrowly averted or, as in Anpo's case, extreme good fortune. Few women attempted the ritual, and Inyan could not recall a time in history when a *winkte*, Anpo's masculine counterpart, had done so. She had much to be thankful for – the coming of her vision, the honor of the white buffalo, the yellow haired woman's powerful presence, and a child in the future. Not many attempted the ceremony at such a young age, however, and he wondered if she had the stamina and courage.

It was not his choice. It was hers. He could choose to deny her his wisdom, and that would only force her to find another path, for he was certain of her adamant desire.

"I will teach you what you need for the Sun Dance, Anpo. You will show your honor and respect to *wakan tanka* at summer camp."

Anpo let out a pent up breath, obviously pleased and struggling to not yip with joy. "Thank you, *wicahca*. Thank you."

"You are welcome, Anpo. Now go. I must prepare." Inyan waved her away with a mock glare. As she rose and trotted off, Inyan remembered a similar moment. When a *wicincala* was once told she could seek a vision in the way of her father. He smiled to himself.

~ * ~ * ~ * ~ * ~

Scouts pointed the way, but the smoke from many fires was what truly led the people toward Summer Camp.

Kathleen, midway along the mile long length of Wagna's traveling band, finally crested a hillock, leading the pony that Anpo gave her. She gasped at the number of *ti ikceyas* present in the valley below. *Goodness! There must be hundreds of them!*

"Ketlin," Hca said with a laugh. "You must keep walking, or we will never get there!"

She blushed as she realized she had frozen in place. "*Ohan*, Hca," she said with a rueful smile.

The advance leaders far ahead were the elders and important men. All were bedecked in their finest clothing and regalia. Their presence spotted by the camp's inhabitants, Kathleen saw groups of riders coming to meet them. She shivered. *What happens when they see me?* she worried, remembering the instances of pinches and hair pulling and unwanted touches before she came to Anpo. She searched for the *wicakte* but could not locate her.

Soon the riders came close enough to speak to those near Kathleen, welcoming them to the gathering. She kept her head down and swallowed a lump in her throat. Young warriors full of excitement circled the group, whooping and yipping as they raced one another or teased arriving friends and family. Several started up conversations with other warriors of the camp, but a few noticed her.

Four of these rode their ponies up to her, their hooves prancing about dangerously close to her feet. Her horse tried to shy away, and Kathleen spent a great deal of energy holding onto his reins to keep him from bolting at the sudden attention. She heard the women of Anpo's family haranguing the riders for their rudeness, though it appeared to do no good.

One rider ignored the women and hopped off his pony, intent on getting a closer look. He took a step forward before a horse purposely sidled into his path and forced him back.

"Leave her alone."

A wave of relief swept over Kathleen as she recognized Anpo's voice. She risked a glance and saw her glaring down at the man on foot. *Thank God!*

He returned Anpo's glare and tried to step around the pony, only to have it backed into him, pushing him away again.

"I said leave her alone."

"Who are you to order me?" he demanded.

Anpo grew taller in the saddle. "I am Anpo, and she is my woman. You will not touch her."

His chin went up at the challenge. "What if I do?"

"Then you will die."

He scoffed, tossing a look of disbelief over his shoulder at his friends. Turning back to the mounted woman, he said, "I know you. You are *wikoskalaka*. You will not kill me." He barked a laugh. "Besides, any who kill our people will be banished."

Anpo's face developed an ugly smile. "Then I will be banished, and I will live with my *winuhca* elsewhere. You will still be dead, hearing the whispers of your ancestors as they remind you of your dishonor with a joined woman."

The man's eyes narrowed as he considered whether or not she was bluffing. A flurry of hooves interrupted his thought, and all eyes turned to the arriving horses.

Mani pulled his pony up short of the tableau. Other elders from the summer camp arrived with him, as well, everyone curious as to what held up the arrival of Wagna's people. Surveying the situation, he jumped from his mount and approached the two disputers. With a great smile, he reached up to take Anpo's forearm. "Anpo! My heart warms to see you, my friend!"

She blinked at him before grasping his arm in return. "Thank you, *wicahca*."

He made a show of looking around Anpo's belongings. "Where's the robe of *tatanka ska*?"

The other man's jaw dropped.

"The robe is with my *winuhca's* lodge," Anpo said.

"*Winuhca!*" Mani peered over Anpo's horse to see Kathleen's hanging head. "So you are joined? That is very good news!"

"Thank you, *wicahca*."

"You are the one who killed *tatanka ska*?" the warrior on the ground finally sputtered.

Warming to his task, Mani turned. "*Hau!* There were four of us who tried, and Anpo's spear throw was true! I will tell you the story when we get back to camp." He remounted his pony and waved the man to follow. "Come, we will talk at my fire."

The warrior appeared to debate the issue, looking from the leader to Anpo. He looked across the horse and saw Kathleen. With a frown and negative gesture with his thumb, he glared up at Anpo. "I challenge you for the *winyan*."

Not understanding the word spoken, Kathleen was aware the tension in the area increased threefold. She studied the people, trying to comprehend what was going on and being said.

Mani made a last attempt. "Let the people of Wagna settle down in camp. You can challenge later, if you wish. Come with me."

The warrior stubbornly stood his ground.

Face grim, Anpo looked to her nearby friend. Nupa edged his horse forward until he was beside her. She handed the reins of her pony to him.

"You will win, *tanksi*," he insisted as he took her pony. "I have seen him wrestle before. His arms are weak."

Anpo nodded and grinned. "Thank you, *tiblo*." She hopped down from her horse.

As the people cleared a space, pulling back from the two combatants, Hca urged Kathleen to one side. "What is happening? What is Anpo doing?"

"She has been challenged for you, Ketlin. She will wrestle the warrior for you."

Kathleen remained confused. "What is that word, Hca?" she asked, repeating the one that baffled her.

"Challenge." Hca thought for a moment. "My *mitan* has been challenged, asked to fight for you."

"Fight for me?" Kathleen looked at the two warriors who now circled around the open area. *Oh my God! Anpo's been challenged!* As fear filled her heart, she watched. *What if she loses?*

The two weaved and dodged, grabbing at each other and feinting as they moved in the hot sun. Around them, bets were cast and items wagered. With a fierce cry, the warrior pounced on Anpo, chest butting her in an effort to drive her to the ground.

She met him, internally wincing as her breasts crushed between them. With a growl, she kept her feet, wrapping long arms around his ribcage. Locking her wrists, she exerted pressure.

He was not wearing a shirt and sweat covered his body. He twisted in her grasp, causing her to lose hold. Standing sideways to her, he brought his elbow down hard onto her neck and shoulder juncture.

Letting go of her opponent, her left arm tingly and weak from the hit, Anpo felt more than saw as he reached for her head. Rather than get caught in a headlock, she dropped to the ground with a suddenness that surprised everyone. Before he realized she had ducked, his legs were swept out from beneath him and he fell.

Anpo watched him roll over and try to regain his feet. She launched herself and landed on his back, forcing him into the dirt. Her left arm felt better, but she decided not to chance it, and wrapped the right around his neck, using her left hand to brace him in a hold.

He felt her grip tightening on his throat. Attempting to use his strong legs to stand, she kept him off balance enough to make such a move impossible. He began to struggle, his breathing coming in gasps as she blocked his air.

"Are you finished?" When there was no response, Anpo squeezed harder. He could barely move from the hold, but she knew the fight had not left him. Grimacing, she continued to apply pressure. "Stop fighting, and I will let you go."

Unable to lose face with his people, he refused. His struggles weakened, but he continued on until he finally passed out from lack of oxygen.

As soon as the man fainted, Anpo released him. She rose to a squat beside his body and gently turned him over. A hand held over his face assured her that he was still breathing. Around her, the watchers were quiet.

Anpo rose to her feet and stood over the body of her challenger. Her gaze raked dangerously over the people surrounding them. "Who else wishes to challenge me?"

No one stepped forward.

With a curt gesture, she left the clearing, intent on her family and friends. Around her, the young warriors of her camp whooped in celebration of her success.

Ah, who needs a knight in shining armor? Kathleen wondered as Anpo neared her. *I've got one in buckskin and that's much better!*

"Ketlin? Are you all right?"

She slipped into Anpo's arms and smiled. "*Ohan*, Anpo. I am much better now."

"I said you would beat him," Nupa exclaimed with a grin. He handed Anpo the reins of her pony and clambered onto his own. "I now have a new spear and a bone necklace."

Anpo released Kathleen and mounted. "You always bet well, *tiblo*."

"*Hau, tanksi*. I always wager on you."

Behind them, the challenger's friends scooped him up and tossed him over his horse for the ride back into the summer camp. Mani's eyes held a flash of approval for Anpo. Then he turned away and led the parade down the hill.

Looking at her woman, Anpo smiled fondly. "Take my hand, *winuhca*," she said. "You will ride with me so that all might know we are together."

Still holding the reins to her pony, Kathleen grasped Anpo's forearm and was hoisted up behind. She settled herself in place, wrapping her arms around Anpo's waist.

"Are you ready, *winuhca*?" Anpo asked, her arm placed over the pale ones.

Nodding, Kathleen replied, "*Ohan*, Anpo. I am ready." As the pony began to move, she snuggled closer. "Thank you."

Anpo squeezed the arm. "I will always protect you, Ketlin. You will be safe with me."

Chapter Twenty-Two

Upon the village's arrival at their area on the southern arm of the huge encampment, the women set up their *ti ikceyas*. Several from the surrounding lodges pitched in to help. Most of the men wandered off to other camps, greeting old friends and making new ones. There were a handful of more responsible men with black stripes painted across their faces, the *akicita*, who stayed behind to organize the camp and ensure all went smoothly.

Kathleen found herself with a number of new friends now that she was an officially recognized member of Anpo's family. Every woman in her *tiospaye* had one or two friends or family relations who came to visit as the village settled into place. Many hands made the work go quickly, and the women spent a good deal of time in gossip – stories regarding their children or men, comparing the young warriors good looks and abilities, and passing news of the other bands of their people.

In no time, Kathleen learned how lucky she was to belong to Anpo. She heard more about the *winkte* and *wicakte*, finally understanding the terms and their meanings. It amazed her to no end how special the Lakota felt the two-souled people were; she knew in her culture, Anpo would be denigrated and ridiculed. Having come to know Anpo intimately over the last weeks, Kathleen was happy Anpo was held in such esteem among her people and not a member of white society. The thought of "her" woman being treated so poorly made her heartsick.

Kathleen also discovered more about the premier ritual held during summer, the Sun Dance. Speculation was rife as the women discussed who the dancers were. When Anpo's name entered the conversation, she flushed from the sudden attention she received from the others. Their expressions of happiness and envy for her seemed odd. *If Anpo is the one to participate, why do they look at me so? Is it such an honor?*

Anpo returned from wherever she had been, effectively stopping the gossip. The older women wandered away to carry on their conversation elsewhere, and the young maidens giggled and made eyes at the *wicakte* before dispersing. Kathleen frowned at their interest, surprised to find a flower of jealousy blooming in her heart. Anpo's warm greeting did nothing to dispel her sudden remembrance that many Lakota warriors had more than one wife, including Anpo's father.

The following days were a blur. There were many nights of reveling around the fires of Anpo's friends, and several days spent building a large bark enclosure. It took nearly two full days of feasting, singing, and ceremony before a center log needed for their dance was cut down and set up inside this space. The log protruded far above the height of the structure, the roof only in place around the edge. Kathleen gleaned from her eavesdropping and questions that those who danced had to be under open sky, but those watching would have shelter from sun and rain.

More ceremonies followed, the log decorated with heathen talismans and paint. Anpo disappeared into a large sweat lodge with a dozen men where she remained for four days. Nupa moved into Kathleen's lodge, taking the traditional male's sleeping place until his friend finished the ritual. Kathleen fought off nightmares in silent misery while he slept. Her waking hours were spent at Gi or Hwa's lodge as she remained busy in an attempt to keep her fears at bay.

Other ceremonies for the Sun Dance were welcome distractions. Kathleen thought all the singing and dancing quite interesting. She occasionally saw Anpo, though they could not speak to each other. Her heart soared when their gazes met.

One day, Nupa, following proper protocol by not addressing his friend's woman directly, trotted towards her lodge. "Today is the day," he said to the fire. "Anpo dances and shows her gratitude to the spirits."

Kathleen stood, heart thumping in anticipation. Tonight Anpo could come home. A feast held in her honor was probably already in the making.

His enthusiasm was contagious, and Kathleen excitedly followed him toward the special lodge. Most of the population joined them, all congregating happily into the structure, singing a song. Male voices lifted in chant, supported by a circle of drummers, with female trilling interspersed. Kathleen spotted Anpo among the dozen candidates by the center pole. Before she could note much more, young Hinhan found her in the crowd and grabbed her hand, leading her to the rest of her family.

Anpo looked exhausted, but healthy. Her clothing was odd – her shirt was painted red and a blue skirt hung from her waist. Her exposed skin had been painted a ruddy color as well. Hca grabbed Kathleen's arm when she neared and explained that red was a sacred color, that the shamans painted all dancers during the purification rituals before the dance itself. Additional adornments of fur and sage circled Anpo's wrists, ankles, and head. A cape draped about her shoulders, and she carried a hoop covered in the same material.

When her hungry gaze was temporarily full with Anpo's presence, Kathleen finally glanced around the cleared dance area. The pole in the center had been decorated since its cutting and placement. What was once a tall, straight cottonwood tree was stripped of all extraneous branches and leaves. The fork at the top was painted red, and various items could be seen there – sage, fur, and other fetishes. Quite a number of braided thongs hung down to wave gently around the base, and she wondered what they were for.

There was plenty of singing, drumming, and dancing by the shamans and the candidates. It seemed to go on forever, and Kathleen grew tired simply watching. Hca and Hwa flanked her in the tight quarters, with arms about her waist as they shuffled in time with the drums. They swayed together as the shamans chanted.

"Now the Sun Dance begins," Nupa murmured loud enough for Kathleen to hear.

The level of anticipation intensified in the shelter as the candidates circled the pole. Four shamans stood at the four directions, as the dancers made four circuits of the dance area. Each approached one of the garish dancers, pulling on the braided thongs hanging from the log above.

Kathleen's gasp of horror was clearly audible to those around her as she watched the shamans slice into the chests of the candidates with stone knives, and attach the thongs to their skin with sticks.

Concerned, Hca peered closely at her. "Ketlin?" she asked quietly.

How...how...barbaric! No other thought could be had. Her mouth moved, no sound issuing.

Realizing that Kathleen's response was not a good one, Hca squeezed her stiff shoulders. "Ketlin!" she urged in a tight whisper. "Anpo needs you to be strong for her!"

The words slowly sank in. *Anpo needs me. Be strong.* Swallowing hard against her rising bile, her eyes bright with unshed tears, Kathleen nodded and pulled herself straighter. *I will be strong.* She welcomed the supportive grip of both her sister friend and Hwa.

The first four began to dance, pulling back and away from the pole, blood flowing down their chests and skin straining from their bodies. Anpo continued to shuffle around the clearing with the remaining candidates, keeping time with her feet as the singing and music continued.

The shamans picked four more individuals from the group. These removed their shirts, but were not attached to the ropes swinging from the pole. Instead, each had four buffalo skulls attached to their backs. They began to dance around the pole, counter to their uninjured companions, dragging the skulls along the dusty ground behind them.

Acid rose in Kathleen's throat as she watched the gory proceedings. *How can they do this? It's disgusting! Torture, plain and simple!* Her heart thudded heavily in her chest as she saw the shaman approach Anpo. *Oh, my God! What will they do to her?*

Anpo removed her shirt, revealing a soft leather band wrapped tightly around her breasts. The shaman's obsidian blade was sharp, and he split her skin with an economy born of experience. He attached two thongs to her chest and circled behind her.

Kathleen watched blood trickling down Anpo's chest, staining the leather wrap. She swayed a little, and only the people surrounding Kathleen kept her from running to Anpo's side. The shaman made two more incisions on Anpo's shoulder blades, and attached two more thongs. Anpo appeared to be strung from two continuous ropes starting at the top of the log, penetrating her through the chest, and exiting from behind to stakes pounded into the floor. She stared into the sun and began to dance, pulling at the cords.

Around Kathleen the people continued singing, repeating the same song over and over as the dancers danced. One by one, the participants pulled away from their bonds, ripping themselves free. At each instance, the people cheered, their yips and trills deafening. The four dragging buffalo skulls were also verbally supported as they went past, and as the weight of the bone pulled the thongs free, leaving ragged wounds in their wake.

Three other warriors shared Anpo's fate, each one swaying back and forth to the beat and staring upwards, but Kathleen's attention was only for her warrior. She stopped trying to keep up with the tune around her, concentrating solely on Anpo's misery. *Ah, my poor love!*

One by one, the dancers freed themselves from the *wakan* tree. Soon, only one remained. Kathleen watched in anguish, her entire body humming with the need to rush out and protect Anpo. The only things holding her back was Hca's arm firmly wrapped about her shoulders and the apparent acceptance of the others at this barbarity.

The spectators gasped as Anpo jerked backwards with a purpose, ripping the thongs from her chest simultaneously. A loud cheer rang out, filling the lodge.

Kathleen grimaced and moaned low in her throat.

"Anpo is very powerful and honored," Nupa said from his place behind her. "Not many are so strong as to do what she has done."

The praise did nothing to ease Kathleen's disgust. Despite her desire to not see anymore of the savage display, she could not keep her eyes from the lone dancer still in the clearing.

Anpo appeared to brace herself and surged forward. Her skin

ripped, and Kathleen swore she could hear the sound despite the deafening roar surrounding her. Fresh blood coursed down Anpo's back as she stumbled and fell to her knees.

"Anpo!" Kathleen cried, her voice drowned from the cheering of the onlookers. She ducked away from Hca and Hwa, pushing through the people and into the clearing.

Everything went silent as her presence was noted. One of the shamans stepped in front of Kathleen before she could go more than two paces. His visage was a fierce one, his body covered only with a breechclout and paint. A buffalo head mask covered his head, hiding his identity, and he carried a crooked staff.

Kathleen tried to dart past, but his staff blocked her way. Behind him, Anpo struggled to her feet. Her bloody chest heaved as she panted from her exertions, but she appeared strong enough to continue. Kathleen suddenly felt the eyes of the people penetrate her. She turned in a circle, imagining their expressions would be savage and filled with anger at her disruption. Instead, she was met with vague disapproval and perhaps a modicum of understanding.

She finished her survey, meeting the eyes of the shaman standing before her. They reflected stern kindness from behind the mask. He seemed familiar to Kathleen, and her mind flashed to the shaman, Inyan. He used his thumb to make the negative gesture.

Kathleen swallowed, dropping her gaze. She backed up until she stood at the edge of the circle of spectators. Those around her made noises in the backs of their throats, something she had learned to associate with approval of her actions. Casting one more look at the shaman, she stepped back again, returning to her place with Anpo's family.

The other dancers circled close to the pole, and Anpo joined them. The drummers began another song, the beat reminding everyone present why they were here. At the pole, the dancers began a final song of thanks to the spirits, their voices growing stronger as they sang. Others caught up the chant, and soon the bark shelter was as raucous as it had been before. Eventually, the song finished and a hush covered them. The dancers circled once before filing out the eastern opening.

Tears coursed down Kathleen's face as Anpo shambled by, exhausted and hurting. She started to reach a hand out to touch her, to assure her that she was there, but pulled back. *Don't dishonor her. Be brave. She needs me to be brave.*

Once the dozen candidates were outside, the people followed. Kathleen looked to Anpo's sister, her face anguished and questioning.

Hca, who had returned her hold on Kathleen when she came back from the sacred circle, released her. "Go, Ketlin. She needs you now."

Anpo stood tall, but had some difficulty. Many people passed her, offering kind words and smiles. But none had the face of the one she wished to see. Awareness seemed to caress her from one side, and she instinctively turned that way. An arm wrapped around her waist, and Kathleen shouldered some of her burden.

"Anpo!" Kathleen said in a breathless tone. "You and I will go home now."

"I love you, *mahasanni*," Anpo said, allowing herself to be led away.

Kathleen paused for just a second before continuing on her path. *That's what 'tis then? Love? Anpo loves me?* A tiny smile curled her lips, and she said, "I love you, too. More than you will ever know."

Part 7: Wakan Waste
Good Energy

Chapter Twenty-Three

1778

Anpo quietly smoked a pipe. She had a buffalo robe wrapped about her to keep out the chill of the late winter evening. Before her a fire crackled and popped.

She was not alone. Her sister bustled about the fire, and her half brother, young Cetan, played close to the warming flames. As Hca finished preparing food, she filled a clay bowl of stew and handed it to the Anpo. "Here, *mitankala*. Eat."

"*Ohan, cuwekala*," Anpo said. "Thank you." Worry lines marred her face, and she set the bowl to one side. In silent contemplation, she finished smoking her pipe.

About thirty *ti ikceyas* lay around the cleared area of Wagna's winter camp. The entrance faced east toward the rising sun. Thin snow covered the forest outside the village, the interior ground mostly bare and hard packed. Smoke rose above the lodges, and the occasional man or woman shuffled from one to another to visit. No one else gathered outside, only Anpo and Hca stayed in the waning light of a gray sky.

Finishing her tobacco, Anpo emptied the ashes and set the pipe aside. Hca watched Cetan and stirred the stew.

Behind Anpo was Kathleen's *ti ikceya*. The designs painted on the buffalo hide were visible in the dim light, one of the many projects Anpo had given herself as her people whiled away the winter. The leather skin covering the *tiopa* was closed, but it did not stop the noises coming from within. A man's voice, the healer, sang. Another's, the shaman, chanted a spell of protection. Beneath those sounds a woman moaned in pain.

Anpo ate her meal quietly. As the voices from Kathleen's lodge became louder, families gathered outside their *ti ikceyas*. Wrapped in furs to keep warm, none were rude enough to stare at Anpo's fire, but all of them showed their support of her by their presence. At Wanbli's fire, Anpo's father did the same, his youngest daughter serving him a hot drink. The big bellies gathered at the main fire by the council lodge, smoking their pipes and discussing where to set up the summer camp in the following months.

In the lodge behind her, a sudden howling rent the air. The camp seemed to freeze, all appearing to hold their collective breath in trepidation. Then a wail from an indignant newborn christened the night sky, and the camp returned to its activities in relief. A few more moments passed as the men inside finished their prayers and incantations. The babe's voice died down.

When the shaman and medicine man stepped out of the *ti ikceya*, Hca left the fire and went inside. This broke the tableau around camp. As the two men sat at Anpo's fire, women from other lodges trailed closer, intent on offering assistance to the new mother.

The trio sat in contemplation. Inyan pulled a bundle of fur from a pouch and carefully unwrapped a pipe. It was made of an antelope antler, intricately carved and decorated. He crouched forward and, with aged fingers, used two twigs to lift a burning ember, lighting the pipe.

He spoke a prayer as he offered the smoke to the four directions. Then he took a puff of the pipe, using his free hand to guide the smoke towards his head and beyond.

Handing the pipe stem first to Anpo, she repeated the process of smoking and guiding the cloud closer. It was passed to the healer, Osni, who did the same. They continued this ritual until the bowl held nothing but ashes.

Anpo appeared to wait patiently, although her worries grew by leaps and bounds the longer the men remained silent. She breathed a faint sigh of relief when Osni cleared his throat to speak.

"You have a strong *cinksi*, Anpo," Osni rasped, his voice almost a whisper from extended use and the cold of winter.

"And Ketlin? How is my *winuhca*?" Anpo asked, leaning forward with intensity.

Inyan chuckled as he rewrapped the pipe. "She is well, Anpo. The labor was long, but the birth was quick." He slipped the bundle into a pouch.

"*Hau*," the healer agreed with a snort. "The *wakanyeja* was stubborn until he made the decision to leave his mother's *san*."

Anpo's face held a mix of concern and confusion. She had seen babies before but had never seen a newborn display obstinacy. "Stubborn...?"

Inyan did not laugh at her consternation, but his humor was evident as he put a reassuring hand on her shoulder. "*Hau*, Anpo! Your son will be stubborn, just like you and his *ina*! He will take a long time to set his path, but he will follow that path to the end when he finds one!"

Still not sure if this was a good character trait or not, Anpo's accepting gesture was a bit weak. Sitting still at her fire, Anpo fought with her natural inclination to dash into the *ti ikceya* and check on Kathleen herself.

Seeing the whites of Anpo's eyes, Osni smiled and waved her away. "Go, *wicakte*. Go see your family before you shake apart from within."

A quick look at Inyan, who also nodded and urged her with a wave of a hand, and Anpo was up and into Kathleen's lodge, scattering the other women like quail in the tall grass.

Inside, the *ti ikceya* was warm from the fire. Gi and Hca both chattered and cooed at Kathleen, something Anpo found puzzling. *They have never treated Ketlin like that before.* Hwa, Hinhan, and even Cetan gathered around Kathleen while other women tended the fire or tidied up. Everyone stood aside with smiles on their faces when Anpo approached.

The small crowd parted, and Anpo saw the yellow of Kathleen's hair. "Ketlin?" she asked, her voice tentative as the flushed face and tired eyes met hers.

"Anpo," Kathleen responded. "Come see your son." Despite her obvious weariness, she chewed her lower lip, her uncertainty obvious.

As Anpo settled down beside her, she saw the reason for her family's strange behavior. Something wrapped in a skin squirmed on Kathleen's chest; small suckling noises and a tuft of black hair were all that could be heard or seen. She reached out but pulled her hand back at a sudden movement, startled.

Kathleen's chuckle was a tired one. She took Anpo's hand. "He is fine." Bringing their hands to the wriggling bundle, she brushed aside the skin, revealing the newborn. "You can touch him, Anpo."

He is so... His skin is so wrinkled! Her fingers brushed against the baby's back. *And soft!* she thought, her face showing wonder. Growing a bit bolder, she placed her hand on his head, covering it completely, the hair tickling her palm. As her family hustled the remaining women out of the lodge, a smile grew on Anpo's face.

"Oh, Ketlin! He is beautiful!" Anpo breathed. She stroked Kathleen's cheek. "As are you, *mahasanni*."

Tears spilled over and Kathleen sobbed even as she laughed. "I am so happy you think so," she said.

"But, how could I not, Ketlin?" Anpo asked. "You are the most beautiful thing I have ever seen. And this child is from you."

Kathleen cried a little harder at the sentiment. Anpo decided it must be her exhaustion at the difficult birth causing her emotional upset. She lay down beside Kathleen and gathered both of them into her arms, gently helping to adjust the babe still feeding. She brought the sleeping robes up, to cover the three of them, and sang a lullaby as Kathleen cried herself out.

When her woman's tears subsided, Anpo leaned back to look at her.

"Are you all right, *winuhcala?*" Her long fingers brushed the tears from Kathleen's face.

"I am more than all right, Anpo," she responded with a smile. "I am very, very happy now." She closed the distance between them.

Anpo's eyes widened as Kathleen kissed her. The lips met hers for just a moment, and then were gone. She felt a flutter in her chest, and she peered at the woman in her arms.

Kathleen's smile was a shy one. It was answered by a silly grin. Anpo hugged Kathleen tight until a squirming newborn showed his displeasure with a grumble.

Anpo backed off so quickly, Kathleen laughed. She readjusted their son to the other breast and covered him again. "What will we call him, *winuhcala?*" She took Anpo's hand and pulled her close again.

She resettled herself, keeping the new arrival in mind. "I have thought long and hard on this, Ketlin," she said, watching their son. "Inyan told me he would be stubborn. And *tatanka ska* brought you and him to me." She used a finger to brush the dark tuft of hair. "I would like to call him Tatanka Teca."

Kathleen's eyes drifted closed. "Tatanka Teca."

As Kathleen fell asleep, their son drowsing as he fed, Anpo held them both close and sang a song of joy. Soon her voice faded, and the small family slumbered together.

~ * ~ * ~ * ~ * ~

The infant picked up a small stone and stuffed it into his mouth.

"Teca!" Kathleen scooped him up, fingers delving into the small orifice to fish out the offending rock. She tossed it away, settling her son in her lap.

The boy immediately began fussing, wriggling in an attempt to get away from his mother and explore further.

"Give him to me, *winuhcala,*" Anpo offered with a smile. She set her empty bowl aside and held out her hands. "I am full. You eat now."

Relieved, Kathleen handed over their bundle of joy and picked up her half eaten food. She watched with wonder as Teca ceased his cranky behavior, giggling at the faces Anpo made for him. *I can't believe how lucky I've been, finding her. Would Adam have made as good a father?*

Anpo played with their son as she finished eating. Teca was settled on one bare leg that moved lightly, causing him to bounce. He was still a bit unstable as he sat, and Anpo held onto his small hands to keep him upright. "You will be a great pony rider, *cinksi,*" she informed him.

Teca gurgled his agreement, two bottom teeth shining brightly in the late afternoon sun.

"He will take after his *inanup*, his second mother," Kathleen said with some authority. "He will be a strong warrior and hunter." Leaning close, she caught the baby's eye. "Am I right, Teca?"

His gaze focused on Kathleen, and his smile widened. He answered with an adamant string of syllables that made no sense.

Laughing, Anpo picked him up and held him high overhead as he chuckled with pleasure. "And he will speak many words like his *ina*. Both Lakota and English."

Kathleen looked at the warrior. "Are you saying I talk too much?"

Anpo brought the baby back down and tucked him into the crook of her arm. "*Hiya*, Ketlin!" was the mock sincere response. "I would never say that!" She looked at the child and, in a loud whisper, said, "Remember, Teca. They are *winyan* and do not make sense."

An eyebrow rose. "I believe that you are *winyan*, too," she suggested.

Anpo's smile widened and she scooted about to lie down, her head in Kathleen's lap, the baby straddling her belly. "*Hiya*, I am *wicakte*, and I make very good sense." At Kathleen's look of askance, she insisted, "I speak true! Wanbli told me so!"

Kathleen shook her head, knowing that there was no winning this "argument". With a smile, she bent closer and brushed her lips across Anpo's forehead. Movement from the corner of her eye caught her attention.

The baby rocked, keeping Anpo's interest. His movement a little sporadic, however, he fought sleep. Anpo hummed softly and pulled the boy forward until he lay across her stomach. The song rumbled deep in her chest, and Teca's ear, pressed against her sternum, picked it up. He began to relax against her.

"What is Nupa doing?"

With idle strokes along Teca's back, Anpo turned her head to see what was going on.

Nupa paced in front of Gi's *ti ikceya*. Despite the heat of summer, he was fully dressed in decorated moccasins, leggings and shirt, a large buffalo robe wrapped about his shoulders. A quilled breastplate hung down his chest, various designs painted along the leather edges in blues and reds. His hair was neatly combed and braided, three small quills dangling and two larger ones with red tips standing upright. The garish colors on his face seemed to glow in the evening sun, reds and yellows and greens appearing to leap away.

A slow smile crept across Anpo's face. "He woos my sister."

"What?" Kathleen looked down in puzzlement. "What was that word again?"

"Woo. He is going to see if she will join with him."

Kathleen repeated the word. She saw movement at the *tiopa*. Nupa continued to pace back and forth. *He's courting her! How interesting!*

Wanbli sat in front of his fire, watching with half an eye as the young warrior paced back and forth, moving closer and closer to the entrance of the lodge. The word spread with some speed and soon others idled in front of their *ti ikceyas*, offering their silent support.

Kathleen watched with interest as her friend stepped from the lodge.

Hca had a shy smile, and she stood demurely just out of reach. Nupa's pacing continued, inching closer with each pass. Then he pounced. A small scuffle ensued, though it did not appear that she made any real attempt at freeing herself. When it stopped, Nupa wrapped the large robe around the two of them and began speaking softly to her.

"Do not look at them now, Ketlin," Anpo said, glancing away herself.

Kathleen looked off to one side, seeing the couple out of the corner of her eye as she looked without looking. "Do you know what he is telling her?" she asked.

"An old story. I do not know what. I think all *wicasa* decide which story to tell their *winyan* when the time comes." Anpo peered down the length of her body and smiled. Teca slept peacefully on her belly, a thumb firmly planted in his mouth.

Using her left hand to support herself, Kathleen leaned back. She brushed hair from Anpo's forehead. "What happens now? Do they join?"

"*Hiya.* First he will visit a few more times, woo my *cuwekala* in a manner fitting to a Lakota maiden. Then a price will be settled between Wanbli and Nupa's family. When that is paid, a feast will be had and then they will join."

After considering this, Kathleen looked at Anpo. "But you and I did not do this because I had been given to you, a slave?"

"*Ohan, winuhcala.* You were not a Lakota maiden. There were no family members to negotiate a price or have a feast." She met Kathleen's gaze. "I would have wooed you, Ketlin, had I been able. I would have let you see how much I love you."

Kathleen's heart warmed at the earnest comment. "I love you, too, Anpo," she said. "Very, very much."

They engaged in the same thing a newly betrothed couple nearby was involved in. Lips met in a long kiss, tongues exploring familiar ground.

When they broke off, it was with two breathless sighs. Kathleen kept her eyes closed and leaned her forehead against Anpo's. "I do so enjoy kissing you." *Now if I could just figure out what to do next....* A flash of remembered sensation, Adam's lips teasing her throat and shoulders, caused her to shiver as she wondered how it would be if Anpo did the same.

An impish grin crossed Anpo's face. "Not as much as I enjoy kissing you, *winuhcala.*"

Teca chose this moment to shift his position, putting him precariously close to sliding off his *inanup's* stomach.

Anpo caught the baby and eased him back into place.

"Let me take him," Kathleen said, seeing the problem. "I will put him in his sleeping robes. He should sleep for the night."

Chapter Twenty-Four

Teca enjoyed the complete attention of his grandmother as Gi shook a rattle at him. He laughed and rocked, arms flailing in excitement. Nearby, Kathleen and Hca served the meal to the three warriors at Wanbli's fire while Hwa and her daughter continued cooking.

"Your *cinksi* grows strong, *tanksi*," Nupa commented, watching the proceedings. He accepted a piece of fry bread from his betrothed with a smile.

As her friend wrapped boiled meat into his bread, Anpo said with pride, "Teca will be a fine warrior when he is grown."

Wanbli made an approving sound in his throat. "He is much like you at that age, Anpo. Very alert and curious."

"I will have strong children, too," Nupa said to Hca who blushed and smiled, casting a sidelong look at him. "Many strong *cinksi* and beautiful *cunksi!*"

Blowing on a piece of meat to cool it, Kathleen watched the young couple. She had heard that the people gossiped about Nupa and Anpo joining when they were children. She popped the meat into her mouth and chewed in thought. *Does Nupa want Hca because she looks so much like her sister?* The resemblance between the siblings was a strong one. It made sense. She certainly could not blame him if this was so. Anpo was quite a catch — strong, good-humored, handsome, and not prone to bouts of melancholy or anger. She was a good provider, always able to find food for their meals. Popular with her people, Anpo even spent some time counseling couples, teaching the men what it meant to be a woman, and vice versa. *And her kisses!*

Kathleen felt blood rise on her face as she banished the memories of their heated exchanges. Yes, despite Kathleen's fondness for Nupa, she was quite glad he had not set his hat for Anpo. The mere thought made her stomach clench.

She poured some broth into a bowl for Teca. Once she skimmed the grease from the top, she would soak bread in it for him to eat.

Gi smashed a berry between her fingers and brushed the pulp onto the baby's tongue. With great pleasure, Teca gummed the treat. He shook his rattle, demanding more.

"Ah, you like berries," Gi said. Another bit of fruit found its way to the waiting child. "Teca has a liking for sweet things," she announced to the others.

"Just as his *inanup*," Kathleen said, lips twitching with a grin.

Anpo reacted with lightning speed and pulled her woman into her arms. Falling backwards and tickling her, she said, "*Ohan*, Ketlin! And you are the sweetest."

Kathleen blushed furiously but tickled back for all she was worth. Gi shook her head and clucked. "Your parents are both crazy, Teca."

The baby decided to forego the berries as he watched his parents play. Gurgling happily, he crawled towards them, his movement still unsteady, intent on joining the fun. He was intercepted by Hinhan and showed his displeasure by trying to get down. His grunts were soft, hardly noticeable over the sounds of his parents. Still, his voice halted the tickle free-for-all. Both of them stopped to check on their child, verifying that he was all right.

Kathleen held out her arms. "I will take him, Hinhan. He is hungry." As expected, when Teca was in her arms, he tugged at the front of her dress. She bared one breast and helped her son suckle. Across from her, Anpo sat up and dusted herself off, picking up a meaty bone to chew on.

Conversation continued among the men as everyone ate. Cetan was nowhere to be seen. He had reached the age where he spent his time with other boys as they roamed the villages in search of adventure. Kathleen wondered how it would be for Teca when he became older. Would he be as rough and tumble, or have a quieter nature? He already seemed quite bold, but Kathleen's experience with children was limited. She only had Gi and Hwa's experiences to draw upon.

It had taken most of the winter for Kathleen to understand the subtleties of these people, and she knew she still had a long way to go. As her command of the language grew, she began to notice differences in the culture itself. The Indians had no concept of guilt, did not make promises, and could not understand the simple phrase "to forgive and forget". They did not even have a corresponding word for an apology.

As alien as they seemed, Kathleen began to realize the true freedom they had. People were allowed to be whom they were, no questions asked. Oh, certainly there was plenty of approval and disapproval of someone's actions; it was the mainstay of their society, the one way to keep everyone civil. She chuckled at the thought of heathens being civil. It was a sure bet her da would have lots to say on *that* subject.

Anpo rarely received disapproval from anyone. Kathleen wondered if it was because of the mystery of her being *wicakte*. Fortunately, Anpo was a strong and caring personality; she instinctively did the right things as befitted a warrior and hunter in this culture, with little need for sanction from her people. Still, she behaved as no one else did.

The men were stoic, rarely laughing outright as they strutted about exuding confidence. Anpo's self-assurance radiated from her with little of the pompous aura. She rarely argued to get her way, yet the leaders heeded her quiet words. The women laughed and giggled among themselves, but were less frivolous around men, becoming docile in their presence. Again Anpo broke that mold, as the latest tickle attack attested. She did not care who witnessed her break with tradition or their opinion of such. And she never demanded Kathleen act as a typical woman.

Kathleen's musings were interrupted by Anpo's voice.

"The Sun Dance begins tomorrow. After it is done, I will hunt for more food."

Wanbli rumbled. "That would be good, *cunksi*. The *tatanka* have been few this season. It has been too hot. I do not think there will be enough food for winter."

"Will the winter be so bad?" Nupa asked, his face becoming serious.

"The last lean winter was many, many winters ago," Wanbli said. "I fear our bellies will be empty again."

"Nupa and I will hunt after the dance," Anpo said, seeing her friend gesture in positive response. "All that we can collect for our people will be needed."

The thought of attending the Sun Dance chilled Kathleen. Memories of Anpo falling to her knees in the dust, blood pouring from her chest and back, still plagued her sleep. The ugly scars left behind were a constant reminder. As the conversation washed over her, she looked down at her son. *Will you dance for the sun when you are older, Teca? Will you hurt yourself to show your thanks for a favor from the spirits? Will it be worth it?*

Teca drowsed as he suckled, his eyelids drooping.

~ * ~ * ~ * ~ * ~

Despite her misgivings, the four days of the festival were good ones. Kathleen realized it was far more enjoyable this time around because she knew the language better, and Anpo was beside her. The *wicakte* spent their time at the celebrations, teaching her the many songs required by the spirits, and explaining the reason behind their practices.

All children who had been born over the last year were gathered together. Teca found himself surrounded by babies, and he eyed them with avid curiosity. When Inyan picked him up, he frowned but did not fuss until an awl was pushed through his earlobe, and a small piece of sinew inserted to keep it from growing back. Then he was placed in his *inanup's* hands, tears of anger and pain coursing down his tiny face.

Anpo comforted her son, jostling him and distracting him with berries. As he snuffled and gummed the fruit, still cross, she said, "You will be a strong and proud warrior, Teca."

"Like his *inanup*," Kathleen added softly. She gently wiped the tears from his face.

Hearing his mother's voice, Teca immediately demanded to be taken into her arms, leaning his body precariously out towards her. He cried and babbled softly in Kathleen's arms while his *inanup* wrapped them both in her long arms and held them.

When Teca had cried himself out and nursed in emotional exhaustion, Anpo led Kathleen towards the large bark structure. "It is time for the Sun Dance, *winuhcala*."

With great reluctance, Kathleen followed.

Watching the Sun Dance still gave her shivers. Kathleen wished she were anywhere but in that huge clearing watching those men mutilate themselves in the name of their *wakan tanka*. She was glad Teca was asleep in her arms and not witnessing the carnage.

It was decidedly easier to watch than the first one. Anpo stood behind her, hands on her shoulders, whispering in her ear the belief behind many of their actions. But when the first cut on the first dancer came, Kathleen shivered and dropped her gaze.

Anpo must have felt her stiffen. "Ketlin?"

Kathleen head shook. "Nothing, *winuhcala*. I will speak of this later."

"*Ohan, winuhcala.*" Then the gathered people cheered, taking her attention to the dancing field.

~ * ~ * ~ * ~ * ~

Later that evening, as stars filled the night sky and the regular dancing continued on with the younger people at the council fire, the small family settled at their own. Teca slept soundly, curled up on a robe beside Anpo. Smoking her pipe, Anpo watched Kathleen sew a pair of small moccasins for their son.

"Why did you not watch the Sun Dance, Ketlin?" she asked.

Ah, here it comes. Kathleen braced herself, not looking at her. "I...I do not think your people...need to...to hurt yourself for the spirits."

"Not needed?" Anpo's voice held a puzzled quality.

Kathleen shook her head and kept her eyes focused on the small pieces of leather in her hands. "*Ohan*, Anpo. Not needed."

She heard Anpo draw upon her pipe in thought. "If the spirits give me a gift, a favor, how else can I repay them?"

"I do not know, *winuhcala.*"

There was further silence as Anpo digested this idea, and Kathleen fervently wished the discussion had never come up. Teca, sensing the tension from his *ina* in his sleep, fussed a bit on the edge of wakefulness. He calmed when Anpo rubbed his belly with her fingers, and soon was slumbering again.

"What spirits do your people talk to, Ketlin? Do they know of *wakan tanka*, the great spirit?"

Kathleen chewed her upper lip. *Well, now you've gone and put your foot in it, lass! Nothing like a bit of religious difference to complicate things!* Her ability to discuss the topic was hobbled by language; as far as she could tell, there was no Lakota word for "believe". There were no beliefs among them, only what was and what was not. The spirits existed because they did, and no one questioned them. "My people talk to a being they call God, Anpo. He is very powerful and mysterious, like your *wakan tanka*. He knows everything and is in everything."

"This God is a man?" Anpo cocked her head. "How can your God be a man? How can he know everything and be everything if he is only one sex?"

"I do not know, *winuhcala*. But that is who my people speak to." Kathleen thought a moment. "He is not a man. He just...is." A Bible verse came into her head. "He is the beginning and the end. He is in all things."

Anpo tapped the bowl of her spent pipe into the fire. "Is this God in me, then?"

"He is in all things, Anpo. Even you."

Leaning forward, she peered intently at Kathleen. "Then why has he not spoken to me? Why has he never given me a vision?"

Kathleen shrugged, discomfited with the conversation. "I do not know. He does not talk to everyone. He only speaks to those special *wicasa* who are shamans."

Anpo sat back. "He only speaks to shamans? To special *wicasa*? Not *winyan*?"

She knew how such a concept seemed bizarre. Anpo was a two-souled person, both male and female. In her people's eyes, the *wicakte* – and their feminine counterparts, the *winkte* – were the ideal, blessed by the spirits and very powerful. "There have been women He has spoken to. There was a woman once who led many warriors in a war party. Her name was Joan of Arc, and she heard His voice."

Always interested in other women warriors, Anpo leaned forward. "Really?" She nodded in grudging respect. "She must have been a very sacred *wicakte*. Did she win many wars, receive many honors?"

"*Ohan*, she did."

"Your people must have been very proud of her."

A miserable look crossed Kathleen's face. "*Hiya*, Anpo. The people killed her a year later."

"But...but why? She was a shamaness and a warrior! She was *wicakte*. The spirits – your God – had shown her much honor, helped her."

"Most did not understand she heard God's voice."

Silence reigned around the fire once again as Anpo considered this. Kathleen diligently focused on the small moccasins, refusing to look at her.

Anpo's low voice drifted across the fire. "Do your people ask favors of your God?"

"*Ohan*, we do." Kathleen risked a glance, their eyes locking.

"And are these favors granted?"

Kathleen shrugged slightly with one shoulder. "Sometimes. Only if He deems so."

"Then how do you repay your God for his help?"

How do we? Kathleen tried to find an answer in the flames between them. Finally, she said, "I do not know, Anpo. We serve Him and pray to Him and be good for Him."

Anpo nodded slowly. "When we ask the spirits for their aid, they gift us. But, that is because we are willing to give back anything we can for their help. For very special reasons, a few do the Sun Dance to show thanks to *wakan tanka*." She pursed her lips as she pondered some thought, unconsciously rubbing her chest where one of the scars hid beneath her shirt. "Perhaps your God does not answer your prayers because you do not show him thanks."

Sighing, Kathleen responded, "Perhaps, Anpo. I do not know."

"I love you, Ketlin. But I do not like your God."

A ghost of a smile crossed Kathleen's lips. "I love you, also. Let us not talk of God or spirits any more."

"No more talk of God or spirits."

Very close by, Kathleen heard the sound of a flute. Relieved by the distraction, Kathleen turned towards it. "That is not at the council fire. Who plays music?"

Anpo smiled. "That is Nupa. He is wooing my sister."

"He is?" *By serenading her? How sweet!*

"*Ohan*. She will go to him, and they will talk long into the night together." A smirk crossed her face. "And other things."

A blush tinted Kathleen's fair skin. "And what 'other things' would there be, warrior?" she asked, setting the leather and rawhide to one side.

Reaching out a hand, Anpo guided her close. Wrapping long arms around Kathleen, she whispered, "Things like this." Their lips met in a long kiss, their hearts reaching for one another in the evening light.

Kathleen lost herself in the intimacy, loving the feel of Anpo's arms protecting her. Kissing Adam had never brought such vivid emotions, and she had to wonder. It seemed the longer time went on, the more excited she became over Anpo's touches and kisses. Was that because as women they could do nothing to ease the fire of arousal? Was it punishment from God for this unnatural love?

Regardless of the religious pall over her heart, Kathleen lost herself to Anpo's lips, a part of her wishing there was more to be had, more to share with this young *wicakte*.

Chapter Twenty-Five

Anpo rode into Wagna's camp, worried about her failure. This had been one of many scouting attempts since they had left summer camp nearly a moon past, and still there was no sign of buffalo. The food levels had not dropped enough to worry the majority of her people yet, which was not necessarily a good thing. They would continue to eat as if all were well and be ill prepared for the coming cold.

Anpo had spread the word to the other young men of her father's memories, memories of a time when there was not enough food, when a harsh winter had killed many. It took all her persuasion in some cases, for would not the big bellies have said something if famine were imminent? Anpo's standing was high among her people; now a handful of those young warriors who heeded her words went out every day, looking for the animal that was their life's blood.

No doubt the leaders of their people were aware of her activities. Not much escaped their notice. Sometimes Anpo wondered what they thought of her. She rarely received disapproval for her actions or words, and she was well aware that her status as *wicakte* was the reason. With no other *wicakte* to learn from, however, Anpo had to make her own way, find her own path. To do so, and yet not betray the teachings of her people in her heart, was a difficult and twisted trail.

As she neared Kathleen's lodge, she located the other two hunters that had gone out that day with her. Both gave her a slash of their thumbs, and she felt her spirits drop a little more. *We will need at least two more good hunts to make it through the winter.*

The sound of Teca's fussing drifted to her ears as she stopped in front of the *ti ikceya*. She slid from the wooden saddle with a sigh and untied the two rabbits hanging from it, dropping the carcasses by the fire. Anpo ducked into the lodge.

Kathleen looked up at the change of light and shadow inside. Her face reflected exhaustion and relief. Their son was in her arms, tears in his eyes and his *ina's* finger gently massaging his tortured gums. "*Han, winuhcala,*" she said softly.

"*Han, winuhcala.*" Anpo knelt down beside her family, a hand gently rubbing Kathleen's shoulder as she peered down at the baby. "His teeth still hurt him," she said.

"*Ohan*, Anpo. And they will for awhile." Kathleen sighed and dipped her fingers into a bowl of water that was slightly cooler than the lodge's interior before returning them to Teca's mouth.

"Have you spoken with the healer? Maybe he has something to help."

Kathleen nodded. "*Ohan*, I have. Hca is with him now. He is going to give me something to help numb the pain and ease his stomach and fever."

Seeing his *inanup*, Teca mumbled over his mother's finger and reached out a small, pudgy hand.

Anpo smiled at him, taking his hand and shaking it gently. "*Han, cinksi.*" She caressed his head and face. "You are a strong young warrior and brave."

He seemed to agree with her, mumbling further, and easing up on his whimpering. Kathleen used the opportunity to wipe his face clean of his tears before replacing her finger in his mouth.

As Anpo watched and rubbed their son's arm, she said, "I have brought two rabbits to eat. I will skin them later."

"I will fix them for our meal tonight. Maybe roasted with the *wagmu ohanpi*?"

"That would be good, Ketlin." She kissed her woman's temple, returning the gentle smile bestowed upon her. Here was another reason to find her path through the twists and turns and snarls blocking her way. Despite Kathleen and Teca's presence, the vision had not lessened in strength. Anpo could close her eyes now and see the wounding, the changing happening before her, hear Kathleen's voice whisper in her ear.

There was a sound of wood on wood as someone knocked against the stick holding the leather covering across the *tiopa*.

"Ketlin? I have what you needed from Osni," Hca said.

With a final squeeze of Kathleen's shoulder, Anpo rose and made her way out of the *ti ikceya*. She held the covering aside for her sister, closing it behind Hca and going to her best hunting pony. There, she removed the saddle and halter. She used handfuls of grass to rub him down before sending the horse to the remainder of the herd with a gentle slap on his withers. Anpo then settled down beside the fire to begin skinning the animals.

After a few minutes, Hca and Ketlin both left the lodge, the baby on his mother's hip. Hca smiled at Anpo before turning away towards her mother's *ti ikceya*. As Anpo finished with the butchering, Kathleen neared the fire and set Teca down. The child promptly crawled closer to his *inanup* to see what she was doing.

Taking a moment to wipe blood from her hands, Anpo scooped up the baby and held him high as she grinned at him. "You look much happier, *cinksi*," she said.

Teca responded with a giggle and chattered at her. An excess of drool came from his lips, but he appeared to be over the worst of the pain.

"Osni had medicine that numbed Teca's mouth," Kathleen informed her as she set water to boil. "And he gave me a tea that will help with his stomach and fever."

Anpo settled the baby in her lap, and returned to her work, giving him a fine view of the proceedings. "Does the healer know how long this will last?"

Kathleen watched her two favorite people. "*Hiya*. Sometimes this lasts many moons and other times this is over sooner. There is no way to know." There was silence for a few moments as the animals were skinned. "Did you find meat?"

Anpo's face turned solemn, knowing she asked about larger game than the one she butchered. "*Hiya*, I did not. No one else did as well." She looked up. "I am afraid we will not have enough for the winter."

"Teca will have enough," Kathleen vowed.

Their eyes locked.

"*Ohan, winuhcala*. Teca will have enough."

From a distance, a voice shouted, "Anpo!"

She broke their gaze to look for the speaker, finding a young *hoksila* of about eight running towards the fire. He stopped at a respectful distance and waited for Anpo to wave him closer.

"My cousin, Nupa, asks for you at your father's fire," he said, excitement in his voice.

A grin slowly spread across her lips, and Anpo nodded. "I will be there soon."

He smiled as he turned away. "I will tell him!" Then he pelted off.

An amused expression perched on Kathleen's face as she looked back and forth between her *winuhca* and the disappearing boy. "What is happening?"

Anpo finished with the rabbits, wiping her hands quickly. She rose, swinging Teca up into the air and holding him high. "Nupa wants to talk to me about a bride price for my *cuwekala*!" she said to the chuckling baby.

"Oh! That is wonderful!" Kathleen said.

"*Ohan!*" Anpo brought the child back down and looked around. "You and I will go to Wanbli's fire. You will help with the feast while I speak with Nupa and his family."

Kathleen took the water from the fire and rose. "I will make the best rabbit stew," she said as she put the newly dressed meat in a basket to carry.

Nupa's father, Sape, was already seated in the honored place to the left of Wanbli. Also in attendance was Hca's only other male relative in the village, a cousin named Ahi. When they arrived, Kathleen offered to take their son with a questioning look.

Anpo shook her head with a grin. "Teca will stay with me. All the men of our *tiospaye* will be needed."

Kathleen nodded with a smile and approached the cluster of women at the front of Gi's lodge. A blushing Hca pulled Kathleen into the *ti ikceya*, followed by the others.

Anpo ignored the giggling from her mother's lodge and settled down at her *ate's* fire with a grin. "*Han,*" she said, settling Teca in her lap.

There were murmured greetings.

With his *wicakte* daughter now present, Wanbli nodded a greeting before lighting the pipe he held in his hand. Eyes twinkling, he smoked before offering it to Anpo with a wink. The pipe made its slow way around the circle in silence, a ritual of calming and focusing.

Just within earshot several *hoksila*, including Nupa's young cousin, hovered with avid curiosity. Teca ignored the boring proceedings, pre-ferring to play with the necklace of quills and buffalo teeth hanging from his *inanup's* neck. He babbled to himself softly.

Once the smoking was finished and the bowl tapped into the fire pit, Sape spoke. "My son, Nupa, would like to offer the father of his betrothed six fine buffalo hides for her."

Wanbli looked to his kin. "My *cunksi*, Hca, is worth that and far much more," he said.

"*Ohan,*" Anpo agreed. "This shirt I wear was made and painted by her. She is a good worker, and her fingers are very agile."

Sape considered this for a moment. "Seven buffalo hides. And a shield of rabbit hide."

"Does my cousin have her own *ti ikceya*?" Ahi asked. "Or will Nupa become a buried man by living at Wanbli's fire?"

"Nupa would only be buried long enough for my *cuwe's* lodge to be completed. The lodge is nearly done now." Anpo jostled the baby in her lap as he began to get bored. "The women of my family will help to complete the *ti ikceya*."

"I do not want my *cinksi* living as a buried man for long," Sape frowned. "The offer stands."

Wanbli considered this. His nephew drank from a water bladder and passed it to him. The elder drank deeply before handing it off to

Anpo. Looking at both of his family members, he begged the question.

Ahi shrugged and gestured in one firm movement.

Anpo looked to Sape. "The joining could be delayed until the lodge is complete," she suggested. "Someone could ask my *ina* how much longer this will be."

Nupa's father thought for a moment, his face clearly showing his acceptance. "If this is good, Nupa will pay the price and wait until Hca's *ti ikceya* is done before the joining."

"This is good," Wanbli firmly responded.

The two older men rose, smiles on their faces, as they grasped each other's forearms. The nearby *hoksila*, full of new gossip, whooped and raced off to spread the word of the impending union.

The remainder of the evening consisted of a feast held at Wanbli's fire. Most of the camp dropped in at one point or another to help the couple celebrate the agreement, but the primary revelers were the immediate families. Nupa himself, the rest of his family in tow, delivered the bride price of hides and shield. The *winyan* cooked and dealt with the young ones while the men sat at the fire to talk, the boys hanging on their every word.

As she had promised, Kathleen produced a magnificent rabbit stew for the meal. The other women were amazed at her use of spices, it being different from their usual fare. Many times through the cooking process, elders and *wikoskalaka* alike quizzed her.

Teca eventually found his way back to his mother's side. When he was not suckling, he was held close to her body in a sling like piece of leather. There were a few interruptions because of his teething, but the ointment and the tea seemed to help the worst of it.

Anpo laughed and joked with the rest of the men, happy with the knowledge that her best friend and her sister were going to join. A niggling bit of jealousy was rooted out as she realized that Hca and Nupa both would have less time for her. But then Anpo saw the couple looking at each other with love in their eyes and set the negative feelings aside. *They will be very happy together!* Her gaze found Kathleen's. *As we are!*

Part 8: Sunka Wakan Natan Ahi
The Year of the Horses

Chapter Twenty-Six

1780

The village meandered along its path, stretching far in the distance. Behind them lay the past two winters, one of famine and one of feast. Before them was the promise of summer camp, reportedly stretched out in a valley between two river forks.

Kathleen led a pony, her lodge suspended between two large logs and dragged along after. A pregnant woman rode beside her, a similar household dragging behind.

"I am happy the sickness is gone," Hca said. She smiled down at Kathleen. "I did not know you felt so badly with Teca in your belly!"

Grinning, Kathleen scratched her arm, no longer noticing the deep golden tan she had developed after three years in the wilderness. "I do not think my sickness was as difficult as yours, Hca. And I was frightened much of the time – I did not pay as much attention to how I felt."

Hca dismissed her words with a wave. "Still, Ketlin. Your sickness was hard enough to call the healer."

Kathleen nodded, her mind casting back to her pregnancy. She sent a silent prayer to the old man, Osni, who had died that following terrible winter. "As was yours, *stepan.*"

She patted her large belly with a chuckle. "As was mine," Hca agreed. Her smile froze in place. "Ketlin!" she said, waving Kathleen closer. "Feel! The baby kicks!"

Having gone through this many times in the last few months, Kathleen nonetheless put up her hand and let it be guided to the area in question. Feeling the spasms beneath her palm, she rubbed it gently, and said, "He is moving very much. I think you will have a strong boy."

"Oh, I hope so!" Hca answered, her eyes showing her excitement. "Nupa would be so happy to have a *cinksi*!" She paused a moment. "He would be happy with a *cunksi*, too," she allowed.

Laughing, Kathleen said, "But a *cinksi* would be better."

Hca blushed a little, though her smile was still in place as she nodded. "*Ohan*, a son would be better."

"Well, if you give birth to a girl, you can always make more," Kathleen offered.

"*Ohan*. And we will!"

They laughed as they continued on their way. The sound of approaching hoof beats drew their attention, and the women looked around to see their warriors returning from the rear of the moving camp.

"*Han, winuhcala!*" Anpo said as she neared, coming to a halt beside her woman. Beside her, Nupa did the same.

"*Hau, ina!*" a small voice piped up.

"*Han*, my two warriors," Kathleen responded, smiling. She pulled her pony to a stop as Hca and Nupa continued on their way. Holding up her arms, she caught their son, Teca, as he dived off the back of his *inanup's* horse. "Did you have a good ride, Teca?"

"*Hau, ina!*" the toddler nodded, a huge grin on his face. He hugged his mother's neck with one arm, waving the other at Anpo who was dismounting. "*Inanup* pony big!"

"Very big," Anpo agreed. She heard their son repeat her words as she bent down for a welcoming kiss. "And we went very far," she informed Kathleen with mock seriousness.

"Very far," Teca agreed.

Looking from Anpo to Teca, she tsked gently. "You must be hungry, *cinksi*." The solemn nod she received in answer caused her to quirk her mouth. "Come then. We will find you something to eat."

As Kathleen turned to approach the household strapped on her pony's back, the boy tugged at her dress. "Want you."

"*Hiya*, Teca. Later tonight when we make camp. You know I cannot travel with you like that anymore."

Before the toddler could make an issue of it, Anpo scooped him up and tossed him into the air. The child laughed softly in pleasure. "You are very big, *cinksi*!" she proclaimed as she caught him in her arms.

He giggled up at Anpo and tugged on one of her braids. "I very big!"

"*Ohan!*" Kathleen agreed. "You will be a tall and strong warrior, Teca."

"Big warrior!"

"Big warrior!" Anpo repeated, swinging the child around as he laughed.

Thankful for the distraction, Kathleen approached her packed lodge and rummaged about in one of the baskets for something to eat. Pulling out some *wansi* and leftover fry bread from breakfast, she called her family closer.

Anpo settled Teca onto the household, in a spot designed specifically for him to sit in while they moved. He settled comfortably and took the pemmican and bread handed to him. Kathleen found a water skin and set it close. As they ate, the camp continued to move, passing around them.

"Nupa and I are going west," Anpo stated as she chewed her food. "If there is any game, we will hunt and bring meat for tonight's feast."

Kathleen nodded. "May the spirits lead you true."

"Want to go!" the toddler demanded, spilling half the *wansi* from his mouth as he spoke.

Kathleen cocked an eye at Anpo. *It's all yours....*

"*Hiya*, Teca. You will stay with your *ina*."

"Want to go!" The tiny face began to screw up in anger and frustration, his food forgotten.

Anpo's face became stern, an expression rarely displayed. Her voice rumbled unpleasantly. "*Hiya*. Your place is with your *ina*, not on a hunt. When you are older and have a pony and weapons of your own, you can hunt."

Teca blinked at her, his emotional tempest pausing at her uncharacteristic disapproval. "*Hau, inanup.*"

"You stay with your *ina*. When I return, I will take you riding again today."

Sensing her easing mood, he relaxed. "*Hau, inanup.*" Teca scooped up his pemmican and began to eat again as if nothing had occurred.

Kathleen mentally wiped her brow at a temper tantrum averted. *Was I ever that mule-headed?* She could see the reflection of her relief in Anpo's gaze, and they grinned at one another. *She's beautiful.*

The passing years had seen Kathleen's initial relief of being rescued from an unbearable future evolve into a deep and abiding love. Anpo's unconditional acceptance of Teca, admittedly a child not of her blood, combined with her natural ability to empathize and show kindness had captured Kathleen's heart. About the only obstacle they faced was one of physical intimacy. It seemed no matter how much Kathleen pressured Anpo for something – anything – beyond their gentle kisses, the *wicakte* balked. She had tried to escalate things on her own once or twice, not knowing what she was doing, only to have Anpo thwart her by pulling away with a reluctant expression.

Some days it made Kathleen wonder if Anpo thought her ugly.

But, no. Anpo always claimed she was beautiful, her eyes brimming with emotion, her heart neatly sitting upon her non-existent sleeve. Kathleen would see the love and feel ashamed of her baser and unnatural demands, promising herself yet again to refrain from attaining something that was not possible.

Instead, Kathleen enjoyed their time together; the gentle love between them, the feelings of family drawing the three of them tight to one another, and the acceptance of the Lakota for almost anything

Anpo chose to do.

It'll just have to be enough.

Most of the travelers had passed by the time they finished their meal. Anpo kissed both of them farewell and mounted her pony. Before she left, she firmly told Teca, "I will return and take you for a ride, *cinksi*!" Then she sped off in search of Nupa.

Teca frowned and fussed a bit, still wanting to go with her. He sat back with an air of impatience as his mother began walking the horse again. Soon his eyes drifted closed.

~ * ~ * ~ * ~ * ~

Anpo sat amidst a handful of male relatives taking their ease near a river. They lounged about, discussing past deeds and future plans for the Sun Dance to be held several days from now. Her father and his brother from another village remained silent, listening to those younger than themselves, keeping their counsel. Anpo followed Wanbli's example, letting their words wash over her as she listened.

Those younger than her were hardly more than boys, still childish and prone to sudden bouts of excitement. Even the men slightly older than her — her cousin, Ahi, who was twenty-one winters — seemed immature. She puzzled over this, wondering how she was different from them.

Among her people children remained children until they proved themselves as adults. A boy took risks in these attempts, defying authority, sneaking away to join hunting and war parties. If he were successful, he would gain respect; if not, he would be shunned for his ignorance and foolishness. Sometimes a man would decide a boy was trustworthy enough to come along on one of these excursions, handling the horses and carrying the extra moccasins of those older and more experienced.

When Anpo was fourteen winters, her uncle had brought her along on a hunt as one of three to watch the horses. Unwilling to be left behind, she had deserted the boys to their task, once the hunting party left, and tracked them to the killing field. She had nearly been stampeded in her efforts, coming out of the adventure with a lump on her head and a bruise on her side from a fleeing deer. Trudging back to the horses and the expected disapproval of those older and wiser than her, she was not disappointed. It was the only time she had felt as if she had failed her people, her uncle.

But a man needed to follow his path, no matter the consequences. And she was *wicakte*, two-souled, with a path more twisted and narrow than most.

Rather than bow her head in shame, Anpo stood tall before the glares of the men, ignored their words of disgust at her behavior. The two boys, sons of one of the hunters, had mixed reactions, alternating between pleasure at her trouble and fear it would be turned on them by their association with her. Anpo did not care. She was not a boy and not a child. Her destiny lay before her in the brightest vision, and nothing the men said changed it.

Anpo did not volunteer for another hunting party until the following year. Three times before that she was volunteered to join a hunt as a horse tender, called forward by the village crier to join the hunters. Three times she refused. She had heard the words of some, who said she thought she was better than others of her age. Their words hurt, but she did not dwell on them. Nor did she heed the others who spoke of her position as *wicakte*, the potential of her vision and future.

Splashing water brought Anpo back to the present. Two young men wrestled with each other in the river, receiving sharp words from their elders to leave. Both of them were older than Anpo. Chagrined, they did as asked, taking their competition elsewhere as talk resumed once more.

Was her two-souled spirit an old one? After several discrete inquiries, Anpo had come to the conclusion that no other had the wealth she had at nineteen. She was only sixteen winters when Kathleen came into her life, seventeen when Teca joined them. Her first hunt had been a disaster, the great *wicakte* returning empty handed. Yet, the second had brought her *tatanka ska* and the white woman of her vision. She had two good riders and one hunting pony, and her woman had a good lodge and a pony of her own.

To further her honors, the White Badges, a society based on visions of the white buffalo, and the Brave Hearts, an ancient society of warriors who took particular care to defend the helpless and elderly, offered Anpo honored places among them. Despite pressure from her people, Anpo had refused to join either of them. She took her position as *wicakte* seriously. She belonged to all her people, not just those of a particular group.

Others joined them, a handful of men from a village that had recently arrived. Several bypassed the gathering to strip and jump into the river. The remainder took up positions near their friends, bringing news of people not seen for many moons.

Anpo drifted along their discussions, hardly noting the words. Did the *winkte* feel this way? Did they feel as separate from the women they emulated as Anpo did from the men about her? She debated with searching one out; certainly one of the three known wants-to-be-woman would have arrived by now.

Her musings were broken by the most bizarre words.

"*Hiya*. The *wicasa* was white."

Anpo's eyes found the speaker with sharp intensity, a man a bit older than herself, one of those recently joining them.

"What did he look like?" another asked, puffing on his pipe in concentration.

The first pursed his lips in thought. "His hair was like ours but curly like the *cana*," and he indicated the area between his legs. "It covered his face. He smiled too much and stank."

A few of the men chuckled at the sentiment.

Mani spoke up from his place nearer Anpo, startling her. She had not known he was there.

"And you say this white man is north?" At the positive gesture, he said, "What is he doing there? Has he no hearth? No family?"

The first man shrugged. "He does not. He said his people were to the east, and he was a trader." A grin crossed his face as he pulled out a knife, holding it up for all to see. "I traded him two wolf skins for this."

The metal blade caught the afternoon sunlight and reflected it back at them all.

Chapter Twenty-Seven

"*Hau*, Nupa! *Hau*, Anpo!" a voice called.

The two friends looked from their game of throwing spears to see Mani approaching them, a wide smile on his handsome face. Following behind were four of his men.

"*Hau*, Mani," Anpo responded, turning to the leader. She held out her hand, and grasped the offered forearm.

Nupa took the opportunity to throw the spear, hitting the targeted tree with a solid *thunk*. He, too, turned to the others and grasped forearms with Mani. "*Hau*, Mani!" Grinning at Anpo, he added, "I beat you, *tanksi*!"

With a careful eye, she studied their target. "You did, *tiblo*. The spear is yours."

Pleased at besting her, he trotted forward to yank the spear from the tree.

Upon his return, Mani said, "I would ask you and your *tiospaye* to join me at my fire tonight."

Anpo looked at her friend who reflected her curiosity. "I...would be honored, Mani," she said.

Nupa echoed her agreement.

The leader's smile broadened, and he clapped both of them on the shoulder. "Good! I look forward to seeing that fine young *cinksi* of yours, Anpo!"

A grin creased her face. "And I look forward to you meeting him."

Obviously pleased at their acceptance, Mani said, "Until tonight." Then he left them, speaking quietly to his men as they walked away.

Once they were gone, Nupa turned to Anpo. "Why does he want to feast our families?"

"I do not know." Anpo turned away from the retreating forms. "You and I must tell our women to prepare."

"*Hau*." As they walked away from their contest, Nupa hefted the spear, a thoughtful look on his face. "Do you remember our first meeting, *tanksi*?"

Memories of a young *hoksila* who had taken the spear her father had given her filled Anpo's mind. With a rueful smile, she nodded. "I do, *tiblo*."

"I finally got that spear!"

Anpo laughed. "*Ohan, tiblo*! You did! And I will not fight you to get the spear back this time!"

~ * ~ * ~ * ~ * ~

Mani's fire was big, a fairly large gathering of his people present. With Anpo and Nupa's families, the crowd nearly doubled, and the atmosphere was jovial in nature. A handful of the men were elders, most others being of an age with the chief or younger. Wanbli and Nupa's father, Sape, sat with the big bellies, passing the time in talk. The women served the men and gossiped among themselves. Several took it upon themselves to speak with Kathleen, having not had the opportunity to meet her before. Boys sat as close as they could to hear the words of the warriors they wished to become, and talk revolved around many subjects – hunting, travel, weapons, and ponies.

Eventually all had been fed. It was late in the evening as the setting sun cast brilliant oranges and reds across the surrounding *ti ikceyas*. Kathleen settled down behind Anpo, leaning against the strong back with one shoulder as she nursed Teca. While the toddler was far past the need for breast milk, he still desired it upon occasion.

"Anpo, Nupa," Mani spoke up, drawing the crowd's attention. "You both have very handsome families."

"Thank you, Mani," Nupa smiled. He gently rubbed Hca's belly. "And mine will be growing soon."

Hca blushed, but smiled at the general murmur of amusement.

Grinning, Mani took a puff off his pipe, his face becoming thoughtful. A comfortable silence reigned about the fire as the rest of Mani's people kept their counsel and waited for him to speak again. "I am going north when the Sun Dance is complete," he announced. "I am going to see this white trader they speak of. I would like the two of you to join me."

Anpo blinked at him. "You would have me join you?" she asked, her tone not quite one of surprise.

"*Hau*, Anpo. And Nupa, too."

She looked at her friend, seeing a sparkle of excitement in his eyes. Behind her, she felt the comforting weight of Kathleen leaning against her and heard the sounds of Teca as he suckled his way to slumber. Anpo glanced at her father. His face was unreadable.

Sensing her hesitation, Mani leaned forward and tapped the ashes of his pipe out. "Anpo, you are a fine warrior and hunter. I witnessed you slaying *tatanka ska*! The spirits have honored you with a *winuhca* and a *cinksi*." He paused. "I would have you come with me."

Her eyes narrowed. *He states the obvious and he tries to sway me with his pleasing tongue.* "You speak sweet words, Mani. But even honey cannot sweeten rotten meat. What do you mean to say?"

A tension filled the air, directed at the visitors. The rest of her family bristled in defense, even Teca fussing a bit at the subtle clues from his mother. Anpo refused to look away from Mani, keeping her eyes locked on his.

He stared back, gaze flinty as the steel knife that had been shown them days earlier. Then a slow grin washed across his face. The heavy atmosphere lessened, and the people responded to his smile. "Nothing and no one sneaks past you, Anpo!" he exclaimed. "You have a pleasant nature and appear as soft as a *wikoskalaka*!" His voice lowered and his tone became serious. "But deep inside beats the heart of a warrior, and that is why I would have you join me!"

Despite her relief at his response, Anpo continued to stare at him without an answering smile. Behind her, Kathleen's presence bolstered her. "Your words are still honey, Mani. Speak your heart."

Mani's smile turned rueful, and he cast a sly look at his people. "You know my heart, Anpo." He jutted a chin at the blonde woman sitting behind her. "I would have your woman be with us as we speak to the white trader. Topeya's people had great difficulty making themselves understood. Your woman may make understanding easier."

Anpo considered her next words carefully. "Tonight we are feasting at your fire, Mani, as invited guests. You have honored me with your invitation." She glanced behind her to see Kathleen looking back, love and acceptance and trust emanating from her. "I will think on your words, Mani. I will not answer you this night."

"That is good, Anpo," he said with a respectful expression. "You do not act or speak without thought. You will be wise counsel in the future."

The subject was dropped and the feast continued until there was no food left. As the next morning was the beginning of the four days of Sun Dance rituals, the reveling ceased early. Eventually, the visitors said their good nights and drifted off to their own camp.

"What do you think your decision will be, *tanksi*?" Nupa asked as the warriors trailed behind the rest of their family members.

"I do not know, *tiblo*," she said. "I am curious. But Mani only wants Ketlin there. If she does not wish so, we will not go."

Her friend searched the distant horizon in thought. "I believe that I will go. I wish a knife of that strange stone." Pulling his own obsidian blade, he said, "Topeya said the stone does not chip or break as fast.

And he only traded two wolf skins."

"That is very good for something so valuable," Anpo murmured.

"*Hau*. Very good."

~ * ~ * ~ * ~ * ~

Arriving at their respective lodges, the people separated for the night. Soon, Teca was sleeping in his robes within easy reach of his parents. Anpo and Kathleen cuddled together, enjoying their privacy before the toddler woke in the night and joined them in their robes.

"Do you wish to see the white trader, *winuhcala*?" Anpo asked, lying comfortably on her back with her woman draped across her.

Kathleen had received a lot of attention from the other *winyan* as news of the white trader washed through summer camp. They asked her about the things they had heard about, and she had done her best to inform them of the various items in the white world created to make a woman's life easier. As she had spoken of metal laundry pails, fry pans, scissors, and boots, a certain feeling of nostalgia had stolen over her.

Upon hearing Mani's plans, her wistfulness warred with her common sense. While it would be nice to see one of her people, she feared for her new family. "*Ohan*, Anpo. But do not think I can speak his words. Many white people have different words from each other." She snuggled closer, a contented sigh escaping her as warm hands moved along her spine. "Much like the Lakota and the Hahatunwan – two different people though your skin is brown."

Anpo said, "You speak truly." One hand reached up to finger yellow hair.

"And do not think that this white trader is as honorable as your people, Anpo," Kathleen said with gentle insistence.

"What?" Anpo frowned down at her, brows furrowed. "I do not understand."

Kathleen squeezed Anpo in a hug. "I know you do not understand. That is why you need to know." She inhaled deeply. "The white men can be very mean, very hurtful. To their own kind as well as others."

"Why?"

"I do not know, *winuhcala*," Kathleen answered, a sorrowful tone to her voice. "This has always been so. Remember the stories I have told you."

They had spent many evenings with Kathleen entertaining Anpo, telling stories of her people; battles fought over a simple piece of land that belonged to no one but the spirits; whole wars that continued on for years because one man was jealous of another. Sometimes Kathleen wondered if Anpo realized the true seriousness of stories, the reality they were based upon.

Her head tucked underneath Anpo's chin, Kathleen traced the pattern of scarring on her chest with light fingers, no longer repelled by the reminders of her first Sun Dance. "Not all white *wicasa* are bad, Anpo. But not all are good."

Running a hand along Kathleen's forearm, Anpo asked, "Do you think there will be trouble?"

"I do not know. I fear there could be. The trader is there for a reason – to make himself wealthy. And wealth drives a white man more than any other thought." *And your people are all babes in the wood and ripe for the taking,* Kathleen thought, unable to find the right words to explain herself.

"All men wish to make themselves wealthy," Anpo said.

Kathleen drew herself up onto her elbow, brushing hair behind one ear as she peered down at Anpo in earnest. The hand returned to lay palm down on her chest. "Do not make light of this, Anpo," she said, her voice firm. "The white *wicasa* would own everything in the world if he knew how."

Anpo tilted her head to one side, blinking. "How could a man own the world? The world belongs to the spirits."

Seeing the alien concept confused her, a small, sad smile crossed Kathleen's face. *Oh, I wish that were true, love. I hope that your future with my people will be a good one.* "*Ohan*, Anpo. The world belongs to the spirits. But the white *wicasa* does not know of your spirits."

"Perhaps Mani is right. You must go with him this season to the white trader." She covered the hand on her chest with her own. "You know so much about your people that he does not. Even if you cannot speak the trader's words, you will be helpful to Mani with his understanding."

"Then we will go with Mani this season," Kathleen agreed with a slight nod. The smile that greeted her caused her breath to catch. *God, she is more than beautiful!*

Anpo pulled her down for a lingering kiss, their lips and tongues meeting and sliding together. Kathleen's hand moved up to tangle in her dark hair. She moaned slightly at the feel of Anpo's body along hers. *She feels so good, tastes so good....*

The heated kissing went on for some time with lips occasional distracted by ears and necks and faces. Hands roamed along bare skin. But Kathleen's aching body did not receive relief. Anpo pulled back, as she always did, her touches calming, her kisses turning chaste. Their intimacy eventually cooled until they both relaxed in each other's arms to catch their breath. Kathleen did not know whether to laugh or cry any more. Either Anpo had no idea what to do, like her, or refused to bring things to the next level. Despite troubling thoughts, Kathleen could not help but let exhaustion wash over her. As she lay drowsing, she heard a low rumble from the chest her head was pillowed on.

"I love you, *mahasanni*."

A sleepy smile graced her features. "And I love you, *mahasanni*."

Chapter Twenty-Eight

The two warriors rode together the following day. One had dark hair going gray with age while the other was young and vibrant. Regardless of their age difference, they sat their ponies almost identically, lending long familiarity to their presence together.

Coming to a small creek, the man pulled up. "You and I will rest the ponies here," he said as he slid from his wooden saddle.

With a bit more energy, Anpo hopped off her horse, signing agreement. She untied a leather sack from her pony before loosing him to graze nearby. Wanbli gingerly sat in the shade of a medium sized boulder, drinking deeply from a water bladder. He handed it up to his daughter with a smile as she joined him.

Trading items, Anpo gave him the sack. "Ketlin made you and I something to eat before I left."

"She is a good cook," Wanbli said with a grin. He opened the leather bag and pulled a small, wrapped bundle from it. As he peeled leaves aside, he saw a roasted quail nestled within. "A very good cook."

Anpo chuckled and drank from the skin. She closed and set it between them, taking the bag from her father.

They ate in silence, watching the ponies and tossing the tiny bones into the nearby creek. Words were rarely necessary between them. Anpo had spent her life in Wanbli's presence, striving to become an extension of him, to follow in his moccasins, to make him proud. She wondered if Teca would grow to do the same with her. Would he be a fierce warrior or a great hunter? Perhaps his skills would lie in tracking and he would spend a lonely life as a scout, ever in search of dangers to his people.

Whenever Anpo thought of her *cinksi*, Kathleen also came to her mind. Three winters had passed, and she had yet to hurt her woman as her vision warned her. Was it going to happen at all? She wondered how much longer it would be before Teca was old enough to no longer want his mother's nourishment. That was the only thing stopping Anpo from doing more than tasting Kathleen's skin. A woman with child needed to focus on the baby, not on the passions of a warrior.

Anpo had always wondered why men had more than one wife. Hwa had been her father's second wife for as long as she could remember. She knew that occasionally Wanbli would visit Hwa's lodge and lay in her robes as he slaked his passions. Her father spent just as many nights in Gi's robes. Anpo saw with fresh eyes now. If she had a second wife, this need to touch a woman's skin would not be so strong; she could indulge herself in her desire and not interrupt the natural cycle of mother and child. An added benefit was the extra hands for Kathleen to use in their day-to-day existence.

The thought of bathing another woman paled. No other woman held Anpo's two souls. No other would do except Kathleen. Was that because she was *wicakte* and not a true man? Anpo needed to think more on this.

Once their meal was finished, they returned the detritus of it to the leather pouch. Anpo drank her fill of fresh water from the creek and returned to lounge beside her father. They both unwrapped pipes, and Wanbli started a tiny fire using bits of twigs and kindling to keep their tobacco lit.

"*Ate–*" Anpo began.

"Go, *cunksi*. Your *ina* and I will be fine."

Anpo looked at him, startled. "You know what I would ask? You have learned to hear my thoughts?"

Chuckling, Wanbli shook his head. "*Hiya*, Anpo. I only know that Nupa is already going with Mani. Where Nupa goes, you go. And where you go, Nupa goes. This has always been so." He puffed in reflection. "And your *cuwe* has been talking of nothing else."

Relieved and irritated at the same time, Anpo stopped just short of grumbling. A hand resting on her shoulder brought her back from uncharitable thoughts.

"Hca is a woman. Her nature is to chatter like the birds. Do not make your heart stone towards her for following her nature."

Immediately contrite, Anpo dropped her gaze. "*Ohan*. Your words are true."

Nodding, Wanbli continued to smoke, idly watching his world of the plains. When the tobacco was gone, he dug a hole in the ground with his heel and tapped the ashes there, covering them with dirt. "You worry about me. Why?"

Anpo dragged the words from within, not wanting to utter them and thereby make them real. "You are getting old. Your hair changes colors and your bones ache in winter. I worry about you and Gi this season."

Wanbli solemnly mulled her words over. "This is the way I felt when my father was my age and I was yours, Anpo. I will tell you what he told me."

She leaned closer. Anpo had never met her grandfather. He had died before her birth, a great warrior. Stories were still told of his final fight with the enemy, how he killed many warriors with only his voice. It was rare her father spoke of him.

"The cycle of the world is to be born, grow old, and die, Anpo. Nothing will change this cycle. Whether you stay with Wagna's camp this season or go with Mani and Nupa, we will still grow older. And maybe we will die in your absence, I do not know." Still strong despite his age, Wanbli stared intently at her. "But you will not follow the path you were meant to follow by letting fear rule you."

Anpo searched her father's face, finding nothing but love and pride. "Do you know my path, Wanbli?"

He gave a slow grin, and nodded. "*Hau*, Anpo. You are to be a warrior and a hunter, like your father before you. Inyan saw this. He heard the scream of the *igmu* in your cries." Wanbli broke eye contact, looking out over the water. "Tell me, *cunksi*. Have you ever seen a family of mountain lions together?"

"*Ohan*. When the female has her cubs."

"And when the cubs are grown?"

Thinking carefully, she considered the question. Her eyes widened. "*Hiya*, Wanbli. The *igmu* live alone."

"Your path is not with mine," Wanbli said. He leaned forward. "At least not now. Go with Mani and be easy in your heart – your *ina* and I will be strong until you return."

His larger hand patted her leg in reassurance as she slowly nodded. "I will go with Mani this season, *ate*. But next season, I will be at summer camp and rejoin you."

"You will do what you must, warrior. And you will be brave and strong as I have taught you."

Part 9: Wicasa Ki Ska
The White Man

Chapter Twenty-Nine

1780

Anpo pulled her pony up as she crested the small hill. Turning, she looked out over summer camp. Around her, Mani's camp flowed past, moving north. As these people who were strangers – yet not – passed by, she surveyed the encampment. With ease she spotted the lodges marking her *tiospaye*, her family's dwellings. She also saw the empty void where her woman's *ti ikceya* had so recently been.

It felt strange to be leaving her home, leaving her family. *I am not yet away and already I feel lost. What will I feel when I cannot look up and see* ate; *when I cannot hear* ina's *or Hwa's voice as she speaks to Ketlin and Teca? Hinhan will be a full woman before I see her again, and Cetan already runs with the* hoksila.

A hand on her bare calf caught her attention. Dark blue met her gaze and a gentle, understanding smile graced the lips of the woman who stood beside her mount. *Mahasanni*, whispered a voice in her head, and Anpo felt a rush of...something fill her – love, fear, desire, tenderness all frothing together into a heady mix.

"We can stay," Kathleen said.

The suggestion gave Anpo the freedom to turn it down. "*Hiya*, Ketlin. We will go with Mani and meet this white trader." She looked at summer camp a final time. "My parents will be well in our absence."

Kathleen nodded and rubbed the brown skin beneath her fingers. She received a smile and a caress on her cheek before Anpo urged her mount to catch up with Nupa's.

She's nineteen years old, Kathleen thought, keeping the yellow shirt in sight. *About the same age as I when...* The distant memory of a dying man's scream echoed in her mind, and she shook her head, long yellow braids shifting in front of her. Kathleen turned away from the sound, searching for something to latch onto, finding her son chatting amiably with Hca.

They were on the back of Kathleen's lodge, being pulled by the strong mare Anpo had given her. Nearby, a grey colt frisked as it trailed along with its mother. Hca held the reins of another pony wrapped around her wrist, another *ti ikceya* dragging behind. She and Teca sang a child's song about animals.

Kathleen's face lost its tenseness, and she grinned at them. *My fam-ily. I will always have Teca and Anpo.*

~ * ~ * ~ * ~ * ~

The warrior swooped in from the south, screaming her cry as she attacked tatanka ska *with a spear. Her hit was solid, and the white buffalo was mortally wounded. With sadness and elation, she watched* tatanka ska *stagger closer to her younger self, blood pouring from its side, its nostrils flaring wide as it panted for breath. It fell to the ground with a solid thump, dust rising about its carcass. The Sun flared again, and she lost the image, turning away from its brightness. The light faded and she looked again, only to find the white buffalo gone.*

Anpo was her younger self once again. In the buffalo's place was Kathleen. The woman's hair was long, longer than her own, and a yellow the color of the Sun itself. Her eyes were the blue of a deep lake, still and clear. She wore the standard dress that all Lakota women wore, buckskin and moccasins, her hair flowing freely in the breeze.

The child Anpo watched in horror as the strange apparition rose from where tatanka ska *had been, blood pouring from the side where the white buffalo had been wounded, walking gently closer. Then the woman knelt and put a hand to her wound, bloodying her fingers. She reached forward and brushed the blood onto the young girl's face, two thunderbolts beneath the dark eyes. She could see those brilliant blue eyes staring at her intently and hear the words whispered into her ear.*

"Mahasanni." The white woman rose to her feet. From behind her emerged a hoksila *who watched with solemn eyes.*

"Teca?" she murmured.

Smiling fondly down at the childlike Anpo, the woman with yellow hair caressed her cheek. "Mahasanni," she repeated. She took the toddler's hand and walked away.

The light intensified until it surrounded the mother and child, so bright Anpo had to hide her eyes. When she was able to see, there was nothing there.

"*Hiya!*" Anpo gasped, fighting herself awake.

The sleeping robes pooled about her waist, her breasts hanging free in the cool early morning air. Beside her, Kathleen rumbled and rolled onto her back, holding Teca to her like a doll.

A dream. It was a dream! Anpo insisted, reaching a hesitant hand out to touch the blonde hair. *They are still here, still with me.*

Teca woke a bit. He sprawled across his mother's belly, thumb tucked firmly into his mouth. Solemn eyes stared at his *inanup*, more asleep than awake.

The look haunted Anpo. *So much like the dream.* She stilled the fear and caressed her son, rubbing his back until his eyes closed and his breath deepened into sleep.

With slow, careful movements, Anpo eased out from under the covers. When she was clear of the bedding, she dressed. She left her hair free and stealthily stepped out of Kathleen's *ti ikceya*.

The sun had yet to rise, and no one was about except those *akicita* and clubmen assigned watch through the night. On the outskirts of the village, younger men guarded the herd, their presence keeping the camp and its inhabitants safe.

As Anpo passed the fire, currently a mound of ash surrounded by rock, she scooped up one of her robes. With long strides, she left Mani's camp behind.

Soon, she stood at the side of a river. It was deep and swift with a small falls rumbling in a tenor voice. The sky was beginning to lighten, midnight blue giving way to the gray of dawn. Puffs of steam from her breath filled the chill air. She found an outcropping that was not getting much spray from the water, and sat down, wrapping the robe about her.

Scouts had returned the previous day with good news. After a full moon of travel, they had found the white trader they sought. The morning would be exciting, people dressing in their finest, preparing their skins for trade, packing their lodges.

Anpo's family had spent quite a bit of time at Mani's fire after the scouts reported. The chief learned all he could from Kathleen. The picture she painted of her people was not a pretty one. All the elders present at the council lodge were uncomfortable with the dangerous potential for misunderstandings.

The point was moot. There was no turning back now. Mani was wise enough to know that whether he made contact with this trader or not, others would. They would end up with the benefits that Topeya's camp had already attained. To not gain them for his village would cause him to lose his place as their leader.

A whisper of the dream tickled Anpo's mind, and she tried to grab at it, make sense of it. For seven winters the vision had remained the same, even in her sleep. *Why is the vision different now?* All that she had thought regarding the vision was put into question. *Do I hurt Ketlin? Or does she hurt me?*

Her heart felt the remembered hollowness as her family disappeared into the brilliant light. *Will she decide to leave me for the white trader?* she worried, pulling the robe tighter against the cold. Anpo immediately discarded that possibility. *No. Not after what my* winuhca *said last night about her people. I do not see her wishing to remain with men such as that.*

Closing her eyes, she heard Kathleen's voice, "*Mahasanni*," and saw her walk away with Teca. *And though she leaves me, she still loves me.*

"*Ate*, Inyan," Anpo whispered to the morning as she opened her eyes. "I wish you were here now to give me counsel."

~ * ~ * ~ * ~ * ~

Kathleen peered into the small clearing as the camp broke through the tree line. The forward scouts were already there, whooping and riding around the large cabin that belched smoke from its chimney. It was a ramshackle building made of thin logs, the entire building twice the size of the usual family settlement.

The area around the trading post had been cleared of tall grass and trees. A woodpile squatted beside one door with a large stump in the front yard obviously used as a chopping block. Already, two *koskalaka* had pulled the axe from it and were studying the blade closely. A separate, smaller shack was to one side. A horse snorted from within as it nickered at the ponies of the circling scouts.

Mani led his people down the gentle slope, resplendent in his red and yellow painted chest and a headdress sporting many eagle feathers. Fanned out behind him were the important men of his camp, all the big bellies wearing their best clothing and paints, hair and bodies adorned with the proper badges and feathers of their accomplishments.

Kathleen felt a sharp sense of loss as the camp neared their destination. *Nothing will be the same,* she mourned, unsure where the emotions and thoughts came from.

"Ketlin! Look!" Hca exclaimed in a soft voice.

The trader had come out of the cabin. He strode a few feet out into the yard, his arms wide in welcome and a smile on his face. Of average height, he wore a homespun shirt and wool pants, suspenders holding them up. His hair was dark and shaggy, as curly as his beard, and parted in the middle.

Hca juggled the baby she carried in a sling across her body. "What is that on his face?"

"Hair," Kathleen answered.

"Do all your men have hair on their faces like that?"

Despite her misgivings, Kathleen smiled. "No. Sometimes the men shave the hair all off. Or they leave some above the lip or over the cheeks." She trailed off, men's beard styles too numerous and distracting to get into.

Hca stared at the wonder of it all, following the people as they continued their trek.

Anpo rode with Mani and the elders. She cast one long look at Kathleen as they neared the white trader. A reassuring smile was sent her way and she returned it before pulling her pony up and dismounting with the rest of the party.

"*Hau, wicasa ska,*" Mani intoned, raising his hand in the sign for peace.

"How," came the response and the mirrored gesture. The trader smiled with encouragement, showing stained and pitted teeth. "You've come to trade?" he asked, using sign language as he spoke his strange tongue.

The elders murmured a grudging respect for his knowledge, though Anpo studied him with careful eyes. *He is not speaking the words that Ketlin speaks.*

The chief signed back, "We come to trade."

Showing off more of his ugly teeth, the trader's grin widened, and he clapped his hand together in delight. "Good! Good!" Thumping his chest, he said, "I am Jacques!"

"Mani."

The trader shocked the gathering by slapping their leader on the back. "Mani! Let's go see my wares!"

Only Mani's warning glance kept the warriors from attacking. Arm firmly wrapped about the native's shoulder, Jacques ushered the leader into the cabin. Seemingly ignorant of the tension he provoked, the trader continued to babble in his language, only releasing Mani when he stopped to throw open the door. With a flamboyant gesture, he indicated Mani was to step inside. The elders followed.

The remainder of the village halted their progress upon reaching the clearing. Women made last minute checks of the items they had brought to trade and chattered excitedly with each other. The children, sensing the emotion, ran rings around the adults and horses. The *koskalaka* roamed the area, studying the cabin and its environs with interest and suspicion.

Anpo drifted towards her family. She caught sight of Nupa speaking with another warrior and holding the trader's axe. A grin was shared between them.

As she neared Kathleen's pony, Teca crowed, "*Inanup!*" from the packed lodge. He stood on unsteady legs and held out his arms with insistence.

Anpo grinned and sidled her pony beside the logs that held her woman's *ti ikceya*. With a strong hand, she grabbed her son up to straddle the horse before her. Clucking at her mount, she urged it around the lodge until they were beside Kathleen. "*Han, winuhcala,*" she greeted. "*Han,* Hca, nephew."

"*Han, mitankala,*" Hca answered. Jostling the sleeping baby. "Yus'as'a would say *hau* if he were awake." She grinned at her sister.

"*Han,* my warrior," Kathleen returned with a smile. Leaning against

Anpo's leg, she looked up at her with a worried expression. "All is well?"

"*Ohan*, Ketlin. All is well." Anpo adjusted herself in the saddle as their son bounced up and down in an attempt to urge the pony onwards. "I do not think he speaks your tongue. I did not recognize any of the sounds."

"This far north, he would be from the French, I think."

"You cannot tell what tribe he is from by his clothing?" Hca asked.

"*Hiya*. Not often. Sometimes it is easy to know what a white man works at by his clothing but not what tribe he is from."

Hca quirked her eyebrow and shook her head at the marvel of white society. In her arms, the baby fussed to wakefulness, and she became distracted from the conversation.

"What happens now, *winuhcala*?" Kathleen questioned as they both looked to the trader's cabin.

Anpo sighed. "Now we wait, Ketlin. When Mani and the elders have decided to trade with *wicasa ska*, we will be told." She looked down at Teca who bobbed intently in her saddle, unable to make the horse go. "But first I must take my *cinksi* for a ride so that he will know the feel of a pony beneath him running like the wind!"

Used to the sudden change of topic for Teca, Kathleen grinned and stepped back. "Our son is already one of the best riders in camp," she insisted, her smile widening as the toddler puffed up in pride.

"*Ohan*, he is."

"*Hau*! I am!" the boy exclaimed with excitement. "Teca big warrior, *inanup*!"

"Big warrior," Anpo repeated with conviction as she pulled the steed away from her woman. As she kicked it into a trot, she glanced behind with a wink and a smile.

Chapter Thirty

It wasn't long before some of the elders emerged from the cabin with a different white man. This one was older, with graying hair and craggy face. He lugged a heavy bundle to the chopping block, settling it carefully before unwrapping it. The warriors around him yipped with enthusiasm as the midday sun reflected off steel blades.

Some of the big bellies stepped out and gestured their people to come inside. While most of them stepped in that direction, a few of the *koskalaka* elected to remain with the older trader and his knives. Nupa and Anpo both decided to follow their women.

Teca lay in a cradleboard across Kathleen's back. Though he fidgeted, he alertly studied the wonders in the cabin. Shiny pots and ladles hung from the rafters, all manner of strange tools and utensils lay upon the heavy wooden tables, thick blankets and shirts of all imaginable colors, wooden boxes of different designs, a riot of color and shapes that boggled the Lakota minds. As Kathleen made her way along the tables, a melancholy twinge plucked at her heart. She became the center of attention as she answered questions about the strange items and their functions, putting her interpretation skills to quite a bit of use. With gentle fingers, she caressed a tin whistle that looked like her grandmother's.

She smelled him first, a dusty odor of sweat that indicated someone who did not bathe often. A vague memory of her husband flitted through her mind as Kathleen looked up from a grinder, a discussion with Hca trailing away. The younger trader stood across the table from her, watching curiously. A trickle of unease caused her to shiver.

Seeing her attention was his, he spoke.

French. Definitely French, lass. Kathleen shook her head. "I do not understand," she replied in Lakota. Beside her, Hca watched with intent curiosity.

The man's brow quirked, obviously not expecting the barrier. Again he spoke, this time with a heavy accent. "You speak English?"

Blinking in surprise, Kathleen nodded.

"I am Jacques," he said. "What is name?"

"Kathleen," she said. She felt a presence behind her, heard the toddler call to his *inanup*, and relaxed.

The trader eyed the sudden appearance of a possessive warrior with misgiving. He stood straighter and raised a chin in response to Anpo's presence. "This your buck?"

A slow burn sparked in Kathleen's heart at the phrase. Her eyes flashed, and she nodded again. "Yes."

Realizing he had offended her, Jacques shrugged an apology. He scooped up the tin whistle and held it before her. "You play?"

Despite herself, Kathleen's anger dissipated, and she gave the instrument a wistful smile. "Yes. It's been some time, though."

"Four rabbit skins and yours."

Her sentimentality was chased away by common sense. "One rabbit skin will buy you five just like it in Boston."

Jacques' face melted into a rueful grin. "*Oui*." He set the whistle back down on the tabletop. "But here worth four."

Lips thinning in distaste, Kathleen shook her head and stepped away from the table. Hca followed as she moved to the other side of the cabin.

~ * ~ * ~ * ~ * ~

The trader watched her go, shaking his head. *Why would a woman like her be with a bunch of animals?* He could tell she was beautiful beneath the dirt and ointments these people used to drive away insects. Before he could entertain much of a notion to liberate her from theses people's clutches, he looked at the yellow shirted warrior who owned her. Swallowing nervously, he forced himself to return the gaze. *You can't show fear to these heathens. If they smell a hint of it, they'll murder you and leave you for the crows.*

The buck leaned forward, his face stern, a feral smile growing on his face.

Jacques' heart beat double time at the implied threat. Without thought, he backed a step away from the table, away from the warrior who studied him as if he were lunch. He watched as the yellow shirted man picked up the tin whistle his woman had been eyeing and tucked it into a pouch. A wince crossed his face at the loss of a trade, but he kept his silence, knowing the savage would kill him as soon as look at him.

The warrior straightened. With obvious disapproval for the trader, he tossed a bundle of furs onto the table and stalked away.

Jacques slumped in relief, pulling a dirty handkerchief from his pocket to mop his brow. Unable to escape his greedy nature, he scooped up the bundle and unwrapped it. Unfurled, he discovered four rabbit skins. His eyebrows shot up as he realized how much the warrior had understood of the conversation he had had with the white woman. *If these natives understand English...*

Nupa, who watched the exchange from nearby, looked up from the strange utensil he examined to see the white trader stumble out into the yard. Hearing the other trader's name called, he ignored it and set the fork down, continuing his path along the tables to a heavy wool blanket.

~ * ~ * ~ * ~ * ~

They wandered away from the still celebrating Lakota. Teca was cuddled in one of his *inanup's* arms, exhausted from the excitement of the day, and Kathleen was wrapped in the other. She enjoyed the intimate contact, liking the feel of Anpo's heat against her side as they walked.

Once the initial trading sessions were complete, the women of the village set up their lodges nearby, and the traders were invited to feast with the people. They had accepted with wreathes of smiles on their faces. After the *ti ikceyas* were up and the fires lit, another bout of trading occurred.

It's almost like a fair, Kathleen mused, leaning into the strong arm draped across her shoulder. *The only fly in the ointment has been the guns and whiskey.*

At the proper time, the traders had come out of their cabin and joined the natives at their council fire. Along with them came their rifles and an innocuous wooden keg. They offered Mani a drink before passing the whiskey around to the other warriors, laughing uproariously as brown faces grimaced at the burning sensation.

Behind Kathleen, another rifle went off near the fire where Mani was being taught how to shoot. She jumped in reaction before relaxing into the gentle squeeze Anpo gave her. Smiling, she squeezed back where her arm lay about a firm waist.

Fortunately, the traders could not understand the native language. It was easy enough for Kathleen to warn Anpo and have her relay the information to the rest of those gathered at the fire. After one round of the keg, no one would have another drink. The two Frenchmen seemed a bit put out, but the younger smiled and winked at Kathleen with grudging admiration.

Reaching her lodge, Kathleen held the leather covering aside for Anpo to duck in with their important bundle. Soon, Teca slept soundly in his furs and the couple sat outside by the fire. She watched as Anpo struggled with the unfamiliar whetstone.

"*Hiya,*" Kathleen said, reaching out her hand to stop Anpo. "You need to hold the knife this way." She showed her the proper angle on the whetstone. "And use pressure as you push."

Anpo nodded and did as instructed, a strange sound emitting from the flat stone she held in her hand. "Like when I sharpen my spears?"

Kathleen smiled. "*Ohan*! Just like that." Watching as Anpo repeated the process several times, she added, "And then you do the same on the other side until the edge is sharp."

They sat in silence as the honing continued; the only sounds to be heard were the gentle rasp of metal on stone, the singing and drumming at the council fire, and the occasional gunshot.

"What did the younger man say to you?" Anpo broke the silence. She did not look up from the knife, concentrating on the task at hand. "I could not understand him well, his words are different than yours."

"He told me his name. Asked if you were my *wicasa*." An impish grin crossed her face. "I told him you were."

Chuckling, Anpo tested the edge of the blade with her thumb before sharpening the other side.

"He offered me something for trade and I told him no." Kathleen returned her gaze to the orange and yellow flames, leaning back and resting her weight on her palms.

"What did he offer for trade?"

"Nothing important. Nothing useful." Kathleen closed her eyes, remembering the tin whistle. "Just a toy."

When she was little, her grandmother had a tin whistle. Before she had died, the old woman had taught Kathleen how to play. The instrument brought back many warm memories. She could not help but fall sway to the sadness threatening her now that she was reminded of her people. It was one thing to miss her family and friends, it was quite another to be slapped in the face with strong memories the trading items brought to her.

Anpo stopped her task and looked at her. "What did you trade for today?"

Sitting forward, Kathleen tucked her legs beneath her. "I traded for a stew pot and a cook knife," she said. "Did you trade for just the stone and knife?"

"I did trade for something else." Anpo pursed her lips in thought, squinting at distant stars in thought.

Kathleen chuckled at her parody of deep thought. A smile broke across Anpo's face, and she wondered again how she had gotten so lucky to have this woman, this *wicakte*, be hers.

"I traded for something I think you will enjoy."

She scooted closer, showing eager curiosity. "I will? What did you trade?"

Anpo set the knife and whetstone aside. With agonizing slowness, she pulled her surprise from a pouch, hiding it in the shadows of the evening. She presented the tin whistle with a flourish, her smile wide as firelight reflected off the metal surface. "What will you trade me for this, *winuhcala?*"

Kathleen burst into tears.

Anpo was unprepared for the response. Her smile faded away, and she swept Kathleen into her arms, holding her close. The whistle was still clutched in one hand, forgotten. Eventually, Kathleen's tears faded off. "Ketlin?"

She pulled away slightly and used the end of her dress to clean her face, sniffling. Kathleen cursed the lack of language; there were no words in Lakota to express apologies. "Thank you, Anpo. My heart is happy you are with me."

"*Ah-ah*, shh. My heart is happy also." Anpo pulled her closer, helping Kathleen readjust her seat until she leaned comfortably against the long frame. She still had the whistle and held it in view. "What is this toy? In what manner do you play with this thing?"

Kathleen smiled gently as she peered at the instrument. Anpo had adorned it with three strips of leather, each holding respectively a feather, a quill, and braided horse's hair. "It is called a tin whistle in my tongue. My grandmother, my *unci* taught me to play music, and I was given hers when she died."

Anpo hugged her closer. "You loved your *unci* very much," she said. "You must have been lonely without her."

A few more tears trickled down Kathleen's cheeks. "*Ohan*," she whispered. "I still feel lonely without her sometimes."

"Your grandmother is in your heart, and her spirit will forever be alive." Anpo studied the whistle. "She wanted you to have this. That is why the trader was here, and why I traded for the tin whistle," she said, stumbling over the English words.

Kathleen took the item pressed into her hands and gave Anpo a look that held a mixture of longing, sadness, and joy.

Anpo used the edge of a robe to wipe off Kathleen's face and laid a tender kiss on her forehead. "Play for me."

Feeling drained but much better, Kathleen smiled. She brought the whistle to her lips and began a simple tune, one of the first her grandmother had taught her when she was small.

As the instrument emitted a sweet tone, Anpo closed her eyes and let herself be carried away on its melody.

Chapter Thirty-One

1781

Winter camp was established in the foothills of a low mountain range. Many stories were told around the fires about the sacredness of these hills and that the Lakota would walk among them forever. Each village settled near others, allowing the occupants to visit back and forth over the season. Things went along as they should, with snowfall and colder temperatures. Plenty of food held off starvation for another season. Winter was a time for rest and renewal as the people told stories and gambled, laughing and enjoying their families and friends.

Anpo had word that her mother's lodge was several days west on the sluggish, half frozen river. Heavy blizzards had made the way very difficult and, though she missed her people, she decided to wait until spring to return to them. The vision remained in its changed state, confusing her with its message. She spoke with Mani's shaman, and he said he would seek council from the spirits. He had not yet returned with any new knowledge of what plagued her.

The problem started with a dry cough and slight fever. Teca whined and would not get out of his sleeping robes, claiming his head hurt. Concerned, his *ina* fed him broth and kept cool rags on his forehead. Nearby, Anpo watched as she worked on various tasks, not wanting them out of her sight.

Two days passed with no changes, and both parents decided it was a cold, nothing more. The toddler seemed to do fine with the teas and compresses from the healer, sleeping the days away in relative comfort. Still, Kathleen slept fitfully, rousing often during the night to check on her only child.

Anpo woke from a frantic shaking. Looking blearily into her woman's face, she shook off sleep in alarm. "Ketlin! What is wrong?" She looked about the *ti ikceya*, a sense of danger filling her as she heard a strange barking sound.

"Teca! Teca!" Kathleen insisted, answering in her native tongue. "He needs a doctor!"

Frowning at the unfamiliar word, Anpo could not question it as Kathleen shook her once more.

"Now! He's dying!" the panicked mother cried. Kathleen literally launched herself away from Anpo, shoving her down as she dived back to her son's robes.

Dying? Teca! Anpo scrambled to her feet, automatically grabbing for her shirt as she stumbled forward, finding the source of the strange sound.

The boy coughed hard now, very dry hacks that seemed to boom from deep inside his little chest. He grasped at his throat as he tried to get air into his lungs, his lips tinted slightly blue. His eyes were barely open, giving the impression he still slept despite the rigors his small body was putting him through.

As Anpo could only stare in shock, Kathleen helped her *cinksi* sit up.

"He's burning up with fever!" Kathleen insisted, running her hands over his body. "We've got to get him to a doctor!" Glancing over her shoulder, she saw Anpo standing slack jawed. A fury came over her and she rose, clutching the coughing boy to her chest and shoving the woman towards the *tiopa*. "Get help now!"

Her befuddlement broken, Anpo dashed out of the lodge. The cold winter air struck her, and she realized she was still naked from the waist down. Grabbing up a robe near the embers of her fire, she wrapped it about her waist as she pelted off for the healer's *ti ikceya*.

Several minutes passed before she returned, dragging the elder with her. The older man sputtered a bit in indignation at the rough treatment, but did not stop their progress. Behind them came his woman and son, both carrying his medicine pouches and adjusting their hastily donned clothing.

Anpo ducked into the lodge, pulling the healer after her. She saw no one. *The vision! They have left me!*

"Where is your *cinksi*?" he questioned, looking around them. "You said he was sicker. Where is his *ina*?"

Nearly staggering in fear and confusion, Anpo reached the sleeping robes of her family and knelt down to feel them. *Still warm!* "They cannot be far," she whispered, more to herself than anyone else.

"Eh?" the healer asked, not hearing. He took a step closer only to be nearly bowled over as a frightened Anpo dashed past, flying through the doorway to the outside. There was a squawk as his family was upset by her passage, and he followed.

Anpo barely missed crashing headlong into the healer's woman as she stood at the entrance. *Where would she go? Where would she take Teca?* She replayed the last few minutes in her memory, hearing her woman's voice. *"He's burning up with fever!"* ... *Somewhere cold. ... The river!*

Grabbing the healer's son by the shoulders, Anpo said, "Wake

Nupa and Hca! Bring them here! Tell them Teca is sick, and Ketlin is crazy with fear! Go!" She spun the *koskalaka* about and pushed him in the direction of her sister's *ti ikceya*. Not seeing if her order was obeyed, Anpo spun on her heel and ran for the river, leaving the healer and his *winyan* to stand and stare blankly after.

As she had hoped, Anpo found her family at the river. Kathleen had waded out waist deep, holding Teca so only his head was above water. Tossing the robe aside, Anpo followed, swallowing her curse as icy water hit her bare skin like a thousand knives. Coming close, she heard Kathleen singing a soft Irish lullaby through chattering teeth. Teca appeared to be unconscious, his dark eyes closed as he trembled.

Kathleen looked up from her son. Her eyes were wide with fear, her lips turning blue from the cold. She could not control her shivering, the nearly freezing waters taking their toll on her body. It took a few seconds for Kathleen to actually focus on Anpo, realizing there was a warm body pressed against her side and dispelling a minute amount of the cold. "You found a doctor then, lass?" she asked.

"Come, Ketlin. We must return to your lodge," Anpo said softly. She wrapped an arm about her *winyan's* shoulder and urged her towards the riverbank, relieved when Kathleen allowed the direction.

"His fever's so high, love. My mum once did this with da when he was half out of his mind," Kathleen explained, continuing to speak in her native tongue.

Anpo nodded in understanding, glad she knew most of what was being said. She guided them up to the bank where she had left the buffalo robe. Ignoring her naked lower half, Anpo wrapped her woman and son in the robe and lead them back to the *ti ikceya*.

By now, Hca and Nupa had been roused. The fire in front of the lodge burned merrily, and the young mother prepared a pot of water for the healer. As they neared, the two families around the fire rose to their feet, stepping forward to help.

Looking wildly about, Kathleen's eyes widened in alarm, and she clutched Teca closer. "Where's the doctor?" she demanded, her voice rising in panic. "You said you found a doctor!"

"I do not know what a doctor is, *winuhcala*," Anpo soothed. "I have brought the healer to help Teca with the coughing sickness. He will know what to do."

"No!" Kathleen pulled away, staring at the gathered people in anger. "No! Teca needs a doctor! A medical professional! Not some heathen dancing about a fire and mixing herbs and poultices!"

Anpo did not understand all the words, but the intent was clear from the amount of scorn put into them. *Ketlin is afraid. She only reacts to her fear.* She stepped forward, trying to look intently into Kathleen's frightened eyes.

Taking a step back and refusing to meet Anpo's gaze, Kathleen readjusted Teca's weight in her arms. The heat radiating off of him warmed her body and fueled her fears. When the toddler began to cough once more, she could only watch with a wave of helplessness rushing through her soul. A low tenor voice grabbed her attention, dragging her tear-filled eyes back to her warrior.

"*Mahasanni.*"

Dark blue met the deepest brown and Kathleen sobbed. "He can't die, love," she whispered frantically. "My family's not yet seen him! My mum doesn't know she's a granny!"

Anpo used the opportunity to step forward and pull her *winyan* back towards the fire and the waiting natives. "Teca will not die, *winuhcala*. And I swear that we will find your family so that he may meet them."

Peering up at Anpo with haunting fear and a faint flicker of hope, of relief, she asked, "We will?"

"*Ohan*, Ketlin. We will travel to your people as soon as winter is past."

Teca coughed again as they neared the fire. The healer immediately reached out to take him.

"I will need to bring the child inside," the elder stated. His arms were around Teca, but Kathleen's embrace tightened.

"Ketlin," Anpo said. "Let Teca go. Let Wayawa heal him."

The long moment stretched between the three of them. Then the tableau broke when Kathleen released the child and sagged against Anpo. The healer wasted no time as he took his charge and ducked inside the *ti ikceya*, his son following with precious medicine pouches.

Breathing a faint sigh of relief, Anpo held the shivering woman in her arms. Feeling a warmth envelope her, she found herself wrapped in a buffalo robe, as well, her *cuwe* tucking it close about both their shoulders. An uncontrollable shivering shook her body at the unfamiliar warmth.

"I will get you both warm clothes," Hca informed them, pulling them towards the fire. Once they were both settled, she ducked into the lodge.

It was not long before they were both completely dressed, though Kathleen was hardly any help. She seemed to shut down in exhaustion and worry, and both Hca and Anpo had to get her out of her wet dress and clothe her. Soon, the couple were wrapped once again in dry robes and cuddled together before the fire while the healer and his son could be heard chanting inside the lodge. Wayawa's woman returned to her own lodge to await her family.

Hca puttered about the fire while her *wicasa* smoked a pipe. She prepared hot water for Wayawa and delivered it to him inside. Then, water was boiled for a soothing tea.

Sitting in the honored space to the left of Anpo, Nupa continued to puff the tobacco, lending silent support to his best friend and *hunka*, his adopted sibling.

Anpo held Kathleen close, gently rocking them as she whispered an appeal for protection for themselves and their son. Kathleen's head was tucked beneath her chin, and she felt warm breath as it brushed her neck. When the tea was done, Anpo held her woman's cup, blowing on it and forcing her to drink.

The night passed into daylight with the two couples huddled together in their robes and staring at the crackling fire as they awaited word from the healer inside.

~ * ~ * ~ * ~ * ~

It was the fifth day of Teca's illness. The lodge reeked of the pungent herbal mix that Wayawa had instructed be placed on his chest, but no one really noticed it any more. Hca and her babe had moved into the *ti ikceya* to help, while Nupa spent more time ice fishing and hunting for rabbits that could be made into nourishing broths for the sick toddler.

The extended family took turns watching the child, washing his body with cool rags to counteract the fever, replacing the poultice on his chest, feeding him the medicinal teas and broths. Additionally, the healer made two or three visits a day to check on his charge and adjust the balance of herbs in the tea.

Anpo drove herself to near exhaustion as she kept an eye on her woman. It had been struggle after struggle as she cajoled, badgered, demanded, and pleaded for Kathleen to sleep and eat. Even now, she dozed in her arms only fitfully, as if deep inside she knew she had to remain available for Teca.

"*Mitankala*."

Opening her eyes, Anpo peered at her older sister. As the woman came into focus, she noted a beautiful smile that plucked at her heart.

"The fever has broken, Anpo," Hca whispered. "I have already sent for Wayawa."

Anpo blinked rapidly, trying to clear her sleep-filled eyes. As the words became clearer, she surged upwards from the robes, pulling her woman with her.

"Wha–?" Kathleen mumbled at the interruption. Almost immediately, her face filled with fear. "Teca–?" She looked wildly at her *cinksi's* robes.

Hca rubbed Kathleen's shoulder. "He is well. The fever has broken!" As the mother hurried to Teca's side, she continued, "Teca is cooler and breathes well now. I have sent for the healer to check on him."

Kathleen collapsed in a heap beside her son. As tears of relief coursed down her face, she bit back sobs so as not to wake him. Kathleen gently brushed his soft, dark hair away from his brow, relaxing deep inside as she noted the coolness of his skin. Warm hands were on her shoulder, and she smiled up at her warrior.

Anpo felt an icy ball inside melt away at the sight of Kathleen's smile. She knelt down behind Kathleen and rubbed the shoulders in her hands. "Teca will grow strong again," she insisted, peering at their son. "And we will travel to your people so that your *ina* will know she is an *unci*."

Leaning back into the embrace, Kathleen quietly cried in relief and hope and love. "Thank you, *mahasanni*. Thank you."

Part 10: Tiospaye Wakuwa Chasing Family

Chapter Thirty-Two

1781

The remainder of the winter stayed mild, and Anpo used her time wisely. She spent it quizzing Kathleen about her family and preparing for a long trip.

Where the McGlashans were located was the biggest issue. It was apparent to both of them that finding her parents' homestead was going to be difficult. Kathleen had no idea of exactly where her family had settled. She knew there was a fairly large river nearby that the area natives called the Ohio, but that was the only landmark of which she was aware.

Anpo spent time with the elders of Mani's camp and several others within visiting distance, trying to discover if any had heard of this river. None had. The only river that they could speak of was called Mississippi, though none had ever seen it before. Kathleen was of the opinion that there would be plenty of people to guide their way once they neared hers. While Anpo was uncomfortable with the idea of putting her faith in any of Kathleen's people, remembering the stories and warnings, there did not seem to be many other choices.

With great reluctance, Anpo agreed.

Early spring colored the air with the smell of growing things and the crisp scent of morning dew. The small gathering of people was wrapped against the brisk chill of the morning. The baby, Yus'as'a, fussed a bit though he calmed when he was distracted by his mother's breast.

A large red stallion and a spotted mare stood nearby, saddled and with various bags hanging from them. Additionally, a grey yearling colt frisked, pulling at the rope about his neck as he sensed the anticipation around him.

"I will miss you, *tanksi*," Nupa spoke with a solemn face.

"I will miss you, as well, *tiblo*." She grabbed her friend into a fierce embrace.

Strong arms held Anpo close. "Do you know this will be the first time we have been apart since we were children?" he asked in a husky voice.

Anpo nodded. "I know." She pulled back, and grasped Nupa by the shoulders. "We will be together again."

Nupa gestured sharply in agreement.

"As will we, *mitankala*," a voice insisted from beside them.

Anpo turned to her sister, a reassuring smile on her handsome face. "*Ohan*, Hca. We will be together again." Using a long finger, she gently chucked the baby's cheek. "I must see how big my nephew grows in one winter."

"We will speak of you to Wanbli and Gi," Hca said with a sad smile. "They will be unhappy to not see you this summer." To Kathleen, she added, "We will keep your *ti ikceya* safe until you return to us, Ketlin."

"Thank you," Kathleen responded, stepping forward for a warm hug. "I will miss you while I am gone."

A toddler barreled his way into the press, not wanting to be left out of the affections. The women broke apart, laughing, and Nupa scooped him up and tossed him high in the air.

"You be strong, *tunska*!" Nupa stated firmly, holding the boy up. "Learn from your *inanup* and take good care of your *ina*!"

"I strong warrior, *leksi*," was the serious response though Teca currently dangled above Nupa's head. "I take good care of *ina* and help *inanup*."

Nodding with grave dignity, he settled the toddler onto the back of the spotted mare. "That is good, Teca. You are very helpful and wise."

Sitting as tall as he was able in the saddle, the boy simply stated, "Thank you."

Anpo raised an eyebrow at their son's humble manner. Looking to her woman, she begged the question.

"I have been teaching our *cinksi* about accepting compliments well," Kathleen answered with a faint smile.

With a thoughtful nod, Anpo looked back to the toddler. She smiled approval and watched Teca's broad grin form. "You are better than most warriors, Teca. Never forget that."

"I will not, *inanup*."

There was a pause in the conversation, and the four of them looked blankly at one another. The red stallion snorted, breaking the silence.

"Go, *tanksi*," Nupa said in a low voice. "Or you will not leave at all."

Her smile was half amused and half chagrined at being discovered. "*Ohan, tiblo*." Anpo helped Kathleen onto the mare, steadying their son until she was in place. She then leapt onto her mount and whirled him about. "I will see you at summer camp after next winter."

The family left behind nodded. "We will see you at summer camp after next winter," Hca repeated.

Knowing she had to leave now or lose her nerve, Anpo swallowed the lump developing in her throat. With a deep breath and a fond smile to Kathleen and Teca, she urged the stallion forward.

~ * ~ * ~ * ~ * ~

For well over a month, the small family traveled across the Great Plains. Steadily, they rode their ponies towards the rising sun. As the days grew longer and warmer, the signs of spring were everywhere – from the dusky green of sage to the brilliant fields of flowers they came across.

Every few days, they remained camped, allowing themselves to recuperate from long hours of riding and walking. Always near a river or creek, the small family relaxed into a natural rhythm of life.

Teca was well over two winters now. He could sit his *ina's* horse alone and, when in camp, spent much of his time with his pony, the yearling colt Anpo had captured for him the previous year. There was great disappointment he could not ride his own horse, but his *inanup* told him in great detail how a young colt, even a yearling one, could be ruined forever if ridden too soon. With reluctance, Teca had accepted the restriction.

During their lull times, Kathleen insisted that everyone bathe, and she cleaned all their clothing. Anpo used the break to hunt and repair tack, tools, and weapons. Teca followed his *inanup* about like a puppy or played by himself nearby.

They ran across the occasional village, as well. Most were offshoots of the Lakota – primarily of the Dakota tribe – and the family was welcome to join them for the night. Despite a few language differences, all went well during these visits, especially when it was discovered they had a *wicakte* in their midst. Anpo regaled the gathered folk with news of her people. She also spent time counseling both men and women in how to deal with one another, her position as two-spirited making her a bridge from one gender to the other. Men who did not understand their wives asked questions, as did women who found their husbands incomprehensible. At first, Anpo felt uncomfortable in this new role, but soon grew to understand its importance among her people.

Kathleen always garnered much attention with her fair skin and hair. Not surprisingly, her existence only heightened Anpo's status. Two-spirited, slayer of the sacred white buffalo, and joined with a white woman – up until now, Kathleen had not realized how truly important Anpo was in this society. It was one thing to know that Anpo's family accepted her strange ways and cared for her. It was quite another to appreciate those strange ways made her a very popular and a highly sought after advisor among other bands. Kathleen had no idea what to make of the whole thing.

Eventually they reached the Mississippi River and camped for three days. Anpo slew an antelope that fed them well and replenished their dwindling supplies. Additional repairs and preparations were made while she ranged a half-day's ride north and south along the riverbank, searching for a likely crossing. None were forthcoming; the travelers were at an impasse.

On the third day in camp, a visitor arrived. An Ojibwe hunter shared their fire that evening. Though the languages were different, signing kept them conversing through the night. Kathleen was more surprised to see that Anpo's status crossed more boundaries, the hunter's deference to her a revelation considering he was not a part of the Lakota people. An arrangement was made to help Anpo and her family cross the large river in their path. Several days later, they continued their trek eastwards alone. Teca had an Ojibwe charm about his neck for protection, as did his mother. Anpo was the proud owner of a new pipe made of beech wood.

Following an offshoot of the Mississippi, the family saw the vegetation change from tall grasses to trees. As they veered away from the tributary, more and more they traveled through wooded growth, traversing game trails as they continued east. Though it was mid summer, the leafy trees provided welcome shade and kept them cool. Many small streams along the way kept them in water, and game was plentiful.

Other native tribes encountered them – the Huron, Kickapoo, and Illinois. Many carried muskets with them, and Anpo became concerned for her family's safety. Through sign language, it was discovered that the English were once again at war, and the fighting was hot and heavy. Kathleen's fears grew with Anpo's. If her people were at war, where would her parents and brother be? Who was fighting whom? Who would they side with?

After two weeks of travel through the woods, they came to a vast lake. Another rest was called for and they enjoyed the deep blue waters of Lake Michigan. A Huron scouting party happened upon them, joining them for several days as they quizzed each other. When the Ohio River was mentioned, one of the warriors said he had heard of it. He suggested continuing their journey to the south and east.

Anpo lead her family onwards. They skirted the lake until they crossed a river leading from it. From there, they turned southeast, continuing their trek through forested lands. A few days passed before they saw the smoke of a fire. As they neared its source, strange music reached Anpo's ears and odd aromas filled her nostrils. Kathleen's spirits perked as they got closer, as she explained it was a homestead of her people.

Their arrival was met with mixed responses. Apparently, a celebration of some sort was going on, and the sudden appearance of strangely dressed natives was a call to arms. With some quick talking, Kathleen dispelled the worst of their fears as she explained her circumstances. While the warrior stood stoically nearby with the horses, she spoke with three men about her family.

Anpo studied the cabin and barn, wondering how a person could live cooped up in the same place all the time. She watched the men with the same suspicion they showed her, constantly alert for any perceived danger. Eventually, Kathleen's conversation ended, and she returned to Anpo with a smile. This family didn't know hers, but they knew of the frontier attacks that had resulted in her capture a few years earlier, and where those had been located.

By evening the trio camped near the Ohio. Kathleen excitedly chattered on about the people at the cabin, explaining that there had been a wedding. It seemed they were now only a few days away. All they had to do was follow the river south.

Eating her meal in silence, Anpo listened to her *winuhca's* voice. It was full of passion and anticipation. The lilting accent that would occasionally peek through was in full view now, even though Kathleen spoke Lakota. Anpo decided it was good to see her woman this happy.

But a gnawing pain grew in her heart and dread filled her mind.

Chapter Thirty-Three

Anpo led her pony along the trail, her hand on his muzzle to keep him from making noise. Behind her, Kathleen did the same, occasionally checking on Teca who rode her grey mare.

The settlements became thicker as they traversed the river and much more dangerous. Local natives who had raided the homesteads along the frontier a few years previously still did so. The small family had been shot at once, Anpo narrowly being missed as a lead ball bit a chunk of wood out of a tree behind her. Signs of war parties were everywhere in the area, so they slowed their pace to better cover their tracks and avoid them. They were lucky so far, but Anpo hoped to find Kathleen's family soon. Even her status as two-spirited might not have any power among these furious people set on destroying the whites encroaching on their territories. Since the shooting three days earlier, Anpo skirted all settlements they came across, only stopping long enough for Kathleen to verify that her family was not there.

The telltale odor of wood smoke beckoned them forward as they edged towards yet another homestead. All of Anpo's senses were alert as she scanned the wooded area they traveled, searching for anything out of the ordinary that signaled danger. She caught the smoke on her nostrils as it mixed with the odd aroma that signified Kathleen's people. Eyes narrowed, she studied the trees carefully, hand still covering the red stallion's muzzle.

She heard the sudden click of a hammer pulling back, the crackling of undergrowth as a white man appeared. He was hiding in the bushes to one side of the trail before them and rose with a fluid motion, his musket aimed at Anpo's chest.

Anpo's only thought was to protect her family. She took a step sideways, forcing her steed to turn and block the trail before she froze. Having seen what damage a musket could do, she had no illusions about her chance of survival. Perhaps Kathleen and Teca could get away.

"Aye, you better stand still, you damned animal," the man agreed, his accent much like the others of this area. He regarded her as he kept careful aim with his weapon, noting the strange clothing. "Don't know who you are, dog, but you're definitely in the wrong place at the wrong time." One eye closed as he sighted down the barrel of the musket. "If you've any gods, you better say your prayers to them."

As Anpo's mind raced for an avenue of escape, a voice drifted from behind the red stallion. "Stewart?"

The man's eye reopened, his finger relaxing on the musket trigger. He lifted his cheek from the stock, suspicious.

"Stewart? Is that you?" Kathleen eased around the pony blocking her path, her heart thumping double time in her chest.

Anpo's heart rate increased as Kathleen came out into the open. She watched the white man slowly lower his weapon, his mouth dropping open in amazement.

"K-K-Kath?" he asked in a choked voice.

Kathleen smiled as she stepped forward. "Aye, Stew. It's me."

Stewart McGlashan blinked back sudden tears. He stumbled forward only to find his way blocked by a very large, very protective native brandishing a knife. He took a step backwards, lifting his musket, but not quite setting it on his shoulder.

Anpo glared at the armed man. She did not speak, but her threat was very clear.

Placing a gentle hand on Anpo's arm, Kathleen moved around her. She rubbed the arm gently and waited. As expected, the *wicakte's* attention flickered from her target to Kathleen.

Kathleen smiled reassuringly up at her, hand still caressing. "He is my *misun*, Anpo. He is your brother-in-law." With firm pressure, Kathleen forced the arm holding the knife down. "He is family. I will be safe."

Anpo's gaze darted back to the young man. She found the same color eyes looking at her, the same color hair on his head, the same general features of her woman on his face. Reluctantly, she sheathed her blade. Her face was of stone, her body tensed to attack, but she nodded with a stiff neck and took a short step to one side.

Sighing quietly with relief, Kathleen turned to her brother once again. A welcome smile spread across her face as she closed the distance between them.

He barely had time to drop the musket barrel as his sister leapt into his arms. For the first time in over three years, the siblings embraced. Joy filled Stewart's heart, and he let the weapon fall to the ground as he picked Kathleen up and swung her round and round.

To give them a modicum of privacy, Anpo returned to the horses and checked on Teca. She watched with some wariness from the corner of her eye, however, not trusting this man who had endangered her family.

"*Inanup?*" the toddler asked in a whisper. "Who that?" He curiously stared as his mother cavorted with this stranger.

Anpo looked fully at the siblings, a part of her heart warming at Kathleen's delighted giggle drifting towards her. "He is her *misun*, Teca. Your *leksi*."

Teca considered this for a moment. "As Nupa?"

"*Ohan*, young warrior. As Nupa."

With quite a bit of interest, the boy watched his *ina* as she greeted his uncle.

Tears spilled freely from both their eyes as Stewart set his sister down. He grabbed her shoulders and held her at arms length. "Where have you been, Kath? We thought you dead like all the others!"

"It's a long story, Stew," Kathleen said, a wide, silly grin plastered on her face. "I'll tell you all about it later." Kathleen looked behind her, waving her family closer. "First, let me introduce you to someone."

Steeling herself, Anpo swung their *cinksi* into her arms and carried him closer.

Stewart's eyes widened in surprise at the toddler. He quickly glanced at his sister, searching for confirmation.

A satisfied grin crossed Kathleen's face. "Stewart, I'd like to introduce you to your nephew, Teca. Teca, this is your uncle, Stewart."

"*Hau, leksi*," he said, holding his hand up in the signal for peace.

"English, *cinksi*," Kathleen murmured. "Stewart does not understand Lakota."

Surprised, Teca blinked for a moment before repeating himself. "Hello, uncle."

The man's face broke into a wondrous grin. "Hello, nephew! It's good to meet you!" His attention turned to Kathleen. "I'm so happy for you, sis!"

"Thank you, Stew," she said with a blush, dropping her gaze for a moment.

"And who is this?" Stewart asked, indicating the tall, silent warrior, his voice lowering in distaste.

Caught up in her own thoughts, Kathleen did not hear the change in his voice. *Aye, lass, explain this one, eh?* "This is Anpo." Kathleen chewed her upper lip in thought. "My...um...Anpo is my partner," she finally blurted. *Oh, that was good.*

"Partner?" Stewart's brow furrowed in confusion. "Your husband, then?"

"*Hiya*. Uh...I mean, no, Anpo's not my...uh...husband." *How to explain to your little brother that you've been sleeping with a woman for the last three years?*

Anpo's attention slowly turned to Kathleen, watching as she

blushed and fidgeted, wondering what was the problem.

Stewart did the same, lower lip pursed in thought. He looked suspiciously at the native, beginning to bristle. "Well, if he's not your husband, then what is he?"

Refusing to look at either of them, Kathleen stared off into the woods, still gnawing on her upper lip.

Anpo decided to take matters into her own hands. "I am her woman as she is mine," she stated in English.

If anything, Stewart's forehead became craggier as his frown deepened. He reconsidered the native's gender. "You're a woman then?" he asked. Full of disbelief, he looked her up and down.

"*Ohan.*" Looking to Kathleen, she was surprised to find the pale skin was flushed even darker. Confused, Anpo reached out and touched Kathleen's shoulder. As her woman inched away from the hand, a thought hit her with sudden ferocity. *Ketlin is ashamed of me!* Anpo almost took a step back from them as the shock filled her.

Sensing the sudden tension, Teca in Anpo's arms said, "*Inanup?*"

"Do not worry, *cinksi,*" Anpo said in Lakota. "This is nothing of you." She gave him a gentle squeeze of reassurance.

Not quite convinced, Teca nevertheless remained silent.

Stewart puzzled over the woman's phrase, not understanding its meaning. With a shrug and a shake of his head, he set it aside. "Well, Kath. Let's get you home, then! Mum and Da will be so surprised!" He stooped, and grabbed up his musket.

The mention of their parents brought Kathleen's attention away from her distress, a welcome distraction. "They are well?" she asked, peering at her brother.

"Aye, though older." He reached for her hand and drew her along. "Mum always knew you were alive. She's told us so many a time over the years."

"Really?"

Stewart nodded. "Aye, lass. She never doubted for a minute."

Watching the siblings move away, Anpo felt the burn of anger enter her heart, something she had never felt for her wife before. *Ketlin is ashamed and does not even care if we follow.* She looked to the toddler in her arms, seeing his mother in the shape of his face. Fighting the irrational emotion down, she smiled at Teca and brought him back to the horses. *She is too excited about seeing her* misun, *her parents after so long. That is all. My* winuhcala *does care.*

With that firmly in mind, Anpo planted their son back on his mother's saddle. "You will meet your *unci* and *tunkasila* now, Teca. The ones who raised your *ina.*" Grabbing up the reins of all three mounts, she followed the trail ahead of her.

~ * ~ * ~ * ~ * ~

Rachel McGlashan worked the slab of bread dough with some force. She was up to her elbows in flour, a smudge of white on her cheek. Thumping on the porch heralded the arrival of her son, and she ignored it as the door swung open behind her.

"Mum! You'll never guess what I found while hunting!" Stewart exclaimed.

"Aye, lad, and that's a fact," the older woman responded, her voice vague with distraction. "I don't have time for guessing games, Stewart. This dough's got to be set to rise for tomorrow's baking."

"Mum?" came a tentative voice.

With an audible gasp, Rachel froze, floury hands grasping the edge of the table. Her heart tripled its beat as she recognized the voice, recalled the many times it had spoken to her in the past and in her dreams. She almost stopped breathing in the silence that followed.

"Mum, turn around," the voice said, soft and familiar.

The older woman refused, shaking her head. Her body tensed, she was trembling, and tears filled her eyes. From behind, she barely heard the whisper of soft footsteps approaching her. A warm hand touched her shoulder, forcing her to turn, to see who it was though she knew without a doubt.

"Mum." Kathleen sighed, a bittersweet smile on her face. The smile faded to concern when her mother collapsed into her arms. Great sobs emanated from the older woman, and Kathleen pulled her close.

"I knew you weren't dead, Kathleen! I knew it!" Rachel babbled through her tears.

"Shh, Mum. I know. Stewart told me." She maneuvered the two of them to her parents' bed in one corner. Sitting down, she held her mother tight, rocking slightly.

Standing awkwardly by the entrance, Stewart mumbled, "I'll go help with the horses." He dashed out, closing the door behind him.

Chapter Thirty-Four

Anpo led the ponies into the yard as she saw the man exit the cabin. They stared blankly at each other, unsure. Teca bounced on the saddle of his mother's mare, causing the pony to nicker and get Anpo's attention. When she looked at him, he held out his arms in demand.

Anpo quickly scanned the dooryard, appraising it for danger. She found what seemed to be common among these folk – a neat stone well, a chopping block with a pile of wood, a cluster of tame birds scratching about. She measured Kathleen's brother once again before making her decision.

"Stay close, *cinksi*," she said, lifting Teca from the saddle. "We are not safe here."

Teca nodded, making a beeline for his colt as soon as his moccasins hit the ground. There was a small trough to one side of the well and, as the child's pony caught a whiff of water, it circled about and buried its nose in the welcome wetness. The sounds of drinking perked the ears of the other two mounts. In response, Anpo led them forward, as well. Soon the three were enjoying their fill, Teca whispering in his colt's ear and petting its mane.

Stewart finally stepped down from the porch where he had been staring at them. "You said you'd help with the horses. So...help," he said to himself, apparently not aware of Anpo's command of English. Skirting around the woman, he dropped a bucket into the water below, and hoisted it upwards. With a practiced hand, he emptied it into the trough before repeating his action.

Once the trough was overflowing Stewart pulled up a final bucket and dipped himself a bit of water using a ladle that hung nearby. As he leaned his head back to drink deeply, he saw the woman watching him. Swallowing, he flicked the ladle downwards, removing the dregs of water before handing it to her.

Keeping a wary eye on him, Anpo took the utensil. Dipping it into the fresh bucket, she asked, "Teca, do you want water?"

The child looked up from his pony and gestured yes with a thumb as he approached her. Slurping mightily on the ladle, water ran down the sides of his face and sprinkled his bare chest. "Good, *inanup!*" he insisted before returning to the yearling. He led the animal away to a bit of grass.

Anpo felt Stewart studying her clothes, her bearing, and her weapons. His stare was bad mannered, but she consoled herself with the memory of Kathleen's rudeness when she first arrived at Wanbli's fire. It was not discourtesy, but uncivilized behavior among the whites that caused such actions. Rather than return his unconscious insolence, she busied herself with the horses, finding grass at the edges of the cleared yard for them to graze upon.

A sudden squawking grabbed her attention, and she whirled to see Teca chasing after the strange birds in the yards. Chickens, Kathleen had said. They created quite a stir as he attempted to catch one, scrabbling away from his entertaining efforts with ease.

Stewart took a step forward, and Anpo watched the play of emotions cross his face. Her heart became colder as she witnessed the curled lip of disgust and anger that quickly washed away into a stubborn acceptance. *Why would someone look at a child in such a way?* "Teca," she called. "Come with me. You and I will ride my pony."

The promise of a ride with his *inanup* snagged the boy's attention, and he raced to her, leaping into her arms with a whoop.

~ * ~ * ~ * ~ * ~

Kathleen held her distraught mother, rocking gently and murmuring soft words in response to the choked questions.

"Where've you been, lass? What happened to you?"

She continued her rocking. *Probably best not to tell her everything,* she considered. "I was captured by the Indians, and they took me away."

Rachel nodded against Kathleen's chest. "Aye. We found Adam in the field. The animals had left him there!" Her voice burred with anger. "It was two days before we heard of other attacks and checked on you." She ducked her head back down, hugging her daughter close. "I'm so sorry, Kathleen," she whispered.

Returning the hug, she smiled sadly. "There's nothing to be sorry for, Mum. No one knew the Indians would range so far north." *And where would I be if it had been stopped before I was captured? What would I have?* Rachel's voice broke into her reverie.

"Aye, lass. The men folk all took up arms after that. Hunted that pack of heathens down and killed them all!"

Kathleen stopped rocking, confused. Brow furrowed, she pulled away from her mother. "When was this?"

Using her apron to wipe her face, still snuffling a bit, Rachel said,

"Why, two or three days after we found Adam. That's why everyone thought you dead. You weren't with them anymore." She paused in thought, her own face puzzled. "But what happened to you, lass? Why weren't you there?"

Kathleen closed her eyes in pain. *That's why we kept moving west. They were running away from the attacks by my people.* Hitching in a breath, Kathleen opened her eyes and looked at her mother. "I wasn't there because..." A well of sadness filled her heart. "Those weren't the Indians who took me, Mum. The men killed a village of innocent people." *Oh, God! Why'd they do something so idiotic?*

Rachel stared at her blankly for a moment before her face crumbled. "God ha' mercy," she whispered, eyes wide.

Kathleen nodded in agreement. She pulled fully away from her mother, remaining seated on the bed with her hands in her lap. "It's no wonder attacks have continued up and down the frontier."

They sat in silence for a moment. Sounds from outside filtered into the quietness, distracting them from their thoughts. A horse galloping and a child crowing in delight drifted in from the open windows.

As Rachel's mouth pursed, she asked, "What in blazes is that?"

"The reason I'm here," Kathleen responded, a huge grin taking residence on her face. She rose to her feet, and held out her hand. "Come with me, Mum. I need to show you something."

As they stepped out onto the porch, a reddish blur raced by. Stewart was out by the well, his attention on a large horse and its occupants as they trotted around the yard.

"What the...?" Rachel asked, stepping forward and off the porch.

An Indian rode around the yard, his short sleeve shirt painted yellow with some kind of designs on white strips. He wore a breechclout, a dirty white color hanging from his waist. His bare legs showed brown skin and dust, white moccasins on his feet. A yellow feather stuck upright from his head, and an eagle feather hung down, his dark hair pulled into two braids and wrapped with buckskin strips. About his neck were several necklaces – two or three it looked like – and a pouch that held a very modern hunting knife.

As Rachel registered what she was seeing, she gasped and stumbled backwards.

Surprised at the response, Kathleen caught her mother before she could fall.

Rachel turned, her expression panicked. Stepping back onto the porch, she hustled her daughter backwards toward the door. "Get inside! Quickly!"

Kathleen took two steps back before stopping in alarm. "Mum! It's not what you think!" She fought off the frantic hands that pushed at her. "It's not an attack, Mum! You're safe! I'm safe!"

Seeing the altercation at the cabin, Anpo rode directly towards it, slowing as she neared. She uncertainly watched an elder woman struggling with Kathleen and pulled the pony short. Kathleen spoke to the older woman, soothing her as Anpo watched. Sliding from the back of her steed, Anpo took a step forward. "Ketlin?"

Kathleen saw her worried expression and spoke over Rachel's stiff shoulder in Lakota. "All is fine now, *winuhcala*. My *ina* is frightened and thought you were here to attack her."

Hearing the strange words from her daughter's mouth gave Rachel pause. The fight drained out of her as she peered closely into Kathleen's face.

Anpo's head tilted, and her lips pursed in puzzlement as she considered this. "Why would she think I am on the warpath? I do not know her."

"My *ina* has heard of many attacks over the years, Anpo," Kathleen continued, her face a reflection of serious concern. "And you have seen evidence of many on the path of war here. My *ina* mistook you for one of those."

Anpo understood an honest mistake and accepted her explanation.

Stewart approached during the conversation, listening to the words roll off his sister's tongue. "What are you saying, sis?" he asked.

"I'm telling Anpo that Mum is concerned for my safety and has made a mistake," Kathleen said. Looking at her mother, a distant part of her was astonished to realize she was eye to eye with the older woman. "You have made a mistake, Mum."

"*Ina!*" Teca called from the pony. "Who that?"

The sound of the child's voice broke the reverie that mother and daughter had fallen into. Kathleen's face broke into a smile as she looked over the older woman's shoulder. Despite her fears, Rachel curiously turned to see who was speaking.

"Teca! This is your *unci*!" she called back. She moved forward, steering her mother back out into the yard.

Anpo held out her arms as Teca dived into them. She set the child on the ground and watched as he approached the women. Seeing Kathleen's mother fully in the daylight, she watched her from the corner of her eye, noting the resemblance.

Kathleen knelt down and held her arms out in encouragement. She hugged Teca to her, the grin threatening to split her face in two. "Mum," she said, looking up at the older woman. "I'd like you to meet Teca. Your grandson."

Her legs faltered, and Rachel stumbled. Stewart dashed forward to catch her before she could do herself damage, easing her to the ground where she sat in astonishment. She was eye to eye with the child who now leaned against his mother, a hesitant thumb stuck in his mouth, regarding her solemnly.

"Teca. Say hello to your *unci.*" As an afterthought, Kathleen added, "In English."

He decided to be bashful. He pulled his thumb out, a shy smile crossing his face before he buried his head in the crook of his mother's neck.

Rachel finally found her voice, though it was shaky and weak. "My...my grandson?"

"Aye, Mum," Kathleen, sitting down onto the ground and pulling her child into her lap. "Your grandson."

Watching the two together, Rachel had no doubt her daughter was speaking the truth. As Kathleen brushed his unruly hair away from his face, the boy settled into his mother's arms and played with a necklace of some sort about her neck. While the coloring was definitely not of her family, Rachel could see the glimmer of her eldest in the child's facial structure. "How old is he?" she nearly croaked.

"About two and a half." Kathleen smiled. "As near as I can tell, he was born in January or February."

The red stallion snorted, drawing Rachel's attention. She eyed the stoic native holding the reins nearby, a shiver of fear coursing through her blood. "He the father?"

Kathleen blushed, dropping her gaze and looking away. *And I haven't even told Stewart!* she worried. *How am I going to tell my mum and da?*

When no answer was forthcoming, Stewart piped up, "No, Mum. That's a friend of Kath's. She's a woman."

The savages kidnapping her daughter was bad enough. Obviously for her to have a child so soon after her capture, they had raped her. But, allowing women dress and act like men, as well? *Heathens.* Anpo watched the disapproval settle onto her *uncisi's* face, and wondered why it was there. A glance at Kathleen showed the same sort of befuddlement that had occurred earlier with her brother.

Dismissing the Indian, Rachel dusted off her hands and rose to her feet with the help of Stewart. "Well, lass," she said briskly. "Come inside. I've got to get the dough ready for tomorrow's baking still, and then start on your father's dinner."

"Da?" Kathleen asked, allowing herself to be sidetracked from her thoughts yet again. "How is he?" she questioned, rising and holding Teca's hand.

The three drifted into the cabin as the women talked.

~ * ~ * ~ * ~ * ~

Anpo could not stop the pang of fear and anger as her dream/vision returned to her.

Smiling fondly down at the childlike Anpo, the woman with yellow hair caressed her cheek. "Mahasanni," she repeated. She took the toddler's hand, and walked away.

The light intensified until it surrounded the mother and child, so bright Anpo had to hide her eyes. When she was able to see, there was nothing there.

The door closed and, though she could still hear her woman's voice inside, it was as if the dream became real.

Beside her, Stewart moved, gesturing toward the barn. It caught Anpo's attention, and she turned to look at him, her eyes distant yet piercing.

He shuddered. "Well, if you want, we can get your horses something to eat...." He waved at the barn once more.

Anpo considered his statement, her gaze drifting away from him to the building he pointed out. The smell of horse and cattle dung was strong from it, and she suspected that was where they kept their animals. *Just like themselves. Cramped into their lodges and away from the world.*

Stewart waved again, his eyebrows lifted in question. It was obvious he was not sure she understood his words. Relief colored his expression when Anpo took her pony's reins and moved toward the barn. With a sigh, Stewart scooped up the reins on the spotted mare and followed, the colt trotting to keep up with its mother.

Chapter Thirty-Five

It was full dark, and Anpo smoked her pipe as she sat on the ground near the porch. She soaked in the solitude, her soul needing the respite.

The day had been full of strain and discomfort. She had met her *tunkasi* when he returned from the fields. It seemed he liked her even less than Stewart and Rachel. She had endured as much of his rude stares as she could stomach, despite Kathleen explaining he should not watch her so intently. Anpo finally fled to the comfort of the darkness.

While normally Anpo as *wicakte* could traverse across the gender division of her people and converse with men, she found it very uncomfortable to do so with Kathleen's father. As in her family, Wanbli did not speak with the white woman. Her status as his daughter's woman put her out of his reach. Too often the close quarters of a *tiospaye* in winter camp produced illicit relationships between its members. The way of their people was a survival tactic that had developed over generations. Anpo wondered how much of her distaste was from McGlashan's relationship as her father-in-law, and how much was a reaction to his dislike for her.

The only natural light was the waning moon overhead. A warm glow came from the windows of the cabin where the sounds of talking and laughing were heard. Anpo took another puff of her tobacco, listening to her woman's laughter. *She is happy now. She is with her family.*

An irrational melancholy hit Anpo as other thoughts invaded. *She is ashamed of me. Her family is not mine; they hate me because of what I am.* Anpo grumbled irritation. *How can they hate me if they do not know me? I do not understand.*

Watching the tendrils of smoke rise from her beech wood pipe, her mind was far away. *Is that why Ketlin is ashamed of me, because of what I am?* That did not sound right, however, else she would have been shamed in Anpo's presence long before they arrived here. *Why is she ashamed of me here and not elsewhere?*

She recalled McGlashan intently questioning her about their relationship. When Anpo had told him they were joined, Kathleen dived into the conversation and deflected his queries elsewhere. *Being joined as a Lakota is the same as being married for Ketlin's people. Is she ashamed that we are joined? Why?* So many questions roiled about her thoughts, all of them aimed at Kathleen's strange behavior whenever mention of their bond came up. None of the questions were good ones, all casting shadows of doubt on what Anpo had always thought was firm and solid.

In an effort to distract herself from the melancholy, Anpo began to plan their return trip.

Going back through the hostile territory immediately surrounding them would be difficult, but not impossible. With careful forethought and planning, it would take less than a week to travel through the worst of it. The further away from the conflict they went, the less likely they would be attacked by other bands. Anpo fully expected to gain the assistance of the different peoples they met just as they had to arrive here.

The horses needed resting, and Kathleen needed to spend time with her family. Anpo decided they would remain for a hand span of days. Maybe the McGlashans would decide in her favor once they knew her well enough. Certainly when Kathleen told them of Anpo's status among her people, the two-spirited soul in her body, they would realize how lucky their daughter truly was to be Anpo's woman.

Their rude behavior came to mind, and Anpo attempted to avoid the doubt plaguing her. If Kathleen was ashamed of her here, could it be these people did not think *wicakte* and *winkte* were of high esteem? The mere thought brought a vague wave of nausea to Anpo's gut. These people had no manners, did not understand the simplest of things, and leapt to the warpath with little provocation. Why would they believe in the sacredness of a two-spirited person?

Again Anpo forced the thoughts from her mind. She mentally went over their supplies, wondering if Kathleen's family would supplement what they were missing. With everyone expecting an attack, she did not think she would be free to hunt for meat on her own. It would not do for her to be captured by the rampaging Indians in the area and made a slave. What would happen to Kathleen and Teca then? It could be years before Anpo could learn their ways, and become a member of their people, to become free.

No, it was best to take what Kathleen's family could offer. They had two horses and a number of domestic animals called cattle. By Lakota standards, McGlashan was quite rich indeed. Still, his wealth seemed coupled with stinginess. These whites did not share among their neighbors unless it was an emergency. That they survived together for as long as they had was startling. Among her people, Anpo knew she could give everything she owned away, yet still have food in her belly, moccasins on her feet, and a place to sleep warm. In fact, it was a point of honor to give away the best of what you had, to share with those less fortunate, and to prove your generosity to your people and the spirits.

Anpo inhaled deeply, catching a whiff of animal dung from the barn. She did not relish sleeping near the cabin, but expected Kathleen's desire to be near. For her woman, Anpo would stay in the clearing. Perhaps they could set their camp behind the cabin, where ropes hung between two trees. They would be upwind of the barn at any rate.

As she considered where to make camp, Anpo refilled her pipe from a pouch at her side. The gesture soothed her, reminded her of mellower times, sitting before the council fires, music, dancing, and feasting. Her family must be at summer camp by now, preparing for the Sun Dance and gossiping about the previous winter. She wondered how her father looked. Did his hair get grayer? Or did he look the same as when Anpo left? Her nephew must be walking now, and she saw the proud smile on Nupa's face in her mind's eye.

Her breath hitched with emotion. Anpo so missed her family. She wondered if Kathleen had felt the same when they had met. Was it as painful to be away from these people as it was for her to be away from her *tiospaye*?

The door to the cabin opened, and a stocky man was silhouetted in the firelight before he stepped onto the porch and shut it behind him.

Anpo braced herself as Kathleen's father stepped into the yard and sat down nearby on the chopping block.

"Nice night," he said, pulling out his pipe.

She knew she could not ignore him. *He's my* tunkasi! *A big belly!* But her culture forbade her to speak or look at him. Swallowing hard, she indicated she understood by gesturing with her head. Kathleen called it "nodding".

McGlashan eyeballed her as he loaded the bowl with tobacco. "Don't talk much, do you?" When no answer was forthcoming, he said, "No, don't answer that. I just like stating the obvious." He reached for the burning stick Anpo had used to light her pipe, pulling it from the ground and puffing contentedly.

They sat in awkward silence, smoke from their pipes mingling high above their heads. Oddly enough, Anpo found it relaxing, similar to many nights with her people. She slowly began to relax.

The man sighed explosively. "Look, lass, I don't like your kind," he said, pointing his pipe at her, his face showing annoyance. "Haven't since they killed my son-in-law and stole my daughter." He glanced back at the cabin, hearing Kathleen telling a story to his family. His face softened somewhat as he looked back at the woman seated half in the shadows. "But you brought her back to me, to us. And for that, I'm grateful."

Again, Anpo nodded. She understood that this was his way of thanking her. As difficult as she found him, she at least felt just as strongly as he for Kathleen. She would feel the same to anyone who returned her woman if she became captured.

"You let me know if you need anything before you leave in the morning," McGlashan said, tapping the pipe against his boot heel. "We ain't got much, but we can give you some kind of reward for bringing Kathleen home to us."

Anpo blinked, not comprehending his words.

Rising to his feet, the older man put his pipe away and peered out over his dooryard. "You can sleep in the barn tonight." No further words were spoken as he returned to the cabin and went inside.

Anpo frowned in puzzled thought. She replayed the short conversation in her mind several times, pulling out the bits and pieces and fitting them together. Anpo's eyes widened when the connections were made. *My* tunkasi *thinks I am leaving my* winuhca *here! That I brought her home to stay!*

She surged to her feet in surprise and denial. "He does not understand," she said aloud. "I must have Ketlin tell them we are joined, that she is my *winuhcala*." But the memory of meeting Stewart, of trying to explain to their parents, of Kathleen interrupting and changing the meanings of her words stopped Anpo.

Ketlin had no choice but to join with me, Anpo mused as she stepped silently onto the porch. *She had been captured and was a slave. I won her in a wager.* Anpo eased closer to the window and peered inside. *What if she does not want to be with me?*

Kathleen was telling her family about one of Teca's many inquisitive altercations. This one was about the time he found a basket of huckleberries and ended up inside, purple from head to toe. Her eyes sparkled in joy as she held her sleeping son, the lilt of her accent sounding like music to Anpo's ears.

She is so happy here, more happy than I have ever seen her. A lump developed in Anpo's throat. The vision reared its ugly head once again.

Smiling fondly down at the childlike Anpo, the woman with yellow hair caressed her cheek. "Mahasanni," she repeated. She took the toddler's hand and walked away.

The light intensified until it surrounded the mother and child, so bright she had to hide her eyes. When she was able to see, there was nothing there.

Inside the cabin, Kathleen wound up her story, obviously delighted at making her parents laugh. Anpo could not help but smile in response, feeling the joy flowing off her woman, glad despite her reservations that Kathleen had the opportunity to visit her family.

McGlashan, who had settled on a stool when he returned from speaking with Anpo, rose and stretched. "Well, I think it's high time to be off to bed," he said.

Rachel put her project to one side. Anpo wondered what it was, seeing the firelight glint of two sharp sticks and piece of cloth. "Aye." Rachel stood. "Kathleen, you and Teca can have your old bed in the loft. Do you need help getting him up the ladder?"

Kathleen turned her head to look at a strange contraption against one wall. Her smile was soft with memory. "No, Mum. I can make it blind with my hands tied. Teca won't make a difference."

When she looked out the window into the night, Anpo ducked out of view. Leaning against the rough wood of the cabin, she wondered why. Confused, she kept her ears fastened on the conversation inside.

"Where's Anpo?"

McGlashan said, "Told her she could sleep in the barn tonight."

"It's good to have you home, Kathleen," Rachel said. "Good night."

"It's good to be home, Mum. I've missed you all so much."

Ketlin is home. Her home is not with me. Anpo turned away from the window and trudged back out to the yard, her shoulders sagging. *When she comes to sleep, I will speak with her on this matter.*

Chapter Thirty-Six

Stewart waited until he was on the porch to put on his boots, not wanting to rouse the rest of the family from slumber. False dawn crept across the sky, as he slipped his feet into the cold leather, stomping into the yard as he settled into them. Regardless of the early hour, he could not sleep, the excitement of having his sister home coupled with the unusual sounds of someone sleeping in the loft nearby. It had been far too long since he had had to share the space; five years or more since Kathleen had married and left for Stevens' homestead.

He stretched with an audible groan and hiked his suspenders over his shoulders before heading toward the barn. *Da said the night before he had told that Indian to sleep there.* He wondered if she had or if she bunked down elsewhere. Besides, Stewart was eager to get a closer look at those so-called ponies.

As he walked, he considered his sister's odd behavior whenever the subject of Anpo came up. He had heard her words, plain as day, when the native said they were joined. He would be damned if he knew what that meant, but whatever it was could not be good. Kathleen blushed furiously and changed the subject to something else. Stewart kind of felt sorry for the Indian, though. She seemed to be put out by his sister's tactics.

Wonder what that means, though? Partner? Maybe it just meant they lived together to raise the boy. Or how about adopted? Now there was a thought, Kathleen adopted into an Indian family and all. And who was the father of Teca, anyway, some member of Anpo's tribe? He discounted that thought almost as soon as it surfaced. The woman dressed in no recognizable style; she obviously came from far away.

The barn door stood slightly ajar, and Stewart pulled it further open. *Just like a heathen,* he mused. *Not even enough sense to close the damned door.* He shook the uncharitable thought from his mind. It was not Anpo's fault she was an Indian, just an accident of birth. Besides, she had Kathleen's friendship, so she could not be all bad.

The interior was murky, and he stood still to allow his eyes to adjust. Soon, he made out the stalls where the horses stayed, and he eased closer. Somewhere in here was Anpo, and he did not want to scare her into something rash.

His fears were baseless, however, when he saw her watching him from the last stall. Her horse was saddled with one of those uncomfortable looking contraptions, her belongings tied in place. As his sight grew better, he realized she looked ragged. *Doesn't look like she's slept at all.*

"Where is Ketlin?"

It took a moment before he recognized his sister's name. "She's still asleep," he said, wondering at the hoarseness of her voice. If he did not know better, it appeared Anpo had had a difficult night. Her eyes were reddened, her face looking gaunt and drawn. "Want me to wake her?"

"*Hiya.*" She made a sharp gesture with her thumb and turned away.

Deciding her response was negative, Stewart leaned against one of the stalls and watched. Her movements were rigid, hard edged. He had no experience with her people, but he could almost swear the Indian was close to tears. Scoffing to himself, he put that thought out of his mind. From what he had heard over the years, these people did not cry or mourn, at least not in a way he was familiar with.

She bundled up a fur, lashing it tight to her saddle. Then she backed the horse out of the stall, leading it toward the door.

Stewart frowned and followed. "You going for a ride?" he asked. He would have thought she would stay around longer, at least to say good-bye to Kathleen.

"I am going back to my people."

Not for the first time, he considered that these people were bizarre. *Didn't they have emotions like everybody else?* Stewart could tell that Kathleen thought highly of Anpo; it was evident every time she looked at the native the day before. He had assumed Anpo felt the same way. *If she did, she sure had a funny way of showing it, though.*

They came out of the barn together. Stewart saw the yard clearly, the sky beginning to turn pink with dawn. Without further discussion, Anpo mounted her animal, pausing to stare at the cabin.

"Are you sure you don't need anything? I know Da wouldn't mind giving you supplies for your trip."

"You have nothing I need."

The voice was icy, and Stewart felt a wave of anger. *Ungrateful animal,* he thought. "Then maybe you have a message for Kathleen?" he asked, his voice echoing Anpo's. He must have hit a nerve because she froze, hardly breathing, and her dark skin paled. Shocked, he wondered if she was going to faint.

"Tell her—" Anpo's voice broke.

Stewart stared at the emotion running just beneath the stoic surface. *Good heavens, she's really torn up about leaving.* He urged himself to step forward, to offer consolation to this stranger who had helped his sister survive the wild frontier.

Before he could act, Anpo regained control of herself. She dug into a pouch attached to her saddle, pulling out a tin whistle. The instrument had been decorated with leather and feathers. She held it out to Stewart.

He stepped forward, reaching for the toy, barely catching it as it tumbled from Anpo's hand.

"Tell her she is happier here. Her home is not with me. Tell her I throw her away," she said, jaw clenching.

Before Stewart could get her to clarify her statement, she wheeled her horse and rode away from the cabin.

"Throw her away?" he questioned the empty dooryard. "What the hell does that mean?" A horse nickered in the barn, and he shook his head. He would ask Kathleen when she woke. For now, he pocketed the whistle and returned to the animals, remembering his desire to get a closer look at them.

~ * ~ * ~ * ~ * ~

Kathleen rose early, as was her habit. The sky was lightening, barely visible through the cracks of the shutters that covered the window. With slow, gentle movements, she eased away from Teca and covered him with the blanket.

It had been a long and exhausting night. The combination of a stuffy interior, a strange bed, and nightmares had made it difficult to sleep. That Anpo was not with her certainly had not helped matters any. *It was only the one night, lass,* she consoled herself as she slipped her leather dress over her head.

Deciding the child would remain asleep a while, she made her way to the top of the ladder. Peering past the hastily created divider – a sheet hanging from a rope – she found Stewart's bed unoccupied. *Must be already up and about then.* Kathleen quietly made her way down the rungs.

Kathleen stepped out onto the porch, slowly closing the heavy wooden door so as not to disturb her parents sleeping nearby. Inhaling the cool morning air, she stretched before relaxing to look about.

The sky was lighter, turning from gray to blue, and the colors of the yard began to coalesce. She heard a chicken clucking nearby and the stamp of a horse echoing from the barn. Kathleen wondered if Anpo was awake yet and stepped off the porch. *Hmmm...time for a cuddle, lass.*

A flash of Anpo's confused face drifted across her vision before she banished it. *Aye. You've got to explain what happened yesterday!* She shook her head ruefully. *Why did it not occur to me that I'd have to clarify Anpo's presence with my family? I was too excited to get here, I suppose. And I certainly wasn't thinking too well last night.*

With memories of the reunion playing in her mind, Kathleen approached the barn, a small smile on her face. The door was ajar, and she slid inside without disturbing it. The warmth drifted over her as she stood still for a moment, allowing her eyes to adjust to the darker interior.

One of the ponies nickered, and she moved towards it, the smile still on her face as she recognized her mount. Movement in the stall further on caught her eye as she held her hand out to the spotted mare, getting a welcome nuzzle in response.

"Stewart?"

A blond head popped up from the other side of Teca's pony. "Morning, sis!" her brother said.

Kathleen continued forward, a curious grin on her face. "What are you doing in there?"

As her sibling came into full view, he shrugged sheepishly and stepped forward to lean against the wooden railing. Stewart held up his hands, both adorned with brushes. "Just thought I'd have a look at your horses. They're pretty dirty," he added, turning to look back at the yearling. "Don't those people know how to take care of them?"

Not liking his tone about "those people", Kathleen's smile faltered. "It's a completely different way of life, Stew. The horses get quite a bit of attention." She shrugged as well. "And the Lakota don't have horse brushes."

"Nor shoes, by the looks of it," Stewart agreed, heedless of the cultural lesson. He reached out and patted the gray on his neck. "Got to admit, though, this fellow's a pretty healthy one. How long you had him?"

Kathleen looked away, distracted. "Just over a year. Anpo caught him for Teca." Scanning the barn, she asked, "Where is she? I don't see her pony."

"Pony!" Stewart exclaimed, turning around again. "That red bugger was huge! Hardly a 'pony'!"

Kathleen rolled her eyes. "You know what I mean, brat." Her eyes searching the interior again, she continued, "No, really...where's Anpo?"

Stewart turned back to the grey yearling. "Already left."

She felt the world fall out from under her and caught the stall to remain on her feet. "Wh—what?"

Unaware of his sister's anxiety, Stewart's attention remained on the horse. "She was all packed up when I got in here." Taking the brushes, he began to vigorously move them across the gray hide. "I offered some supplies, but she turned me down. Honestly, sis, after she left I had a look around. I don't think she slept last night. At least she didn't look it this morning. She gave me something for you, though."

She left me? Kathleen shook her head, trying to rid it of the numbness that threatened her vision. *She left me!* "Did she...did she say anything?" she asked, surprised her voice didn't crack.

"Aye, she did." Her brother turned to look at her, his face becoming concerned. He hastily dropped the brushes and moved forward. "Kath? You okay? You look like you've seen a ghost!"

With surprising strength, Kathleen grabbed Stewart by the arm. "What did she say to you? *Exactly!*"

Stewart winced as fingers dug into the skin of his forearm. "Something about you being happier here, and your home wasn't with her. She said she was throwing you away, but I took that to be her ignorance and not knowing the right words." His eyes widened as he watched his sister turn even whiter. "Sis?"

Kathleen's fingers released his arm, and she turned to stumble towards the door. She barely made it outside before she fell to her hands and knees. Strong arms held her shoulder and she could hear her brother's voice from a distance. His words were indistinct, drowned out by her thoughts.

She threw me away! Divorced me! She thinks I want to stay here! Oh my God! I should have come to her last night! I should have talked with her, slept with her, held her! How could she do this?

Curling into a little ball, Kathleen felt as if her head and chest and throat were going to explode. Great braying sobs racked her body, and she trembled with their force. Something metallic was pressed into her hands, and she found the tin whistle with its braided leather decorations.

Miles away and heading north, a reddish horse galloped at full speed, its rider barely keeping attention on the terrain. The rider wept for the loss of a loved one, a heart closed away from the pain. Anpo was too far away to hear her *winuhca's* scream, too far away to feel its power.

"*NO!*"

Part 11: Mikiyela Ksto
She is Near Me

Chapter Thirty-Seven

1782

Kathleen's sleep was shattered by a quiet whimper. As she floundered awake, she heard the grumblings of her brother nearby. Instinctively, she reached for Teca as he cried again.

With practiced movements, she pulled the rigid little body into her arms and began rocking and singing in an effort to dispel the nightmare. The child fought her off, his sobs fading to quiet gasps as he whispered in Lakota.

"*Hiya*! *Hiya*, go away!" Teca battled his imaginary attacker, scoring a fist to his mother's temple before she could pin his arms.

Kathleen did not quite see stars, and it amazed her again how strong her son was. She continued to rock and sing, holding him as still as she was able while he cried.

Teca had been raised to keep silent, to not give away the village's position with loud shouts or cries. Kathleen had no doubt that had he been raised in the white world, he would be screaming at the top of his lungs. Regardless of the lack of decibels, however, he still managed to wake others in the cabin. Stewart tweaked the divider in the loft to one side and eyeballed the pair, his face haggard. "What's he saying?" he grumbled. He received a glare in response and held up his hands in surrender. "Alright! I won't interrupt you at work!" He pulled the sheet back into place.

More sounds of movement below alerted Kathleen to her mother's presence, and the ladder creaked.

A grey-blonde head poked over the edge of the floor. "I'll set the water to heating," she informed her daughter with a weary voice.

Kathleen only nodded, not breaking in her ministrations to her son. As her mother disappeared back downstairs, she peered into Teca's face.

His eyes were wide with fear, seeing things no one else could see. It had been this way all winter, these nightmares that rousted him and all in the house to wakefulness. It would take several minutes for the boy to wake, despite his activities and crying, and he never remembered what it was that he dreamed.

Soon, Teca no longer fought her, curled up into a fetal ball in her arms to sob uncontrollably. Kathleen continued to speak in his native tongue, telling him a story of the creation of the world. Her voice soothed him, eased him, and the crying eventually drifted off.

When there were no more sounds but the hitching of his breath, she adjusted her hold on Teca, cradling him. She peered down into sleepy red eyes. "*Cinksi?* Are you well?"

Having some difficulty focusing, he nodded and hugged his mother's neck. "Tired, *ina*," he mumbled.

With a relieved sigh at another crisis averted, Kathleen laid her son down in her bed. She kissed his forehead and tucked him in as he reached for the rag doll he now slept with, cuddling it to his small chest. She continued to hum an Irish tune, caressing his soft hair until he fell back to sleep.

Kathleen sighed again and closed her eyes. The thought of climbing back into the warm bed and returning to sleep was very tempting. She heard her mother puttering around downstairs, however, and she forced her eyes open. *Now's not the time, lass.*

She pushed herself up and grabbed her robe, pulling it about her. With regret she eyed the bed as she walked to the ladder and eased her way down.

"Good luck, sis," Stewart whispered just before her head dropped below the loft floor.

A quick glance to the right, and she saw her brother wink and smile encouragingly. She smiled thanks as she continued on.

The coals had been stirred back into flame, the only light in the cabin. In the murky shadows, Kathleen saw her father facing the wall in his bed, pillow held firmly over his head. *Sorry again, Da.*

Her mother finished putting tea into two cups on the table. She waved her daughter to a bench and retrieved the kettle before it could boil over and douse the flames. Rachel poured the hot liquid into the cups, the tea leaves swirling about with the steam.

Kathleen sat, her profile to the fire. She idly peered into the cup pushed in her direction. *Gypsies can see my fortune in tealeaves,* she mused. *I wonder what kind of bad luck they'd see tonight.*

"Don't let it worry you none, lass," Rachel spoke in a low voice. "'Tis the curse of the O'Neill's and that's a fact. The lad will get over it in time."

"Curse?" Kathleen looked up from her cup, concerned. "I've not heard of a curse before, Mum."

Rachel shrugged. "You're the first born, Kath. You had the night terrors as a child, too, though you don't remember. As did I and your granny's brother, Malcolm." Rachel lifted her cup to blow on the tea.

"The boy will outgrow it in a year or so."

Irritable, Kathleen shook her head. "He has a name, Mum."

"A heathen name," her mother murmured before taking a sip.

Kathleen rolled her eyes and looked away, pushing the cup to one side. Silence filled the room, tension ringing in the air as the tired argument was met once again.

Rachel set the cup down, her face one of concern. "Why don't you give the boy a Christian name?" she asked for the hundredth time. "And stop letting him speak that gibberish?"

"That 'gibberish' is Lakota and it's Teca's language," Kathleen responded, her voice low and hard. Before her mother could speak, she held up her hand. "I know, I know! He's Irish, too. But that's neither here nor there. He knows English, as well."

The older woman sighed explosively, her mouth pursed in disapproval. "Aye, but there's no one here that speaks Lakota, lass. In case you haven't noticed," she said, her tone sarcastic.

Kathleen's heart ached at the dig, but she refused to allow her mother to see the damage. "I speak Lakota, Mum. And someday, Teca will want to know about his people. I *will* keep that alive for him."

Another silence drifted over the table. Finally, Rachel reached out and took her daughter's hand. "Kathleen," she said, her voice soft with caring. "I love you. And I love the boy. But he'll not fit in at this rate." She waved her hand vaguely. "At weddings and barn raisings and such, he'll be a stranger to the rest of his people."

It was Kathleen's turn to sigh. "I understand your concern, Mum. But, I will not change my mind on the matter." She squeezed her mother's hand. "I don't know how to explain it to you. I don't feel that Teca's meant to be here."

"That woman won't be back to get him, if that's what you mean," Rachel snapped, pulling her hand away. She missed the look of pain that flashed across her daughter's face.

"Aye," Kathleen whispered. Her voice firmed as she continued. "But I expect Teca will want to know of his people, of his *inanup*. I'll not keep that from him. They are good people."

Shaking her head in disapproval, Rachel looked sidelong at her eldest child. "Do you know what the Widow Smythe has to say about it?"

Burning with anger, Kathleen's eyes flashed. "No, Mum. And I don't care to know. I've told you before, I'll not marry again. Least of all, the Widow Smythe." Kathleen pushed away from the table, her cup still sitting full. "I'm to bed. It's late."

She was halfway up the ladder when she heard her name called. Looking over her shoulder, she saw her mother. *Sweet Jesus, she's getting old!*

"I love you, Kath. You know that?"

Kathleen ducked her head a moment before peering down at her mother once again. "Aye, Mum. I know. You want what's best for me and mine, just as I want what's best for Teca."

Rachel awkwardly nodded, not liking the comparison but accepting it nonetheless.

"Good night, Mum."

"Good night, Kath."

~ * ~ * ~ * ~ * ~

Nupa sat in silence as he watched the proceedings across the fire. It had warmed considerably in the last moon, and Wagna's people prepared to leave winter camp in the next few days. Nupa was worried more about the woman across from him.

His woman, Hca, spoke in calming murmurs to her sister, brushing unruly mahogany hair.

When Anpo's pony had stumbled into camp the previous moon, everyone had been surprised. To travel alone through the winter was unthinkable, stuff of which only legends were made. The *wicakte's* health had reflected the hardships she had put herself through – her clothes more rags than not, hair filthy and matted, cheeks gaunt from lack of food.

No one knew how Anpo had found winter camp. No one knew what had happened to Kathleen and Teca. She would not speak. Her tongue had frozen in her mouth – no amount of gentle questioning or prodding brought an answer.

She is only half a person, came Nupa's stormy thought.

The people spoke of the white woman and her child being dead, and that Anpo was in mourning. But her hair was still long, her arms showing no signs of the cuts she would have inflicted upon herself in her lamentation. There was some confusion because of this – only *winyan* did these things in mourning, *wicasa* did not. Anpo was an enigma in that area, being neither wholly female nor male. If something had happened to her family, in what manner would she respond?

When she had first awakened in her mother's lodge, she had immediately staggered out of her sleeping robes and stepped outside, robes in hand. Her feet took her to where Kathleen's *ti ikceya* would have been, and she curled up on the cold, hard ground. Since that time, the women of her *tiospaye* had set the lodge as if Kathleen was still present, and Anpo resided there.

The shaman, Inyan, had spent time with her and proclaimed her own evil spirits haunted her. With food and love she would eventually fight through and return to them. All his visions attested to this.

And so, Nupa and his family spent their nights more often than not at Kathleen's *ti ikceya*, taking care of Anpo. The regular feeding had done her much good; Anpo's skin no longer hung on her bones. Her sisters and mothers repaired or replaced her clothing, and kept her clean and warm. Wanbli and Nupa sat with her in silence, emanating a quiet support.

Nupa stared into the flames. His woman's voice sang a low song to Yus'as'a, the baby asleep in her arms. Anpo's gaze was also on the dancing fire, her hair now neatly braided.

Movement caught his attention, and he looked up from the fire at his *tanksi*. He watched as she pulled the rawhide ties from her hair. Long fingers raked through it, freeing her tresses from the braids as she always did.

A thought came to Nupa's mind, and he blinked in recognition. A warrior who wore his hair loose only meant one thing. "You are willing to do desperate things, *tanksi*," he said, his voice low.

Hca's voice faded as she looked up at them, a puzzled expression on her face. She let out a soft gasp as her *mitan* slowly gestured yes.

His heart in his throat at the first response Anpo had given since her return, Nupa leaned closer. His friend's gaze was still on the flames, but he could see them shining and tiny muscles in her face twitched as she tried to keep control. "Why?" he whispered.

There was a long silence, as there always was with Anpo. Nupa almost gave up, preparing to straighten and continue his worrying. A sound stopped him.

With a voice that had not been used in months, Anpo croaked, "*Mahasanni*."

Frozen, Hca and Nupa stared blankly at each other. Neither wanted to move or speak, to disrupt this first contact with the emotionally wounded *wicakte*. Anpo said nothing further so Nupa took a bracing breath.

"Why is she not with you?"

Another long quiet that left Nupa thinking she would not answer.

"*Winuhcala* is ashamed of me."

Nupa's brow furrowed, his mouth pulling down in a frown. Searching his mind for something to say, he finally spoke. "I do not understand, *tanksi*. Ketlin has always been proud of you. You are a great leader to your people, a voice of reason and wisdom."

The tears finally spilled over and ran down Anpo's face, twin streaks of light reflecting from the fire. "*Hiya*, she is not proud of me," she said, her voice strengthening with conviction. "She is ashamed."

Unable to simply watch, Hca settled the baby down on some nearby furs and scooted closer, draping an arm about her sister's shoulder, her hand rubbing Anpo's upper arm. "Why do you say this, *mitankala?*" she prodded gently.

"She would not speak to me, would not explain to her *ate* and *ina* that we were joined." Anpo's tears increased their pace. "Her *ate* thought I only brought her home to them. That we were not just visiting."

Hca's eyes narrowed at Kathleen's strange behavior. "That makes no sense, Anpo," she murmured.

With a forlorn shrug, Anpo dropped her head. "I was left to sleep with the animals. She did not even come to speak to me, to sleep with me. I was not welcome in her parents' lodge."

"What happened to Ketlin and Teca, *tanksi?*" Nupa asked, his gaze intense on his friend.

A sob could be heard from the mass of dark hair hanging down across her face. "Ketlin said she was happy to be home." The head shook. "She would not come to me. I threw her away," came the whisper.

As more sobs racked Anpo's body, her sister cuddled her close, letting Anpo cry onto her shoulder as a small child.

Nupa knew Anpo needed more than a friend to help through the raging emotions. "I will get your mother," Nupa said to Hca, rising to his feet. At her nod, he left the fire, striding toward Gi's lodge.

How could Ketlin do this to her? the angry thought repeated in his head.

Chapter Thirty-Eight

The Crow horse thieves were put down, the stolen ponies returned, and the warriors victorious against a vicious foe. Anpo killed two of the enemy herself, shining through the battle with furious skill. The celebratory feast was in full swing as night fell. The council fire burned high, and the *wicasa* danced about it, dressed in their finest clothing and war paint as they reenacted their deeds of the day.

Despite the noise of drums, flutes, singing, and whooping, a bubble of stillness surrounded Anpo. She sat with her family and friends, smiling pleasantly and responding to their comments. She did not participate in the celebration, instead floating along as a spectator.

It had been many moons since her return home. Now, the air was heavy with late summer, hot and dry in defiance of the evening breeze. Summer camp and the Sun Dance ceremony had come and gone. In that time, Anpo had basked in the love of her family, regaining her emotional equilibrium. She never laughed and rarely spoke first.

And she never danced.

An *akicita* roamed the fire, a carved stick and a crooked staff in hand. He was the leader of the dance, his staff showing his high rank among one of the warrior societies. As one warrior finished dancing, he threw the stick to another, inviting the man to jump into the circle, tell his story. All tales of daring had to be witnessed by another, and invariably, a second person would join the dance as witness and counterpoint to the spectacular events unfolding before the people. The women trilled approval, clapping and shuffling to the sound of the drums while the men whooped and yipped acceptance of the daring feats.

Retrieving the carved stick from the latest dancer, the *akicita* threw it into the dirt before Anpo. A hush fell over the crowd, as everyone wondered what she would do. To pick up the stick would be to acknowledge its demand. Word of Anpo's bravery had already spread among the people, as witnesses danced their view of her victory. She had single handedly ridden down to of the enemy, clubbing one and breaking the other's neck with her bare hands.

Anpo ignored the stick.

The people stared at her, the tension rising as she refused an order from the *akicita*. Obviously, he was displeased with her behavior as he stomped back and forth in front of her. He was well within his rights to punish her for disobedience. The *akicita's* word was law; to ignore his demands courted disapproval of the people, something no one could afford in such a communal culture.

She showed no indication anything was wrong, regardless of the stick before her. Anpo continued to watch the fire, not even deigning to meet the *akicita's* gaze with her own.

A young man whooped, interrupting the tableau. He wore a mask over his face as he leapt into the cleared area. The lower half of it was painted white, two red and yellow thunder bolts drawn beneath. Everyone knew his mask imitated Anpo's war design. He swooped forward and grabbed up the stick, turning to dance about the fire, his hair free flowing. Two "died" under his knife and the surrounding spectators cheered, their eyes drawn to whom the dance represented.

Angered, the *akicita* could do nothing about this upstart standing in for Anpo. He shook his staff at her once before stomping around to the other side of the fire. Oblivious, Anpo accepted the praise from her people with grace, a slight smile on her face. Not many noticed that it didn't quite reach her eyes. No one knew how heavy her heart was. *I still live.*

When the masked dancer finished, two others joined to witness Anpo's acts of bravery. The *akicita* remained unhappy, but apparently decided to leave the situation as it was. Everyone knew Anpo did not dance, had not since her return from her trip to the rising sun. Before the leader tossed the stick to another, Wanbli stepped into the circle of light.

Excitedly, the people quieted to hear his words. It was not often that the big belly interrupted the celebration. Surely his presence marked something of importance, and his timing indicated it had everything to do with his *wicakte* daughter.

"In honor of Anpo's kills, I give away three of my best ponies," he said. He threw three small sticks into the crowd, promissory notes to those fortunate enough to catch them. A cheer rose from the people, pleased with his obvious pride in his daughter's performance. "I honor my child, but she is no more a youth. She has grown into a fine hunter and warrior for her people, fierce and proud and strong. I give her a new name. She is no longer Wi Ile Anpo. She is now Psatoka Ktepi, Kills Crow Enemy."

It was not often a naming occurred, and the people showed their approval of the new title. In the uproar, Anpo rose to her feet, her face grave. She held her hands up, asking the celebrants for their attention, eventually receiving it as they quieted down to hear her words of acceptance.

"My name is Wi Ile Anpo. I will use no other for my entire life." Her expression was grave as she looked at her father. "I am honored, Wanbli, but my vision holds my spirit. I cannot release the vision from my heart." Around them, the crowd murmured among themselves in wonder. To refuse a name was a rare thing. Perhaps the *wicakte's* vision was too strong for ordinary people. Perhaps she needed to keep her name in order to control its power.

Her father studied her. Finally, he gestured acceptance and turned to the audience. "I still honor my daughter's bravery with three of my best ponies."

The people whooped and hollered, the three lucky individuals proudly holding the slips of wood to be used in the future. Waving his staff, the *akicita* ordered the music to begin anew and threw his dancing stick to another warrior.

Eventually, it became late and the elders drifted away into the darkness. Young mothers took their children away to sleep. As soon as it was polite to do so, Anpo left as well.

She did not know where she was going. Her only goal was to remain away from the *ti ikceya* for as long as possible. She let her moccasins guide her, following a game trail once she was away from the encampment. Anpo ended up on a small hill near a tree. Here, she settled down to watch the camp, long fingers idly shredding twigs.

The memory of another tree, another vigil came to mind and she could not help but allow a sad smile cross her face. After sitting there all day on her maiden's vision quest, she had had nothing to show for it. *I was so determined to have a vision. Nothing else would do.* The smile faded, and her face relaxed into its now normal distracted frown. *My vision was my curse. I should never have demanded one.*

Anpo watched as the merriment at the council fire continued, a slightly wistful glow to her expression. As usual, her thoughts rambled over the same well-worn path, the one that took her where she did not want to go.

Would things be different if I did not have the vision, if I did not kill tatanka ska? Her *ate's* voice filled her head. *"Be still in your heart, cunksi. Do not worry the vision so. The vision will not change and will only make you crazy with grief and fear."*

"*Ohan.* I am crazy with grief and fear," she whispered aloud, her voice harsh in the quiet.

Her father had been wrong. The vision had changed, her *cinksi* becoming entangled in her dreams as he held his mother's hand. Now it had changed again, never giving her peace.

The woman wore the dress of her people, green gingham, her hair long and hanging free. A man had his arm about her waist, grinning at Anpo as she knelt in the dirt. It was a white stranger, leering and possessive of the blonde, his meaty hands holding her close.

"Mahasanni," Anpo croaked, her voice ragged. She raised a bloody hand in supplication, a sharp pain lancing her side from where she had speared tatanka ska.

The woman either did not hear or ignored the cry. She turned away, walking into the brilliant light on the arm of the man with her, a sweet smile on her face.

Teca was nowhere to be seen.

Anpo shook her head to clear the vision. With weary eyes, she looked up at the moon. "Take this vision from me." Silence was her only answer, and she sighed heavily, bowing her neck and staring into her hands as another twig was shredded. "Please..."

~ * ~ * ~ * ~ * ~

It was dark, the breeze coming off the nearby creek cooling the oppressive heat of summer. Kathleen lay on her back, staring up at the moon as she finished her tale. Nearby, Stewart sat with his long legs crossed at the ankles, leaning back on his hands. The boy had his head pillowed on Kathleen's stomach, his eyes closed and his breathing even. The three had fled the cabin after a fine Sunday supper, preferring to be away from their elders and the heated interior.

Kathleen gently brushed long dark hair from her son's forehead, her other hand supporting her head. *He's grown so big!* she marveled. A melancholy washed over her. *I wish Anpo could see him. She would be so proud!*

"What does that word mean?" Stewart asked. "*Inyan?*"

Distracted from her thoughts, she craned her neck to peer over at her brother. She could barely see him in the dark. "It means 'stone'."

Puzzlement crossed his face. "Isn't that the same word you use when you tell about the creation of the world?"

Kathleen was pleased her sibling had made the connection. "Aye, it is." She relaxed to look back up at the lunar orb hanging far away. "*Inyan* didn't used to be like it is, brittle and hard. It was the first and began creation by draining its blood to create *Maka.*"

"Earth," Stewart supplied.

"Aye, the Earth. And, as more things were needed for *Maka, Inyan* continued to drain its blood, losing its energy along the way." Kathleen inhaled deeply of the cool air. "When everything had been made, *Inyan* was scattered all over the world."

A comfortable silence fell between them. Teca mumbled and rolled over, tucking a hand beneath his chin. His breathing deepened as he slipped into the land of dreams. Kathleen continued to gently caress his temple, brushing the hair away from his face. Her brother sat forward and pulled out a pipe and tobacco.

The months had been long, longer than Kathleen could ever remember them being. Never a day went by that she did not think of Anpo. Her initial feelings of abandonment and anger had given way to a deep sorrow that would not let go. She felt so hollow some days that it hardly seemed worth getting out of bed. Only Teca kept her going. His welfare and well-being was above all other considerations.

I'd have been dead long ago without him.

To pass the time, Kathleen resumed old chores within the household, helping her mother with the work. She also spent quite a deal of time trying to change Stewart's mind about the "heathens". She had even gotten him to begin speaking Lakota — but only when he was not around their parents. There was plenty enough stress regarding that little foible already.

There had been three suitors her parents paraded before her. Kathleen had scorned them all, much to her mother's distress and fury. *"You've got to have a husband, Kathleen Sarah McGlashan!" Rachel exclaimed.*

"Why won't you remarry, Kath?" came the soft question from the dark.

Kathleen closed her eyes against the sudden lump in her throat. "I've told you before, Stew. I belong to another."

He puffed his pipe in thought. "Aye. That you've said. But you haven't told me who. Or why you're here instead of with him." They listened to the crickets singing in the coolness. "It's eating you up inside, lass! You've got to know that you can talk to me about anything."

Inhaling deeply, Kathleen's breath hitching in her chest as she fought off tears. "I know, Stew," she whispered, barely audible. Her mind was awhirl with thoughts, her heart heavy with emotion.

Stewart scooted closer, peering down at his sister, his pipe forgotten in one hand. "And don't think you can distract me from the subject again," he informed her in all seriousness. "I'll not be chased away this night."

Kathleen did not know if she should laugh at his tenacity or cry. She opted for neither, preferring to worry her lower lip. *You've got to tell someone, lass. The question is what will the brat think of you now? Falling in love with a woman, for pity's sake. Marrying her...* She closed her eyes, smelling Anpo in the night breeze, feeling warm skin against hers, holding her, protecting her. *God, I miss her so much!*

"Kath?"

Opening her eyes, Kathleen looked up at her brother silhouetted against the moon. She studied him closely, not knowing what she was looking for, nor if she found it.

Stewart's voice lowered. "Sis? It'll be okay, I swear it." The pain and concern for her was evident as he reached out a hand to brush his knuckles against her temple.

Despite herself, a sob welled up from Kathleen's throat at the touch. She sat up, gently easing Teca's head into her lap as she fought with the tears. Her back was now to Stewart and she felt his hand on her shoulder.

"I love you, you know," he murmured. "I want to see you happy, Kathleen. And you're not happy here. Tell me?"

"You've already met who has my heart."

Stewart's hand continued to rub his sister's shoulder as he turned that around in his head.

When the hand on her shoulder froze, so did Kathleen's heart. *He knows. He understands now.*

"That Indian you came with...Anpo?" Stewart asked, confusion in his tone.

She could only nod, the struggle with her tears capturing her voice.

"B-but...Anpo's a woman, Kath. You can't belong to her. Not like that."

Kathleen pulled away from his hand, glaring at him over her shoulder. "I *do* belong to her!" Kathleen insisted. "She might have thrown me away, but she owns my heart and soul." *She threw me away!* The thought echoed in her head, and she turned back around as tears began to course down her face. *I was so stupid!*

Stewart discarded his pipe and scooted closer, pulling the crying woman into his arms. "Shh," he murmured as she relaxed into his embrace, babbling.

"I was so stupid that night, Stew. I should never have left her alone, left her to sleep in the barn. I should have told you and Mum and Da about what she meant to me from the beginning. Anpo tried, I know, but I kept interrupting and changing the subject. I didn't know what to say, what to do." Kathleen finally buried her face in his chest as she wept. "She thinks I don't love her. I can never forgive myself."

The crying went on for some time, though Kathleen's sobs were quiet. It was no different than most of her lonely nights in bed, crying once everyone else had gone to sleep. Her brother's embrace seemed to help, nonetheless, and she felt a lessening of her burden.

"*Ina?*" Teca whispered, his hand reaching up to touch his mother's cheek. "Do not cry. *Inanup* loves you. And she loves me, too."

This only served to strengthen Kathleen's tears. She gathered her son into her arms, and the three of them cuddled together to support her maelstrom of emotion.

Chapter Thirty-Nine

1783

She approached the figure huddled on the hillside, pulling her shawl closer with aching fingers. It was inadequate protection against the icy tendrils of wind that whipped about her, freezing her very soul as it howled. Coldness also gripped her heart as she neared the familiar figure. The warrior's back was to her, a thin robe ruffling loosely as the wind teased its edges.

"Mahasanni?" she breathed.

There was no answer. With hesitant hand, she reached out to touch the warrior's shoulder, to urge her awake, to make some sort of contact.

The warrior was ice.

Unable to pull away, to flee what she knew she would find, she shook the warrior. With absurd slowness, the warrior toppled backwards into the snow. The naturally dark skin was pale and gray, the eyes open and unseeing with a thin layer of frost covering the lenses.

Feeling as if she had been punched in the stomach, she stumbled back a step, gasping for air. Her lungs ached from the winter cold, and she whirled to run away.

Below her she saw a small hollow full of Lakota lodges, many of them familiar. There were no warm fires, no sign of movement, not even the nicker of ponies. Frozen bodies lay everywhere in the camp.

"Anpo!" Kathleen gasped as she sat up, wildly searching the loft for the scene she had just left. Darkness met her gaze, a claustrophobic sensation washing over her. Heart thumping madly, she tossed off her blankets and fled down the ladder.

Standing outside on the porch, Kathleen gulped the cold air of early spring. She shivered with fear and cold, her breath drifting away in clouds of steam, her feet bare upon the rough wooden planks. Teeth chattering, Kathleen wrapped her arms about herself as she stared out over the yard.

The nightmare rolled around in her head, not letting her go as it worried her soul with sharp teeth. She could still feel the snow on her face, feel the wind whipping at her clothing, and smell the faint odor of musty decay. Never had a nightmare been so real. Questions whisked in and out between the scenes and emotions that played on, adding to her mental agitation.

Was that a vision? And if it was, what does it mean?

Kathleen took a shaky breath and stepped from the porch. Her feet hardly flinched from the icy ground as she made her way to the barn. Soon, she was inside, the warmth of the animals causing her to shiver even more. She neared the stall where her pony stayed, hearing the soft mumble of welcome and feeling a nose nuzzle her hair. With relief, she hugged the spotted mare's neck and buried her face in the long mane.

If it is a vision...has it already happened? Or is it the future? The sight of Anpo dead and frozen in the snow caused a sob to well in her throat. In silence, Kathleen wept her fear and worry onto the animal.

Is it possible to change a vision?

~ * ~ * ~ * ~ * ~

Stewart milked the cow while his sister collected eggs. Teca visited with his pony nearby, perched on the stall divider, and explaining in patient Lakota how they would ride like the wind this year.

Kathleen heard her son mention *inanup* several times, her heart seizing in her chest with each repetition. *What am I going to do?* she asked herself for the millionth time. *He deserves to know his family...all of his family.*

"Your nightmares are getting worse, sis," Stewart said, breaking the silence between them. He peered sideways at her, his cheek against the cow's warm side as he worked the udders. "You've got shadows under your eyes, and you haven't spent a full night in bed for a week."

She turned away from his gaze, reaching into a wooden box, and pulling a brown egg out. Setting it in her basket, she shrugged. "Aye, I'll not lie to you, Stew. It'll pass."

"Will it?" her brother asked.

Pretending not to hear him, Kathleen finished finding the last of the eggs.

Stewart sighed and changed the topic. "Why do you think she left you here? Threw you away?" he asked.

Kathleen froze at his callus disregard for her feelings, shoulders tense, a lump in her throat. Forcing herself to breathe evenly, she answered, "Because she thinks I don't love her."

"Because you let her sleep in the barn, right? Didn't tell the folks about the two of you? Didn't go to her that night?" he prodded. Behind him, Teca's conversation trailed off into silence as he listened for the answer.

"Aye, Stew," Kathleen said with an explosive sigh, a tenacious hold on her emotions. "And what that's got to do with anything now is beyond me." She twitched her skirts with her free hand and made her way towards the barn door.

"Well, I think it's high time you stopped feeling sorry for yourself and did something about it, is all!" Stewart's voice rang out as she reached the doorway.

Kathleen halted, looking out at the early morning yard, eyes unseeing. Her anger flared, and she whirled about. She set the basket and its precious cargo down, and stomped forward with eyes flashing.

To give her brother credit, he did not flinch away as she loomed over him, rage on her face. Instead, he continued to milk the cow, his body language showing unconcern.

"And what would you have me do, Stewart Franklin?" she demanded.

He swallowed but refused to turn. As he finished with the cow, he shrugged and spoke with apparent nonchalance. "Make up your mind, sis. You won't remarry, though Mum and Da have paraded half the eligible bachelors through here the last year and a half. You won't give Teca there a Christian name, or forbid him to speak that infernal language. You won't even let Mum cut his hair!"

As he rose to his feet, pulling the pail out from under the cow, his sister stared at him in shock. After a moment passed, she sputtered in fury, unable to speak through the emotion. They were both surprised when she slapped him across the face.

The sound of flesh hitting flesh rang through the suddenly quiet barn. Stewart did not respond, only looked down at his sister as a red handprint blossomed on his cheek.

Teca interrupted their argument as he threw himself from his seat and wormed his way between them. "You leave my *ina* alone!" he insisted with all the scorn he could muster, pushing his uncle away. "You will not touch her! *Inanup* said to protect her!"

Stewart took a step backwards to appease the boy, his mouth quirking in a crooked smile. "My *hanka*, has raised him well," he told Kathleen in Lakota.

She blinked, confused as she placed the word. The fury drained from her face, and she reached down to touch her son's shoulder. "Thank you, Teca. Things are not as they seem."

Anxiously looking up to his mother, the boy studied her face for clues.

Kathleen smiled at him and squeezed his shoulder. "You have done a fine job of protecting me, *cinksi*. *Inanup* will be very proud."

Teca allowed his stern look to fade into a pleased expression, and he turned to Kathleen, hugging her close. "When will we see *inanup* again?" he asked, his voice muffled against her skirts. "I miss her."

"I do not know, *cinksi*," Kathleen murmured, her throat tight and eyes burning.

Stewart settled the pail of milk down. Draping an arm across the broad back of the cow, he leaned against it as he watched the pair. "What's stopping you from going to her, Kath?"

With a weary sigh, she shook her head. "What do you think, Stew? It's not easy for a woman to travel so far without horrible accidents befalling her." She looked up at him, her lips pursed in exasperation. "Would you have me take my son into the unknown? We'd be dead inside of a week."

He sighed as well, stooping to settle the stool and sit. "Way I see it, you'd do worse by staying here." With a gesture to his nephew, he continued, "You want to see Teca become a farmer? Or a warrior?"

"A warrior!" the boy exclaimed. "Like *inanup!*"

Stewart chuckled. "What's it going to be, Kath? You can't have it both ways for much longer."

What's it going to be? she wondered, a glimmer of hope sparking deep in her soul. "She threw me away, Stew. That's the way they divorce," Kathleen argued.

"Aye, so you've said. Way I see it, though, it was a misunderstanding."

Kathleen made a dismissive noise in her throat and looked away, her eyes lighting on the spotted mare. "It's not that easy, Stew. It took us two months of travel to get here, and I don't even know where she is!"

"But, they get together each year for that summer camp, don't they?" he asked. At her nod, he shrugged. "If'n we hooked up with any Lakota between here and there, they'd show us the way, wouldn't they?"

"Well, aye, but..." His words reached her, and Kathleen's face became cautious. "What was that again?"

A smug grin sat on his lips. "I said, if we found any Lakota they'd lead us to where summer camp was."

"You said, 'we'," Kathleen clarified.

"Aye. That's what I said."

~ * ~ * ~ * ~ * ~

Once they made the decision, Kathleen was amazed at how easily their plan fell into place. Over the following week, she went through her and Teca's belongings, digging out the buckskin clothing. Their moccasins were horribly worn, and she felt a twinge of guilt. When had she last ensured her son was cared for in the Lakota way? Since most travel was done on foot or horseback, moccasins were considered very important. No well-loved man ever suffered holes or torn stitches in his footwear.

Taking one of her spare dresses, Kathleen picked out the rawhide stitching. She used the leather to make new moccasins for her and Teca, wishing she had the time and supplies to decorate them appropriately. The work was familiar and comforting, reminding her of how much she truly missed her life with the Lakota. She eagerly looked forward to seeing Hca and Hinhan, wondering how big Cetan had grown and whether or not young Yus'as'a had grown to look like his mother or father.

She was also happy that Stewart had taken an interest in the native riding gear. Long ago, he had stowed her wooden saddle instead of throwing it away as their father had wished. It took little effort on her part to show him where repairs needed to be made. With only the one saddle between them, the siblings decided Teca should use it; Kathleen and Stewart would use the ones they were raised with.

Stewart spent more and more time away from the homestead, taking Teca and his speckled pony out to a natural pond. Between the stories Kathleen had told her brother and Teca's close connection to the animal, they proceeded to break the pony for the boy to ride. Putting the animal into water until he was breast deep made it hard for him to fight against the odd sensations of a saddle and rider.

In less than two weeks, all was ready. Kathleen would wait to make the various medicinal items to ward off insects and the like once they were on the way. Everything that could be fixed was, and those items needing to be recreated were either complete or awaiting the proper materials from the wild. There was nothing left to do except tell their parents.

"No! I'll not have it," McGlashan said, jaw clenched. "Wherever did you get such a fool notion to begin with?"

Kathleen growled in frustration, startling Teca who sat beside her.

Night had fallen some time ago, and the remains of their supper was still scattered about the hardwood table. Rachel, who had been in the process of cleaning up, slowly sank back to the bench, still holding plates in her hands.

Stewart never looked more like his father as he did now. His jaw jutted out just as far, his lips thinned in stubborn defiance. "It's not like you've much choice, Da," he said. "Kathleen and I aren't children any longer. We're adults and can do what we please."

"And it pleases you to go off into the wilderness on a wild goose chase?" his father demanded, his voice rising uncharacteristically.

The effect caused Teca to shrink closer to his mother, the volume hurting his ears. It was rare for his grandfather to yell regardless of his Irish temper. Kathleen put a calming arm around her son's shoulders, knowing he was still unused to the white man's way of loudness over the safety of quietness. "It's not a wild goose chase, Da," she said. "I'm going home."

"This *is* your home, damn it!" McGlashan pounded the table for emphasis, rattling the crockery and causing his wife to jump. "Not some flea ridden heathen campsite."

"Kathleen, don't you remember when you returned?" Rachel asked, setting the plates down. "You were bedraggled and dirty; you hadn't had a bath in months. Why, the boy had mosquito bites all over his arms and legs."

"It wasn't that bad, Mum," Kathleen said, shaking her head. "And we'd bathed just the day before. Don't judge what you don't understand."

"I understand plenty," her father cut in. "I understand that you were a sensible girl until those damned Indians kidnapped you. Now look at you! You won't even consider remarrying. What's wrong with you?"

Kathleen felt her heart race. "I'm already married, Da. Just because I'm not with her, doesn't mean I'm not."

Silence reigned for the space of a moment. "Her?" Rachel asked.

"What are you talking about?" McGlashan demanded. "That filthy heathen Indian who brought you here?"

Anger fortified Kathleen. "She's not a heathen, she's my wife and Teca's mother. I should have told you to begin with, but I didn't know what to say. Now she's gone and I've spent the last two years in Hell."

"Oh my God," Rachel whispered, blood draining from her face.

"You've gone and upset your mother! I'll not have another word of this. Kathleen, Stewart, mark my words. The answer is no. Kathleen will marry the Widower Smythe by next Sunday."

The threat of a forced union seemed to bring everything into focus for Kathleen. Her father sputtered in fury, but it was all posturing. She knew this. He had no control over her and had not since her return. *He's scared of me, scared of the strength that Anpo and Teca have brought me.*

Kathleen looked at her mother patting her face in some misguided attempt at calming herself. She remembered her childhood in Ireland, making mud pies with Stewart, Rachel helping to put together the "desserts" by baking them in the fire. *When did Mum become so unhappy?*

She drew herself up, giving Teca a reassuring hug. "I'm sorry you feel that way, Da. And I'm sorry to upset Mum. But the fact of the matter is that I'll not remarry anyone. I leave tomorrow morning with or without your blessing."

Before McGlashan could get past his rage at being defied, Stewart stepped forward from his place at the fire. "And I'm going with her to make sure she arrives safely. You can't tell me no; I'm a man now, and one of those horses is mine. What I do with my life is none of your concern."

Rachel no longer appeared worried about her emotions, more concerned with the alarming shade of purple her husband turned. "Stewart Franklin! How could you?"

"It's easy, Mum. I love Kathleen and I want to see she's happy. She's not happy here, and the Widower Smythe ain't going to help."

McGlashan was finally able to speak, though his voice was as mottled as his complexion. "Get out of my house, *both* of you. You'll not spend another night under my roof, you ungrateful dogs."

"Jonathon!" Rachel gasped.

Stewart's face fell at the pronouncement, but he did not falter. "You don't mean that, Da. You're just angry." He raised his hands in supplication as his father prepared another outburst. "But Kathleen and I will leave now."

Since most of their things were already packed for the trip, it took little time for Stewart to collect their belongings from the loft. Teca carried a sack with his things and a rolled up blanket, Kathleen following him outside with two saddle bags. Stewart brought the rest of their bedding and his gear. McGlashan refused to look at his mutinous family, glaring stiff necked at the hearth as they left.

Outside, the air was noticeably more relaxed. Tears formed in Kathleen's eyes. The last thing she had wanted was to hurt her family – any of them – but this was something she had to do. She could not live without Anpo; two years of trying had shown her the truth. As much as she wanted her parents to understand, she realized it was time to let them go.

Stewart saddled the horses, muttering under his breath at McGlashan's stubborn spite. Only Kathleen heard the catch in his voice and knew how close he was to tears himself. She said nothing, however, letting him mourn in peace as she helped Teca into his saddle.

"Are we going to see *inanup* now?" he asked, his voice hardly above a whisper.

"*Hau*, Teca. We are going to see *inanup*. But the journey will be long."

His excitement overshadowed the subdued fear from the argument. "I am big and strong," he said. "The journey will be easy."

"Let's hope so," Stewart said, leading the horses from the barn.

They stopped at the well to fill their water bags and give the horses a last minute drink. The cabin door opened and Kathleen braced herself for another onslaught.

"Kathleen?" Rachel called softly.

She swallowed against the burning in her throat at her mother's tone. "Aye, Mum," she said, leaving the horses to step closer.

Rachel stood, uncertainty in every line of her body. She hugged her arms, shivering though it was not cold. "Kathleen, your father–"

"It's all right, Mum. I understand," she said, tamping down her anger. "He'll either get used to the idea or he won't. Nothing I can do or say will change his opinion."

"I can't say that I'll get used to the idea," Rachel said. "But always remember that we love you, no matter what you do."

Unable to stop the flow, Kathleen began to cry. Rachel stepped forward and took her into her arms. She hummed a lullaby, just as she had done through years of cuts and scrapes and hurt feelings.

"I love you, too, Mum. Both of you."

"Make that two of us," Stewart said, having come to the porch.

"Me, too, *unci*!"

Rachel laughed and sniffled, releasing Kathleen to pick up her grandson who had dismounted to join them. "Don't let grandpa fool you, Teca. He does care. He just worries about you, about all of you."

Kathleen wiped her face, stepping back to give Stewart room to say farewell to their mother.

"Now, Stewart, you come back as soon as you're finished," Rachel said, straightening the collar of his shirt with nervous hands. "I expect your da will be all over his mad by tomorrow and regretting every word of this night."

"Aye, Mum. McGlashans are true Irish, ain't they? Quick to anger and just as quick to forgive."

"Aye, that they are."

They finished their good byes, and Kathleen found it harder to leave after the kindness and understanding. If it wasn't for Teca's obvious eagerness to depart, reminding her of what awaited them, she might have capitulated for another night. Her last glimpse of the homestead remained etched in her mind. Her mother stood on the porch, gentle moonlight illuminating her as she waved at her departing children. In the window, firelight glowing behind him, was the silhouette of her father watching them go.

Part 12: Wana Yagli
Coming Home

Chapter Forty

1783

Holding her breath, Anpo released the bowstring. With a sharp whisper, the arrow flew through the still air and hit its intended target. The antelope had time for only a few surprised steps before it collapsed to the ground. Bow strung across her back, she jogged towards her prey, pulling her hunting knife.

The animal lay on its side, breathing labored and liquid brown eyes wide with fear and confusion. Anpo approached from its back, mindful of the antlers, and knelt near the head. With a solid, quick motion of the knife, she slit the buck's throat. As blood gushed onto the ground, she murmured, "Thank you, *nigesanla*, for your sacrifice. My family will feed well and long on your flesh. Your bones and sinew will be used as tools to keep us strong. You will always be with us in our hearts."

Within a few minutes, she had the antelope gutted, the entrails that were not useful scattered further away – an offering to animals living in the area. It was a bit of a struggle, but Anpo lifted the carcass onto her pony, lashing it down behind the saddle. She jumped atop the red stallion and slowly began the return trip home.

It was good being alone out in the hills near summer camp. Since Kathleen, Anpo had found it harder and harder to be around people. She rarely spoke, even to her own family, preferring to watch from a distance. *Because you have difficulty hiding this cloud hanging over you*, Anpo thought.

She steered her thoughts to her well-worn daydreams. *Ketlin...have you joined with another? Have you given him sons? And Teca...how do you fare in the white man's world?*

With only half a mind on her destination, she allowed the pony to take her where he may.

~ * ~ * ~ * ~ * ~

Kathleen led the spotted mare along the creek. Ahead of her rode Stewart and Teca, the boy proud to be on the back of his own pony. Around her were others headed for summer camp, some familiar and some not.

The return trip not surprisingly had taken a month longer than the initial one. Where Anpo's *wicakte* status eased their progress in many instances, a white couple and an Indian child brought more trouble than Kathleen had expected. Only her obvious knowledge of native culture, language and – more importantly – sign language had gotten them through the worst of the encounters. In one case, the Ojibwa fisher she had met with Anpo remembered her when they arrived in his village. As they traveled further from established white territory, their danger lessened, but not by much.

It had been the most outrageous of fortune that after close to three solid months they stumbled across the camp of Mani. There had been quite a tense moment upon their arrival, the leader having heard a version of what happened between Kathleen and Anpo. However, Mani felt obligated to Kathleen for her help with the white traders and allowed them to join. Kathleen was allowed to retain her status as Anpo's woman, giving her more freedom than she should have had as a non-Indian. Stewart was accepted as her brother and, while he was not shunned, he became the butt of a few jokes among the men. He took it with good humor, telling his sister that it was not any worse than what she used to throw his way when they were children.

The one who was welcomed back with open arms was Teca. The first three nights, he was a guest of Mani and sat with him at his fire, being regaled with tales of his *inanup* and how proud and brave she was. Kathleen watched fondly, serving her brother and son their food, glad for this connection.

Now they were almost to summer camp. Kathleen swallowed, feeling the butterflies in her stomach. *Has she joined with another? Maybe adopted another child? Will she be happy to see Teca, or too angry at seeing me?* Thundering hooves interrupted her thoughts as the first of the welcoming committee found them. As expected, the circling warriors caught sight of Stewart on his horse and, within minutes, two were within reach of him, staring at his clothes and coloring. Kathleen hustled forward, dropping the reins of her pony.

"Are the people always this rude to a guest?" she demanded, hands on her hips and glaring up at the riders.

They looked at her, recognition on their faces. One pointed at Stewart, his dark eyes narrow. "He is not my guest!"

"He's mine," came a low voice. Mani kicked his pony into the gathering, forcing one of them back. "Do you wish to challenge my right?"

Unsettled, the two warriors dropped their eyes and pulled away. "*Hiya*, Mani. I do not wish to challenge."

The other gestured no with his thumb.

Nodding in satisfaction, Mani said, "Good. Now, go tell the people at camp that we are coming." He turned his steed away, resuming his path.

Reprieved, the two warriors threaded their way out of Mani's traveling camp and rode with their comrades back the way they had come.

Stewart blew out a breath and rolled his eyes. "Thanks, sis," he said.

"I felt the same way the first time I came to summer camp, lad," she answered with a smile. "It can be a bit overwhelming." Memories of her young *wicakte* defending her assailed Kathleen's heart.

"Aye. And that's a fact," Stewart said, not seeing the pained expression on his sister's face.

Once they had made it to summer camp, Kathleen thanked Mani for his help and invited him to eat at Stewart's fire in the future. He appeared to give the thought serious consideration before signaling assent, studying them.

They then parted ways, Mani moving his people towards their usual place and Kathleen leading her family to Wagna's village. Along their way, children danced alongside, laughing and joking at the strangers' yellow hair. When Kathleen responded to their rude comments, explaining the nature of politeness to them, the youngsters amazed she understood the language. For the remainder of the short trip they plagued the trio with questions, one or two finally admitting to remembering her.

It was a good distraction for Kathleen because, as she neared Wagna's village, her stomach became more upset and she could feel a headache developing at the base of her neck. *I don't know which is worse...the idea of seeing Anpo again or facing Gi and Hca!*

When familiar *ti ikceyas* came into view, Kathleen's heart flip-flopped in her chest, and her responses to the accompanying children dried up. Questions no longer being answered, the children raced away to spread the news of Kathleen's return.

The tension in the air increased as the people of Wagna's camp noticed the new arrivals. Fortunately for Stewart, there were no warriors about, most having gone hunting or spending time at the main council fire with their friends. Kathleen was glad she would not have to worry about defending him from some well-meaning *wicasa* protecting Anpo's honor, thinking her brother was her husband.

Instead, they began to gather into clumps of spectators, watching the newcomers' progress. Kathleen knew most of them, could remember picking berries with that woman, helping this one with the birth of the toddler on her hip, laughing and swimming with the third. Yet no one spoke to them. No one came forth in welcome. It was unsettling that the people she had felt were friends and family for years would not approach. When Gi's lodge came into view, Kathleen stopped.

Stewart, riding behind his sister, pulled his horse up when she halted. Something in the line of her body warned him, and he jumped down from his mount, stepping up to her.

Kathleen was pale, her eyes locked on the *ti ikceya* before her. She drew in a shaky breath, remembering to breathe when she felt her brother's hand on her arm.

Following her gaze, he looked at one of many conical tents. The leather flap in front of the door opened, and an older woman bustled out with a basket on her hip. "Who is she?" he asked.

"Anpo's *ina*." *My uncisi*. Regaining her senses, Kathleen turned to her brother and spoke in urgent tones. "Do not look at her, *misun*. Treat her as your *uncisi* for now. Remember what I said?"

Stewart averted his gaze and nodded, responding in Lakota, "*Hau.*"

Gi set her basket of corn down by the grinding stone. Something in the air tickled her senses, and she realized that it was quiet – far too quiet for a pleasant day in a camp this size. With a frown, she straightened and looked around.

Other people in the camp clustered here and there, whispering among themselves and watching her, watching something nearby. Turning, she looked to where they looked. Three ponies stood before her lodge, a man and woman leading two of them, and a child on the third. Something was odd about the pair.

Gi took a step forward, her eyes squinting as she focused her failing eyesight. "Ketlin?"

Hearing her name spoken with the Lakota accent brought warmth washing over her. "*Ohan.* I have returned."

Gi wavered in her shock, her mouth dropping open. Steeling herself, she drew upright and inhaled deeply. "Why are you here, Ketlin?"

Several reasons flew through Kathleen's mind – worry for Anpo, the vision that threatened her every night, the hollowness in her chest for these people and this life, the almost tangible memory of strong arms wrapped around her in sleep. Kathleen discarded them all. "I have brought your *takoja*. He needs to know his family."

Gi's attention was drawn to the small figure on horseback, and her face softened into a smile. Approaching them, she took Kathleen by the shoulders and peered at her. "Are you home?"

It was getting harder and harder to keep from crying. Kathleen dropped her gaze and nodded, fighting with the lump in her throat. She felt Gi pull her into an embrace, and a piece of her heart returned to life. To do her credit, Kathleen did not fall apart with tears, but she could not help but allow a few to leak out.

"This *wicasa* brought you here?"

Sniffling and nodding, Kathleen pulled back. "*Ohan*, Gi. He is my *misun*, Stewart."

The old woman noticed the stranger would not look at her, and she nodded in satisfaction. "You have taught him well, Ketlin. Tell Stu'et that I welcome him to my lodge."

Kathleen nodded and smiled, relaying the already heard message with a murmur. She also repeated her brother's thanks, wondering if all this would be necessary in the future. *Anpo might not have me back. Then Stew and Gi won't be related...* She quickly stifled the negative thoughts and returned her attention to Anpo's mother.

Gi moved to the gray pony, peering at the child perched on its back. Her wrinkled face broke into a wide smile as she recognized her grandson, seeing his mother's features in the dark face. "You are Teca," she said.

"You are my *unci?*" he responded, his statement also a vague question.

"*Ohan*, I am."

Lips pursed in concentrated thought, Teca studied her. Finally, he smiled. "You gave me berries when I was little."

"*Ohan*, Teca! You have always had a liking for sweet things!"

Satisfied, he held out his arms and slid into his grandmother's. After a long hug, he was set on the ground and studied. "You have grown big and strong, *takoja*. Soon you will be a great warrior and hunter."

"Just like *inanup*," Teca insisted with a nod. A thought evidently crossed his mind because his face became serious, and he tilted his head. "You are *inanup's ina?*"

"*Ohan*, and she will be very happy to see you!" Gi brought her attention back to Kathleen and her brother. "Come to my lodge and accept food and drink. Anpo has gone hunting and will return soon."

Chapter Forty-One

Anpo's pony meandered through the camp on course for her *cuwe's* lodge. Since she had no woman of her own, she tended to split her hunting prizes between Hca and her two mothers, Gi and Hwa. She was so deep in her daydreams and apathy, the curious looks and whispers of others failed to grab her attention as she drifted past.

At Hca's *ti ikceya*, the fire burned merrily. It did not appear she was there, however. Anpo dismounted and untied the antelope carcass. She set it downwind of the fire so the smoke would deter the worst of the flies, and used a stick to knock on the *tiopa*.

She may be at ina's, Anpo thought when there was no answer. She dropped the stick and returned to her horse. Taking the reins, she led the animal towards her lodge. Once there, she pulled the saddle and reins off the red stallion and sent him towards the herd with a smack on his flank.

Turning back to her fire, Anpo noted that it had burned down to coals. Rather than restart them, she settled down in her place and prepared a pipe. She smoked as she stared at the dead and dying embers, her thoughts in a place just as dead, just as smoky.

A burst of laughter perked her ears, and she glanced towards her mother's lodge. She could not quite see the fire from this angle, but she could tell there were several people about it. Another camp must have arrived. *Maybe Gi's* maske? Anpo puffed as she watched, her heart leaden and a little wistful at the gaiety she heard.

A child emerged from the group, peering in her direction. He looked vaguely familiar to Anpo, but she could not place his face. Most children were familiar at summer camp, though, seen every year as they grew to adulthood. She watched as his face broke into a smile, and he trotted closer.

With a concerted effort, she put a mild look on her face, hiding her melancholy behind a pleasant exterior. The boy stopped just outside the circle, his eyes roaming up and down the seated *wicakte* before him. Anpo finally tilted her head and said, "*Han*, young *koskalaka*. Come sit by me."

The child grinned and leapt forward to do just that. He settled down to the left of her, in the honored place. "You are Anpo?" he asked. "*Cunksi* of Gi and Wanbli?"

Anpo smoked her pipe. "*Ohan*, I am. What is your name?"

He puffed his chest out in pride, thumping it once with a small fist. "I am Teca! *Cinksi* of Ketlin and Anpo!"

The pipe sat forgotten in her hand as she stared at him.

"You are my *inanup*!" Teca crowed. "I have missed you very much, *inanup*!" He wrapped his small arms about her waist in a hug.

At that exact moment, Anpo heard a familiar voice calling from her mother's lodge. "Teca?"

Before Anpo could respond, the boy called, "*Hau, ina*! I am with *inanup*!"

Kathleen appeared, stepping from the front of Gi's *ti ikceya*, and Anpo's breath caught in her throat. *Mahasanni*! Hungry eyes took in the woman form, recognizing the yellow *cuwignaka*, noting the new bead-work that had been added along its length. Her hair was longer, and the braids still hung down across her chest, indicating her status as that of a joined woman. *She has joined with another?* Anpo's heart twisted in her chest.

She looks so sad, Kathleen thought, scanning the woman before her. The shirt was new with blue and red quills decorating the chest and fringes hanging from the sides. In her hair two upright feathers had joined the yellow one, and three quills hung down. The hair was loose about Anpo's shoulders, and Kathleen fought an irrational urge to rush forward and run her fingers through it.

Anpo was not sure how it happened, but she found herself standing, Teca wrapped firmly about her muscled thigh, her hand in his hair. The pipe was left on the ground, its smoke drifting off to the spirit world. Struggling with her emotions, she finally croaked, "*Han*, Ketlin."

Kathleen inhaled deeply to gain some emotional control. Hearing her name roll off Anpo's lips cracked the hollow in her chest, allowing the ache to rise closer to the surface. "*Han*, Anpo," she responded softly. Looking to their son, she smiled. "I see that Teca has found you."

"I have missed *inanup, ina*," he said, hugging the leg tighter. "She will teach me to be a great warrior!"

"*Ohan*. She will." Kathleen looked at Anpo. "But, *inanup* and I must speak alone, *cinksi*. I want you to go back to *unci's* lodge."

Teca frowned and shook his head, holding Anpo's thigh tighter still, nearly cutting off the circulation. "*Hiya*! I want to stay here!"

Despite herself, Anpo smiled at his adamancy. She gently disengaged the boy and knelt to peer into his eyes. It truly *was* Teca! *How I have missed him!* she thought as she grasped his small shoulders. "Obey your *ina*, my son. I will come for you when we are done speaking."

The crack in Kathleen's heart opened further as she heard Anpo call Teca her son.

"Can we go riding again? I can ride my pony now! You and I can go very fast!" he rattled off.

Anpo's smile widened. "*Ohan*, Teca. You go to my *ina's* lodge now, and I will take you riding when I am finished."

With some reluctance, he nodded, eyeing his parents. Slowly, he shuffled away, shoulders drooping and looking over his shoulder at them until he arrived back at the *ti ikceya*. There, he was immediately picked up by Hca and distracted with his young cousin.

Kathleen turned back to Anpo, and they stood in awkward silence for several moments. "May I sit down?" she finally asked.

Her nod almost frantic, Anpo said, "*Ohan*! Sit!"

A small smile quirked Kathleen's mouth as she stepped into the circle of Anpo's fire. She did not sit in the honored place to the left of the warrior, nor did she settle down to the immediate right where Anpo's woman would. Kathleen stayed directly across from her. She glanced at the smoldering embers. "Your fire is going dead."

Anpo, who had returned to her own seat, hardly spared the fire a glance. "*Ohan*, I know." Her eyes continued to feed on the woman before her.

Kathleen blushed a little at the intensity of the dark gaze. *Get to it, lass! Ask what you've come to ask!* Looking away, she picked at her dress. "Stewart said you left me a message when you went away," she said. "What did you tell him to say?"

For a second time, Anpo felt her heart clutch her chest and her breath freeze. Her mouth worked but no sound came out. She dropped her eyes, staring forlornly into her hands.

"Anpo," Kathleen said in a soft, calming tone. "I need to hear the words from your lips."

"I...I throw you away," Anpo croaked out.

Kathleen closed her eyes in pain and nodded, taking a deep breath to still her nerves. "I see."

Movement caught Anpo's eye and she looked up to find Kathleen pulling her braids to her back. *She is not joined with another? Ketlin thought we were still joined? Why?* "Did your *misun* not tell you my message?"

"*Ohan*, he did. But I could not believe that my *mahasanni* would leave me without speaking to me."

It was Anpo's turn to wince in pain and look away. "You left me to sleep with the animals. You would not come to me. I was alone."

"I know," Kathleen said, leaning forward to stare with earnest into

Anpo's eyes. "What I did was the biggest mistake I have ever made. I was confused, unable to explain to my family what you meant to me."

"Why, Ketlin? Why were the words so hard to tell them we were joined?" Anpo's face showed all the lost bewilderment of a child. "I do not understand."

Kathleen so wanted to rush to Anpo's side and hold her. *No, lass. She's not yours any longer.* "To be a woman intimate with women goes against my God's teachings, Anpo. I know that we did nothing besides kiss, but even that means I will be punished forever by Him. My parents would never have understood."

There was a long silence as Anpo processed this. "If you stay with my people, will you still be punished by your god?" she finally asked.

"I do not know."

Another pause as the pair lost themselves in their thoughts. Finally, Anpo nodded a chin at the blonde. "You are not joined with another?"

"*Hiya*, I am not, Anpo."

"Why? You are a good woman. You cook well and love your family. You have taken good care of me." *And I miss you so — your touches, your kisses, your laughter.*

"Wasn't from lack of trying on my mum's part," Kathleen muttered in English with a crooked smile. "I belong to only one. That will never change."

Moisture welled up in Anpo's eyes. "Even if you are punished forever by your God?" she asked.

"Even then. I will go to the ends of the earth for you, *mahasanni*."

Blinded by the tears that filled her eyes, Anpo shook with sobs. She wrapped long arms about herself, hugging with all her might.

She might not be mine, but I can't just sit here. Kathleen felt tears of her own and moved to Anpo's side, gathering the larger woman into her arms. The *wicakte* curled up and leaned into her, shaking with the force of her weeping. Rocking gently back and forth, Kathleen crooned a song that she had been taught by Gi long ago.

The familiar song, the familiar arms only served to intensify the feelings of loss. Anpo was overcome with crying, unable to stop as she poured out the last two years of pain and anguish. They sat this way for some time. Eventually, Anpo's tears faded, and she lay in Kathleen's arms, staring dazedly at the reddish coals of the fire pit. Kathleen continued to sing softly, brushing her fingers through the dark hair.

Anpo felt numb now that the fierce emotions had flown through her. "I have missed you, *mahasanni*," she whispered, sighing at the fingertips that grazed her temple.

"I have missed you, *mahasanni*," Kathleen answered.

"Will you join with me again?"

I'd love to, lass! Kathleen inhaled deeply. "I am no longer a slave, Anpo. And you are living in my *ti ikceya*. I have a place in this camp." She looked at the woman she loved. "Whether I join with you or not remains to be seen."

Sitting up, Anpo studied her. *She wants me to court her?* Another thought came to mind. "How did you get here, Ketlin? Did you travel by yourself?"

"*Hiya.* My *misun*, Stewart, brought me. He knows of my joining with you, and I have taught him many Lakota words and things."

Hope blossomed in Anpo's heart, and she wiped her face clean, her mind whirling a mile a minute. With a curt gesture, she rose to her feet. "This is Stu'et's fire and your lodge. I will stay with *ina*."

Kathleen's mouth dropped open as Anpo ducked into the *ti ikceya*. *That's not what I meant!* She rose to her feet and almost collided with Anpo as she barreled back out of the lodge. "I did not mean for you to leave this lodge, Anpo—"

"*Ohan*, Ketlin." She juggled her personal possessions. "This is better." Her handsome face creased into a grin. "I will take Teca riding now." She marched off towards the people at her mother's lodge.

Kathleen stared after her, breathless with confusion. Looking about, she saw the scattered people loitering around their lodges in silent support, Kathleen mumbled, "What in blazes just happened?"

Chapter Forty-Two

In Wagna's village, the night rang with music. Everyone celebrated the return of Kathleen and Teca, and welcomed Stewart into their lives with gusto. The smell of roasting meat filled the air, the antelope Anpo killed feeding many hungry mouths. Kathleen's attention was divided between her family and friends. Women asking questions about her travels and the availability of her brother surrounded her.

But not everyone was happy.

Nupa left the firelight and stood on the edge of it as he watched. Someone dragged the white man into the circle to dance, ignoring his awkward laughs. The men hooted uproariously at his antics as he tried to copy the steps of the other dancers. After several attempts, he gave up and began kicking his feet up in an Irish reel. Around him, the people howled and trilled their approval.

His expression solemn, Nupa looked at his *tanksi*, watching as she enjoyed Stewart's antics and joked with her *ate* beside her. On her other side sat Teca who had not left her side since she had taken him riding in the afternoon. *She looks so much happier now. She is a whole person.* With a frown, Nupa's attention drifted to the cause of this change.

Kathleen sat behind her son, watching her brother play with the Lakota. Her long braids were behind her, indicating she was unmarried. Her face was happy and her smile brilliant as she responded to something Anpo said about the white man. Other than the difference with the style of her hair and the age of Teca, tonight could be as any other night in the past. Nupa had seen many just like this one.

Why did you return? Will you hurt my tanksi *again?* Nupa's head whirled with questions. While he was undeniably relieved to see his friend actually participating with her people again, he could not help but worry that Kathleen was still ashamed of Anpo and would be the cause of more pain. He did not think Anpo could survive another separation.

Kathleen's gaze met Nupa's, and he watched her smile fade, replaced by concern. She rose to her feet and said something to Teca, who was too enamored of his *inanup* to pay any mind. Kathleen eased out of the press of celebrants and toward Nupa. Upon reaching him, she stepped to his side and turned to watch the camp in silence.

"Two winters ago, a woman arrived at our camp, frozen and starving, dressed in rags. She would not speak to us, would not sign. Her spirit was dead, and she only saw their world." He glanced sideways at her. "Anpo did not speak for a moon."

Kathleen dropped her head. "I did not know."

"She told us of a stranger who was ashamed of her, that she was not welcome in her *uncisi's* lodge."

Kathleen's head jerked up, eyes flashing. "I was never ashamed of Anpo! She is the best thing that ever happened to me!" she insisted. Looking at the warrior in question, her shoulders slumped. "I was ashamed of me, *tiblo*. In the white world, things are different. My parents would not have understood our joining. I did not know how to tell them."

"And have you told them now?"

"*Ohan.*" She studied the ground at their feet. "They were not happy." Pushing whatever plagued her from her mind, she raised her head, chin jutting out in defiance. "I made a mistake that night long ago, Nupa. And so did Anpo by leaving as she did. She and I have paid the price for our misunderstanding. She and I must learn from our mistake."

Nupa nodded in grudging respect. *She has grown stronger.* "I do not want to see another 'misunderstanding,' Ketlin. I fear another will destroy Anpo."

"I know. I cannot say that we will never have a misunderstanding, *tiblo*. But, I will never allow things to go so long again. I did not follow her immediately and explain what happened, why I was confused. That was my second mistake."

Mollified, his worries put to rest, Nupa placed an arm about Kathleen's shoulders. "Do not worry the past, *tanksi*, you will go crazy. Keep your eye on now and the future."

They stood together and watched the celebration continue.

~ * ~ * ~ * ~ * ~

She approached the figure huddled on the hillside, pulling her shawl closer with aching fingers. It was inadequate protection against the icy tendrils of wind that whipped about her, freezing her very soul as it howled. Coldness also gripped her heart as she neared the familiar figure. The warrior's back was to her, a thin robe ruffling loosely as the wind teased its edges.

"Mahasanni?" she breathed.

There was no answer. With hesitant hand, she reached out to touch the war-

rior's shoulder, to urge her awake, to make some sort of contact.

The warrior was ice.

Unable to pull away, to flee what she knew she would find, she shook the warrior. With absurd slowness, the warrior toppled backwards into the snow. The naturally dark skin was pale and gray, the eyes open and unseeing with a thin layer of frost covering the lenses.

Feeling as if she had been punched in the stomach, she stumbled back a step, gasping for air. Her lungs ached from the winter cold and she whirled around to run away.

Below her was a small hollow full of Lakota lodges, many of them familiar. There were no warm fires, no sign of movement, not even the nicker of ponies. Frozen bodies lay everywhere in the camp.

Kathleen sat up, shivering. *I thought it would go away!* she cried to herself. She huddled under the blanket, holding her knees to her chest as she calmed down.

Around her she heard the soft sounds of others sleeping. A light snore emitted from a wool blanket with a tuft of yellow hair sticking out of it. Nearby, Teca had thrown off his covers, hugging his doll to his chest.

She disentangled herself and pulled her son's blanket up over his shoulder, brushing hair from his face. After watching Teca sleep for several minutes, she sighed and dressed, stepping outside into the cool summer morning.

As usual, the sun had not risen though the skies were grey with impending dawn. Kathleen set herself to work getting the fire burning and preparing for breakfast. As she worked, her mind worried the problem of the nightmare.

Obviously, the dream had not been of the past as she had been so frightened of. Having started just after the worst of last year's winter storms passed her family's homestead; that had been Kathleen's greatest concern – that it was what had happened, and she would find everyone dead. *Anpo dead.* She shuddered and veered away from the thought.

Does that mean it's a dream about the future? And if it is, can it be avoided? Or does it have to remain as it is and everyone dies? Kathleen mixed porridge out of grains and set it to cooking over the fire, unconsciously shaking her head at her thoughts. *I can't believe I've come here to watch it happen! Doesn't that mean that Teca and I die, too?*

The sun peeked over the horizon, bathing her in warm, reddish light. Despite her worries, she lifted her face and basked in it, pausing in her chores for just a moment. A noise grabbed her attention and she opened her eyes, finding she was not alone in enjoying the dawn.

The shaman, Inyan, had grown old, his steps shuffling and his dark hair grey. He stood in front of his woman's *ti ikceya*, arms wide as he welcomed the sun with a prayer and a song. Dancing a bit, he shook a rattle in the four directions before sitting down with obvious pain in front of his fire.

Perhaps this nightmare is a vision. Kathleen considered, her eyes widening at the thought. "I must talk to Inyan about visions."

~ * ~ * ~ * ~ * ~

As Wanbli and Anpo left camp, she watched with curiosity as she passed the shaman's fire. There sat Kathleen in serious discussion with the old man, a curious thing. Brow furrowed in concern, she continued her course as she followed her *ate*. *Why would Ketlin need to see Inyan?* she wondered. *She has never met with him before.* Anpo forced the thoughts from her mind. *My place is not to question her path. Ketlin will tell me if she wishes.*

When they were a way out from camp, the two warriors urged their ponies into a gallop, which turned into a race. With wild abandon, they whooped and chased each other about until their mounts became winded. Wanbli steered them towards a nearby creek, and they let the horses drink their fill.

Seated on the back of the red stallion, Anpo's eyes wandered about the area. She saw the smoke from summer camp to her right and heard the water as it gurgled beneath her horse's hooves.

"What will you do now that Ketlin has returned, *cunksi?*" Wanbli asked.

Anpo inhaled deeply of the fresh air, a smile on her face. "I will woo her." Turning to her father, she continued, "I ask that you speak for me with her *misun.*"

Wanbli cocked his head. "Do you think this is wise?"

Becoming serious, Anpo searched his countenance, finding only concern for her. "*Ohan, ate,*" she said softly. "Ketlin is my *mahasanni.* I cannot be without her."

"You have been without her for two winters, Anpo. Things were hard, but you have survived the pain." Wanbli made a negative sign. "I would not have you return to that dark place, and I fear that Ketlin will hurt you again."

"*Ohan,* there will always be that possibility. But, I was not alive." She looked away to the distance. "I only waited for the time of my death, hoping something would come soon to end my misery."

"And that has changed, Anpo?"

"*Ohan!*" Her smile returned. "What happened between Kathleen and I was our mistake, each responsible for a piece. Ketlin and I will work hard to not let that happen again."

Wanbli came to a decision. "I will speak to Stu'et for you."

"Thank you, *ate*!" Anpo responded, gratefulness coloring her words.

Their horses continued to drink deeply, and they sat in silence for a few more moments.

"*Ate?*"

"*Hau*, Anpo." Wanbli turned to his daughter and saw the familiar frown of thought on her face.

"What is the story you tell a woman when you court her?"

"Only you can know, my *cunksi*. The story you tell your woman is one close to your heart, one that tells her the type of person she will join. Ketlin already knows what type of person you are."

Anpo was not reassured, her frown deepening. "I am no longer that person. I was foolish and allowed my emotions to destroy my family, *ate*. I do not want Ketlin to hear a story of my shame and fear."

Wanbli studied the back of his horse's ears, unaware that his expression matched his daughter's. "Perhaps you must tell Ketlin why you allowed your emotions to destroy your family."

Aghast, she focused on Wanbli. "Tell her?" she asked. "Describe why I let my feelings cause me to throw her away? Tell her I was not strong enough, my spirit unable to defend against my confusion? Show her my weakness?" Anpo looked away with a scoff. "Ketlin will decide she must wait for a strong man to join with her, instead of me. Someone without a vision like mine."

"You are wrong."

Anpo had never had a firm declaration such as this one in her life. Her status as *wicakte* allowed her the freedom to act differently than other men and women, rarely bringing the subtle means of control among her people – their disapproval. Hearing such adamancy from her father shocked her to silence.

"Your vision told you this would happen, Anpo," Wanbli said. "The sacred white buffalo brought Ketlin to you. You are responsible for her pain, her wounding. And still she sees you as her *mahasanni*, as you see her."

As quickly as that, she saw the original vision in her mind, as clear and as strong as it ever was. "But she disappears, *ate*. She goes into the sun."

"The vision and the circle of life continue, whether you see or not. Maybe you need to seek another vision."

Was that true? Had the vision reached its natural conclusion, and no longer held power for her? While Anpo mulled over the repercussions of such an event, her father offered his wordless acceptance and support. Finally, she said, "Thank you, *ate*. You have given me much to think on."

"You are welcome to all that I have, Anpo. You are my *cunksi* and a fine warrior and hunter. You have many honors for one so young. I believe the spirits are strong within you and, if you listen closely, they will tell you what you need to know."

Chapter Forty-Three

It took a very short while for Kathleen to fall back into the pattern of Lakota life. Despite the many similarities between the two cultures, when it came to women's work she thought the native lifestyle less stressful. *Maybe it's the many other hands to help*, she mused, thinking of how the women all worked together towards a common goal. *So much more different than homesteading, lass. There you'd be, all alone except your immediate family.*

She took even less time to reacquaint herself with her *ti ikceya* and its household items. It was a sign of how well Anpo had been taken care of, her sisters and mothers keeping the usual tools of a woman's trade in good condition, dry food stored, cooking herbs available, old and worn items replaced. Kathleen went through some baskets on the right side of the lodge, seated in her place near the central fire pit. With some surprise, she even uncovered one that held pieces of leather and feathers for a project she had been working on before leaving to visit her parents. She fingered the quills of a crow, trying to recall what she had planned for it.

Outside, Stewart sat at the fire, trying to get used to the loincloth he had been put into by Anpo and Wanbli. The hair on his pale legs tickled from the breeze, and he constantly rubbed his shins to relieve the itch. There had been a while where he could not quite get comfortable, not wanting to show off his wares to the passing young women who giggled and pointed at him. He paused in the sharpening of his knife to twitch the leather and readjust his seat. *It's positively indecent!* he griped. *Mum would have a conniption if she saw me now!* In contrast to his sun deprived legs, his chest and arms were tan from many years of farm work in hot fields. His longish hair was pulled back into a tail and tied with rawhide.

The Lakota were gearing up for their major celebration, the Sun Dance. Within the next couple of days, the shamans were supposed to be finished with their vision quests and the celebration would begin. Stewart looked forward to it, despite the horrid descriptions his sister had painted. *Should be interesting to see how they worship their gods.*

A shadow fell across him as he worked the sharpening stone. Looking up at the silhouette, he peered at the dark figure until he could make out the features. "Anpo!" he said with delight, setting the blade down. "*Han*! Sit at my fire!"

She did not answer, sharply signing no with her thumb.

Puzzled, Stewart put his hand over his eyes to see better.

Anpo was dressed head to toe in her leathers and leggings, despite the heat of summer. Her hair fell loose about her shoulders, and two lightning bolts of red and yellow slashed down her cheeks. To top her outfit off, she wore a shaggy white robe.

Stewart blinked. Uncertain, he looked around to see others of Wanbli's village gathering to watch. Still confused, he turned to Anpo who had moved away, and now stomped back and forth. "Uh...Kath? I think you'd better get out here," he called.

Hearing her name, Kathleen set the basket she searched through to one side. At the *tiopa*, she lifted the leather cover aside, mouth open to ask what her brother wanted. Her mouth remained open as she stared in shock at Anpo, pacing back and forth as if angered. *Oh, my God... Is this what I think it is?*

"Kath?"

She tore her gaze from Anpo to glance at Stewart. The expression of bewilderment and worry on his face almost caused her to laugh. Biting her lip, she smothered her mirth. "Do not worry, Stew," she murmured as she stepped from the *ti ikceya*. "Ease your heart and remain still. Everything is fine."

With a reluctant nod, Stewart agreed. He kept a wary eye on the agitated native, however, glad that his nephew was off visiting Hca.

Kathleen saw others of Wagna's camp as they appeared out of nowhere in support of Anpo before her. She reddened at the attention but stood tall, her head held up as the courtship dance continued.

Anpo's dark eyes glittered in happiness though her face remained stoic. She paced back and forth in mock anger, "hunting" her prey as she moved closer and closer to the *winyan* standing before her lodge. She felt the strength from her people as they stood witness, and it filled her heart with pride.

With a sudden move, Anpo was upon her prey, long arms wrapping about the smaller form. Kathleen put up a struggle, trying to free herself despite the overwhelming urge to melt into Anpo's grasp.

The speed of the attack startled Stewart, and he jumped to his feet, the knife held in a white knuckled fist.

"*Stu'et, hiya*," said someone to his left.

Shaken, he turned to find Hca smiling at him. She held Teca by the hand, her son on her hip, and they were smiling at him. "But...but,

Anpo's..." he stuttered as he gestured to his right with the knife.

"This is what our *wicasa* do when they choose a woman, a wife." Hca released Teca and held out her hand. "All will be well, Stu'et. Anpo will not harm Ketlin."

Stewart swallowed and turned back to the couple. He chewed his lip, flustered, as he saw his sister wrapped in a calm embrace with Anpo. Frowning, he scratched at his neck, mind awhirl as the white buffalo robe engulfed them both.

"Do not look at them now, Stu'et," Hca instructed. "This is a moment of privacy for them. Sit. I will get you and Teca something to eat."

He looked away and blew out a breath. "I'll never understand all these customs," he muttered in English. He sat beside his nephew who peeked around Stewart at his parents with a wide smile. "Least she could have done was warn me!"

~ * ~ * ~ * ~ * ~

Kathleen closed her eyes, a wave of emotion rolling over her. She felt relaxed, satisfied, hopeful, and nostalgic all at once. She inhaled deeply of Anpo's scent, laying her head against the strong chest. Familiar arms wrapped about her and, though she began to perspire from being covered in a heavy robe, she did not want to be anywhere else. Beneath her ear, she heard the thump of Anpo's heart, and the rumble of her low voice as she began to speak. *That's right! She's to tell me an old tale!*

"Many winters ago, a warrior's *winuhca* bore his third child. Despite his desire for a *cinksi* to teach and take care of him in his old age, a girl was born. But the shaman had a vision when he held the newborn. He heard the scream of the *igmu* in all her mystery as the child cried out for life. The shaman said that the girl would be *wicakte*, two-spirited, taught by the warrior to hunt and fight though they were not the traditional ways of a woman.

"The child grew strong over the winters. She learned the ways of *wicasa*, developing great skill in all areas of men's work. When she was eleven winters old, she began wearing a shirt for her body grew into that of a woman's. As she reached twelve winters, the bleeding time began for her, and she was taught the ways of women in this matter. She was confused for a time, her lifelong teachings at war with her body's changes.

"As is usual for the *wicincala* of the Lakota, the *cunksi* took her first bleeding and found a tree. There, she climbed as high as she could and placed the bundle into the branches. Then, she sat at the base of the tree and asked the spirits for a vision. All day she sat there, looking down at summer camp, feeling confused and lonely. No vision came to her."

Kathleen's heart reached out at the sense of hopelessness that shimmered off the woman holding her. She hugged Anpo closer, eyes closed as she envisioned the solitary figure under a tree.

"The *wicakte*, her vision denied, thought that she had gone about things the wrong way. She might be *wikoskalaka*, but she was raised as *koskalaka*. The only way to receive a vision was to do what her father and his father had done. With some fear, she braved the fire of the shaman and asked to be guided in this manner. After some thought and questioning, the wise *wicasa* agreed to teach her the way of the vision quest.

"Happy, she went to the *oinikaga tipi* after much preparation and cleansed her body and spirits for the vision quest. Dressed in a loincloth, moccasins, and a robe, she left the summer camp in search of a likely place. Several hours of travel passed before she found a hill that felt right, a boulder jutting out from one side that looked like a cougar. She began her preparations. She cleared an area of all living things and entered it, placing the spirit banners given her by the shaman at each corner. She began a small fire and burnt sweet smelling herbs to entice the spirits. She smoked a pipe in honor of them, offering it to the four directions as she waited for her vision."

Kathleen could almost feel the confidence rolling off Anpo, knowing deep down inside that she had had no doubt she would be granted a vision by the spirits. This story intrigued her. Kathleen had known for years that there had been a pretty serious vision in Anpo's past, but she had never been told what it was, always assuming it was a personal, private thing and not to be shared. That Anpo was telling her now was a great gift, and her heart thumped in happiness that it was being given to her.

"For three days the sun rose and set as the *wicakte* prayed to the spirits, asking for a vision. Three days of no food or water, little sleep, all alone. This was a difficult time. She knew if she did not have a vision soon, she would have to return to camp without one or die there on the hill. She was facing east as the sun rose when the vision happened.

"The Sun flared into a brilliant white light. She had to squint to see through the light, one hand raised to shade her eyes. As the light faded, she saw a cloud of dust rising and felt the ground beneath her shake at the stampeding of a thousand buffalo. They ran towards her, led by the most sacred animal of all, *tatanka ska*.

"Watching in dazed awe, she saw a warrior woman swoop in from the south, screaming her cry as she attacked the white buffalo with a spear. The warrior's hit was solid and *tatanka ska* was mortally wounded. The remainder of the herd simply disappeared, as did the warrior woman. The white buffalo staggered closer to the young *wicakte*, blood pouring from its side, its nostrils flaring wide as it panted for breath. *Tatanka ska* fell just outside the cleared area and looked so real that she could almost touch the hide. The Sun flared again, and she lost the image, covering her eyes with her arm. The light faded, and she looked again, only to find *tatanka ska* gone."

Anpo paused in her narration, drawing in a deep, steadying breath. Kathleen was stiff with curiosity, having shifted her stance to peer up at her with intent eyes.

"Someone was in *tatanka ska's* place, a strange woman with pale skin. Her hair was long, longer than the *wicakte's*, and a yellow the color of the Sun itself. Her eyes were the blue of a deep lake, still and clear. She wore the *cuwignaka* and moccasins, her hair flowing freely in the breeze."

Kathleen's mouth had dropped open in shock. *She saw me in her vision? When she was...only twelve?* Her mind kicked into gear. *I was only fourteen! We'd just settled into the cabin on the river!* Hearing Anpo's voice continue, she forced herself to pay attention, thoughts whirling about in her head.

"This strange apparition rose from where *tatanka ska* had been, blood pouring from her side where he had been wounded. She walked closer to the *wicakte* staring at her in wonder. Then the woman put a hand to her wound, bloodying her fingers. She reached forward and brushed the blood onto the *wicakte's* face, two thunderbolts beneath her eyes. As the Sun flared again, she saw those brilliant blue eyes staring at her, and heard the words whispered into her ear."

Anpo dropped her head, bringing her lips closer to Kathleen's ear. She whispered the word from her vision. "*Mahasanni.*"

Kathleen nearly swooned, her arms tightening about the woman's waist. "Oh, Anpo," she whispered, full of disbelief, desire, and wistfulness. The arms holding her shifted, and she felt a finger on her lips. She looked up into a smiling face.

"The *wicakte* returned to camp, singing a song of her vision to all that would hear. She was happy the spirits had gifted her, but unsure of their meaning. When she came upon the shaman, she sat and smoked with him, telling him what had happened. With his help, she was able to understand some of the vision – that *tatanka ska* was to point the way to this strange woman, that she would meet this woman in the future, that she would be loved by this woman very much." Anpo closed her eyes in pain. "That she would hurt this woman, though she would be loved despite the pain she caused."

"I love you, Anpo, with all my heart."

Anpo pulled on a blonde braid with affection and continued her tale. "The shaman changed her name to reflect the vision of that day. She was no longer known as Cinksi. Her name forever after became Wi Ile Anpo. She continued on as a *wicakte* in her village.

"Four winters passed. The vision returned to her in her dreams and, sometimes, when she was awake. The shaman told her that this strange woman was very powerful to be so strong for so long. Many do not remember their visions with such clarity as time passes, but hers remained strong and real. Maybe this strange woman was a spirit that would be revealed to the *wicakte* when the time was right.

"And then I saw you," Anpo said, changing the point of view of her tale. She brushed her knuckles against the soft skin of Kathleen's face. "And you were real, not a spirit. I knew I had to have you, that you were mine forever. When I killed *tatanka ska* and Yatke challenged me, I wagered a pony against you. He did not know of the vision, and I felt if I was meant to have you as was shown me, I would not lose.

"I had spent many winters worrying about hurting the strange woman of my vision. I then spent more winters worrying about hurting you, Ketlin, *mahasanni*. My vision never left me – the vision stayed with me when I was asleep or awake, haunting me with a puzzle. When we left to see the white traders, the vision changed. Teca appeared beside you and the two of you would walk away into the light without me." Anpo could feel a lump in her throat, and she swallowed around it. "I did not know what to do. My *ate* and Inyan were far away. I could not talk to them...."

Kathleen reached up a hand to caress Anpo's cheek. "Shh, Anpo. I understand. Let me finish your story." When she received a hesitant nod, Kathleen smiled. "Teca almost died, and I became hysterical, demanding to have my family see him. You gave up your people and family to bring me to my parents' lodge so that your *cinksi* could meet his family. I was confused, unable to speak to my family about us, about our joining. I allowed my *ate* and *ina* to make my decision for me, allowed them to put you in the barn for the night, followed their command to sleep in their lodge. I left you alone with your vision and your fears."

Tears welled up in Anpo's eyes.

"So your vision became true – Teca and I left you. You hurt me, though I loved you afterwards." Her voice dropped to a whisper. "But we are here now. And I am healing." She pulled Anpo's head down, closing her eyes with a sigh as their lips met for the first time in over two years.

Chapter Forty-Four

Over the next several days, Stewart received an in-depth education in Lakota ceremonies and mating rituals. There were four days of preparation for the Sun Dance with plenty of singing, chanting, and dancing. Everyone was involved in building the bark lodge, the Sun's *ti ikceya*. Afterwards there were three more days of celebration inside the new construction, culminating in the Sun Dance itself. Stewart was not sure which was worse – the men disfiguring themselves or Anpo holding Teca so the boy could get a clear view of the proceedings.

This was the first Sun Dance that Teca could remember. When the new babies received their ear piercings, he fingered one of his lobes in vague memory. He enjoyed the games and singing, spending quite a bit of his time reacquainting himself with his *inanup*. By the end of the ceremony, he whooped and cheered with the rest of his people as they honored the dancers.

Kathleen found herself enjoying a strange level of giddiness she had never experienced, despite the pall of the gory celebration. Her time with Anpo was markedly different than before. When she had first become Anpo's woman, it was her responsibility to take care of the *wicakte*, to fix and serve her food, to keep her clothed in a manner that befitted her status in the camp.

Now she awoke to find small gifts of flowers, food, or adornments in her place at Stewart's fire. Anpo ate most meals there, getting to know the white man and entertaining them with stories. After Teca was put to bed, Anpo would return and sit just outside the firelight, playing a Lakota flute to draw Kathleen out into the darkness.

A sweet grin crossed Kathleen's lips as she heard Anpo's flute. It was earlier than usual, and Teca perked up at the sound as well. Kathleen glanced at her brother to find a matching smile on his face.

"Go, Kath," Stewart said. "I'll get Teca to bed tonight."

Her smile widened and she scampered off, feeling very much like a child given a reprieve from an onerous chore. Following the sound of the music, she found Anpo seated on a robe in a dark pocket between lodges. With practiced ease, Kathleen settled down, leaning into her as the tune finished.

Anpo smiled at her as she set the flute aside. She pulled Kathleen into her lap, holding her close and inhaling deeply of her scent. "I have missed you, *mahasanni*."

"You just saw me a short time ago at our meal, Anpo." Kathleen chuckled. "You had seconds and thirds, too."

"That was a long time ago!" she insisted, stealing a kiss. "And I am only hungry for you."

Kathleen felt a shiver rush down her spine. Warm lips caressed her face, and she closed her eyes. Her mouth opened slightly in invitation as they were brushed in turn. She felt a familiar twist in her stomach as Anpo delved inside with a tongue. The heat of summer was nothing compared to the flames that burst from within as their kisses became ravenous.

With some surprise, Kathleen broke off from the breathless intensity to find herself in a wanton position. She had turned in Anpo's arms, her dress hiked up to her upper thighs, and her legs wrapped firmly about the *wicakte's* torso. Blushing in surprise and embarrassment, she started to cringe away.

Strong hands held her close, refusing to let her go. "*Hiya*, Ketlin. Stay." The hands moved on her back and shoulders, massaging the suddenly tense muscles there. "I know that you have been hurt in the past by the *wicasa* who captured you. I know that your people do not speak of this or act in this manner." Anpo peered at her. "But, you must know that I will not hurt you. Teca is no longer a baby in need of his mother's breast or attention. He is a *hoksila*, a boy beginning to be curious about the world and other boys. I *will* pleasure you on our joining day."

Kathleen's blood burned at the promise. The hooded brown eyes looking deeply into her soul did not help, serving only to fan the flames of her desire. Trembling, she pulled Anpo close into an embrace, gathering strength from the long arms that surrounded her, protected her. Anpo continued to caress her, easing her nervousness yet inciting another rush of arousal. *Why had it never felt this way with Adam? Good heavens, the sheer emotions alone seem like to kill me! What will it be like on our joining day?*

After a time, Anpo said, "Tomorrow, my *ate* and Nupa will speak with Stu'et about your price. They will negotiate with your *misun*, and then we will have a true joining ceremony."

She nodded her head against the shoulder she leaned on. "I will tell Stewart."

Anpo smiled as she felt the weight of her woman against her, trusting her to keep her safe from harm. She tasted the tender skin at the juncture of Kathleen's throat, and felt more than heard the woman's quiet moan. She enjoyed the excitement the sound awoke in her, urging her to continue her oral explorations. Arms and legs clutched at her, pressing their bodies close. Anpo's heart raced, and she felt the answering beat of Kathleen's. "*Mahasanni,*" she breathed.

While it would not be the first time a young couple consummated their relationship prior to the nuptials, Anpo reined herself in before things went too far. As much as she wanted to taste every span of skin of the woman in her arms, she knew Kathleen's people were far different in many ways. This one was no exception. She knew Kathleen would gladly allow the dalliance, but was instinctively aware it was not something to be done. Perhaps it was the *wicakte* spirits alerting her to the dangers; Anpo's unique place among her people gave her insights to both men and women. Her extensive knowledge of the white man, gained through Kathleen, gave her the advantage of knowing how her actions might affect the woman.

Kathleen murmured her disappointment, but remained in Anpo's arms as they relaxed together, catching their breath.

~ * ~ * ~ * ~ * ~

As was foretold, Nupa and Wanbli arrived at Stewart's fire a short time after the morning meal. They were followed by a trail of *hoksila* interested in the proceedings, and Stewart felt a circus like atmosphere coming from the children. Teca responded to their excitement by hopping about the fire, unable to sit still. With proper hospitality, Stewart asked the *wicasa* to sit at his fire, giving Wanbli the honored seat to his left.

Kathleen served the men some tea and fry bread, careful to not look at Wanbli.

The shaman, Inyan, shuffled up to the fire and awaited an invitation. Nupa and Wanbli, while not overtly showing their emotions, appeared puzzled at his arrival.

Confused, Stewart asked Inyan to sit with them and gestured for Kathleen to bring food and tea for their new guest. When the elder settled down on his right, the place reserved for family members, he frowned.

Kathleen appeared surprised, but gave the shaman some fry bread and tea, receiving a smile in thanks.

The men then had the traditional pipe, smoking in silence as they all reflected on why they were there. When it was finished, they looked to the elder, Inyan, to begin.

"I adopt Ketlin as my child, my *hunka cunksi*. She is my daughter by choice, and has had a vision that is very disastrous for our people. Her return and telling of this vision may mean that we will survive the coming winter." Aged eyes looked about the circle of *wicasa*, finally settling on the woman in question. A smile crossed his face at her shock. "I have no children, and I am getting old. You are young and strong, yet have no Lakota man to speak for you in this matter." He patted Stewart's bare knee with a wry grin. "You have done well, *wicasa ska*, but you are not Lakota," he said.

Stewart felt relieved the burden of these unfamiliar situations would be lifted from him, and nodded. Remembering his Lakota, he said, "I am honored, Inyan."

The shaman returned his gaze to Kathleen.

She swallowed, her heart soaring with fondness for the old man. Her face creased in a soft smile, she went to him and hugged him. "Thank you, *hunka ate*," she whispered into his ear.

The embrace was returned. "Thank you, Ketlin," Inyan said. He peered into his adopted daughter's face. "You must go now. This is men's work."

Nodding, Kathleen paused only long enough to give her brother and son a hug, as well. She then left in search of Anpo.

The negotiations continued in earnest for quite some time. The worth of Kathleen, fairly high on the overall scale of Lakota society already, nearly doubled now that she was the daughter of the shaman. Inyan and Wanbli did the primary dickering, with Nupa putting in his opinions here and there. Stewart remained silent for most of it, watching the proceedings with avid interest. Soon a price was agreed upon, and the men of Anpo's family took their leave.

Stewart offered more tea to the shaman who had remained behind. "Thank you very much, *wicahca*," he said. "I would have made a mistake if I were alone."

"I know," Inyan replied with a chuckle. He pulled out his pipe and loaded the bowl. "And though both Nupa and Wanbli care for Ketlin, they would not have offered as much without me. And she deserves all and more."

"*Hau*, she does," Stewart murmured. He stared at the fire for a few moments. "What you said about her vision...she truly had a vision?"

The elder nodded, a cloud of smoke drifting from his mouth. "*Hau*, she did. She sees a very bad winter coming. I have sought visions on this and found this to be true." He handed the pipe to Stewart. "I do not know why the other shamans and I were not given this vision, why we were not told to prepare our people for the coming bad times. Perhaps this was the spirits' way of bringing Ketlin back to us."

Stewart nodded in thought. "Perhaps."

Chapter Forty-Five

The joining day dawned bright and warm. Left pretty much on their own, several *wicasa* of Wagna's village spent their day speaking with relatives and acquaintances from other bands preparing to leave. Others proceeded to go hunting and fishing, anything to get them out of the encampment for a while. Many elders surrounded the council fire and discussed the coming worries of a harsh winter. Finding enough food and robes would be the primary goal for the remainder of the season.

Kathleen was surrounded by a flurry of activity that surprised her. When she had become Anpo's woman before, the only women that prepared her were Anpo's family. This time, however, she was a full Lakota woman with all the rights and benefits that incurred. It seemed that every woman from the entire summer camp had dropped by her lodge to help with preparations or give gifts. Stewart fled long ago, keeping company with Wanbli at the council fire.

Alone on a hillock overlooking summer camp, Anpo sat and watched her people. The melancholy that once held her had disappeared since Kathleen's return, yet the need for solitude remained. A small smile crossed her face as she saw the telltale yellow hair when a group of *winyan* herded her betrothed towards the river to bathe. She debated briefly about following along to watch but decided against it. *I will have her to myself soon,* she thought as the gathering disappeared around a bend of the river.

The morning progressed well. As the sun rose to its zenith, Kathleen finally stood alone in her lodge. She wore a new *cuwignaka* decorated with paint and quills of green and yellow. Her hair had been combed with animal fat until it glistened, and put into braids wrapped in otter fur. Her *ti ikceya* was clean and stocked with all the gifts the women had brought. Outside at the fire, a haunch of deer roasted and was nearly ready. Teca was with his aunt for a few days.

Kathleen felt butterflies in her stomach as she paced her lodge, brushing at imaginary dirt on her dress. She was breathless in anticipation, forcing herself to inhale deeply to get enough air. There was a knock at the entrance, and her heart leapt into her chest.

Hca pulled the leather cover aside and grinned in at her. "Anpo is at my father's fire," she said.

As her friend dropped the covering and left, Kathleen thought, *Am I doing the right thing?* Two years of pain and emptiness flashed through her memory; the many nights crying, the nightmares, a forlorn desire for someone to cuddle, the taste and smell of her warrior just out of reach. Inhaling deeply, she shook the memories off. "Aye, lass. There's no doubt about that. You are doing the right thing." She slipped out the *tiopa*.

It was almost surreal, this feeling of *deja vu* overcoming Kathleen as she made her way to Gi's lodge. She saw the entire camp out and about in support, and she smiled. When she neared the lodge, she saw her family seated about the fire, smoking and talking. But she only had eyes for Anpo, the confident *wicakte* comfortably telling a story to her son and nephew.

Anpo must have felt Kathleen's presence. She looked up, her handsome face breaking into a welcome smile.

Silence fell about the fire. Kathleen spared a glance at the others there, finding a wreathe of smiles. With no words, she reached out her hand, sighing as Anpo's warm skin touched hers. She turned and led the way back to her lodge, the butterflies in her stomach raging.

She held the leather cover aside for Anpo before following her. With sure steps, Kathleen led Anpo to the place across from the entrance and helped her sit. Kneeling before her, she gently removed Anpo's moccasins and replaced them with new ones. "We are joined, *winuhca*."

Anpo reached out and pulled the braids forward to hang down Kathleen's breasts. "We are joined, *winuhca*," she repeated with a smile.

~ * ~ * ~ * ~ * ~

The afternoon was another whirlwind of activity. Wagna's village celebrated the joining of the couple with a fine feast. Many of Mani's people joined them as well as a few others from the summer camp. Anpo ate her midday meal at her own fire in front of Kathleen's *ti ikceya*, her woman serving her with gentle grace for all to see. After all had served witness to their domestic bliss, Anpo took her by the hand and led her into the lodge.

Kathleen chewed her lower lip with a heady mix of fear, anticipation, and arousal. She was reminded of the first time they had ever been together, before she understood the words spoken to her or the intentions of the strange warrior in the yellow shirt. Remembering her surprise at finding a woman, not a man, she grinned.

Anpo drew her to her sleeping robes. The fire burned low, more for light than heat, and the bottom of the *ti ikceya* had been rolled up a few inches to allow a breeze to cool the interior. Stopping at the robes, Anpo turned her attention to Kathleen. She recalled their first night together, as well, and proceeded to deliberately copy it. Her hands touched the pale skin, caressing, studying, bowing her head to peer closely at the small hairs decorating it. *So long...* Once again, she marveled at the movement of the hair as her breath brushed across.

Kathleen sighed and closed her eyes at the sensation, a shiver running up her arm to her heart. A vague throb developed between her legs, and she pressed her thighs together to ease it. The feeling of lips on her skin startled her and her eyes popped open. *She's never kissed me there!*

With tender curiosity, Anpo nibbled the pulse point at Kathleen's wrist, tasting the skin. Her body smoldered, her heart fluttering in her chest as she proceeded to lick and kiss a line towards Kathleen's elbow. The hand she held curved about her head, fingers grazing her hair. Hearing a whispery sigh caused her blood to pulse hotter in her veins.

Kathleen crooked her arm, planting her hand firmly behind Anpo's head. With a craving that surprised her, she forced Anpo's mouth to her own, demanding a kiss. Their lips met, voracious appetites whetting. Hard arms wrapped about her and pulled her tight, one hand behind her head, the other squeezing her rear. The wave of passion that assailed Kathleen almost made her swoon, her knees becoming weak from the rush.

Anpo freed the delicious mouth from her attentions, her motions fierce and frantic as she blazed a trail to the lithe neck. She felt smaller arms clutching at her waist and head, could hear a moan force its way from Kathleen's throat, and she bit down on the skin there, feeling the sound in her teeth. The muscles beneath her hand tightened as Kathleen pushed her hips forward.

The unfamiliar sound rising from her throat shocked Kathleen even as it excited her. She looked about in confusion as if she were just waking. A war erupted in her head, her desire fighting with the puritan upbringing of her parents. The teeth nibbling her neck, and the resultant growl from Anpo sent a flood of heat to her thighs, an ache to her breasts. *What's wrong with me? I've never felt this way! Not even with Adam!*

Feeling the woman in her arms begin to struggle weakly, Anpo released the smooth neck and pulled back. Kathleen's eyes brimmed with fear and arousal, and Anpo's heart went out to her. "*Hiya*, Ketlin," she whispered, peering into the stormy eyes. "*Ah-ah.* You are safe with me, *mahasanni.*" With slow, deliberate movement, Anpo moved the hand kneading a full buttock. As their eyes remained locked, she traced a path over the swell of hip, the curve of waist, brushing a breast.

The fear receded at the gentle touch. Kathleen's breast ached even more as Anpo's hand barely caressed it, and she found herself opening her mouth in a soft sigh. She licked her lips, feeling thirsty and hungry all at once.

Seeing Kathleen's fears were calming, Anpo's hand wrapped about the neck, her thumb caressing the reddening mark where her teeth had just been. "I love you, Ketlin. I will not hurt you." The thumb roamed up to follow the jaw line, her other hand caressing the back of Kathleen's head. "We will give each other pleasure on our joining day."

Kathleen swayed a bit when she was released. With concentration, she focused on Anpo who was removing shirt and breechclout. She blinked, and a memory flitted across her mind's eye – the man in the yellow shirt becoming a woman after removing his clothing. The gentle dark eyes that promised when no words could be understood that nothing would harm her. With a smile, Kathleen pulled her dress over her head and kicked off her moccasins.

Smiling in return, Anpo took her by the hand and sat on the sleeping robes. They faced each other in the dim light of the fire, sitting cross-legged, knee-to-knee. Again, she reenacted their first night, reaching out to touch with inquisitive hands. There was a difference, however. As her hands roamed pale skin, her eyes locked with Kathleen's, watching the blonde's responses.

Kathleen sat very still as she was caressed. Touches trailed along her arms, gently massaged her shoulders. They brushed her neck, and she arched it as a cat receiving a scratching. She tried diligently to keep visual contact, but when Anpo's touch drifted to her aching breasts, it was too much, and she let out a soft moan as her eyes closed.

Anpo's heartbeat increased at the sound. She dropped her gaze and watched her brown hands against the light skin, circling the soft roundness, watching the nipples pucker in anticipation. Curiosity washed over her, and she leaned closer.

A familiar sensation occurred, and Kathleen's mind frantically searched for the memory. *Nursing!* She opened her eyes to see Anpo suckling her left breast. The *wicakte's* eyes were closed, and her hands had reached around Kathleen's back to support her. The sheer eroticism of the moment flushed through Kathleen, and she tossed her head backwards, her hands pressing her lover's head closer. "Oh, Anpo," she sighed.

The skin was smooth and warm. Anpo heard the rapid heart beat, felt it on her lips as she sucked on the small bud. Hearing Kathleen's response, a wave of passion flowed through her and she attacked the right nipple with hunger. Anpo braced her with one arm, bringing her other hand forward to knead the abandoned breast.

Once again, Kathleen lost herself in the intensity. Both her hands were wrapped in raven hair, and she clutched at Anpo, wanting her to continue, wanting her to stop, wanting her to do...something. Teeth grazed her nipple and she groaned, bringing her head forward to rain kisses on Anpo.

With raging appetite, Anpo moaned and avidly attacked Kathleen's chest and neck, finally stopping at her lips. There, her touch became gentle, her kisses teasing, drawing Kathleen out and away from her nervousness and fears.

Expecting the same frenzied attention, Kathleen felt frustration. She tried to extend the kisses only to have Anpo pull away. Her eyes snapped in pique. Hands still buried in dark hair, she forced the desired lips closer and attacked them. Their tongues entwined, she could feel Anpo's moan and it urged her to lean forward.

Losing herself to the sensations, Anpo pulled Kathleen closer. She sat with her woman in her lap, straddling her waist. The shock of their bellies and breasts touching, rubbing, pressing against each other brought another wave of arousal and sound from both of them.

Anpo's hands rubbed pale thighs, occasionally reaching around to knead the rounded buttocks and pull Kathleen closer. She felt curly hair brushing and mingling with hers, felt the moisture there mixing with her essence. Small hands, having finally released her hair, scratched up and down her back and shoulders. *"Mahasanni,"* she whispered between incendiary kisses, capturing one of the hands.

Kathleen found her hand pressed to Anpo's breast. She broke off the kiss, studying Anpo as she brushed her thumb against the darker areola, seeing the erect nipple peaking. She stared into fiery brown eyes and, with deliberate slowness, squeezed the breast, capturing the nipple between thumb and forefinger.

Anpo's eyes closed and she pressed against Kathleen's hips with a groan. *"Ohan, mahasanni,"* she panted as the attention continued, a rush of wetness between her thighs.

It was Kathleen's turn to marvel at the effect of her touch. She lost herself in the wonder as her hands crossed heated flesh, watching her lover's reactions to the different touches. Straying down, she brushed the hair between them, feeling moisture. Surprised, she reached further, scooping Anpo's essence onto a finger and touching the sensitive bud.

Anpo was on fire, her body automatically bucking as Kathleen touched her. She opened her eyes to slits, watching as Kathleen studied the liquid on her finger.

"You are wet," she said, holding the digit up to show Anpo.

Panting, Anpo could not help but chuckle. "*Ohan*, Ketlin. It is what happens to *winyan* when they are aroused." With a sly grin, she brought her hand down and returned the favor, her smile widening at the gasp of surprise as she caressed Kathleen's clitoris. Bringing her finger up, she showed Kathleen that it glistened with wetness, as well.

The jolt of pleasure from her center startled her. While there had been some amount of feeling with her husband, it had never been so intense with just a touch. She watched as Anpo licked her finger clean, eyes closing with enjoyment. Kathleen peered at her damp finger, a maddening curiosity overcoming her. *What does she taste like?* The resulting explosion of saltiness on her tongue amazed her.

Anpo opened her eyes to see Kathleen repeating the action, finger in mouth as she sucked the *wicakte's* essence. Her hands returned to pale skin, pulling Kathleen's hips closer until their arousal mingled. She heard a moan that drove her on and her hands massaged the firm muscles of Kathleen's buttocks, moving slowly south.

As long fingers played in her wetness, Kathleen's hips began to move, pressing herself against Anpo. Not wanting to be left out, she reached between them and caressed Anpo's silky folds, her body on fire at the immediate and carnal response.

They moved together, soft moans punctuating their touches as they thrust against each other. Lips and tongues clashed together in breathless excitement, fingers reaching into places that had not been touched in too long. The pair rode wave upon wave of ecstasy until they cried out in a final spasm, bucking against firm skin in mutual climax.

Anpo was physically exhausted, but her heart was filled to bursting. She eased backwards onto their robes until she lay with Kathleen splayed across her body. Her fingertips idly traced patterns on Kathleen's back and sides.

Kathleen relaxed under the stroking, her body sluggish. A hundred thoughts rampaged through her active mind, foremost being, *Good Lord! What else have we been missing?* She listened to the steady beat of Anpo's heart, slowing to normal after their exertions. Another sound filled her ear, the croon of her woman singing a love song.

When it was finished, Anpo hugged Kathleen close. "I will never leave you again, *mahasanni*. Not even in death."

Though the words sent shivers down her spine, Kathleen lifted her head, falling into deep pools of brown. "And I will never leave you, *mahasanni*. Not even in death."

Chapter Forty-Six

1784

The spring morning was chilly and a little overcast. It had rained pretty steadily for the past month, and Stewart was happy for the break in the weather. Elders among the people were of the opinion the good weather would hold for several days and, if there was one thing he had learned during his stay among the Lakota, the big bellies knew what they were talking about. He tightened the cinch on his saddle and readjusted a stirrup. Certain he and his gear would stay on the animal, he turned to his family with a smile.

As usual, Teca was in Anpo's arms. The boy was six winters old now and becoming more and more interested in the *hoksila* running wild through the village. Beside them stood Kathleen, tears shining on her cheeks in contrast to the happy smile on her face. It was to her Stewart went first.

Kathleen's breath hitched as she was gathered into his arms. She reined in her rampant emotions and bussed his cheek. "You take care of yourself, Stew," she insisted, pulling back to dust and straighten the leather shirt she had made him.

"*Hau*, sis, I will," Stewart responded. He tilted her chin with a finger and stared into eyes so like his own. "And you take care of yourself and your family."

Despite her best intentions, she began weeping and tugged him into another embrace. "I will," she promised in a fierce whisper.

After a few moments, Stewart pulled away, his eyes suspiciously damp. "Here now, lass! No tears!" He helped her wipe her face before turning to Anpo.

The *wicakte* stared at him for long seconds. Her face was unreadable as she set Teca down and reached for a pouch at her feet. She handed it to him, a slight smile gracing her face. "Thank you for bringing my *winuhca* and *cinksi* back to me."

Blinking in surprise at the gift, Stewart opened the pouch. Carefully wrapped inside a fur bundle was a pipe made of bone, yellowed with age. Small animals were carved on the stem, and a second piece of bone had been fashioned into the bowl, the interior blackened from use.

"This is my best pipe," Anpo said, "made from the bone of the *tatanka ska* that brought Ketlin to me."

Stewart gaped at Anpo, knowing the importance of this item among her personal belongings. He automatically reached to hand it back, but Kathleen intercepted him.

"Never refuse a gift," she murmured.

Swallowing, he nodded. "Thank you, Anpo. You do me a great honor with this gift." His mind raced as he considered his belongings. He had little in the way of trade items. What few clothes that survived the harsh winter had been augmented with native wear. "I have nothing to give you in return."

Anpo's smile widened. She picked Teca up again and held out her arm, draping it around Kathleen's waist. "You have given me a great gift, Stu'et, one that I can never repay. You have brought my family home to me."

Unable to top that, Stewart accepted the compliment and gift with grace. He wrapped the pipe carefully and stowed it with the rest of his gear. Final good byes were said and he mounted his horse.

"Give my best to Mum and Da," Kathleen said.

"I will, sis."

Teca, who remained fairly silent through the exchange, finally called out, "*Leksi!* You will return?"

Stewart's eyes took in the boy and his family. He turned a bit to study the winter camp of Wagna with fond eyes. A smile crossed his face, and he looked back at his nephew. "*Hau, tunska!* I will be back to see you."

"Good." Satisfied, Teca asked to be put down and scampered off to his mother's lodge to play.

"Take care, sis. I love you." Stewart urged his mount away, threading through the village. Other families stood outside their *ti ikceyas* in silent good byes. Stewart tipped his hat at Wanbli and Nupa's fires, receiving grunts of approval from the men and muted trilling from the women. Once through the eastern entrance, he kicked the horse into a trot.

On a hill outside of camp, Stewart pulled up short. Turning, he looked down and saw his sister and *hanka* walking arm in arm back to the *ti ikceya*. Teca danced around the fire, pretending to hunt *tatanka ska*.

"Aye, sis. I'll be back. You can bet on it."

He turned the horse for home.

Lakota Indian Names (pronunciation):

Anpo (ahn-**poh**) – daughter of Wanbli and Gi

Cetan (cheh-**tahn**) – son of Wanbli and Hwa, Anpo's younger brother

Cinksi (cheen-**kashee**) – see Anpo

Gi (jee) – Anpo's mother, wife of Wanbli

Hca (hajah) – daughter of Wanbli and Gi, Anpo's older sister

Hinhan (heen-**hahn**) – daughter of Wanbli and Hwa, Anpo's younger sister

Hwa (hwah) – Wanbli's second wife, Anpo's second mother

Inyan (**een**-yahn) – shaman

Ketlin (**ket**-lin) – Kathleen McGlashan

Mani (**mah**-nee) – Chief of another Lakota camp

Nupa (**noo**-pah) – Anpo's lifelong friend

Osni (**oz**-nee) – healer in Wagna's camp

Sape (**sah**-peh) – Nupa's father

Stu'et (stew-**et**) – Stewart McGlashan, brother of Ketlin

Teca (teh-**jah**) – son of Ketlin and Anpo

Wagna (wah-**ganah**) – Chief of Anpo's camp

Wanbli (wahn-**blee**) – Anpo's father, husband to Gi and Hwa

Wi Ile Anpo (wee ee-**leh** ahn-**poh**) – see Anpo

Yakte (**yahk**-teh) – owned Kathleen as a slave

Yus'as'a (yoo-**sheah**-sheah) – son of Nupa and Hca

Glossary

-kala (**kah**-lah)	added to end of familial names, dear one
ah-ah (ah-ah)	hushing sound
akicita (ah-**kee**-chee-ta)	watchman, club man, security
ate (ah-**teh**)	father
cinksi (cheen-**kashee**)	son
cunksi (choon-**kashee**)	daughter
cuwe (choo-**weh**)	older sister
cuwignaka (choo-**wee**-genah-kah)	dress
han (hahn)	female greeting
hanka (**hahn**-kah)	male to sister-in-law
hau (**hah**-oo)	male agreement, yes / greeting
hehaka (hee-**hah**-kah)	deer
hiya (hee-**yah**)	negative, no
hoh (hoh)	negative, no, masculine
hokahe wana (hoh-**kah**-heh **wah**-nah)	let's go
hoksila (hoh-**keshee**-lah)	boy
hunka (**hoon**-ka)	adopted, by choice
igmu (ee-**gmoo**)	cat, mysterious animal
ikceya (eek-**jeh**-yah)	common lodge (a.k.a. tipi)
ina (ee-**nah**)	mother

inanup (ee-**nah**-noop)	mother two
inyan (een-**yahn**)	stone
isnatipi (ee-**shna**-tee-pee)	lodge of women's bleeding
koskalaka (kosh-kah-**lah**-kah)	young man
leksi (leh-**kashee**)	uncle
mahasanni (mah-hah-**sahn**-nee)	"my second skin", very intimate name for one's mate
maka (ma-**ka**)	earth
maske (mah-**shekeh**)	female to female close friend
misun (mee-**soon**)	female to younger brother
mitan (mee-**tahn**)	female to younger sister
nigesanla (nee-**geh**-sahn-lah)	antelope
ohan (**oh**-hahn)	female agreement, yes
oinikaga tipi (oh-ee-nee-**kah**-gah tee-pee)	sweat lodge
pispiza (pees-**peez**-ah)	prairie dog
san (shahn)	vagina
ska (skah)	white
stepan (**sheteh**-pahn)	female to sister-in-law
takoja (tah-**ko**-zcha)	grandchild
tanksi (tahn-**kashee**)	male form of younger sister, close friend
tatanka (tah-**tahn**-kah)	buffalo
ti (tee)	lives in
tiblo (tee-**beloh**)	female form of older brother / close male friend
tiopa (tee-**oh**-pah)	door, opening

tiospaye (tee-**oh**-shpay-ya)	extended family unit
tunkasi (toon-**kah**-shee)	father-in-law
tunkasila (toon-**kah**-shee-lah)	grandfather
tunska (**toon**-shekah)	nephew
unci (oon-**jee**)	grandmother
uncisi (oon-**jee**-shee)	mother-in-law
wagmu ohanpi (wahg-**moo** oh-**hahn**-pee)	summer squash
wakan (**wah**-kahn)	mysterious, sacred
wakan tanka (**wah**-kahn **tahn**-ka)	literally "Great Mystery", the great powers
wakanyeja (wah-kahn-**yay**-jah)	mysterious baby, newborn
wana (**wah**-nah)	hurry
wansi (wahn-**shee**)	pemmican
wicakte (wee-**chah**-ktay)	two-spirited woman
wicasa (wee-**chah**-shah)	man, older adult male
wicahca (wee-**chah**-hajah)	real man, term of respect
wicincala (wee-cheen-**jah**-lah)	girl
winkte (ween-**ktay**)	two-spirited man
wikoskalaka (wee-kosh-kah-**lah**-kah)	young woman
winuhca (wee-**noo**-hejah)	real woman, term of respect
winuhcala (wee-noo-**hejah**-lah)	precious, real woman / term of endearment for wife
winyan (**ween**-yahn)	woman, older adult female

D Jordan Redhawk lives in Portland, Oregon where she makes her living in the hospitality industry. (But don't make the mistake of thinking she's hospitable.) Her household consists of her wife of seventeen years, four attack cats that rampage through the house at all hours of the day and night, two Hermit crabs, and a white buffalo Beanie Buddy names Roam.

You can reach D Jordan Redhawk through her website:
http://www.djordanredhawk.net

Printed in the United States
43587LVS00005B/85